ZACH WILSON

GARDEN OF ASH

DARK SIX IMPRISONED BOOK 1

SILVERSMITH
PRESS

Published by Silversmith Press–Houston, Texas
www.silversmithpress.com

Copyright © 2024 Zach Wilson

All rights reserved.

This book, or parts thereof, may not be reproduced in any form or by any means without written permission from the author, except for brief passages for purposes of reviews. For more information, contact the publisher at office@publishandgo.com.

The views and opinions expressed herein belong to the author and do not necessarily represent those of the publisher.

ISBN 978-1-961093-80-5 (Softcover Book)
ISBN 978-1-961093-81-2 (eBook)

CONTENTS

1. Mourning and Dusk 1
2. Sleeper Awakened 21
3. The Tomb is Full 42
4. Worn Path to Wildercrown 62
5. Council of Twelve 77
6. Deadly Messages 96
7. At a Loss and into Light 124
8. Flight to the Fringe 141
9. Friendly Enemy 165
10. A Gift in the Dark 191
11. Fire in the Highest 214
12. Sorrow and Salvation 239
13. Hammer, Plague, and Storm 265
14. Refugees 288
15. Fight in the Forest 309
16. Hidden City Found 327
17. Last-Hope Beleaguered 350
18. A Day's Duties 375
19. Interlude: Sleepless Dream 402
20. Powers to Bear 407
21. Malice 432
22. Promises 447
23. Threshold 468
24. Descent 480

Glossary and Pronunciation 499

To Christ Jesus, my Lord
and
Lauren, my love.

Without either of you, this book would not be.

I love you both,
—Z

MAP OF LEÓHTENESS-FAL

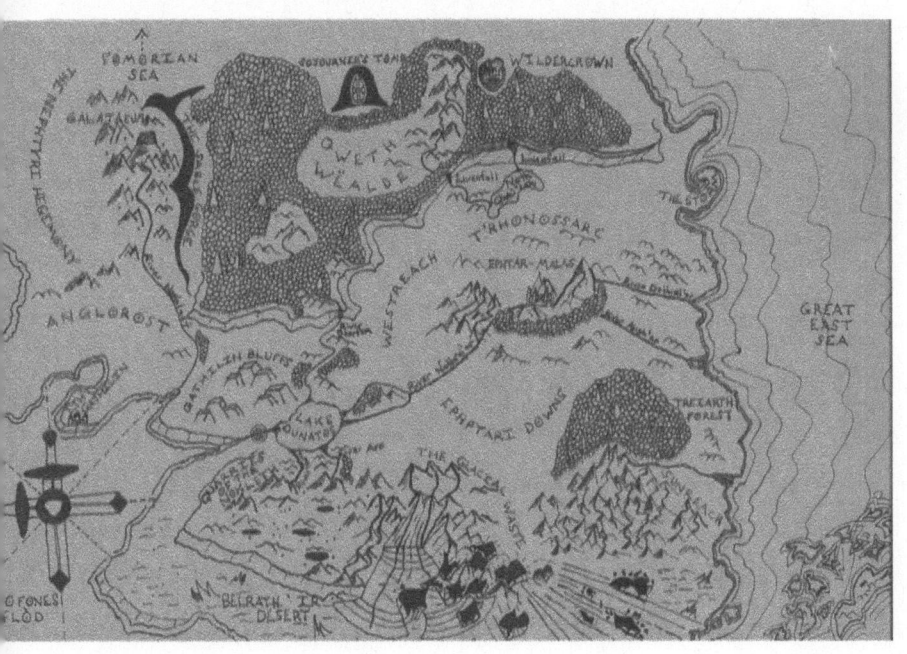

I
MOURNING AND DUSK

"Will it work this time, Dusk?" the dark-haired girl asked the boy whose eyes were lanterns.

She watched as he bent close over his comatose mother, then turned back to her. "This is the f-f-first time I've t-t-tried this one," Dusk said, his halting words far worse than usual.

"You know what I mean!" she snapped.

"I d-d-don't know," he whispered.

"Maybe if you hadn't been gone so long and so far—"

"Aryka!" the boy hissed. "S-s-stand over there."

She glared at the bright-eyed boy but did not move. Maybe she had been a bit harsh, but his temper often rose to bursting, especially after his ma got sick. Aryka had been his longest friend, and she had seen his entire transformation, from bright-eyed boy to fierce young man, all in just three or so years.

And she knew it was not his fault he had been gone so long. She had been the one to come hollering his name, after all. She thought of him and his frantic business on the soaring hills of his homeland. She often watched him gather root, flower, and leaf for his Ma. But his most recent trip had taken him away from the cottage far longer than he had told her it would. And in desperate search, Aryka had found him, half-unrecognizable, and brought him back.

"Dusk! She's screaming!" Aryka had called when she found the feral lad. She remembered hot tears and sweat on her face. But upon her approach, what she had taken for her friend was instead a form of dark obsession, more beast than boy. "She's in so much pain," was all Aryka had managed to whisper to him. But it was enough.

Back home they had raced from the high, dark meadows. Unsure of whether Dusk the boy or Dusk the beast chased at her heels, Aryka nevertheless guided him, his pouches and pockets stuffed with earthy remedies, back to his Ma's cottage. They had stomped, plodded, and swam, sweat stinging their eyes. She had heard him growl and gnash his teeth while reviewing his recipes and rumors of cures, unsure of whether a thing half-wolf or half-surgeon stalked along beside her.

"One of these will work," she remembered him say as they had slid down the muddy slopes high above the little cottage. When the door to the humble house had come into view, she had heard Dusk whisper, "They h-h-have to work. She's all I have left."

"Is it working, Dusk?" Aryka asked, sure now that the boy, not the brute, stood beside her, considering his choices. Dusk stirred from his work and looked back to where she stood at his shoulder in front of the single stone table in the middle of the warm, little house.

"No," Dusk growled. She saw his eyes brighten like molten bronze. "Fever's r-r-rising."

"You tried grayvine, arrowroot, witch hazel, silver-mint, valerian, and ephedra?" she recited, as she stepped toward the ailing woman on the bed.

"All of them," the boy grunted, grabbing up a handful of other ingredients, grinding them in a bowl.

"I'll grab you a cold washcloth for her forehead," Aryka said, rushing out the open door. As she went, she thought of Dusk working frantically, applying poultice, paste, and every new idea of a cure. But the cold stone in her stomach told her his mother would not stop thrashing and burning. Not this time. Aryka snatched up clean cloths from her packs, which lay just outside. She turned, stepping back inside, then stopped, looking toward the sickbed. Sweat poured down the sick woman's lovely face, fighting the losing battle.

"Nearly the third y-y-year." Dusk's whisper came to Aryka from the darkness of the room. She saw him kneeling at his mother's bedside. "The third *year*, yet stricken *Eissyr* has never shown *fear*." Aryka heard him give a grim chuckle that turned into a growl. She saw the shadow return, and beside the woman's bed knelt the beast Aryka had seen claim more and more of him over the long weeks and months of his mother's illness. "St-st-still I've f-f-found nothing to help you," Dusk said through gritted teeth. "But I w-w-won't stop, not s-s-so long as I'm the m-m-man of this house. Not t-t-till Da comes back."

Aryka watched him turn back to the stone table, set to mixing medicines. His humming of little tunes over them chased away the beast for the moment, and she watched her friend invoke all the blessings and enchantments he had ever shared with her. She hoped they would help.

Snapping out of her reverie, Aryka bustled in. "Clean rags," she said, adding a few to the table and plunging one into a basin of fresh water. Wringing it gently, Aryka lay the cloth over Eissyr's hot forehead. Aryka stood close to assist Dusk as he applied his healing arts. *Imagine, a goatherd dressed up with so much shadow and knowledge*, she thought. She remembered when all the cares he bore were for sheep, goat, and slashing stick for the noses of starving wolves.

With his da having left Dusk and Eissyr more than three years back, the big-eyed boy she thought she had known and often played with had changed—and changed fast. She had watched as necessity had forged Dusk into the best healer their village had ever known. She shivered now as that healer, growing a little more feral, a little less human, stood grim beside her, commanding the Wasting Sickness out of his mother with strange, powerful words, to no avail.

Aryka heard Dusk snarl, dash his clay bowl filled with some smelly remedy against the log walls of the cottage, then return to the stone table for a new recipe. She cleaned up the mess and watched as he traced a finger down a sheepskin list of etched runes and other writings. He grabbed another dish and set to mixing another cure.

MOURNING AND DUSK

After two more attempts, Eissyr began thrashing again, shouting vaguely of battle and darkness. Dusk began searching through sacks of ingredients dropped off by men and women of the village who had come by earlier in the day, as they always had. While she worked beside him, Aryka thought of the people of their village, the things they believed, and how they would stand strong in the gap when their neighbors fell infirm. She loved them for that, and she and her parents stood daily in just such a gap for Dusk and Eissyr. Her folk would stop by with sad smiles, bringing anything they hoped would help the young healer in his tragic endeavor. But even the most practiced in healing among them were useless against this powerful plague. So, all the people of the mountains could do was pray and bring Dusk what provision they could. Aryka helped in her best ways as well, holding the woman's arms and feet to keep her from hurting herself, pouring and fetching water, and running for help if needed.

"Because it's what we do," Aryka whispered.

"*Enemy*," the woman moaned, "*marching under earth ...*"

Aryka held Eissyr's arms firmly down while Dusk poured some steaming concoction into her mouth. As the lad worked, and she watched, Aryka thought of the boy's strong da. Dusk's face had gone sharp and rocky, like his father's, and had begun to grow around his saucers of eyes. The boy's arms and legs grew too, beginning to fill his once-loose clothing.

"*Ephtar-Malas!*" Eissyr hissed as Aryka dabbed at the woman's brow again. "*... conceals the Coffin.*"

Thinking again of Eissyr's hale husband, Aryka remembered that the man had spent his younger days as a sort of traveler. Though Aryka had heard little of the hard man's life before his settling in that cottage in the mountains with Eissyr, Dusk's da knew much of the far-away places of the Lower-world. He taught folk how to read and write. When he did, he would have them practice their scribing by telling stories of the good men, women, and fairfolk he had befriended, protected, or served in his travels. He would even tell old stories of war and danger.

"*The prince lies dead!*" Eissyr cried. Dread forced Aryka back to herself for a moment. It was this sort of fever-shout that had sent her running to find Dusk hours earlier. Eissyr was getting worse, had been for weeks. But Aryka held her tight while Dusk worked. She shut her eyes to the woman's ravings, let her mind wander away, back to the strange things that had led them all here. But dread had been there too, when Dusk's da left.

Fearful whispers had crept up the high slopes of Sunreach, their mountain home. When she would come over to talk with Dusk as he gathered his goats, Aryka saw Dusk's da dress again in his old training gear, as if preparing for some looming trouble. Then, on a cold day in spring three years ago, when Aryka had again been on the way over, she saw Dusk's da from afar take up his old armor and cloak. He kissed lovely Eissyr and lay a firm hand on his boy's head. After he had gone, Aryka had run up to Dusk, who cried as he told her his da had ridden off to a kingdom hidden in the mists of the West, speaking of unfinished business with a key and a king. Dusk had told her that it all had to do with what his da had called the Fading and the Star-farer.

These things, Aryka now knew, were somehow connected to the moment in the fall of that year, when the grass-green of Eissyr and Dusk's eyes had burned away, never to come back. Their eyes shined eerily thenceforth; leafy green replaced by irises the color of molten glass. Aryka had always stuck up for Dusk, who had grown up with eyes bigger than most children. But when they turned that burning color, everyone in Sunreach said his eyes shone like lanterns and often picked on him for it. That was when she would step in. While Dusk fended off wolves on the high pastures, she would scare off the jackals who sought to sneer and laugh at him for his eyes and his voice when they thought he was too preoccupied to defend himself. Aryka had never minded Dusk's eyes. They always made it easy to find him when she wanted. And she had often found those lanterns pointed toward the Outer-dark above or gazing on the flowers and creatures of the mountain as he spoke with them, commanding them to grow or heal.

"*In Golden-mount is born an Heir,*" Eissyr whispered.

Thinking again of Dusk's da while she lay a gentle hand on Eissyr's arm, Aryka thought it odd that the man seemed to have taken little interest in his son's strange gifts of mending and speaking with the flowers and animals. But a key to retrieve and a door to open seemed to have taken more of his thought and time. So, Dusk's da had left, and Aryka saw sorrow enter into Eissyr and Dusk's lives. She remembered helping a much smaller Dusk carry in buckets of water, only to find brave Eissyr crying amber tears onto their cottage floor, not ready to raise her boy all on her own. And that was before she had gotten sick.

"*Flee, Treiarn!*" Eissyr screamed.

"Da's gone, Ma!" Dusk shouted back, his composure broken. "He left us, and he's n-n-never c-c-coming back! He-he-he—"

Aryka watched the boy come undone. His body, a moment ago so grownup and strong, shrank and shook with silent sobs. Her own eyes began blurring, her lip quivering. She bent toward him, wrapped him with her arms as best she could.

She felt him freeze, his back go rigid. He stopped his sobs, turned his lantern-eyes upward. "The helm!" Dusk cried suddenly, his fey smile startling her.

"What?" she said, releasing him.

"Aryka!" he said as he continued tending the ailing woman. "The helm! He l-l-left it for me. Quick now! G-g-grab it. Under my bed. F-f-far back. Hurry!"

"I don't—"

"Please," he pleaded. "B-b-bring it here. I have n-n-nothing else to g-g-give her, and the h-h-helm may be the only way!"

Aryka rushed to the little pallet in a corner of the cottage. She dug under the wooden frame, shoving aside trinkets, clothes, tools, and toys. Then she spied it: a gleam of silver on a polished surface. She set her fingers to cool steel and heaved the helm out from under its sleepy prison. She held it for a moment, felt its solid weight, then thought she heard a new whisper, a voice other than Eissyr's as the woman heaved. But her attention returned to the helm, its practical make and solid weight. No doubt it had been designed to protect its bearer from war and a storm of blows and looked to have done its job on more than one occasion. This was not the property of simple mountain herders.

"Hurry!" Dusk called from across the room.

She scrambled over and lowered the helm to the table alongside Dusk's collection of roots and remedies. She studied it while she waited. Its peaks came to steep angles, and its visor hung back on its pivots. Dusk finished applying his mother's medicine, then came over to the table. Setting aside his bowl of liquid and handful of herbs, Dusk wiped stained hands on his heavy apron. She watched him breathe deeply, the lights of his eyes going dark then bright again as he blinked. He raised his hands to grab up the helm as if it were some fragile treasure.

"Last chance," he whispered. Aryka watched Dusk take the helm gently and set it on his head. He shut his eyes, contorting his face as if trying to hear something shouted to him from far away. She shut her eyes, listening with him. A minute passed. Then another. She opened an eye, saw his still closed. She snapped hers shut again. When a second, then a third minute crept by, and only the sounds of Eissyr's thrashing and moaning could be heard, Aryka opened her eyes. Just then, she heard Dusk give a disgusted snarl, making to tear the helm from his head in frustration. Then she saw his eyes snap open. Gooseflesh ran the length of her arms as the lad's blazing pupils quaked, as if he stared into a vision of doom.

Aryka reached out with a wavering hand. But before she could touch him, Dusk set to the table once more, gathering root, water, herb, and a handful of other ingredients. He worked like a man possessed, mixing and heating compounds she had never seen him try before. Dusk's hands drew Aryka's attention, working faster than a person's should. She saw sparks in them, and shadow too. He must have been calling upon his strange powers again, the ones that drew crowds to the mountain, begging for his healing help for their children and elders. She watched him apply this latest batch of medicine to his mother's lips. Suddenly, the woman stopped tossing and went quiet. Her pale face soaked up a little color once more, and she sighed into contented rest.

"Oh," Aryka said, relief in her voice. She bent to whisper in Dusk's ear, "She's gone to sleep, Dusk. You've done it!"

When he gave no response, she looked to him. Before her eyes, the stuttering goat-lad and the wild creature his wanderings often turned him into had both gone away. In Dusk's place stood the strong image of his father. Face drawn, his mouth formed a thin line under his sharp nose. His smoldering eyes were set, and although the helm of his father sat a little askew over his straggly dark hair, Aryka saw for an instant the man he would one day become, given the chance. He only stood there, staring at his sleeping mother. When tears welled in his eyes once more, Aryka grabbed his hand and gave it a gentle squeeze. The touch of his fingers was ice to her hand, but not altogether unpleasant.

"Come on," she whispered and pulled him toward the open door. They stepped softly out through the threshold, crossed the little wooden porch, and stood above a field of glowing grass.

"Just in time to see *last-light*!" Aryka said. "And the grass is just as happy as always to stand and shine for us at the beginning of night."

Pleasant little hearth-lights sprang to life, dotting the hills and steep countryside all around and below them. They stood for a few minutes, saying nothing. And when all had gone dark as pitch, she giggled. "Nighttime now! Though there's little difference to be found between dawn and dusk on Sunreach, is there? Although, I'd say *Dusk* looks rather dashing at this time of day."

Dusk blinked and shook his head. He then turned to face Aryka's sidelong smile.

"I have to leave Sunreach," Dusk said, his words confident and clear.

"You sound like your father," she said. "Though you leave all the time."

"This time for a long time, Ary," he said. "To a faraway country, where blood was spilled."

"What on 'Fal for?" she asked.

"The cure."

"But you've found it!" Aryka cried. "Your mother lies far better in her bed, and all you need do is mix that potion for her again. You've succeeded, Dusk."

"You know I haven't," Dusk said. "I've only staved off what will kill her that much longer. She may live for a while, if well-tended. But she will still die if a proper cure is not found. Aryka, what is it?"

Aryka sniffed back her tears, releasing his hand. "Oh, you've been through it so!" she said, words spilling out of her. "Eissyr was so strong before she got sick, and you mirrored her strength, and your da's, after she did. You bent all thought of light and mending toward saving her. You wandered so far, so desperately for a cure, you went wild, Dusk! I saw you from far away—thinking, praying, pleading. I watched you change as you spent more and more time with stones, flowers, and bubbling springs."

His eyes brimmed, but she saw him master himself, even now.

"There were some nights after you'd been gone for days," she said. "Nights I'd watched over Eissyr, taking my shift alongside the neighbors. Nights you'd come back, and I thought some wild wolf or badger had stolen up the doorstep! But no, it was Dusk, covered all about with dirt and berry juice, twigs in his hair, and mud on his face!"

"Aryka," Dusk said, reaching out to her.

"No!" she cried, pulling away. "And now you're leaving again? Where? To the Lower-world? Where is this *faraway country where blood was spilled*?"

"I must," he said quietly. She saw his usual agitation returning. "It's b-b-below the mountain, and farther north than I've ever s-s-set foot, norther than all the expanse of T'Rhonossarc. I s-s-saw the place when I p-p-put on the helm."

"What did you see? And how did the helm let you see it?"

"I don't know, exactly," he sighed. "But I saw lightning flashing ceaselessly b-b-by the sea. It was like I was there, Ary, in the Storm. The h-h-helm was the only thing Da left me. And he t-t-told me not to put it on until need was g-g-greatest. That n-n-need was just then, when Ma called his name. The helm h-h-helped. It showed me how to c-c-crush berry, root, and bark, how to administer it once it reached the right t-t-temperatures. It sh-sh-showed me everything, even where to find the cure, the r-r-real cure. Or, rather, the p-p-power I need to cure her for good."

"But you *are* powerful," Aryka whispered. "You've got power, not make-believe, but real and great and terrible, like a surgeon's knife ready to cut. Even now, I see it laying about your shoulders, like all the other weights you carry."

"It's not enough," he said darkly.

"And you traveling to some faraway land to get yourself killed in whatever wars the Lower-worlders have gotten themselves into *will* be?"

"There is no choice," he growled. She saw Dusk the man fade away, replaced by the impression of a dangerous, feral will and sharp claws, his eyes flashing fierce.

GARDEN OF ASH

"I see," she whispered. "Then what can I do to help?"

"Only what you and your f-f-family and our neighbors have d-d-done for me, for us, this far," Dusk said, molten eyes cooling a little. "Tell them t-t-to follow my l-l-lists and recipes, give her the m-m-medicine I just made for her. Have them care for her until I return. I may be g-g-gone for a long while, but not forever. I will c-c-come back. And when I do, she'll be right again, and you and I c-c-can go back to the way we were before—"

"No," Aryka spat, her auburn eyes hardening. This was all too much to hear. "Not the way things were before, oaf. You were a silent stick of a boy who cared more for goats and wind songs than his friends. You've become a man in just three years. And I'm certainly not letting you go back, either to boy or beast. And neither secret helm nor adventure nor hidden power are taking you from me. Is that clear?"

"It is," Dusk said. "I journey to the Lower-world for p-p-power and cures, then back to my m-m-mother, then back to you. Short and simple."

"Nothing is ever short or simple with you, Dusk of Sunreach," she snapped.

She saw him lift the helm off his pale forehead, stare at her with his bright gold eyes, then sigh, closing them. She left him then, stalking back down the mountain to her family's house, to be greeted by three happy hounds.

They spent the following days in quiet preparation for his journey. Aryka would sit on a barrel, kicking her legs while reciting lists of supplies. She watched Dusk run around the house and into the village to fetch those things she mentioned when he was not fussing over his mother. He also showed her pieces of gear he had gathered for his journey when he was not standing aloof, looking either to the dark sky or the strange helm left to him by his da. Aryka brought what tools she thought best for him and offered an assisting hand when the crowds came during the day. They begged for Dusk's healing hands and blessed him when their loved ones rose again from fever, rash, or pox. Those he could not help weighed heavy on him, Aryka saw. His shoulders sagged when he delivered the words he hated most: "Nothing more I can do." But even those who were not blessed by Dusk's healing power gave him gifts and many thanks.

Coins were few and far between, but the people of the village and beyond stocked his shelves with new herbs, stores of wheat, and cured meats. Dusk took freely given steaming loaves and fresh spices. The rich, savory stews, he always shared with Aryka, then spoon fed to Eissyr. Close neighbors of Eissyr and Dusk knew of his frequent excursions, and one family of herders parted the crowd to thank him for splinting their father's broken leg a month prior. They gifted him a fine pair of goatskin boots as payment for Dusk's perfect work. Two old sisters who had grown old together after their husbands had passed away presented the healer with a set of tough leather gloves, lined with fur. Aryka saw Dusk flash his rare but brilliant smile when her mother presented a heavy, gray-green travel cloak to the boy as a surprise. Aryka did her best to hide her apple-red cheeks when that smile fell on her, and he hugged her, his tears falling onto her shoulder.

"You've g-g-given me s-s-so much," he whispered.

"You gave us back my da," she replied.

"We've taken our t-t-time to make me r-r-ready," Dusk told Aryka two nights after he had sent Eissyr to restful slumber. Aryka stood with him in the doorway of his mother's cottage. "I'm laden with gifts and grants, and I'm wrapped all ab-b-bout with rope! I have enough f-f-food for a month's hard w-w-walk too. And after I r-r-run out, I know all the b-b-berries and g-g-good mushrooms from bad well enough to s-s-stay fed. You've s-s-seen me hunt too."

Aryka had dropped by earlier that day to help Dusk make final preparations. "I have," she replied. "I know you can take care of yourself. But let me worry a little more after you. I must say, though, you certainly look the part!" she said, beaming. "No doubt thanks to the lovely stitching of my mum and me. Spin for me."

"Aryka," Dusk said impatiently.

"Do it," she said, clapping her hands. "You may be digging in the dirt and carrying deer on your back by the time I see you again."

Rolling his glowing eyes, he spun a quick circle, his new cloak catching the mountain breeze that whispered in through the doorway.

"I didn't know if I liked the look of your presents alone," she mused, "but now that I see you wearing them all at once, and knowing they'll keep you warm and safe, I think they make you look like some traveler of wilds, straight out of the old fey-tales!"

"No fey-tales here." Dusk laughed. "Just a b-b-boy. And my story won't end until I f-f-find the cure for *Eissyr's Blight*."

"Ooh, so the healer has named his foe—*Eissyr's Blight*," Aryka said, nodding at the sound of it. "It's a good name for a foe none but you can defeat. And speaking of names, you shouldn't go by your real name on the road."

"No," he agreed. "Treijan, son of Treiarn isn't exactly a name for g-g-goatherds. It may rouse s-s-suspicion among the Lower-worlders, even when I truthfully say I *am* a g-g-goatherd. I'll s-s-stick with Dusk. You and everyone else c-c-call me that anyway."

"Good." She nodded, folding her arms. "Your eyes will provide proof of that. And what's your story, should one of the prince's knights waylay you below the mountain?"

"I h-h-hardly think it w-w-will be a knight," he said. "A f-f-forester, hunter, or farmer, more's the like." At her scowl, he held up his arms. "Alright. I'll tell Sir Lost-His-Way the truth, or at l-l-least what was t-t-true when I herded my f-f-flock. I'm a herder whose p-p-prodigal goat was attacked by an eagle in one of the high p-p-passes. I saw the poor beast f-f-fall and came all the way d-d-down the mountain looking for it. And if I'm t-t-too far from the mountain to be b-b-believed, I'll just t-t-tell more truth: that I'm on my way to Ephtar-Malas, the Hidden City, to find a t-t-trader along the road w-w-willing to barter a new kid to me in exchange for one of my m-m-many gifts." He drew back the hem of his cloak to reveal pockets filled with healing tonic, coin, string, salt box, flint, steel, knife, and lodestone.

"You think whoever stops you will believe you?" Aryka asked, frowning.

"I had to d-d-do it a few years b-b-back when Da was fire-breathing mad at me for l-l-losing two goats to the eagles. I n-n-never made it to the Hidden City, or even got to s-s-see its white towers. But I t-t-traded three c-c-clay jugs of goat milk for a lame kid on the road that l-l-led to it. Stiff price, but I g-g-got the last laugh. That k-k-kid grew up bigger n' stronger than anyone thought sh-sh-she would! Supplied Ma with all the warm m-m-milk I gave her in her s-s-sickness."

"If you say so," she sighed. "Go on, then, and be happy I don't pack up and go with you, for all the trouble you're sure to get into."

"Ary," Dusk said, fixing her with his firelit gaze. "I will n-n-need you out there."

"You will," she said. "But I have business of my own to tend here. The homestead will be mine soon, and there's still a lot to learn before I can retire Mum and Da. You're ready for this journey. All your time in the high places above the light and your wanderings far from home say so. It'll just be another trip like those ones, with you searching high and low for something to save your mum."

"I know that, Ary," Dusk said.

"I know you know that," she snapped. "I'm just trying to tell myself you'll be fine."

"I will be," he said, patting her shoulder. "I've f-f-fought off wolf, eagle, and winter-wind on the m-m-mountain, and I'll have my s-s-staff and knife with me. I'm small, but I can h-h-hold my own."

"I know you can. We all do," she said, eyes going dark. "Just don't die, by way of bandits or bad weather, yeah?"

"Aryka's famed advice," Dusk chuckled. "Yeah."

"Don't make fun," she said, swatting at him. "I'm being serious."

"So am I," he said, his smile fading. "Aryka, I'll be h-h-home soon."

With pursed lips, she nodded. "You've got the helm?"

He pulled back the hood of his cloak, revealing polished steel.

"Good," she said, moving his hood back into place so that it covered the helm completely. "Need to keep that big head of yours protected."

He gave her a flat look.

"Now, off you get," she said after her fussing was finished. "Ma, Da, and I will stop in when we have the chance, make sure Eissyr is well tended. I'll show the neighbors how to mix your medicines." She gestured at the larder, laden with the fruits of Dusk's healing labors, then gave him a frank look. "Farewell, Dusk of Sunreach. I'm not happy about this parting, and neither I nor things between us will be the same upon your return. The only promise I make is that Eissyr will want for nothing."

"Farewell, fairest Aryka of the Mountain," he whispered, squeezing her hand. "The only p-p-promise I can m-m-make to you is that I *will* return. And hopefully put things to r-r-rights upon that r-r-return. He released her hand and went to his mother's sickbed. His shining eyes fell upon her pale, lovely face as she lay dreaming. With no break in his voice, he said, "Farewell, brave Eissyr, mightiest of shield maidens. Stay strong just a little longer. I shall return to you, this time with a cure, not a respite only." He grabbed the woman's hand, and she stirred slightly.

"*Starlight*," Eissyr sighed. Dusk released her hand and adjusted her cushions.

"What does it mean?" Aryka whispered, coming to his side.

"I don't know," he said. "We will ask her w-w-when she wakes." With that, Dusk turned and walked straight out the door without looking back, just as Aryka had done two nights before. She watched him pass into the night like a shadow, avoiding the twinkling lights of the hundred houses spread up and down the slopes of Sunreach. And by the time half-dawn spilled scant light through the windows of the little cottage on the soaring heights, Aryka could imagine Dusk being far gone. It hurt Aryka's heart to imagine the boy walking alone, with only dreams of white towers, a blood-covered country, and a vicious power as companions.

2

SLEEPER AWAKENED

Rushing feet clattered to a halt, startling the man who lay on a stone slab. "They're breaking in!" cried a young voice.

"How many, Cailus?" barked a rich baritone.

"Thousands, lord: fomori, goblins, armored men, and a thing that stands a thousand feet tall, or I'm not an elf! Can you hear the booming from across the lake? That's it, sir. It hammers the cave's walls and all the earth with its fists, destroying all!"

"The packs and food we set aside from the rest," said the baritone, "with the battle garb, you remember?"

"Of course, sir," said the young voice.

"Bring them here. The day is come, Cailus."

"My lord, Lohrë!" The rushing feet hurried off, and all went quiet again. Except, there came a low, heavy boom from somewhere far away.

Who was talking? wondered the man who lay on the slab. Suddenly he cried out, memories flooding his mind. *Pain! Fire!* His thoughts raced as blood flowed back into ill-used limbs. *Monsters, thousands! What did they do to me? Where have they taken me? Are they here again?*

All was dark, and pain was everywhere. This was not his home. Shining shards of memory collided, each cutting into the other before anything coherent could form. All that was clear was fire and darkness. There had been a crash, then evil things surrounding him, then sleep. He drew a breath, but the mountain on his chest and ash in his throat forced him to convulse. His coughs echoed up and far away, a rhythm of small explosions in a deep, cold place.

Have I awakened only to die? Have I died already?

A lyrical voice, deep and calming, sang him to expectant silence. Its beauty filled his mind, carrying a memory of starlight. But he could not remember, and he could not understand what it said.

"You're finally awake," said the baritone voice from earlier, ending the song. The man understood the words this time, though they were less beautiful than the strange song he had sung. Still, it added a bit of music on the heels of the chaotic beat trotted out by the man's echoing coughs, and things seemed less terrible. "I suppose my true duty begins. And it only took two centuries to see it start."

Who are you? thought the man on the slab, anxiety growing. *Are you going to hurt me? Two centuries?* But only a low moan escaped his lips. *I have no words. Did I have any to begin with?* The rock under his back froze and bit. But before another series of coughs blistered his parched throat, he felt something cool, soothing, and fresh pour into his mouth.

"My name is Lohrë, and you'll have to forgive me," the low voice continued. "I've cared for you so long, and the days run so much the same: dark and quiet. You should have had water hours ago. Drink deeply, but not too much. You've been asleep for two hundred and twelve years, after all. Never know what the body will do if given too much after so long a time, even one so sturdy as yours. Drink now, and food will come later."

Two hundred? the man thought. But the draft, cool and sweet, spilled over his lips, sweeping all thought away, forcing his stinging eyes to water. He could not see, but the drink offered by the voice was a blessing. And he realized it was not the only water close at hand. He heard waves lapping nearby on a shore of stone, pushed by a subterranean breeze. With the wind came the ancient damp of endless water under the earth.

Laying forever beside a lake, he thought.

"Open your eyes, if you can," Lohrë said.

The man on the slab felt his lids flutter as he struggled with the effort. The weight of all the world had dislodged itself from his chest, but no sooner had it been freed than it stumbled and fell gracelessly over his eyes. He was also empty for lack of food and water, but the relentless darkness forced him to realize the thing he truly wanted: light.

Light. It flickered into his vision, chasing away the dark with little bursts of flame as he blinked, throwing off the clumsy weight on his eyes. They were starved of it, and he needed more. He forced his eyes open. But they burned and hurt, drawn to candle-fire after so long lost in the dark, but stung by unfamiliar air. Then, just as when he had been given the drink, he felt soothing coolness, this time flooding both eyes. His tears mingled with the healing solution, and he sobbed his relief.

"That's it," Lohrë said. "Blink, but don't rub them. My folk are well-versed in cures for the eyes, ours being the keenest in all the world. Try to remember, if you're able, anything that came before. Things grow urgent in the Outer-world, I fear. But here and for now, you're safe, watched over by many arrows. We wait for our provision to arrive. So, you must try."

Try what? the man thought. *I don't remember.*

A clacking rush broke the peace created by Lohrë's voice and introduced a frantic melody. "He wakes!" a young man cried, the words sending ghosts of lightning flashing in the dark. The man on the slab had closed his eyes once more to let them revel in the cold relief of this *Lohrë's* counterirritant. But the frantic, melodic voice—the same lad who had spoken of monsters and invading things—continued, forcing the man to open his eyes again in curiosity. All he saw were shadows chased by dim fire in the dark above. "Voices torture the dreams of our people, fomori by the thousand march through the Tomb, *and* the Star-farer wakes."

"You've never seen a star," Lohrë said flatly.

"I've seen *him*."

The lad must mean me, the man thought, blinking.

"He fell from the sky!" the boy continued. "And maybe he brought the last star down with him. What it all must mean. Surely adventures await us now."

"Our *duty*, Cailus, is to leave this place with our heads," scolded Lohrë. Then came a pause. "Though duty and adventure are often close companions. And I don't see why that wouldn't be the case here."

"Ha!" Cailus said. Then came a shifting of cloth and metal links. "Now, before you scold me for disobeying, sir, I've fetched the Sojourner his garb first, since everything you asked for was too much to carry in one trip. Off I go now for the packs and food, and do tell me if he sits up or speaks or eats on his own. In fact, tell me everything he does when I get back!" Booted feet fled, clacking once more into the deep beyond the stone on which the man lay.

Time to leave. Let me go with you. Can I leave? Could I stand if I wanted?

"Good lad, that one." Lohrë chuckled. The man shivered as a hand pulled away his blankets. Then strong arms wrestled him into new clothing. His caretaker continued, "Cailus chose this life as a lad, after we won the War. But, along with me and the rest of our host, he swore to keep you secret. So, to our people and the Outer-world, he's just as dead as the rest of us. He believed in me, and so in you. Here's hoping we did the right thing. If nothing else, I'm glad to see what he'll become now that his fate isn't to serve long years in the dark below the world. But none have eyes like his, or such bow skill, not even our young Messenger." He trailed off, silence washing back with the dark tide.

Hearing the pause, the man opened his eyes, now with cool ease. *Dark above and off in all directions*, he thought. *But*

I see light below me. I'm surrounded by it. Need more. With a will, he sent every signal at his disposal down through his limbs, stretching toes, moving fingers, and the like.

All in your right place, he thought. *And functioning properly. That's pleasing. Now I leave.* Next, he flexed ankle, calf, and shoulders such as he could. He shifted his feet closer to his torso so that his knees bent, facing the black above. Preparing his core for the fire of his next effort, the man hauled himself up on sore elbows, abdomen protesting as he knew it would.

"That's it!" said Lohrë. "Sit up now, and see your secret home."

The man on the slab twisted his torso, knowing the act from a dream or memory but struggling with the execution. He balanced his weight on stinging wrists, but at last, he sat up, legs swinging over his bed of stone. The dark world spun and rocked as blood fled, rushing in all directions. He clenched his eyes shut to the motion, snapping both hands to the sides of his head. Then came the fall, and he began to topple.

Crashing again!

But a steadying hand lay upon his shoulder, grounding him. Feeling as if it were all that anchored him to the world, he grasped at it with both hands and held it there until the chaos churning in his mind and gut settled.

"Well done," Lohrë said. "Some have said you would never wake. Now look at you: not just awake, but dancing before sitting all the way up! You must be one great acrobat or entertainer where you're from."

The sitting man felt his face contort upward, finding the motion pleasant and familiar.

"He smiles as well," Lohrë said. "If you open your eyes again, you'll find there is much to smile on in so grim a place."

The man, refusing to let go of the hand on his shoulder, opened his eyes again. He looked down to see gentle candlelight standing strong against the dark and his dizziness. All about him on the earthen floor stood little melting towers of tallow, beeswax, and cinnamon fruit. Close to them, all around his stone pallet, lay humble gifts of all sorts: tinderboxes, wreaths, flowers, packages of dried fruits and nuts, clay jars of honey and various spices, and many other such wonderful things. The man looked back at his stone bed, seeing it piled high with straw, flowers, and leaves, not half as uncomfortable as it had seemed. He then looked down at himself, seeing he had been dressed in a soft shirt and trousers of matching dark velvet. Then, seeing the tranquil light come to an end at an edge, he found the boundary of his prison. Lapping water stretched far, wide, and away: the placid black lake, his only known companion, that had so invaded his countless dreams. The water, disturbed by a thousand little drops falling from as many growing stalactites, stretched to a horizon so black that to fathom it sent his head reeling once more.

"See, sleeper?" Lohrë said, cutting into his dizzying reverie. "It's not so bad once you get used to it, our little slice of solace under-earth." The man then turned to look into the face of his caretaker, and a strange and wonderful face it was. The figure belonging to the low voice was tall and lean, his dark hair pulled back neatly. It trailed down the length of his back. He had a friendly but stern face, framed by broad ears ending in sharp points. And in his eyes the man saw gray clouds torn by lightning and hail.

I've seen your like before ... before what?

"Listen carefully," the dark-haired man said. "You've awakened in a secret place my people built for you. I suppose you could call me *Tomb-guard*, along with my brothers and sisters. I have kept watch over you for more than two lifetimes by count of Men, fulfilling my secret duty. And don't get me wrong with what I said about serving in the dark and all that. It's my honor, and I do it gladly. But young Cailus, with his sharp eye and quick feet—I see greatness in him beyond this darkness. He just needs to grow into it.

"You'll meet more of us in time, since we, who call ourselves the Qwei-Sillar, keep you. Although in the common tongue, we are called elves. *You* are called many names as well: *Firewalker* and *Lightfall*. *Star-farer* and *Starsailor* for those of us old enough to remember the Old Fires. And *King of Fomori* for those of us with a flare for the dramatic, though I would hesitate to call you something so sinister. We don't know who you are or whence you came, but you fell to our world on a ball of fire more than two hundred years ago, sparking the Fomori War. You understand the common tongue, which I speak to you now, yes?"

The man frowned at him, nodding slowly.

"However ..." Lohrë kept eye contact with the sitting man but tilted his head. Lohrë sang a handful of words that sounded like the music of dreams to the man on the slab. The man, kicking out his legs a bit, simply blinked at the stranger with storm clouds for eyes. Lohrë continued, "You do not seem to understand elvish. This is strange, as it is my language that has gone unchanged since the Devouring War. The tongues of Men have undergone a good many dialectic shifts since then. Though I suppose it is the least of the puzzles laid out for us. One we can solve for now is that of your name. If I were to list all your titles in elvish and mannish, we would stay down here another two centuries. For now, your name will be *Sojourner*. Can you stand?"

Sojourner, the sitting man mused. Then he frowned, considering the elf's question and the distance between his head and the rocky floor should he fall once more. Lohrë smiled, stepping back, offering an outstretched hand as if to shake. Sojourner nodded, focusing only on Lohrë's stormy face. He shifted his weight, feet touching the floor. Then, with courage and effort mingling, Sojourner lunged himself forward, throwing himself into the arms of his benefactor, who caught him.

"And there it is," Lohrë said, smiling down. Sojourner then saw the elf's features grow severe. "This is the first I've ever seen of blood or color in your face. And now that you're truly alive, I see you're not a man at all. Just a boy. Come on, we've little time. Let's see if we can't have you stand on your own. How about it?"

No, don't make me. I can't crash again! Sojourner clung to Lohrë, eyes widening with terror.

"Fear not," Lohrë said solemnly. "I've kept my oath to you for half my life. I will not let you fall now."

Drawing a deep breath, Sojourner nodded, made to push himself away from the tall man, then did so. And on wobbly knees, the man who once crashed to earth now stood aright for the first time in two centuries. Shaking but sturdy, he looked back to the elf, who bowed to him. A single laugh escaped Sojourner's throat, triumph radiating from him. Then he turned to look at what lay behind his resting spot again. The dark enormity of what he saw nearly sent him reeling to the floor once more.

He caught himself before the elf could offer a hand. But his eyes were wide again in awe of the black gulf stretching away in every direction. It overwhelmed him still, but less than it had a moment before, the paltry candle fires and their tiny resistance against the impenetrable dark kindling long-forgotten courage.

"Fall." The whisper barely escaped Sojourner's lips, and he quaked at the sound of his meager voice.

"Leóhteness-Fal," Lohrë said, bustling about and grabbing up odd items after seeming sure Sojourner could stand without help. "Our ineffable world in the dark. This pit of rock and water is named Deeplake. Live down here long enough and you'll see it's not so dreadful. There are patterns up there, little asterisms made by glowing worms, our tiny heroes who dig and eat in the soil and give us a little light. Our world is still a good one, no matter how dark. And those ancient ones who hollowed out these deep places long before ever we came to Leóhteness-Fal kept close hold of their secrets. So, we thought this the perfect place to hide you while you slept. The underground is said to stretch across the breadth of the darkling world, and we can escape when and wherever we so choose. Legends say these depths were home to empires, wars, terrors. Now I fear a new terror kindled from ash of the old, and powers moving in the Outer-world have grown too strong. The fomori have been searching for you since their defeat. They will be coming for you."

As the trembling man frowned at Lohrë, footsteps echoed toward them once more. Sojourner watched a lythe elvish lad trot up. Built the same as Lohrë, albeit a little smaller, the boy arrived, heavily laden. His smooth face would have suggested late teenage years had he been human, and he practically crackled with energy, slung all about with packs of provision and gear.

"Standing upright!" the boy said, smiling ear to sharpened ear. Candlelight sparked in his white-blond hair, reflected off silver tracks carved into an otherwise handsome face. "A miracle from Eternity himself."

"Indeed," Lohrë said. "And we'll need more of those if we're to set this lad on the right path, Cailus."

"What path is that, sir?" asked the elf boy, eyes bright and hungry.

"One to Wildercrown," Lohrë said darkly. Silence bloomed from where they stood. Far off, a drop of water collided with the surface of the black lake, its echo singing in the dark. Then came another deep boom, far off. The elves stirred.

"You mean to go back?" Cailus asked gently.

"I do," Lohrë growled.

"Lord Lohrë," Cailus said, hesitating. "We're dead."

"Then Wildercrown shall witness our revival," Lohrë snapped. "And three thousand elves long thought dead shall rise up from their Tomb to defend her."

"But," whispered Cailus, "seven thousand did die. And so many more before we fought to the Throne. Will our remnant survive?"

"To leave this world is gain," Lohrë said. "We have the promise of hope beyond it. For now, know that our day has come to see at least one miraculous thing: The Sojourner wakes! Let him be armed and garbed in elvish fashion."

With a nod, Cailus dropped the packs. He found another sack, embroidered with cloth-of-gold thread, and worked at its fastenings. Sojourner's eyes darted here and there, chasing the flicker of candle flame. In the empty infinity above, his eye caught a blue spark, then a small flare of gold. He stared up for a little while, his eyes adapting. Soon, a ceiling of sapphires glittered in the black vault, shocked by flashes of topaz and copper. Seams of opal and ice reflected candle-fire in the high ceilings above. Then, as if from a dream, a cloud of fireflies swirled over the lake, pricking fleeting, silver holes in the gloom. Transfixed, Sojourner could only stare in awe, until, from a space far over and beyond the lake darker than night, another booming rumble shook the waters beyond what had been his quiet resting place.

We are not safe here, Sojourner thought.

"Here we are," Cailus said, throwing back the flaps of the embroidered pack. He grew solemn, producing from it a battle helm that glowed golden-bronze in the candlelight. He approached the overwhelmed Sojourner, bowed, then lay the helm atop his head. Its cool weight settled there, and Sojourner was surprised at the lightness of such a fearsome armament. He looked to Cailus, who smiled before returning to the bag. The elf drew out several pieces of golden garb, fixing them in the crook of his elbow.

"By Eternity," a new voice gasped. Sojourner jumped and turned to see a new silhouette standing at the little fire's edge.

"Cyrwedh!" Cailus said, grinning behind an armload of gear and facing the newcomer. "Welcome to the rest of our lives, be they long or short, given what the Sojourner's waking could mean."

Stepping forward, the silhouette melted into a striking woman clad in armor, with weapons sheathed at her waist. Her long, flowing tunic and cloak were shimmering gray, and her boots were black. "I see that," she breathed. "We watched him wake from our post, and I needed to come down. It's been two centuries." Her amethyst eyes were filled with as much wonder as Sojourner's.

"A long time, even measured against the thousand or so years gifted to a Qweieth-Sil," Lohrë said gravely, turning to her. Firelight flared on the woman's cheeks for a moment, then she rubbed a hand under her eyes.

"All has changed, Lohrë," she whispered. "This Tomb is breached. Our enemies are returned. Do we fight them to the death now and make true the lie we told the Qwei-Sillar two hundred years ago?"

"No," Lohrë said. "We return to fight them at Wildercrown."

"Wildercrown?" she breathed, disbelief plain in her bright eyes.

"Our people suffered terrible losses to stem the tide of the fomori," Lohrë said. "Two hundred years will not have been enough time for them to have recovered. If our enemies have found this secret place, then surely they march upon Wildercrown where they know the Qwei-Sillar reside in strength."

"We cannot go back," she said.

"They will need our help," Lohrë replied.

"No!" the woman snapped. The explosion of her answer sent echoes rippling over the subterranean lake. Sojourner listened to the echo slowly vanish. Then he heard something else just as her voice faded beyond the reach of hearing. Another faint boom rumbled over the surface of the lake.

"This is no argument, *reileth*," Lohrë growled.

"You just made it one," she said. "You can't go back, not after what you did to them."

"They live because of us," Lohrë said quietly.

"They thought we all died in battle, after the Elf-lord and the Council ordered you not to go. We were supposed to have returned to our families!"

"The war was not yet won," Lohrë growled. "Our families would be dead if not for our taking of the Fomori Throne."

"What then," Cyrwedh said, motioning to Sojourner, "is your plan for this one?"

"I can only hope he will help disperse the mystery behind the voices that invade our minds and stand with us against the forces that invade our homes."

"They're always like this," Cailus said cheerily, stepping between Sojourner and the arguing elves to make a motion as if reaching to the sky. Sojourner did as Cailus had, and Cailus threw a chilly breastplate of seemingly interwoven strips of metal over Sojourner's shoulders. He shivered at its touch, even through the warmth of his shirt. The golden armor was hard as forged steel but moved over his chest like water, clinging to his body like a perfectly tailored glove.

"The fomori took everything from the Qwei-Sillar," Cyrwedh whispered. "Then *we* dealt them the worst wound of all: removing their greatest general, their *prince*. What would it do to them seeing us return to our city, back from the dead, only to die in battle against the fomori, whom our people also thought dead with our sacrifice?"

"Cyr," Lohrë sighed. "It was a choice."

"Choice?" she asked. A terrible silence descended, the meager light seeming to recoil.

"A choice made by faith," Lohrë whispered.

"Faith," she said, as if chewing the word. "By faith, what did you do, Lohrë?"

Lohrë stood, tall and defiant before her. "Stayed true to what I believed, about the Sojourner, about the Fomori War two hundred years ago cracking the vault."

"Based on some old prophecy only the most decrepit of us remember?"

"A prophecy that has proved *true*, Cyrwedh," Lohrë said, motioning to the frowning man standing in traveling clothes, an elvish helm, and a half-fastened hauberk. "He wakes."

The silence fell again, and all Sojourner could hear was the swishing of cloth, clamor of chain, and snap of buckles as Cailus fastened the elvish garb to his arms, neck, and chest. Moving to see the pair, Sojourner saw the woman's eyes fall, despair rippling in violet pools as she shrank. "I saw the hosts, Lohrë," Cyrwedh whispered. "All is as Cailus told: tens of thousands marching this way. Lohrë, what can one man waking do against the same dark powers we thought we had defeated utterly, only for them to spring up again, stronger than before?"

"He can go with us to Wildercrown, help us find whoever it is that is sending these messages into our minds. There must be a connection between the Sojourner and the *Heir*. The Elf-lord will have answers."

Angst building, Sojourner huffed his disapproval. *Words don't come easily*, he thought. *But who are you that you all make my decisions for me?*

"Will the Elf-lord even believe it is you?" Cyrwedh asked. "As far as he must be concerned, his son and his daughter-in-law are long dead."

"An army of ghosts at his doorstep will claim his attention if my boldness does not," Lohrë said.

"Two hundred years away from home and our families," she mused, turning her back to him. "Two hundred years spent at your side thinking I was doing right by you.

Seems *my* choice was not all to my benefit. I pray yours sees us all to a better end than languishing at the bottom of this dark pit. Know that wherever your choice takes you in the long years of your life, my love, I am with you. Even if it leads you to Wildercrown, against my counsel, I will protect you. But know, too, that I am not pleased."

"Cyr," Lohrë said, reaching a hand to her. With a smooth motion, she backed away, melting into the shadows at candlelight's edge once more.

"Your prophecy has proved right," her silhouette admitted. "And now I've some part to play. I'll begin it by getting you and this Sojourner out of here. Don't make me resent my choice, or you."

Cailus slapped a pair of pauldrons to Sojourner's shoulders and fastened them. Each was mismatched in size for mobility of Sojourner's right arm. He watched the shadow of Cyrwedh's head turn toward another booming thud echoing across the black gulf.

I don't know how, but we are not safe here, Sojourner thought again. *When do we leave?*

"We leave now," Cyrwedh said, gazing across the sable lake. "I fear even this talk has stolen precious time."

Sojourner saw Lohrë nod. "The Elf-lord needs to know of the Sojourner's waking and our enemy marching under earth," he said. "After he hears my news, hears my reasons, I will be there to see his face when he realizes, for once, that I was right."

"And the Warrior must have had his reasons for approaching you back then, showing you all that would come to pass in this age, and *has*," she replied. Sojourner saw her eyes flash at Lohrë's shocked look. "Oh yes, I know of what he told you, my love. And with these voices we hear, reminding us of old oaths, I wouldn't be surprised if old faces, more than just the Elf-lord's, reveal themselves to us once more."

Sojourner's frustration was near boiling, his questions bubbling over. But before he could pull away from the elf-lad, Cailus spun him and fixed his hands and arms with bracers the color of amber. The lad also took each of Sojourner's legs, guiding his feet into a pair of sturdy traveling boots of the same make and hue. And as Lohrë approached the lady, leaning in to kiss her, Cailus threw an argent cloak around Sojourner's shoulders, obscuring the scene.

"You're not off the hook," Cyrwedh said, putting a finger to Lohrë's lips. "You've hurt me. Eternity only knows how many more you've hurt in the spreading circles of your *choices*. Understand that your debt to me is not assuaged, only changed and multiplied."

Lohrë's mouth was a thin, taut line. He nodded to her.

"All done!" said Cailus, beaming. "Garbed as one of us and ready to join me on my sure-to-come adventures." The elf boy stepped back.

Lohrë and Cyrwedh turned to look at Sojourner. "I know why we were sent here, Cyr," Lohrë said. "Though I know not whether the Elf-lord will understand. I see the *Sojourner* of legend, garbed like a hero of the Qwei-Sillar, in this living-tomb under the earth. And my blood is stirred to take my rightful place in this ancient puzzle that just now decides to reveal its shape to us. I know my fate will be intertwined with his, and that I will be reconciled to my father. My brother, as well."

"Then we must away," Cyrwedh said. "I want to see light, true light again. We've a task to complete and places to go in this world that doesn't belong to us. And maybe, once we're free of duty and doom, you'll chase me through the falling leaves, the way you did when we were young and you were but a humble prince."

Lohrë smiled at that. "It would be my honor, lady."

Sojourner heard Cailus clear his throat. "Lord," he said to the pair of them. "It is time."

"We depart, Cailus," Lohrë said. "And no lord stands here, at least not since the days of the Fomori War. Though, maybe I'll need to be one again, for I fear war has already returned. For now, Lohrë will suffice."

"How could I forget?" Cailus laughed. "To the surface!"

With that, the three elves gathered their precious packs, food, and drink. Sojourner watched, his concentration solely upon staying upright under the weight of his new armaments. Soon Lohrë handed a pack to him, which he slung over his shoulders.

"We are off now for my city, friend," the elf said. "It will be a long journey up through the dark, then through forest and swamp, over hill, and into valley. Your full voice may return with time, but for now, you must signal me if you need to rest, understood?"

Sojourner shook his head vigorously.

"Well, some things will have to be revealed as we go," Lohrë said. "A stiff march will doubtless help you remember your old strength."

Finally at the end of his patience, Sojourner stomped his newly-booted foot.

A roaring crash and the scream of a thousand horrible voices cut him off. The four companions looked out over the black lake. What Sojourner had thought an endless expanse beyond the reaches of the waters had been a black wall of solid rock. That wall now crumbled in an avalanche of destroyed stone and soil. Through the breach, countless pinpricks of fire threw up a cloud of crimson that reflected off the stone ceiling a thousand feet above. The fires advanced, weaving a burning path around the distant rim of the dark lake. A host innumerable poured through the tear in the earth.

Cyrwedh readied a war bow that had been hidden amongst the folds of her cloak.

Lohrë stood, jaw clenched, watching the torch fires as their bearers marched along the distant shoreline. Then he remembered himself and turned to his companions. "We leave Deeplake, make for the Sunken Lofts. From there, we get an eye on just what Cailus has told us of that possesses strength enough to breach the walls of solid earth. We'll also need a man to speed word of Sojourner's waking to the Warrior."

"The *surgeon*, as he calls himself in these after-days," Cailus said, fire's reflection catching in his eyes.

"You would know best, with one ear in the Tomb and

the other ever listening abroad." Lohrë chuckled. "Cailus, the task will fall to you. For now, your eyes are best in this darkness. You know where we go?"

The young elf smiled lazily at the taller one, as if his master had asked a question and given away the answer all in the same breath.

"Good," Lohrë said. "Cyr, we rely on your arrows should our enemies draw near."

"Our bows are ready," she replied. "They will die before ever they see us."

Lohrë nodded, drawing his deadly sword. Sojourner, who had lain upon a slab of stone for over two centuries, now standing and decked in the argent and gold of ancient days, drew two swords of his own from his belt. Lohrë smiled at him. "Our gifts suit you well, friend. May you never have need of them while we make the climb out of this place, or even as you escape it and travel within our borders." Then, to both elves and the man he said, "Quietly, now. Away!"

The four companions sprang away, leaving behind the little dais by the black lake that stood surrounded by a hundred little gifts for a man who slept as if dead. And the gentle light of candlewick that had been burning for more than two centuries died as it was overtaken by the marching blaze of ten thousand torches.

3
THE TOMB IS FULL

Their journey took them through narrow passageways, around bottomless chasms, and under ceilings dotted with the light of incandescent fireflies and glowing fungi. The man whose companions had named Sojourner stopped so many times to gawk at such things that he soon forgot his hunger and his host's earlier promise of food altogether. His new friends eventually tied cords to his belts and theirs to ensure he paid attention to hidden dangers and kept up with them as they trotted through the dark.

The torchlight from their pursuers proved a constant companion, Sojourner finding that it gave him new eyes in what he thought a dreary, cheerless place. What he had taken for a hellish, pitch-black cave became quite the opposite when aided by the distant, fiery glow. Although pursued by fear and the strange, marching host, Sojourner's dim prison expanded by leaps into an intricate system of glittering tunnels, halls, and wonders of living stone that shone humbly in their ancient enormity. He spotted rivers aglow with alien fish whose eyes were bigger than his balled fist. The underground world revealed itself to be made just as much of silent waters as of cold, familiar rock. Everywhere his feet slipped, splashing into yet another black pond. A low growl had also grown steadily for hours in his ears as he and his companions ran ever ahead of the torchlight. And when they rounded a corner of jagged rock together, they found a waterfall thundering before them, its river roaring down from higher, darker places before plunging into infinite black below. The abyss beneath them nearly overwhelmed Sojourner, and his collapse forced the group to call an hour's rest.

In the murk of restless sleep and the raging of the falls, Sojourner awoke more than once to see tall figures with bright eyes and faces scarred by golden-silver scrawlings pass through their makeshift camp. He heard them speaking low and urgently in the lyrical tongue of his companions before fading away again like smoke. And when he sat up to watch them go, the only trail left by their passing lay between dream and memory. When Lohrë woke him, Cyrwedh and Cailus were nowhere to be seen. Without a word from Lohrë as to where the others had gone, the elf gave Sojourner a few strips of dried beef, some strong cheese, and a handful of nuts and dried berries. The rustic fair was a banquet to Sojourner, who could not guess the last time he had tasted food. But before he could savor his meal, Lohrë stood him up, and the two of them were off again at a trot under the night sky of the underground.

Sojourner soon found himself pursued by memory of a ship as he fought to keep up with Lohrë. Sails and swirls of mist over endless water were chased by the winds of his mind, while the roars of the invaders who marched below them chased him through this darker, harsher world. The cries of the marching host reminded him of gulls' shrill calls over an ocean, though he did not know what an ocean or a gull were, or when he had seen either. But such thoughts fell away soon enough as the flashing flames, his pouring sweat, and the burning in his legs and chest formed an amalgam of pain as he followed Lohrë. Sojourner found roots jabbing out of the uneven ground tugging at his ankles with what seemed every step. Despite these nuisances, or perhaps because of them, he did all he could to return to thoughts of masts and a solid deck underfoot. Those dreams or memories, and the dull pains of his efforts, lulled him into a waking sleep. In that gray wakefulness, the ocean spoke a name.

Eshra, Eshra, Eshra. Sojourner's eyes had been open, but he now saw for the first time a figure in front of him, keeping pace with every harried step he took. It was a woman, facing him, somehow floating backward as he came on. Then she stopped. He gasped, not at the shadow cast by her concealing cloak, but at the eager smile that split her lovely face, the angry light that pricked her eyes. She held pale hands before her, as if pushing herself up against a pane of glass. A crack formed in the space between them. That was all she needed. Her smile went manic, then a cry of despair pierced his waking dream. The voice was his own.

"Not so loud, friend," came Lohrë's whisper. "They're

close now." Sojourner sat up from a bundle of blankets he had not remembered wrapping himself in. Then he saw the elf in the amber glow, whose brightness had grown. Lohrë, perched in a concealing outcrop of stone, looked down from their high, narrow road. Sojourner rose and crawled on all fours to where the elf knelt.

"Eshra, Eshra, Eshra!" The name, chanted over and over again, echoed up from an endless column of men and monsters, marching under a river of flowing firelight.

"Eshra?" Sojourner asked. The word seemed twisted, somehow wrong in his mouth.

"So, he speaks," Lohrë whispered in wonder. The elf gave the boy a gentle slap to the shoulder. "Seems your nightmare's scared the name right out of you. I don't know what it means. Sometimes they rave about a tree and a king, but always they return to *Eshra*. When some within their ranks stop to talk, I do recognize a few of the tongues spoken, though what they say makes little sense; things out of old stories. Then again, *you*, sleeping under the earth, waking after centuries, makes little sense either, my friend. It would seem we've become wrapped up quite neatly in a tale of our own."

"Wrapped," Sojourner said, holding Lohrë's gaze. He pointed a finger to the blankets, then to his own chest. He made a solemn motion, closing his eyes as if sleeping. Then he frowned at the elf, shaking his head.

Lohrë nodded. "You wandered off last night, turning completely off our road. I followed for a few hundred paces until you stopped before a narrow, deep pool. You were hot with fever, staring as if at something that scared you. Then you dropped. I fished you out of the water then brought you here to rest. We're back on our road, and you've been down about four hours."

"What are you doing here?" came a hiss out of the gloom. The cloaked form of Cyrwedh blurred into being, backed by Cailus and a handful of what Sojourner thought to be tall stalagmites. "We should have come to the Lofts hours ago," she continued. "They're so close, they might catch us if they so much as look up!"

"We needed rest," Lohrë whispered patiently. "With cover of dark, and the shouts of those marching fools, they'll never know we were here. There is still time to talk. What news?"

To Sojourner, the standing rocks behind Cyrwedh and Cailus suddenly broke themselves off from the cavern floor and stepped forward to become a handful of dour elves.

"Qwei-Sillar," Sojourner whispered. This word carried no such shadow as the name chanted by the host marching below and felt light to his tongue. The figures stood as tall and elegant as his companions, the torch fire of their enemies flaring in metallic sparks off the patterns that decorated their faces. The elves, armed and armored, looked upon him with keen eyes that shone like the lights of the silver moths that had greeted him when he awoke on his bed of stone. Some eyes went wide. Others brimmed with tears.

Sojourner heard whispers of, "*He lives, Sky-render, so it was true,* and *legend itself,*" hissed among them. "*Has it* to do with the voices? We've all heard them, Lohrë. What are we to do now? Our people think we died. Who are the First Children, lord, and why do they need our help? And who is the Heir? Will this Star-farer help us?"

"My friends," said Lohrë, standing to quiet the assembled Qwei-Sillar. "Faith is paid in full, but there is mischief about. The Sojourner has awakened, and now is the time for you to know that my intent was never to keep you here, forever sleeping in this burial ground. I do not beg your forgiveness. But I hope you'll come to know that the oaths I swore serve a greater purpose. We leave the deep and return to Wildercrown with our bows. She will need us against this gathering storm."

"We cannot stand against that," whispered an elf missing an ear.

"We cannot," Lohrë confirmed. "But we've done a good thing, just by being here, seeing this. We will be Wildercrown's hope: the lost battalion risen from the dead! I tell you this: I have heard the voices, just as you have. I know not who the *First Children* are, though they be mentioned ceaselessly in our minds. But they beg us to remember an ancient oath, and it is no coincidence that our guest here wakes with their call to us."

"We let our doubts in, lord," said a woman. To Sojourner's ear, she nearly sang the words at Lohrë. "Forgive *us*."

"There is nothing to forgive, Wyndarra," Lohrë said, putting up a placating hand. "Two hundred years you've stood watch, when most of us are given no more than a thousand; more than enough time to call things into question, even for a Qweieth-Sil. Now, what news from the perimeter guard?"

"The fomori have not seen us," said an elf with an open wound that bled from his scalp. "Though we did not expect such devastating strength from their colossus. It could crush a mountain if it wanted. Many of us were wounded when we escaped its wrath. The fomori give the thing a wide birth, so it destroys wantonly as they do their best to control its path."

"But they could not all escape the ruin of the wall at the lakeshore, marching too close together," Cyrwedh said. "We guess some three hundred goblins and fomori died in the falling rocks when they broke through to Deeplake."

"Their pace has slowed, but their host still pours through that gap, with no visible end to their numbers," added Wyndarra. "We don't know their destination, as talk is scarce among them, save the name they chant. The course they take suggests some knowledge of this place, and they seem to march toward the Eastern Window."

Others joined in the reporting, and the group dropped into the musical elvish language from here, and the group, some twelve in all, conveyed other tidings.

Before long, Cailus made his way over to Sojourner, clapping a hand to his armored shoulder. "We've reached the Sunken Lofts, where we can survey all the underground. It marks roughly halfway between *Deeplake*, where you lay, and one of the hidden doors leading to the surface."

THE TOMB IS FULL

Sojourner blinked at the elf, looking after the group of elves who made frantic gestures. He turned then to peer over the edge of the precipice at the horde below.

"It must all be hard to understand," Cailus said, offering him a seat on the ground beside him.

Sojourner stared at the conferring elves, then back to Cailus, blinking.

"I understand only a little of it myself, being one of the youngest," Cailus said. "As you may have come to suspect, our humble Tomb-warden, Lohrë, is more than he appears to be. He sacrificed more than his reputation to be here, to see this very thing, in this very moment. And while I itch to be off, and I find the enemy too close for comfort, I respect his wishes for counsel. And while we wait, I can tell you a little of him and our people, maybe clarify some things."

Sojourner nodded, accepting the elf's invitation.

"There was a war," Cailus began as Sojourner sat. "It was long ago by the reckoning of Men, sparked by *your* arrival of all things. Beasts from the poisoned sea northward took your fiery fall to mean their time had come for conquering. Those beasts called themselves *fomori*, grim and fierce; perhaps our oldest and most incessant foes upon this world. And after many years and countless lives lost, we and the ancestors of Men beat the fomori back in the war they started. We drove them into the sea, where they reside to this day in little caves, scratching a meager living off sea-foam and fish."

A harsh hiss drew Sojourner's attention, and he saw

an elf heavy with muscle point a long finger at Lohrë, who stepped right up to him expectantly. Cyrwedh stepped in between the two fighters, facing the bigger one.

"But something happened in that terrible battle that baffles Qweieth-Sil and Man alike," Cailus continued. "Lohrë, our greatest commander, was struck down by the fomori king. I was not there, only told so as I fought at other parts. But stories say the hulking fomori king, with his single blazing eye, burned Lohrë with the flaming beam it threw forth. And just as the king of monsters made to slay my lord, a warrior of Men, unknown and unlooked for, stepped forth from the fray to do battle with him. So fierce was the battle that a hundred fomori were slain in its wake. Then, delivering the final blow, the warrior struck off the fomori king's head, and the fire from its wheeling eye scorched a hundred more!

"After the battle was won, Lohrë came to, healed by the strange warrior who had slain the fomori king with hands possessing skill both to maim and mend. The warrior, garbed in ancient armor, gave Lohrë a message portending doom. The warrior said that, for all our fighting and dying in that Fomori War, as it was named thereafter, it was only the beginning. The stranger called the fomori invasion a slapdash attempt at domination that would pale in comparison to the final stroke of forces greater, more terrible. But so few of us were left in the wake of war that none would listen. Our warriors saw in the stranger little more than the perceived ramblings of an old beggar. A beggar, mind you, who, by power both ancient and deep, for

THE TOMB IS FULL

that is the only way he could have done so, had wandered deep into our woods and slain our most terrible foe on a nigh unreachable shore. Although, I cannot blame those who refused him. Even then, Wildercrown lay half-empty. By now, entire wards must be reclaimed by the Qweth-Wëalda, our fierce, beloved forest. As Lohrë said, we've had no time to recover our strength, for children come seldom. And when they do, it is cause for great celebration.

"Ragged armies of Qwei-Sillar and Men departed the battlefield after the fomori king's death, forging bonds of friendship and promises of help in dire times, should such things arise again. Peace descended, and folk returned to assemble the shards of shattered lives. But Lohrë, having sworn an oath to the strange beggar for saving him, thought ever on the man's message: The war wasn't truly over, only postponed to be worsened later. Soon, whispers of an Enemy, older and deadlier than the fomori, rode the wind. This new foe had yet to reveal itself, but Lohrë thought back to the signs of your coming: a sky ablaze with fire, a Storm awakening on its heels, raging to this day upon the Dread-Coast. So, instead of simply allowing the battle to be won, the war to be over, Lohrë sought out his rescuer once more.

"Stories say the warrior appeared before Lohrë once my lord had made up his mind to find this Enemy. The pair of them disappeared for whole seasons, hunting answers. While away, they found the greatest source of power given to the fomori. It was a throne, one their ugly king had erected over top of a cataclysmic hole in the earth, where your fire had landed. The place crawled with thousands of the beasts—to what purpose, we know not to this day. Lohrë returned to Wildercrown, mustered as many of us as could be found into his greatest army, and marched upon the throne of the fomori in secret. The battle that ensued there, the graves it dug ..." Cailus shivered, eyes downcast. He fell silent for a while, and the music of the elvish warriors speaking in the gloom, paired with the drumming of the marching host below, filled Sojourner's ears.

Before the silence stretched overlong, Cyrwedh came over and lay a hand on the young elf's shoulder. Cailus shook himself out of his reverie. "Forgive me, Sojourner," he said. "There's hardly a Qweieth-Sil alive who wasn't wounded by that last of all fights."

Cyrwedh nodded. "You have the truth of it, Cailus. I heard your telling and tried to split my ears between you and the news. The conversation over there brought me closer to handing out blows rather than information, so I thought it best to detach myself and help with your telling." She looked to Sojourner.

So many questions, he thought.

"Lohrë and his hosts slew the fomori on the steps of their very throne, defeating them utterly, throwing down their chair, and casting them into the sea forever," Cyrwedh said. "And below the battle, at the bottom of the hole over which they had built their throne, there lay a single man."

Sojourner gasped at a memory of sudden fire, then of beastly things tearing at him, burying him. "Monsters," he whispered, then clapped both hands to his mouth, eyes wide.

The elf boy nodded eagerly, his grief evaporating. "So you *do* speak! Yes. Your arrival, our war, and the damage it all wrought. They broke something in places deeper than this."

Cyrwedh sighed. "Lohrë always held that the break was the releasing of the Enemy, mentioned by the warrior, though perhaps the break was more a crack. He could never prove such a thing to the Qwei-Sillar, only ask those of us who loved and fought beside him to believe him, then to march away with him into the dark, hoping to stand vigil over a man who portended doom and be witness to something worse coming."

Sojourner grasped Cailus' collar, pointed to the river of fire marching in the valley of crystals below.

"Eshra, Eshra, Eshra!" the marching monsters cried.

Cailus nodded again. "We've now all seen worse things. Those torchbearers form a large piece of an even greater puzzle, we think. Oh, and don't think all we've done is sit by your side like solemn embalmers. Nor that the dozen or so of us you've seen so far is the limit of our strength. Fear not! We are exiled, not disbanded. More of our eyes watch under the earth than on the surface. Now, make ready!"

The elvish boy and armored traveler checked their gear and garb as Cyrwedh returned to Lohrë and the other warriors, who broke conclave. Sojourner watched the lithe figures depart like dust in a storm, then Lohrë and Cyrwedh returned to him and Cailus. The tall elf asked with a glance if they were ready. They all nodded, and their leader only told them, "Our kin follow." Then the four of them set off once more, their path flaring bloody by torchlight splashing off the half-buried surfaces of agates.

The rest of the journey brought them into more civilized parts of the deep Tomb. They walked past chiseled columns that leaped from the floor into the black above and climbed granite stairs that curved ever upward. They stopped at several wells and fire pits, and Sojourner spotted carts, moldering ropes, and broken tools outside of what appeared to be long-abandoned mineshafts. Carven tunnels led off their path into other passageways and depths, but Cailus led them steadily upward. Whether by uncanny sense of sight, direction, or both, the young elf never faltered, even when his companions saw bright-eyed figures in gray cloaks gathering and marching silently behind them, growing ever greater in number with each passing hour.

The pace of the journey began again to take on a dream-like quality as Sojourner kept his gaze forward on Cailus' shoulders while all else blurred by in the dark. Whenever he looked back, sometimes he would see Lohrë and Cyrwedh speaking softly to one another. Other times he would find Lohrë gone and Cyrwedh's lean back and arms pulling taught as she aimed her drawn bow into the vague glow of the firelight behind them. Such instances only blurred the line between wakefulness and dreams.

THE TOMB IS FULL

And Sojourner, a little desperate never to let his mind lull too long, lest sleep carry him away down some endless passage and into dreams for another century, made a point to focus on such things to keep himself awake. The soreness of his feet, his burning lungs, and want for water were excellent motivators. As these things drew more and more of his concentration, he hardly noticed the window of light that drew near. Only when it grew large enough to envelop him, his companions, and the stairs up which they climbed did Sojourner see that they had made their way out of the Tomb, and that he was painfully awake.

More light than he had seen in all his days within the waking world dazzled his eyes, and he brought a hand up to shield them. His other, he clasped securely to Cailus' shoulder, dreading that the steadfast elves would force him to continue, even if blinded. But Sojourner felt the young elf stop, then heard Lohrë say, "We've run a good race; gained hours on our friends, and perhaps days on our enemies. But now comes the harder part of our trek home, where all haste will be needed. Rest for an hour. Eat, drink, get used to daylight, then we leave."

"Darker than I remember," whispered the voice of Cyrwedh. "Has the very daylight of the world grown weak in our absence?"

"A connection between the voices, fomori, and the Sojourner?" Cailus asked from Sojourner's side.

"We'd be foolish to dismiss such things now," she replied. Sojourner saw, separate from the golden glare of the Outer-world, pale skin and metallic slivers of scarlet under her gray hood. "I'll look ahead, and to see how our country has changed in all this time."

"I'll scout opposite," said Lohrë. "Cailus, stay a while, until he regains his vision. Then get a view of the wider world for yourself. I foresee little danger here inside the next hour."

Sojourner heard light feet pad away, then the sound of shifting packs as Cailus quested for food.

The first few minutes under free air were bright agony as Sojourner accepted food and water he could not see. He kept his eyes shut while he ate, but after his meal, he opened them to a sprawling forest under jagged mountains and a cloudless sky. Sojourner gazed in wonder at a dozen kinds of encircling trees as they swayed and marched away north and south toward climbing foothills. The scent of sweet spruce was a welcome change to the damp of the underground.

"Qweth-Wëalda," Cailus said with a homesick sigh. "The one and only place the Qwei-Sillar have ever called ours on Leóhteness-Fal. The forest stretches a thousand miles in all directions, and none have ever walked its full length for all its dangers, both visible and veiled."

Sojourner stood, finding himself taking gulps of the rich air as the wind nipped his ears and nose. He looked back to the Tomb's hidden door. A small square of crumbling stonework lay overgrown with scrub and vine. It seemed little more than an oddly shaped well, able to fool the eye of all but the most astute of passersby. He could

THE TOMB IS FULL

scarcely believe a single room, let alone a whole twilit country, lay under the little, stone window.

Sojourner then looked to Cailus, making contact with the lad's silver-gray eyes. "Water?" he whispered.

Cailus nodded as he prepared their packs, along with those left behind by their two companions. "There should be clean streams nearby if memory serves," he said. "Here, fill our bottles, strengthen your legs and eyes, and take in a little more of our home-world-away-from-home. As Lord Lohrë said, you shouldn't run into much trouble in these parts, not until the fomori catch up in a day or two. Go on! I'll have fire and a pipe ready for you when you get back."

Sojourner gave an excited nod, gathered up water skin, gourd, and flask, and made his way through rough scrub and tall, silver grass. Looking eastward to the mountains he had spied earlier, Sojourner caught the knife edge of a river shining as it cascaded down from the high places. He made his way toward the sound of rushing water and dared to look skyward now that the pain in his eyes had subsided. The bright dome above cast a bronze hew over the world, hinting of evening's approach. He wondered briefly if the elves would journey once more through the dark after light had gone down for the day, forcing him to stumble and stave off his walking dreams. But the thought of Cailus' eyesight, Cyrwedh's bow, and Lohrë's strength put his mind at ease as his path emptied him onto the river's noisy edge. He stood on a pebble-shod shore and saw fish leap up the banks in a flare of silver scales as he watched, awe-struck.

GARDEN OF ASH

A smile came to his face then, and he basked in the smell of clear water and the sound of it coursing over stone. He dropped his bottles, then his face, to the water's edge and saw his reflection stare back at him. He was startled to see brown eyes and dark hair flecked with streaks of gold. His cheeks and chin were sharp and pointed respectfully, and he shattered the image as his hands plunged into the cold water. He flushed his face, the cold water making him gasp and shiver. He laughed at the sensation, shook his head, and saw the droplets pepper the water's surface. He saw his own smile in the water then, another first, and felt at ease. But then, another thing he had not seen before appeared, and at first, he took it for the reflection of one of his companions' faces. But this one was dark and gray and crowned with horns. The eyes were fierce, and its smile—too wide, with too many teeth—was no smile at all. From behind him, a baleful shriek broke Sojourner's peace.

A wiry hand tore at the back of his neck and plunged his head underwater. He struggled, terror building as he spluttered and coughed, thrashing for air. But the hand held him.

"Ephtarrath!" roared a high, cold voice when he forced himself up for a sliver of air. Then the strength behind the hand that held his neck multiplied, and he went coughing into the cold water again.

What is happening? Who is this? It's cold. Too much water! Sojourner thought. *If I go on like this, I'll fall asleep again. Anything but that. Anything. Anything!* With the thought, he heaved himself backward, the back of his head crashing into something fleshy that yielded with a crunch. A howl tore through the fresh, bright air, and the pressure holding him to the water's edge disappeared. Sojourner stood upright, whirling. A creature his size and shape, horned, hunched, and razor-toothed, clutched at the flattened wedge of its nose. Sojourner's terror rose at the sight of the thing, and he drew out one of the elvish blades Lohrë had given him at the edge of Deeplake. Beyond its unsheathing days ago in the dark, the weapon felt familiar in his hand. But there was no time to consider the weapon, for just then, the dark man-beast ripped a jagged knife from a scabbard at its side, and it lunged at him with a guttural cry.

Not knowing what compulsion guided his hand, Sojourner struck aside the beast's knife jab. With his back to the water, he pushed away from the thing, keeping the full length of his sword between him and it. This only enraged the beast, and it flailed at him with its knife and gnarled hand. The hand, balled into a fist, swatted aside Sojourner's sword and hit his chest like a hammer blow. He staggered back, driven to the water's edge, gasping. There he fought blade-to-blade with the creature, his feet splashing in ankle-deep water.

I'm your match, he thought toward the beast, though he only reacted to its wild slashing. But just as Sojourner saw the gray-skinned thing's strength ebb against his makeshift defense, it cast aside its notched knife and barreled into him. Cold and wet sloshed over his head again, and he felt water plunge into his ears and nose as the side of his face raked river stones. The beast's hand held him under again, while the other beat at him, striking chest, stomach, and groin. Panic rose, strength ebbed, and dark set in.

Dark! Sojourner's mind screamed. *Dark and sleep!* He caught his attacker's pounding fist in his own and broke its thumb in three places without knowing how. The pressure on his face and neck lessened, and he threw himself up, into air and light. The creature wailed, grasping its hand, and Sojourner flattened its nose a second time. The strength of his blow sent the beast sprawling on the stony shore, but before Sojourner could catch his breath or grab his sword, it was up and running at him with a new dagger in its twisted hand. It made to ram its blade past his weaponless guard, but it stopped short, an arrow sprouting from its throat. Then, to Sojourner's amazement, a flare of light swept off the arm that held the dagger. Sojourner's attacker dropped to both knees before another flash of light tore its throat. It fell at his feet, bleeding and lifeless.

"You're hurt?" Cailus asked, pressing a cool cloth to the side of Sojourner's face as the elf looked over his other scrapes and cuts.

"There will be more," Lohrë said, black blood streaking his blade. "There always are."

There was a crack, then a scream not far away. Sojourner looked away from Cailus to see Cyrwedh, cloaked and shadowed, nocking another arrow to her war bow. "One less," she said.

"No hurts," Sojourner grunted, motioning to the creature's ruin as the Cailus removed the rag.

"Fomori," Cailus said, striking the edge of his sword blade against the beast's gray hide with a metallic ring. The point of his blade found the creature's mouth, revealing rows of pointed teeth.

"Two centuries gone, and no less vile," Cyrwedh said, rejoining the group. "And now ten thousand march through the dark."

"Toward Wildercrown," Lohrë added, turning to Sojourner. "We're sorry for letting you get too far astray, friend. Your fight, and this thing's cry, brought us running. We'll not let you out of eyesight again."

"We swear it," Cyrwedh confirmed.

"He held his own, though," commented Cailus, a wry smile crossing his sharp features as Sojourner clenched his fingers into a fist, then released them. "Seems our Sojourner is stronger even than *he* believed."

"Good," Lohrë said. "We'll all have need of strength if we're to survive the wild."

"Ephtarrath," Sojourner said, pointing to the fallen fomori, then to his chest.

"It called you that?" Cyrwedh asked.

At Sojourner's nod, Lohrë's face darkened. "You're dressed as one of us. No surprise that it called you what we once called ourselves in lives long past. But it only confirms my guesses. The fomori seek the deaths of elves, and they march on Wildercrown. We must beat them there. Forth!"

The companions sprang away again, all four of them at a run. They sped past tree and stone, spurred by duty and fear, reinvigorated by light of a clear, golden sky.

4
WORN PATH TO WILDERCROWN

Days had passed, and Lohrë's pace had taken the elves and Sojourner well over a hundred miles. Instead of the deep atrophy he had expected from muscle and joint, Sojourner found his body ready to test itself against the twisting will of the elvish wild. The constant trot for hours proved no easy task, but he soon found his legs accepting of the challenge, especially when so much beauty readied itself to jump out at every turn. White trees dropped silver leaves as if to guide their way, despite Lohrë insisting they stay off any road, elvish-built or otherwise. Tall stags that glowed with white-blue fire turned hundred-antlered heads at their passing. And once while they dashed through a thicker, darker part of the elvish wood, Sojourner spotted a timber house built high in a sturdy tree. Motes of floating fire danced in the treetops, illuminating a rope ladder that had been thrown down in welcome. But Lohrë refused to stop in such a place, warning that the wood was home to creatures more welcoming and less benevolent than the Qwei-Sillar.

WORN PATH TO WILDERCROWN

Lohrë was the perfect guide, leading them without word along paths hidden from the common eye yet retrieved from well-trodden memory. Cyrwedh followed from all angles at a distance, watching over the three men with stern eyes and a ready bow. And Cailus never left Sojourner's side, often putting a hand to the lad's shoulder to keep him on the path Lohrë had set for them. When travel had run them ragged and their way lay overgrown, Lohrë would draw his sword to hack through the bracken. Often the swipes of his blade brought them away from the great wood and into some private teeming glade or burbling fountain that would provide succor after a long day's trek.

"Sanctuaries, grown and blessed by our people," Cyrwedh had said of such places in one of the rare moments she had rejoined them along Lohrë's path. "Two centuries gone, and these I am *pleased* to see."

"We can rest at ease here," Lohrë added. "No enemy without has ever comprehended the magic of elves inlaid in these places." Sojourner found the elves' confidence well founded, and trusted the quiet, wizened figures a little more with each step he took with them. When they rested by night in these sanctuaries, Sojourner found his nightmares of marching fire, horned creatures, and a leering, smiling woman, kept at bay.

When forced to sleep on the ground outside the eaves of elvish shelters, Sojourner noticed a strange thing. Day and night ran in odd cycles, though the true memory of how they may have run differently eluded him. Much like the world underneath the earth, night seemed to govern the sky above it. To Sojourner's wheeling thoughts, the dark was stronger than whatever diminished brightness attempted to rule the daylight hours. Always the morning dawned dull, with only a dream of orange and gold managing to breach the horizon. And all day, the world seemed locked in an endless evening, as if twilight threatened to overtake daylight at the turning of every hour. Eventually, it would, and night would swallow all light entirely, casting the world in pitch darkness. Sojourner found little warmth when lying in the dark, even amongst his enchanted elvish cloak and the coals of Cailus' well-constructed fires. And just as nightmares startled Sojourner from restless sleep, he would wake to an even darker world surrounding him, whose very air teemed with malice. It was at those times that he would rise to look over the strange elf-lands from a high spot, seeking the marching fire of their enemies. Once there, all he perceived was Cyrwedh hooded and cloaked, who watched a host of her kin, marching as shadows, and winding a slow, silent path a mile or more behind them.

When they rose in the dim mornings, Sojourner found himself unable to put his unease to words, so he ignored the incessant feeling that something was not quite right with this world on which he found himself, either on the surface or under it. Instead, he turned his attention to running, walking, climbing, and concentrating on the words that would come to mind and mouth. As the companions stumbled up rocky slopes under wild orchards, Sojourner would point, calling his companions' attention to, "*apple, oak, stone, sky,* and *boot!*" He had been proud at the thought of his words returning, and the elves would laugh and cheer on his progress. They clapped along with him when he had heard his own voice for the first time rise above a faltering whisper. It was a good, strong voice, he thought; better than what he had expected. And within two days of his first words, he was relaying more complex terms to his companions as they set camp and cooked.

"*Roasted nuts, salted pork, smoldering,*" and "*fey things*" had been the words of one evening's gathering around a refreshing crackle of fire. The last Sojourner had said when he had spotted hooded figures passing at the edge of their firelight. Some, he saw, were horned. Some wore whiskers at the ends of long muzzles. Others looked akin to elves, and these grinned at him, their mouths brimming with vicious fangs. One thing was common among them: All walked on two legs and seemed possessed of a fierce wanting. But when their savage eyes caught sight of the elves' bright swords and vicious arrowheads drawn to shoot, they fled like fire-smoke in the darkling wind.

When Sojourner saw the elves relax, stowing away their weapons, he looked to Lohrë. The tall elf looked troubled, as if not sure how to proceed. "What I said about surviving the wild. It was no jest. Our Qweth-Wëalda is home to sweeter things than shining pools and houses of rest. But under its eaves also live horrors older and viler than fomori. If you let them, they will take you away, and even *our* eyes will never find you."

Sojourner looked to Cyrwedh and Cailus, who seemed

painstakingly interested in the cups of tea they drank, looking anywhere but at him. "Monsters?" he asked.

"Perhaps," Lohrë replied. "And there may come more the closer we draw to Wildercrown. Its power attracts such things. Though those we find there may be less sinister."

Sojourner spent the next black nights glancing over his shoulder, thinking on Lohrë's words. But thoughts of hungry things haunting their shadows fled quickly when Sojourner noted a change in the world's light. Looking skyward as they ran one evening, he found the sky growing brighter. This was odd to him, as the night made its descent as usual but seemed to be somehow resisted. When they camped that night, Sojourner released his stored up words.

"Light too late," he said, waiting for his companions to tell him of the strange sky. Smiling as usual, Cailus nodded to Lohrë and Cyrwedh, who, nodding in return, disappeared to scout or wander ahead together.

"We draw close to Wildercrown, friend," Cailus said as he tended their fire. "The waxing light you see is thrown by Mithweileth-Nal, the Giant's Ring surrounding our city. Legend says when the Qwei-Sillar came to this world with the ancestors of Men, and the war in heaven was finished, they wandered far from battle and woe. Their wanderings brought them to the last of giants."

"Giants," Sojourner recited, standing and extending an arm high as if measuring someone taller than himself.

"Far taller, larger, and stronger than even we of the

Elder Kindred can imagine," Cailus said. "Our sires did well by this last of giants. *Weileth-Zhul* we named him. In return, this giant plunged his flaming arms into the earth, uprooting a jagged ring of incandescent quartz, its value insurmountable. And so, my people, in acceptance of this gift, named the wall after that creature of myth and built their city within the protective ring of glowing rock he had erected for them."

"The giant," Sojourner asked. "What happened?"

"Oh, who can say?" chuckled Cailus. "It's all wrapped in myth. One story says he marched away south, covering a thousand miles in as many steps. When he stopped at the ocean there, he drank so much of it that the Belrath'ir Desert now stands there as a dire warning against gluttony. Another tale says he came across a mountain in his path and decided to level it with a fist, thus creating the Valley of Razors. You know how such tales go."

The man blinked at him.

"Then again, you may not," Cailus said, deflating. "The point is, you have seen a good many wonders in our travels away from your resting place. But none can compare to the Gleaming Wall! Sleep well and fast tonight, for tomorrow we reach Wildercrown."

"Ah, do you hear it, friend Sojourner?" Cailus asked while they walked, tilting his head so that a broad ear pointed to a sky pierced with beams of light.

Sojourner frowned, trying to listen as he followed Lohrë's brisk pace. A full day and some forty miles had passed since Cailus' story of elves and a giant's ring. In all that time, night never fell, the sky only growing brighter. All about the companions, the forest teemed with light and life. Deer leaped in packs over log and stone, fish jumped in rushing streams, and frogs and crickets created a cacophonous chorus as the night hours encroached. He looked back to the young elf and shook his head.

"Come now," Cailus admonished. "Eternity knows your ears aren't as big as mine, but even a deaf man could be stirred to tears by their music. Keep listening!"

Sojourner shut his eyes, feeling the slowing of his heart. Woven into the chaos of animal and cricket cries came threads of song. Sad and lovely, a chorus of female voices wafted with the cool wind. Sojourner blinked and looked to see his companion shading his eyes with a long-fingered hand.

"Lovely," Cailus whispered, lip quivering. "It is so long since I've heard the song. I thought I would never return, never hear them again. Their music hurts my heart."

Sojourner put a hand on Cailus' shoulder, not sure how best to comfort an elf. With his awkward gesture, he felt the air itself hum to life, almost with the promise of lightning. Then he smiled. He could not pinpoint the source of his lightening heart, but Sojourner thought he could feel the oppressive, hungry nature of the night held suddenly in check under this living air filled with light and song.

Cailus turned suddenly to him, laughing. "Elf-ladies of my city," he said eagerly. "Ever the magic of their song hangs over Wildercrown, keeping safe those within, while keeping at bay enemies without. The Giant's Ring, and the end of our journey, are both close."

"Maybe now that we're back from the dead, we'll find one such strong lady as can match that wild heart of yours, Cailus," teased Cyrwedh, who had joined the trio on the ground as soon as the night had been banished.

"I can only hope to find one so wonderful as you, lady," Cailus said with more than a little whimsy. "I simply pray the lady I give my heart to won't cuff me so often as you do our poor lord Lohrë—ouch!"

Cyrwedh had reached out a finger and flicked one of Cailus' long ears. "Manners such as those will never attract a woman," she said with an arched brow and knowing smile.

Rubbing his ear, Cailus said, "I haven't always been hunter, runner, and armor bearer, you know. I can sing and harp as well as any bard."

"Now *that* I would love to see and hear." Cyrwedh laughed. Looking to the stormy elf woman, Sojourner realized it was the first time he had heard such a sound from her. He realized then as well that the sound suited her, as did her smile.

"Easy on the lad, Cyr." Lohrë chuckled. "We need Cailus to arrive unharmed to Wildercrown, not nursing bruised ears and a battered heart."

"I think the *lad* handles himself in a duel of wits with a cool hand," she mused. "He'll need to, given the spark of wit that burns within our women."

The three elves laughed together and even sang a little,

their burdens seeming to ease as they drew nearer their home. But still Lohrë led them all at a hard run for the next hour until leaf and bough parted and wonder sprang up before them. The companions approached what Sojourner thought to be a mountain of glowing quartz. More than one hundred feet high, the Mithweileth-Nal loomed suddenly overhead, sparkling brighter than any light Sojourner had yet seen. The solid rock, imperious, shone with violet and sapphire, run through by rivers of shifting opal.

"Giant's Ring," Sojourner said.

"Sentries still march its length," Cyrwedh said as the group drew within half a mile of Mithweileth-Nal. "I see our kin, cloaked in gray, watching the land. They see us too."

"We are not too late," Lohrë sighed.

Sojourner's eyes narrowed, trying to glimpse the figures Cyrwedh saw so clearly. But towering trees that rose up from behind the shining bulwark drew his attention away from the search. Their boughs bent down from two and three times the height of the beaming wall.

Lohrë stopped his companions a thousand or so paces from the wall. He called a handful of words in the lyrical elvish tongue, adding more music to the already singing air. Sojourner continued gazing upward in bewilderment. Far away and above the wall, through a gap in the soaring canopy, he spotted the snowcapped summit of a mountain. Beams of the Outer-world's dying light stretched like grasping fingers toward the peak, casting the high snows in a bloody glow. Then his ears rang with sudden silence, and his limbs crawled with cold. His feet refused to move. Alarm swept away his admiration, and his gaze fell back to his surroundings. He gasped, finding himself and his companions ringed in by a hundred bright-eyed Qwei-Sillar.

"Monsters," Sojourner whispered, for creatures he had and had not seen stalking the steps of their journey through the Qweth-Wëalda now stood alongside the newcomers. Horned wolves, long-eared foxes, crested rabbits, cats with coats of crimson leaves, and stags whose antlers burned like tongues of white fire flanked every cloaked elf. Even trees blinked deep, amber eyes, their boughs reaching like knotted arms to bar the trespassers' way.

"Allies," Cailus replied.

A rider broke from the fey gathering, astride a catlike beast with wings and claws. He rode forward, then dismounted, approaching Lohrë, who strode up to meet with him.

"Word has reached our ears of dead Men leading a host of wraiths under our eaves," the rider said, his voice caught somewhere between suspicion and wonder. "Now I see for myself you are no Men at all, but our kin. Or at least you appear so."

"He is Lohrë, Prince of Wildercrown, Hero of the Fomori War!" cried Cailus. "It is by his cunning and might that you, we, and our kin breath freely to this day."

"Prince?" said Sojourner, the word barely escaping as he looked to Lohrë.

"Freely now, but for how much longer?" the sentry growled, turning to Cailus. "Two hosts snap at your heels: one small and all made up of creeping spies; the other leaves burning furrows in its wake as its battalions howl under marching fires. How do we know you do not lead them to our doorstep?"

"One we *do* lead to your doorstep," Lohrë said. "Not to conquer, but to protect and to carve a road upon which the Qwei-Sillar may run to safety. We escape fomori, goblins, and Men, bringing help unlooked for to the Council of Twelve. I *am* Lohrë, and I return at a dire hour. See my proof!" He removed the glove of his left hand with a snap, causing the encircling elves to flinch. He then held the hand aloft, and the Wall's light flared off a stone the color of ice set in a golden band. "Behold the ring of the Rheilori, given by our ancestors when we marched into the dark long ago! It is given only by the Elf-lord to his heir and was never recovered from the carnage of the attack on the Fomori Throne 208 years ago."

From the shock plain on the elves' faces, Sojourner thought they would draw weapons. Instead, the rider bowed, and his eyes were wet. His companions did the same, and all the beasts hemming in the four runners lost interest in them, retreating like shadows into the concealing brush of nearby thickets.

"You seem to have overcome whatever foe it was that kept you from home, if not the grave, lord," the rider said. "For worse, I fear, than for the better."

"Worse?" Lohrë asked, lowering his hand.

"Lohrë," the rider said. "The Fomori War, it gave rise to many evils. But the void left by your disappearance and the ruin of the Fomori Throne ... something terrible filled it."

Sojourner did not understand the rider's meaning but saw the destitute faces of the elves around them. *Not tears of relief but of deep sorrow*, he thought.

"The Nephtyr," Lohrë said darkly.

The rider nodded. "Those of us who called for peace with the fomori argued against their annihilation after the death of their king. The fomori possessed some restraining power over the Nephtyr, kept them in check."

"I did what had to be done," Lohrë growled. "Else *we* would have been the ones annihilated."

The rider nodded. "Nevertheless, the war's ending left the North empty. With no fomori left to halt their advance, the Nephtyr seized it, securing their hold on more than half the world. Their power grew and grew. Unchecked, they commanded light and power the likes of which we had never seen."

"Then what?" asked Lohrë.

"War again. Some twenty years ago. The Nephtyr lost in the end. But we, and the world, are diminished beyond grief, even by measure of the Fomori War."

Sojourner watched Lohrë grab up the rider in a rough embrace without preamble, hearing only the words, "Forgive me," whispered from his guide's mouth before the rider pushed him away gently. Tension drained a little from the surrounding Qwei-Sillar, and Sojourner watched them draw close. Some of them shoved playfully at Cailus, while others touched the hem of Lohrë's cloak. Whether the gesture was a token of respect or loathing, or an attempt to prove Lohrë truly was alive, Sojourner could not tell. But still more cried into their hands as they recognized their general long thought defeated.

"You vanished!" Sojourner heard a woman say, to which Lohrë nodded. "We looked to your coming, but you and your hosts did not return. We thought you had been slain by the last of the fomori, or worse."

"For good reason, I assure you," Lohrë said quietly. "Though I am sorry for the grief our vanishing caused. But what worse could have been done?"

"That matter," the rider said. "We will leave for the Elf-lord to explain."

"Much was risked," Lohrë said more loudly, eyeing them all. Sojourner saw the muscles in his companion's jaw clench. "But for the pain we caused, I am most sorry. Alas! I have no time to tarry and explain to you all. The things you first heard about us were not far off. I do bring precious few of the company who went with me all those years ago, who fought and lived to see the fomori toppled. But that is where my good tidings end, for we *are* pursued by a host of many thousands: fomori regrown, goblins, and evil Men. They march here chanting a name we have never heard. Tell me what passes and where the Elf-lord is."

"Much there will be to discuss once you enter the city, and to many of our folk," the rider said. "Things are not good in the world, Lohrë. The sins of the Nephtyr were laid to rest, and some healing was worked on the world. Then, three years ago, a Wasting Sickness ravaged the world of Men. It gnaws at them to this day. Shortly after the Sickness started, the sky itself shattered over Belrath'ir. A shard of it fell on the desert, and the Suthesturrmenn were destroyed. Even now, the sands of the South burn with war and cataclysm. Then came the whispers of oaths, which you no doubt have heard. Other things vex our consciences, but I will let the Elf-lord tell you more, if he would see you. He holds council now at the Oaken Throne, with the Eleven."

"What of Wildercrown's Messenger?" Lohrë asked.

"Your brother is well, though he keeps miserable company," the rider answered.

A brother too? Sojourner demanded. *My host seems to have forgotten to speak on that front as well. Maybe I should trust these new friends a little less moving forward.*

The rider continued, "He returns to Wildercrown from some errand given him by the Council. Get you there now, lord! The Council will doubtless want news of your return and will tell you all there is of our fading world. The Elf-lord has prepared us of the Wall guard and what soldiers he has left for war. He knows the Outer-world brims with it. Go now under the Ring. I pray the Elf-lord won't string you up for what you did, Lohrë. Farewell!"

Sojourner watched the rider remount his cat-steed. But before he could see more of the cloaked elves, Lohrë, Cyrwedh, and Cailus all lay hands on his shoulders. They forced him forward a step, and the power that had rooted his feet a moment before was gone. But when his foot struck the earth, Sojourner fell through a veil of light

GARDEN OF ASH

and shadow. Heat scorched his skin, then a fog of frost snatched the breath from his lips. Then, a sprawling city square adorned with floating lanterns stretched out before his eyes. And when he found the towering Giant's Ring at his back, all Sojourner could do was whisper a single word.

"Magic."

5
COUNCIL OF TWELVE

The four companions passed swiftly through white-cobbled streets. Word of Lohrë's return had already gone ahead, spreading like fire amongst the falling leaves. All manner of folk came to see the exiled elf's return and the rumor of his strange companion dressed like an ancient champion. Gentle winds stirred leaves of silver, gold, and green, carrying curious whispers of all who had come out to see them. Sojourner, doing all he could to keep his mouth from falling open, heard the elfsong flourish. With it, some of the tension he had been carrying over the last exhausting weeks began to melt away. He watched elves dance in the streets and families dining or talking through brightly lit windows. There were elves, old and young, and children playing and learning craft and trade in the autumn glory of Wildercrown.

"Look there!" Cailus said, pointing to a cluster of dark-skinned men and women dressed in bright greens and golds. Sojourner watched the strikingly-dressed folk stare at the wonder of the city with as much stunned awe as he did. "Outer-folk, like you. That's what we of the Elder Kindred call all Men. Those must be from among the Suthesturri tribes. Not many Outer-folk come this far north, let alone those from the desert. And few of us have ever looked upon you Younger Ones at all. Then there are the Bolg, crowned with curved horns for ramming, along with the hooves and golden eyes of goats. Though, don't ever let one of the Fir Bolg hear you comparing them with goats. Never mistake a Bolg for a simpleton, either. They're whip-smart and will leave you feeling a fool with your eyes crossed should *you* cross one of them!"

The four companions came to a great market, Sojourner watching as peddlers shouted, clapped, and whistled. "There's a pretty lot," Cyrwedh said, flashing her rare smile once more. "Cloth-of-gold tapestries and silks from the South Kingdoms in Belrath'ir beyond the ice. They may be all the scarcer given the sentries' news about cataclysms in the desert. And there are daggers forged from good steel by Angloreans to the west. I may need to pick up a few of their arrows, now that some of mine are spent."

"All seems right and close to memory," Lohrë said when they passed a crowded stand whose tables lay decked with toys, games, and contraptions of intricate design. Sojourner's skin then pricked up at the sound of a thing eerie yet familiar: sudden silence. It was an all-too-close companion, one he thought he had left behind in the Tomb. But here it was, an unwelcome travel-mate, laying heavy about the market. Every eye aimed straight for the little group of travelers. Every ear bent toward them, and every tongue whispered.

"So much for secrecy," Cyrwedh said, violet eyes studying every concerned face from under her hood's shadow.

"No other way to get in than by the Wall sentries' leave," Lohrë whispered. "The city was too well guarded."

"A result of precautions taken by a certain elf-prince long ago, no doubt?" Cailus said.

"No doubt." Lohrë chuckled grimly. He leaned in to speak to Sojourner as they bustled away from stalls and shops. "Though we are aloof and tend to be quicker to mistrust new tidings in favor of tried-and-true experience, we Qwei-Sillar do listen when the safety of our families lies at stake. Preservation runs deeply within our blood. And every Qweieth-Sil, male or female, walks about with arms ready to defend our homes. Even now the city stands on guard. The feeling here is not so different from the days of the Fomori War. Tension rides the air, even above the songs of our Singers."

"You think the fomori behind us truly mean to reignite their war?" Cailus asked.

"I pray not," Lohrë said, eyes falling. "Though, if the host pursuing us from the Tomb's depths marches here, I would sooner see the able-bodied flee and fight another day on a better front with united strength."

"So that is why we're here," Cailus breathed. "You mean to regain command."

"I mean to offer strength to our people, accept whatever punishment the Elf-lord may impose upon a general who cast aside the orders of his lord, then ask him what we should do about the Sojourner," Lohrë replied. "We don't have the whole picture. Something strange is at work, both in our Qweth-Wëalda and in the Outer-world. We need answers to the riddles of the Sojourner's waking, the armies marching under the earth, and the name they bear."

"Eshra," Sojourner whispered.

Lohrë responded with a single nod. "Our families must take heart, foster strength. It is the only way both to defeat the evils of our hearts, as well as that which roars in the hearts of the fomori who hated us. I think Sojourner here will be instrumental in helping achieve our goal."

"And what is that goal, Lohrë?" Cywedh asked, coming to a stop.

"Find and protect this *Heir* so incessantly whispered of in our minds," Lohrë replied. "See what the Elf-lord can tell us of Sojourner's waking."

"An Enemy and a goal," Cailus mused. "I'm prepared to go with you, lord. But before we come under the eyes of the Elf-lord's Council, what do you think the sentries meant when they mentioned something *worse* having caused our disappearance two hundred years ago?"

"I think bloated Nephtyri power was but one factor in this world's most recent of wars," Lohrë mused. "But until we know more, I need Cailus the scribe, not the fighter. Your eyes have seen much in the last weeks and will see more in days to come. Your account of things will be important. Understand?"

"What of your own account?" Cailus said as they continued on, passing over bridges and ducking into narrow lanes. "Have things gone as you thought they would?"

"Yes and no," the dark-haired elf said. "I chose to watch over the Sojourner by faith, thinking the story of the fomori's wrath wasn't all there was to tell. To answer your question, my *death*, as it were, seems to have served my prime hope: Our people remain watchful and strong. Men and the Qwei-Sillar are prone to stray given too little duty and dedication. Even in our days of war with the fomori, decadence and complacency would have killed us long before any army would have lain sword to our throats.

"Before our exile, I begged the Elf-lord to consider why the fomori acted as they did, but he was loathe to listen. His stubborn will was bent toward crushing them, not strengthening our people against something more elusive."

"You mean something pulling the strings of the fomori, goading them to invade," Cyrwedh said. "Rather than them seeking to war with elves and rule the North by their ambition alone."

"Yes," Lohrë said. "And while I had hoped that Sojourner would awaken after some time, I never thought he would live more than two hundred years in the state he was in. We've been away far too long, Cyr. And while I'm sorry for that, I also didn't anticipate a new army of fomori and other evil things heralding the Sojourner's waking. But I'm glad we were ready to depart."

"And the voices?" Cailus asked. "The Heir?" Sojourner

got the feeling the young elf was not used to having so many of his questions answered all at once.

"On those fronts," Lohrë said with a smile, "we must be patient, see if the Elf-lord has gathered any news. I don't know whose voices we've been hearing in our heads, nor have I ever heard tell of such a thing, even from the days before we came to Leóhteness-Fal. But with all that now passes within his borders, and with his very house at risk, I will not be surprised to see new plans set in place by our Elf-lord."

Hastening onward, Lohrë led Cyrwedh, Sojourner, and Cailus through a series of marble colonnades, then beneath the boughs of monstrous trees and under the sight of grim watchtowers. As they made their way up staircases of carven stone toward what must have been Wildercrown's center, Sojourner now saw the trees' sentries keeping watch over the city. Elves marched from tree to tree, colossal branches acting as bridges wide enough to allow two grown men to walk fully abreast. Many of them, he realized, were looking at him.

After half an hour's walk up into the shining city, the group stopped at the foot of a great hollow tree. A stately house had been carved into the base of its white trunk. Guards dressed in burnished helms, scale mail, and winter-gray cloaks met them. Sojourner's companions exchanged brief words with the sentries, who stared at him in fascination before escorting them under the eaves of the house. They entered quickly, descending to the tree's roots, which had been hollowed to form twisting hallways. Fey motes lit their way as their feet clacked on chiseled stone steps that wound, spiraling downward. When they came to the heart of the tree, a door wrought of marble, stone, and steel lay open to them. Lavish chambers beyond the threshold beckoned. A bonfire roared in a stone hearth at the edge of the room, and little sap-falls gushed down in corners, sparking with its light.

Sojourner heard Lohrë breathe deeply. The elf's eyes were downcast as he stepped forward, lost in some memory, or perhaps preparing to be tossed out by the one whom Sojourner imagined to be a proud, angry lord of elves with fire in his eyes at the return of a deviant son.

"Lohrë?" asked a deep voice filled with disbelief.

Released from his reverie, Sojourner found himself and his friends facing a throne of thorn and oak. The carven steps that had led them all the way to the tree's heart made their final climb to a lean man who stood before the twisted chair. His eyes were gold, and although he bore the look of a man of thirty or so, his hair was long and icy-gray. Eleven crowned elves flanked him to either side, sitting in smaller chairs. Their sharp faces were young and sad, but their hair was long with age. Some wore robes of dark forest colors; others were armed and garbed in battle mail.

Lohrë dropped to one knee under the standing man's golden gaze, reciting, "Hail, Elf-lord of Wildercrown, Marshal of the Qweth-Wëalda, Keeper of Memories, and Hope of the Qwei-Sillar. I greet you, and you lords of

Argentleaf, Quickstream, Silverwash, Cloudfire, Brokentree, Crystalfall, and all others on earth and under it, with highest courtesies and sincerest apologies for my long absence. I bring tidings in these strange times, for our enemies march under earth and over it once more. But two centuries of waiting has paid off. I will explain myself then accept my sentencing, should it suit my lords."

The Elf-lord, so imperious and full of proud fury to Sojourner, stood wordless. He trembled like a lute string tightened to snapping. Then he took a breath through clenched teeth. "*Tidings*," he whispered. "*Tidings* are naught but ill, ever since my son, his wife, who was my joy to accept as daughter, and a host of my people, all disappeared overnight. To my dismay, they marched against lord and law, toward folly. More *tidings* came hence soon after. And what were they but that all those who marched away—my son, my daughter, my hosts—all died. Two hundred years ago, my grief nearly put me in the grave with you. And now, as foes hem us in and danger draws enough attention finally to leech my grief, lo! My children return, alive. And hope is kindled in my heart. But to what end? That they may be torn from me again as our realm is conquered and run over, roughshod? Will you all die again, this time fighting beside me? Would that I could be happier at my son's miraculous revival, for now I must preside over your crimes and not your safe return! What am I to make of such wonders?"

"Only that our grief was perhaps the greater," Lohrë said quietly. "And that we *are* here to fight beside you, though we will not do the dying this time. We accept whatever sentence you deem right for our transgression."

Sojourner saw a tear fall from Cyrwedh's cheek as she knelt beside Lohrë. He then looked to the Elf-lord whose mouth quivered, though whether under the weight of anger or sorrow Sojourner could not guess.

"Transgression," the Elf-lord practically spat. He drew himself up even higher, a judge prepared to condemn a criminal for deeds most vile. But his golden eyes overflowed, and he burst into sudden tears. The Elf-lord flung his silver crown to the dirt, raced down the steps, and threw his arms around Lohrë and Cyrwedh, who nearly fell over in bewilderment.

"My son!" the Elf-lord choked. "My daughter. Both live!"

"Hail, Lohrë Thronebreakerer!" cried the eleven elvish lords, rising from their seats to draw swords in salute.

"Lord?" Lohrë gasped, awkward in the Elf-lord's arms.

"We have sorely needed you," said the Elf-lord, releasing him, only to crush Cyrwedh in a firmer embrace. "The Qwei-Sillar suffer badly. News of this new fomori threat marching toward Wildercrown is only the latest of many evil signs in the Outer-world."

Lohrë, making to stand, helped the Elf-lord to his feet. He nodded to the assorted elves. Sojourner only then realized that, while most of the Council bore smiles at the return of their general, some wore soaked dressings. Others bled openly. "I am here to serve," Lohrë said.

"As am I," Cyrwedh said.

"And I, lord," added Cailus beside her.

"We travel with those of my host who marched away to end the fomori threat two hundred years ago," Lohrë finished.

The Elf-lord nodded, wiping his eyes. "Reports of your coming arrived after our first battles only weeks ago. But they spoke nonsense: a host of elvish dead sweeping our lands like the shadow before a storm. And at their head marches the ghost of our greatest general, eyes burning with hatred for his people who sent him away to die. It was too farcical to believe. But here you are, not hateful but humble!"

"I thought you would be the one bearing hatred, lord," Lohrë said, tears falling.

"*Never*, my son," the Elf-lord said fiercely, pulling Lohrë into a rough embrace once more. "Your safe return home is worth more to me than all the victories of war and all the light in the world."

"Thank you, lord," Lohrë whispered, returning the embrace.

"Now," the Elf-lord said, releasing him a second time. The cold stonework of his face and ice-white rivulets of his hair reasserted themselves. Once more, the highest lord of the Qwei-Sillar stood before them. "There is much to discuss. Join us for a while, you and your companions. We discuss the dire news of which I just spoke. And we will catch you up on things you may have missed while away."

"Bless you, lord," Lohrë said, regaining his composure.

The Elf-lord motioned to wardens at his door. The tall

sentries fetched chairs and flasks of water for the latecomers before disappearing from the throne room. When the Elf-lord took his throne again, an elf with golden-white hair and blue sigils tattooed across his brows and cheekbones spoke up.

"Argentleaf is fallen," he said gravely. "Our first fight against the coming onslaught was there. I commanded over a thousand bows and three hundred swords. We were overrun by sheer numbers. But there was no pillaging. The fomori overwhelmed and killed any who stood before them, laying waste to our fields and forests. Then they continued on, burning as they went. I sent runners bearing tidings of our ruin to Wildercrown. We gathered all folk we could find and followed."

"Argentleaf's messengers arrived a week ago," the Elf-lord confirmed. "The rest of her folk only arrived this morning."

The elf with the blue sigils nodded. "We are several days ahead of the host, but they march this way, surely to make of Wildercrown what it made of our home."

"The same has happened to Cloudfire," barked a female elf bearing scars on her exposed arms and crimson tattoos across her face. Her hair was all red wine and dark honey, and her teeth were filed to wicked points. "Our mountain burst without warning. Then goblins attacked just as its rivers of fire burned our homes. We stood no chance, and these goblins were not so cordial as the fomori. They took their time raping, stealing, and butchering. What few of us remain are here, with the enemy at our heels."

"Brokentree burns as well," a slight woman sang from under the hood of her gray cloak. "Men of the Northern Isles landed in Graywind, hurling axe and insult. We took no casualties, the Sisters of Graywind being keen enough of eye and mind to see our attackers coming at a distance. Our arrows have not feasted so on Man-flesh for centuries. But too many landed ashore and burned the corpse of our Dead Tree. We fled when our arrows were spent, but we watched the host march southward by the thousands. Whether to Galataeum or Eth-Gathilin they go, we do not know."

"News is much the same from all the northern reaches of the Qweth-Wëalda," the Elf-lord said. "For now, Lohrë, share with us what news you bring. Perhaps I can meet you halfway with reports brought by the eyes and mouths of Mithweileth-Nal in recent weeks."

Lohrë told of Sojourner's waking, of his companions' flight from the Tomb under-earth, and Sojourner's encounter with the fomori by the river. The Elf-lord, despite Lohrë's talk of his severity, sat at rapt attention, considering every word the dark-haired elf told him. Lohrë would ask occasionally for Cyrwedh and Cailus to speak, and they both interjected at times, confirming Lohrë's accounting.

The door wardens returned, bringing porcelain platters of roasted beef slices, pungent cheeses, bittersweet berries, and nuts. For drink, the assembly received ewers of the same honeyed ice-wine Lohrë had given Sojourner to refresh him when he had first awakened.

"Not all your tidings are new to me," the Elf-lord said, offering Lohrë, Sojourner, Cyrwedh, and Cailus a chance to eat. "Some I may inform you of, as the world has changed since you vanished. Away south and west, our allies, the Angloreans of Eth-Gathilin, are beset by goblins and Swardha-Menn. As the Sisters of Graywind reported, the hosts of the Swardha-Menn marched away southward. We know now that their goal is the rape of all Anglorost. As for the South, what do you know of *Second-fire?*"

"Precious little," Lohrë replied. "Our scouts brought messages to our tomb of fire once more appearing in the sky some years ago. Its like was similar to the sky-fire that brought Sojourner to Leóhteness-Fal. When they met us at the seat of the Giant's Ring, your sentries reported this *Second-fire* as having devastated the South."

"Indeed," the Elf-lord said darkly. "The *Second-fire* crashed to earth with such violence that the Glacial Waste to this day is nearly destroyed. The impact and ensuing flood gouged a furrow into the desert that cut straight through to the Great East Sea. The kingdoms of the Suthesturmenn lie in utter ruin. War has consumed all people and fae of the deserts as they battle to see who will become king of sand and cinder. We sent what little aid we could. But the power of the Qwei-Sillar is divided and diminished. What few surviving Suthesturmenn now flee north and westward to the Gathilin Bluffs or eastward toward the Ephtari Downs. They seek new lives and refuge from the hell the desert has become. Those regions, Last-Hope, and our own Qweth-Wëalda, survive unharmed only by virtue of the *Second-fire* striking northwest to southeast. The cloud thrown up in the explosion died under the heights of Sunreach. The mountains contained the blast but flung ash back toward the desert with fury tenfold. I fear all record of the Men of the South lays buried forever.

"But invasions and cataclysms are not all. Another strange thing happened, coinciding with the *Second-fire*. Stone-folk, people hidden from elves and Men when the Kindreds arrived on Leóhteness-Fal, roused us in the night. We awoke to a hail of hammering, unceasing. The racket lay not within the forest, but had been carried on the wind, from the far South. Only when we sought the sound of hammering under the earth did we see fire raging in the southern sky. So, we named it *Second-fire*, and have since prepared, either for another Fomori War or some other doom. Our Messenger went south to bring tidings and gifts from our people to these Stone-folk, who call themselves *Nokleth*."

"The Messenger—" Lohrë said, catching himself.

"He is well, Lohrë," said the Elf-lord. "But there is more to the tale before it turns to your brother."

"Something, too, stirs in the West," boomed an elf with a thick trunk of a chest and arms that looked strong enough to tear trees out from the roots. "News that may not have reached your ears, general, concerns the Nephtyr."

"I heard a piece of this story from the Wall-watchers, too, Lord Ethriri," Lohrë said, turning to the thickset elf.

"It seems the Nephtyr took every advantage of our little Fomori War?"

"They took all the North!" Ethriri snapped. "Shortly after your disappearance, without fomori numbers to keep them humble, the Nephtyr spread through all the North, forming an empire they named the Hegemony. Prideful fools. We and all the Men south and west of us were busy rebuilding in the wake of destruction wrought by our foes. We were paying no heed to a betrayal by friends! We should have known. Who but our *angelic* neighbors sent heralds declaring all lands north of the Qweth-Wëalda, formerly ruled by the Fomori King and his warlords, now belonged to the Nephtyri Hegemony? Who were we to refuse? We had no armies, no children to replace the ones we'd lost. My thinking is, this was their plan from the beginning: looking to rule over all the darkened world once the Kindreds were too weak to resist them. They were too blinded by power not to take advantage of such a crisis."

"The Nephtyr took those lands they desired," said the woman cloaked in gray. "Their expansion sundered Brokentree from the rest of the elf-lands, further dividing the Qwei-Sillar. As Lord Ethriri said, who were we to refuse? We thousand or so she-elves with bows stood no chance against legions of armed and armored angels. They would have made slaves of us all."

"But they didn't," Lohrë concluded. "What happened, then?"

"Legends awoke," whispered an ancient elf with honey-brown hair and a bristling beard that chattered with birds and little creatures. His eyes were closed, but he spoke on. "The sins of the Nephtyr reached their full measure, and their hammer stroke fell hardest upon Men. That is until fifteen years ago. The Men of Ephtar-Malas boiled up out of T'Rhonossarc in a raging flood. Their fury washed the world clean of Nephtyr. They drove the tyrants back to their mountain stronghold at Galataeum. Then, one among the Men of Ephtar-Malas slew the greatest champion of the Nephtyr before Galataeum's gate. With that greatest of angels dead, and his wings torn from his back by hand of a Midlothean from Ephtar-Malas, the Nephtyr withdrew. Their Hegemony fell without further fight."

"The Masters, as the Nephtyr so loved calling themselves, have gone silent since," the Elf-lord said. "In fifteen years, no message has been borne to us by their heralds, and we know not whether they even live. Their gate remains shut. No demand or levy has come down from them since, so we have done as always: fended for ourselves. Though we weaken with each passing year."

"Weaken?" Lohrë asked. "Though you seem not to have lost in this war against Nephtyri tyranny?"

The Elf-lord sighed. "You move us to the next part of our sad tale. Lohrë, light pours out of the world. We know not whether the Fomori War or the War against the Nephtyri Hegemony broke the dam. But as light leaks away, so too does the strength of the Qwei-Sillar. And in the wake of light failing, our people have heard strange voices in our minds. So far, we alone are affected. You know of what I speak?"

COUNCIL OF TWELVE

Lohrë looked to Cyrwedh and Cailus. Together, all three elves recited,

> "First Children paid and were poured out.
> The Second saved but were enslaved.
> Light springs anew, Third take to path.
> Come Qwei-Sillar, O Ephtarrath!
> Remember oaths to ancient friends.
> Door's Key once hid is found again.
> Children of Weileth delve the deep
> While South-Men war, then fall asleep.
> In Golden-mount is born an Heir
> Who seeks the Garden, with our prayer."

Memories of fire, darkness, and a dreadful impact sprang up in Sojourner's mind. "The Heir!" he cried, drawing the eyes of every elf in the chamber.

Lohrë put a hand on his shoulder. "We should have recited the rhyme to you earlier, friend. You may yet play a part." He turned back to the Elf-lord. "We first heard the chant in our minds three years ago," Lohrë said. "The timing matches that which was given by the Wall sentries."

The lords of the elvish council looked around at one another. "Then it truly is both *all* and *only* our people who hear," the ancient, bearded elf said.

"We may have some answers to these questions," the Elf-lord said, to the surprise of the gathering. "I have gathered Wildercrown's scholars to investigate these events, knowing better than to call them all coincidence.

I have checked on the scholars' progress steadily over the past year. You all shall have the latest revisions of their notes shortly. The delay in having them prepared for this Council comes from my ordering of another set of copies drawn up for our Messenger. He will not be returning to Wildercrown, as was his original instruction before I sent him to make contact with the Nokleth."

Sojourner saw Lohrë blink at the Elf-lord.

"Your brother," the Elf-lord said to Lohrë with a knowing smile, "has been a busy runner."

"My gift proved useful, then," Lohrë whispered.

"That and more," the Elf-lord replied. "He is herald of our people, and his travels have become legend to our few children. But he is forced to walk a winding road in service to the Qwei-Sillar."

"Waylaid on his return home?" Lohrë asked.

The Elf-lord gave a troubled nod. "As has been said, the Nephtyr have made no contact with the Outer-world since the shutting of their mountain gate. Yet, a new light has been set above the high towers of Galataeum. It seems enough to keep the world lit as all other lights fail. But I do not trust such a trifle, especially one that nests so high above the unassailable gates of the Nephtyr. Our Messenger was meant to return here after his time spent among the Nokleth. But for the dangers we face and the news we covet, I have sent him away to Galataeum. He is to see what the Nephtyr are scheming from behind their locked gates."

"Troubling news from all corners," said an elf with

short black hair and the broadest ears Sojourner had yet seen among the Qwei-Sillar. His garb was of all black, and blood ran red down the side of his face. "We shall fight for Wildercrown when the time comes. For now, my lords, my wounds need tending to, and my people need feeding and sheltering. We should reconvene before dawn. A few hours' rest should suffice for the wounded and travel weary."

Relief flooded through Sojourner as the elves of the Council muttered their assent. Nothing sounded better to him than a bath and a bed after so long a journey. The lords quickly departed the throne room while the Elf-lord addressed Lohrë, Sojourner, Cyrwedh, and Cailus. "Perhaps the greatest of these riddles sits before us in this Sojourner," the Elf-lord said. "But what little time we have now should be spent resting. Tomorrow I will call, and we may set to solving such mysteries then."

"I would go with you, father," Lohrë said. "I have no need for sleep after meeting my father for the first time since my death."

"With me, then, specter!" said the Elf-lord, a little of his fierceness returning as he addressed his son. "A fitting punishment we might also find for your disobedience, in time. For now, I wish simply to speak with my son." He motioned for his wardens to tend Sojourner, Cyrwedh, and Cailus as the bonfire at the center of the Oaken Throne room burned low.

6
DEADLY MESSAGES

Door's Key once hid is found again.

An elf shut his eyes to the incessant chant. He and his angel passed like ghosts under lightless thickets. He knew they must look a strange pair. The elf ran hard, golden-hair plastered to his forehead by sweat and rainwater. Golden sigils traced his face, the rain striking staccato beats along the patterns as he went. He looked to his companion, who was twice his height, sallow, hunched, and wrapped in an adamant cloak. They said little as they sped their way northward, drenched and cold. The elf thought of their flight from their business in the ruined southlands, the secret paths and ravines carved by rivers they had trodden to stay hidden. Sometimes he led. At others, the angel took point. Their journey had been deadly, but they were hale and fast and bound by oaths. And they had done all they could to conceal the angel's iron wings.

"Arwë," the angel's voice boomed over shards of pelting rain. "We've passed eight days and three hundred miles since the hand-off at Wildercrown."

"We don't stop!" the elf hissed, icy pins biting at his face as he turned to his companion. "I would have fought at Wildercrown, but the Elf-lord's message told us to make for Galataeum. That is our road."

"And I would have gone with you to Wildercrown's aid," the angel rumbled. "But there was more to the message. You've been too silent since you insisted on tearing us out of the South and coming this way by strange roads. You owe me answers."

"Not until we're closer to Hegemonic territory," Arwë huffed. He found himself beginning to want for breath. They had been running for four hours.

"Not far now," the angel growled, eyes cold and bright under his hood. "And the Hegemony is destroyed."

"I'm sorry, Tyrith," Arwë said, relaxing his jaw. "Seeing the scarlet sky over Wildercrown, and an army surrounding it. It—"

"It recalls memories of destruction and death in the wake of tyranny," Tyrith said darkly.

"It does," Arwë said lamely. "Tyrith, I—"

"The Hegemony is destroyed," Tyrith repeated. "And rightly so. But Wildercrown and the Qwei-Sillar do not deserve the same fate as the Nephtyr. All the same, we are far from the danger that surrounds your city, and there may be more that the Elf-lord was trying to tell us with his letters. We've covered more ground than any would have expected of us, thanks to your grit. We should rest, and you should read me all that the Stone-folk and Elf-lord have written us."

"Thank Eternity," the elf breathed, stumbling to a haggard walk. He pointed through the brush as he strung his bow. "There. Those trees and the way they fell will provide as good a cover as any canvas. We'll rest there a while, read, and regroup."

They made their way to a high glade where several trees had been felled by lightning in some long-past storm. When they came to the half-formed shelter, Tyrith, with arms as big around as trees themselves, began hauling the fallen trunks into the shape of a rough house. As he did so, a crunch of brush some hundred yards away in the gloom of the surrounding wood made the skin of Arwë's neck prick up.

Prey. The thought struck his mind, expelling all others. He sucked in a breath, gave a series of hand signals to Tyrith, then loosed a shaft into the murk. Not waiting for the impact, Arwë rushed into the dark, leaving his friend to continue the work of building camp.

Seconds later, Arwë, with trembling hands and wide eyes, came upon his kill. A grin tugged at his mouth as he gazed down at the tall, healthy doe, slain instantly by his single arrow. He released the breath he had been holding, then lugged the body onto his shoulders.

As he walked back toward the glade, the scent of the animal's blood in his nostrils, Arwë saw Tyrith in the distance releasing his great-axe, double-edged and bright. The angel chopped half a massive tree into more than enough firewood to last them the evening. Arwë broke out of the surrounding dark bearing his prize as Tyrith stacked the soaked wood in a pyre, setting it ablaze with a motion from his hand.

"Clean kill?" Tyrith asked, restoring his axe to its resting place on his broad back.

"Into the crease, and right through the heart," Arwë said, dropping the deer and unsheathing a dressing knife.

"Hardly any need for dry food at all, this trip." Tyrith chuckled as Arwë skinned the carcass.

"If the hunt can't be my profession," Arwë grunted through his knife strokes, "I at least aim to keep my skills honed while on the road."

"No grief from me," Tyrith rumbled.

Arwë cooked them a lavish meal of roasted venison, carrots, potatoes, and salted almonds. An hour later, he sat back after he had rinsed his iron pot and cooking utensils with boiled rainwater and ash soap.

"Wildercrown to Westreach," Arwë sighed as Tyrith lit their pipes with his fingers. "Westreach to Glacial Waste—or should I say *Melted* Waste now? From there, to the Gathilin Road, where Suthesturri refugees march by the hundred away from the desert wars. At the end of the road, the Gray Valleys, and at the bottom of those lay the Quarries of our Noklethi friends. Finally, under earth and away from what little light exists *above* it, we found our little hosts and our gift."

Tyrith harrumphed, easing his back against a standing tree and releasing plumes of blue smoke from both nostrils.

"At least we found some rest with them," Arwë continued, "being their honored guests, after all."

"Honored, before having to flee with all haste," Tyrith said flatly. "Come, tell me why we've traveled like hunted men for months now."

"Here is what I wrote of our conversations with the Nokleth." Arwë retrieved a parcel of neatly folded parchments and vellum sheaves, choosing one with tidy, iron-scratch handwriting. "'Tokens of friendship we offer to you and your kin, swift prince of the Qwei-Sillar!' they told us. 'But the greatest of our tokens you must take to Galataeum. You know this already, given the message you and your folk know so well.'"

"The rhyming chants?" Tyrith asked.

Arwë nodded, pipe pinched between his teeth as he scanned the page. "I begged our hosts to tell me any small thing that would help my people decipher the voices. And I received an answer."

"You did?" The angel coughed, suddenly captivated. His armored elbows banged on plate-covered knees as he sat forward.

Smiling, Arwë held up the vellum note once more, reciting, *"Seek the Door under Golden-mount, but trust the road no longer. You, Herald of Wildercrown, are possessed of high reputation among the Kindreds and us, the Forgotten. But that reputation may prove your doom! Announce not your march to Sable Gorge with banners and trumpets. Go swiftly by what secret ways you know, telling no one of your journey. There may be time enough to return to Giant's Ring before seeking the light-long-hidden, but put no faith in false hope!"*

"That explains things," Tyrith said flatly. "Every point

DEADLY MESSAGES

proven right. And even our fastest pace was not enough to bring us back to Wildercrown in time. You received this 'greatest of tokens' the Nokleth spoke of?"

Arwë retrieved a neatly wrapped bundle from his pack and handed it to his companion.

"A cloak?" Tyrith asked, unfurling the sturdy, woolen garment.

Arwë shrugged. "Neither for you nor I, nor for your people nor mine. But it goes to Galataeum."

"Under it," Tyrith corrected.

"Under it," Arwë conceded. "Do you know what it's supposed to mean? Have your folk hollowed out some secret chamber under their beloved capital since their shutting of Galataeum's gate?"

"How would I know?" Tyrith retorted. "Although, we both know Sable Gorge. It's the wedge between western Qweth-Wëalda and the eastern edge of the Hegemony. A great bridge once crossed the gap between our peoples."

"The Men of Ephtar-Malas broke it and threw the stones into the gorge after they destroyed the Nephtyr," Arwë ventured. "None of us now know what Goldenmount actually looks like, let alone most lands beyond Qweth-Wëalda's borders."

Tyrith gave a short nod. "Much was lost in those days. But perhaps our stony, little friends can say more. What else did the Nokleth say?"

Arwë read from his note once more. "*Get you gone, away to the Gorge, and the Light-hidden. But once you've captured the Garden's prize, hurry back to us. For the Nokleth* will have unearthed the greatest gift for all. And with the Lathe shall we form it anew for the deeds of this age. And so, we dig!"

"All that's left is to get to where we need to be," the angel mused. "Only to turn right around and go back the way we came. I'd say we're near the halfway mark."

Arwë snorted. "In our search for the Nokleth's Quarries, we climbed mossy cliffs, crossed icy rivers, and trudged over hill and steppe. Since we made contact and departed, we've fallen into valleys and splashed up streams that shined in the dark. Now we're hounded by masked men and shot at by goblins in this blasted north waste. If we're only halfway done, I'll head for home now."

"What home?" Tyrith asked, a wry smile crossing his handsome, shadowed face.

"Who'd have thought the angel would be possessed of the darkest sense of humor?" Arwë said flatly. Then he heard a rumble like the sound of rolling rocks escape his companion's hood. "Did the angel just laugh at Wildercrown's misfortune?"

"You know Nephtyr are no angels," Tyrith said, growing stern once more.

Arwë let his attention fall to rifling through his stacks of letters and missives to distract himself from the truth his companion let hang.

"What of the Elf-lord's letters?" Tyrith asked.

Arwë picked a vellum page out of the inner cover of a heavy codex. "I've only read a few. Little comes from the Elf-lord himself. Most are records written by our scholars." A hasty note written in a combination of elvish runes and other sigils lay scrawled across the page. He recited, "*Correspondence passed by writ of highest Lord of Wildercrown to Arwë, Herald of Wildercrown and ...*" Arwë cleared his throat, reading, "*his companion, Nephtyr Ithar-fel, Descendant of Tyrants and exile of the Nephtyri Hegemony—*"

"Skip that part," Tyrith snapped.

Arwë continued, reading quickly. "*Torphellan, scholar of Wildercrown, to Arwë: friendly albeit swift greetings to you, for I am out of time. War comes under the forest, and we flee the city. You will know this compendium comes from me, given the code in which I write. See notes appended within marked with my rune.*"

Arwë then opened the codex, paging through the leaves to the intended manuscript.

"Note thirty-three," he said. "'*What we of the Qwei-Sillar have heard in our minds is a revelation passed to us by means of an ancient bond. I hear the voices just as all my kin who reside beneath Qweth-Wëalda and beyond. All report to me the exact words I have heard in my own mind again and again. They bear no repeating here, as every Qweieth-Sil knows them by heart, them having been repeated endlessly, day and night, for three years.*'

"Note thirty-four reads, '*I have found that the chant coincides with what the Outer-folk have named the Wasting Sickness. It is a disease only afflicting the races of Men, causing delirium, prolonged coma, and death if the afflicted are not properly cared for. None have recovered from the disease* that we have found. This plague began seemingly the same day the Qwei-Sillar heard the first chants. The Prince of Last-Hope assigned his finest surgeon to the task of curing this plague. The surgeon came to us two years ago in search of remedies, to no avail. He left, pursuing rumor of a healer who had seemingly met with success against the Wasting Sickness. This healer is said to reside in the far south, where the mountains stand tallest above the Belrath'ir Desert. We know little of so far away a place—only that those mountains are named Sunreach, so named because no earthly light can reach their summits.'

"Note thirty-five: 'Stranger still, our scholars now know that the first chants heard by the Qwei-Sillar, and the advent of the Wasting Sickness, both occurred on the same night the Sky-shard fell on Belrath'ir and the kingdoms of the Suthesturmenn. With the utter ruin of Belrath'ir, the Nokleth, or Stone-folk, were revealed for the first time in history when the Sky-shard rent the earth, exposing their mines. Arwë, Herald of Wildercrown, and the Nephtyri warrior, journeyed south to meet with these folk who had never before been seen in the world by any Kindred. Arwë compiled exhaustive codices on the Nokleth, which he sent back to Wildercrown. These have only just recently arrived and been deciphered. Conjecture dictates that these stone-skinned craftsmen of brilliant metalworks went into hiding long ago, citing betrayal by, what can only be translated into our tongue as, friends-light-the-highest.'"

"And no other note informs us of whom *friends-light-the-highest* may refer to?" Tyrith asked.

DEADLY MESSAGES

"I spelled the word used by the Nokleth phonetically in my message to Wildercrown," Arwë said. "It was *Atrellarrath*."

"I've never heard the term," Tyrith rumbled. He then asked, "What of the Elf-lord telling us to stay away from your city?"

Arwë flipped to the end of the codex, pulling a torn strip of cloth that he had placed between the last page and back cover. "Written in haste, no doubt, and coded," he said, eyeing the frantic characters adorning the woolen scrap. "It reads, '*If Messenger meets runner off-road, city is assaulted. Qwei-Sillar scattered ... Great Hero of old Fomori War revived ... marches with Sojourner, making for Malice. By order of Elf-lord, Messenger and Midlothean make for Ephtar-a-Tyrian Feilleth.*'"

"That's all?" Tyrith said.

Arwë nodded. "Things are straight forward until it mentions the Great Hero and Sojourner. Who or whatever these are, I cannot guess. But *malice* means they make for the refuge of Ephtar-Malas. It is another name for Last-Hope, the Hidden City of Men in the realm of T'Rhonossarc—"

"I'm well aware of the place," Tyrith cut in, "and what its Men are capable of."

"Yes, well, if my people's hope lies in Malas, then they must truly be hard-pressed. And you may be forced to treat with the Midlotheans who rule the city sooner than expected."

"Perhaps," Tyrith mused. "But could the Elf-lord have

meant you are to meet *a* Midlothean at ... what was the name at the letter's end? *'Messenger makes for,'* what?"

Arwë hesitated, then whispered, "Ephtar-a-Tyrian Feilleth. It means, *Tyrant's Fall*. It's what my people named Galataeum after the defeat of the Nephtyri Hegemony."

Tyrith was silent for a while, whether fuming or in contemplation, Arwë could not guess. Then the angel spoke softly. "It would appear the commission of the Nokleth and instruction of the Elf-lord drive us to similar purpose."

"What are you thinking?" Arwë asked.

"I think we go to meet a man, a Midlothean, at the gates of Galataeum," Tyrith said. Then his eyes narrowed to small, bright slashes under his hood. "Or *Tyrant's Fall*, if you prefer that name."

Arwë looked everywhere but at his companion. "Ah, Galataeum will suit it just fine," he said. "But you don't think the Elf-lord was calling *you* the Midlothean in his note?"

"No," Tyrith said. "Your father is cruel, but not so cruel as to name me among the Men who overthrew my people and slew our champions, even in a coded message. No," he said again. "We are to meet a Midlothean at Galataeum. And I shall return to where my people were brought low and speak with one of the Men who did it."

"What good will such a talk earn, Tyrith?" Arwë asked.

"Answers," Tyrith grunted, hauling himself to his feet. "First watch is mine." He stalked into the surrounding hedges with a clatter of mail and no other word.

DEADLY MESSAGES

Knowing better than to argue further with his colossal companion, Arwë took a deep pull on his pipe, then closed his eyes to his weariness.

Come now, make haste to valley-black.
Here is the knight, returned with might.
The Heir comes forth but cannot hide.
Through dark and danger, she must ride.
But man and Heir cannot be swift,
for knight is come without the gift.
O Weileth-Zhul, mercy we beg!
Send Qweieth-Sil on renewed legs.
Come, bring us shroud, for now's the hou'r.
She bears our hope, our light, and pow'r.

"Not the same!" Arwë shouted, startling awake. Terror gnawed his senses as the black before his open eyes grew deeper than the black he had seen behind closed ones.

A shriek shattered the forest's silence.

"Fell asleep while smoking!" Arwë hissed, hauling himself to his feet. Their blazing fire had exhausted itself, leaving only glowing coals, and the forest's net of thick copses had pulled the darkness close. "Tyrith?" he cried. Some screaming, groping thing tore at him in the dark. Arwë roared as it clawed his arm, and he threw it to the ground with a crunch. Booted steps thudded over the logs Tyrith had shaped into their shelter the night before, then three more creatures hurled themselves at him. Arwë's sword sang from its sheath, and three grasping hands fell to the earth, each accompanied by a chorus of deafening wails.

"Fomori!" Arwë spat, catching up his pack and cache of documents as the creatures writhed at his feet. A crash drew his attention. Sheathing his sword, Arwë leaped into the branches above. From the tree's boughs, he looked hard in the direction the noise had come from. Through the inky darkness, his eyes caught torch fire reflecting off the thick forest canopy above. Then he saw sparks fly from an axe's blade as Tyrith hued at the swords of a dozen fomori. With deft fingers, Arwë found his arrows and bow, strung his weapon, then took aim.

"Two-hundred feet," he whispered, and the crack of his string left a fomori dead, an arrow piercing its skull. Arwë watched Tyrith break from the scuffle in the confusion, striking westward. Arwë struck down another fomori before he hopped to a new tree branch, trying to keep ahead of the band pursuing the angel.

He sighted an ugly, hulking fomori as it emerged from the crowd, bounding after Tyrith. Arwë's next shot missed the monster, and it lunged a crooked blade at Tyrith's neck as the angel wheeled about. Before Arwë could scream his outrage, he saw Tyrith batter the blade aside, then catch the beast by the throat with his other hand. Arwë heard a sickening crunch. The fomori, nearly Tyrith's height, clattered lifeless to the forest floor. But six more of the gangly creatures rushed Tyrith, screaming for blood at the sight of their fallen captain. An arrow shot from Arwë's bow took one through the throat, but the others reached the angel. Tyrith wheeled around again, arms rippling as he swung his axe in a deadly arc. Arwë watched the fierce weapon rip armor and flesh, sending fomori, both half and whole, flying through the air to smash into the rushing ranks of their comrades.

Arwë counted thirteen fomori lumbering toward Tyrith, with more and more of them emerging over hill and ridge. Firelight plumed in the sky above the snarling creatures. *First, ten to one*, Arwë thought. *Now twenty, even thirty, to one. Maybe more.* His jaw clenched as he counted more fomori on the ground than arrows in his quiver, and still more issued from the darkness of the wood.

"Eshra, Eshra, Eshra," they cried.

No straggling hunter party—an army! Arwë thought. Then, he spied a fiery glint off the head of a helm. *Not a helm; a mask!* Shrieking cries rose above the chants of the fomori. Arwë saw Tyrith startle a glowing bunch of hundred-horned stags who had stopped to drink at a rocky brook. The creatures' flight from the axe-fighter sent them leaping off, away forward, where they trampled a dozen gray-skinned fomori who had been lying in wait for the angel farther ahead. The cries of their comrades sent a frenzy through the fomori pursuers, and they surged toward the angel.

Arwë bent his bow, and his arrow slew another fomori who stabbed at Tyrith. The angel took his axe in both hands, swinging at his foes as they charged him. They fell, broken. But more poured in to replace the fallen, even as Arwë's keen arrows cut them down mid-run. But only when ten or more fomori lay slain or writhing at Tyrith's feet did they hesitate. And this, Arwë saw, was not for fear of the angel.

A shrill ring lashed Arwë's ears, and he clutched the sides of his head, his arrow skittering off the rusted helm of a fomori grunt. Shielding his ears, Arwë watched the fomori part then grow silent. Through their messy ranks walked a lithe man in sparkling armor and dark cloak. He shambled forward as if drunk. The beasts cowered when he passed, his hands drawing the hood off his head. Underneath was a burnished crown, sitting above a leering mask of gray steel. Its eyeless gaze seemed to fall upon Tyrith, and for the first time, Arwë saw the angel quail. The masked man drew a slender sword, then with elvish speed, launched toward the cloaked axe-fighter.

Tyrith hurled a hand-axe at the man, who sidestepped the whirling weapon then struck the angel head on. Arwë watched the blade clash with the guarding axe stroke, then saw Tyrith fly back as if struck by a boulder. The angel careened past hedge and tree, his girth carving a jagged path in the forest floor. Roots and dirt rained in the woods as the slim man charged Tyrith again. Arwë felled two more fomori who stood slack-jawed in awe of their leader's power, then he followed the fight.

From the ruin of his fall, Tyrith rose, and Arwë felt an icy chill trail the length of his spine when he glimpsed the white fire of the angel's eyes. Tyrith tore the cloak from his shoulders, revealing six sharp wings gleaming brighter than torchlight. Battleaxe in hand, Tyrith charged the slim man, and their battle echoed into the deepest reaches of the wood. Arwë chased and sent down a hail of fletched shafts, slaying any fomori who dared interfere with the fight between the angel and masked man. The slim man seemed to match the angel blow for blow, but to Arwë, the flashing crown made for an easy, if frustratingly fast, target.

Arwë saw the masked man blur forward, and weapons crashed once more below. One of Tyrith's wings batted his attacker's blade aside. Another wing struck the man's feet. The masked man fell off balance but jumped over the sweeping wing, stabbing at the angel's face. A third wing slammed down to deflect the thrust, and a fourth jabbed with lightning speed, crushing the shoulder of the masked man's sword arm. The man's off hand shot up to grasp his shoulder. Another of Tyrith's wings slashed down, cutting the sword from the man's hand. Then, forming an armored fist, Tyrith caved in the steel face. The man flew end over end, then plowed into a horde of raging fomori.

"You lose," Tyrith rumbled. Then the angel's blazing eyes met Arwë's. "Run!" he cried, pointing westward to a sliver of gold light peering through the trees.

Arwë hurled himself from branch to branch, following his winged companion. His bow sang, felling any creature who came within twenty feet of the Nyphtyri warrior. As he took aim at another fomori and jumped again, light flared all around, and Arwë found himself flailing blindly in empty air.

Out of trees! Arwë thought, falling fast. The world shaped itself as his eyes separated land from morning light. A desolate country stretched below him suddenly, split by a wide gulf. A savage cry drew his attention away from the approaching ground. Hundreds of fomori poured from the forest's edge, screaming their outrage. *Can't right yourself this time, Arwë,* he thought. *'If you accept the burden of this gift, then by fall or by sword, and not the thousand years of an elf's life, you may die.' Lohrë told you as much when he fixed your legs. Well, your legs have gotten you into every bit of trouble he said you were bound to find. Forgive me, brother! I've wasted your gift.*

Iron-hard arms suddenly plucked him from the sky. "Tyrith!" he cried. "I thought Nephtyri wings weren't for flying?"

"Your folk aren't the only ones who leap as high as trees with a single bound!" the angel thundered. His wings brought them gliding to the ground. Their feet struck a mess of cobbles half-reclaimed by grass and roots, and they dashed forward under a rain of fomori arrows.

"See the bridge!" Arwë hollered, pointing to a heap of stone steps that ended abruptly in a ruin that fell over the side of the gulf he had seen from above.

"Keep running!" Tyrith shouted, arrows skating off his iron wings.

"Run where?" Arwë bellowed back, mounting the giant carven steps. They passed under a broken archway of stone that looked out over the wide, black fissure below. Fomori screamed behind them.

"Jump!" Tyrith roared. They leaped from the ruined bridge way, and the valley yawned before him. Arwë watched the light of morning fly away to impossible heights above as Tyrith's wings wrapped him in a cage of iron. The elf and his angel plunged into blackness once more as they waited for the crash that would kill them both.

Send Qweieth-Sil on renewed legs.

Arwë awoke surrounded by cold metal. *Caged in the dark*, he thought, rapping a knuckle on a long, crumpled iron plate that lay inches above his forehead. The plate shifted aside at his touch. Wind billowed through the gap in Arwë's prison, the chill dark without startling him to full wakefulness. He sat up, groaning at a hundred little pains. Shallow, sharp, and everywhere, his muscles ached, cuts bled, and joints protested. Fire burned down the side of his face, and his gloved hand came away bloody when he touched it. As he escaped through the gap in the iron plates, Arwë heard a low moan. Then the entire structure surrounding him shifted, folding down into segments until they lay neatly on the back of a massive man who lay beside him.

"Tyrith," he hissed. "The fall didn't kill you either, I hope?"

"No," the big warrior grunted, rolling over with a clatter of mail and wings. "No lasting damage, either; I only landed on my head."

"Oh good," Arwë said, watching the Nephtyr sit up slowly, turning eyes that glowed in the dusty gloom to look sternly upon him. "Where have we gotten ourselves?"

"Sable Gorge, under Golden-mount," Tyrith rumbled, pointing a long finger out into the darkness. He gained his feet gingerly, walked forward, then stood upon the sheer edge of the spot on which they had landed. Blackness stretched far and away below. The angel sighed. "No way into Nephtyri lands from the east without crossing what once was the bridge we jumped from. So, the only way into Galataeum, is under it."

"Well," Arwë said, coming to his friend's side to look out over the black maw that gaped below them. "In all our flailing about, we seem to have unerringly fallen headlong onto our intended path. Ah, what I'd give for a proper rest." He gasped then, clutching at his leg, which buckled under him.

Tyrith grabbed at the elf's arm, keeping him upright. "Broken?"

"Don't know," Arwë grunted, shifting his weight to his other leg. "Can't seem to stand on it without pain shooting. But I don't think splinting it would do any good. How did *you* survive such a fall, let alone protect me?"

"I've felt worse," Tyrith said, releasing the elf to stand tentatively on his own. "So have my people, so *did* my people, fifteen years ago. Though I'd rather be cut and stabbed than endure such a fall again." He took a step, teetered, then dropped heavily to one knee.

"You've kept a stiff upper lip," Arwë observed, wiping blood away from his mouth. "But you're worse off than me. And that says nothing of the terminal pain you and your folk bear without the aid of screaming foes and cutting swords."

"The less said of it, the better," Tyrith growled, whether at pain or at Arwë, the elf couldn't guess. "We've a man to find at the bottom of this pit." He tried again to get up but faltered.

"Half a moment," Arwë said. "My wounds need tending,

and both our faces are bleeding. Let's have a small meal, dress our cuts, *then* be off."

"Fair enough," Tyrith sighed, but he drew a sharp breath as he pressed up from the ground with his wrist. "Not long, though. We may have fallen far, but fomori are nothing if not persistent. They'll be after us."

As they bandaged wounds and shared strips of dried beef from Arwë's pack, the elf asked, "What happened back there in the woods, Tyrith? I awoke from a strange dream, and you were gone. Then I was attacked."

"I'd seen a glow of firelight under the forest canopy, like the one we saw above Wildercrown," the angel rumbled. "I figured you needed the sleep, so I'd gone off to see if I could find anything. Before I knew it, a dozen fomori burst from the hedges, stabbing with knives. I'd hoped my shouts would find you."

"They did," Arwë mused. "Maybe it was your voice that pulled me from sleep."

"Maybe," Tyrith said, dabbing a cloth at the nasty weal that ran from Arwë's cheekbone to his jaw. "What was the dream you had?"

"Voices chanting, like the ones my people and I have heard for years," Arwë said, gazing in remembrance. "But all the words were different; newer, revealing more of the riddle."

"You remember them?" Tyrith asked.

Arwë frowned, then nodded. "They spoke of a knight, and a journey he must make. They said—"

"Light's Heir shall seek for Garden-hid.
Deep under earth, to find her worth.
Stars' Sailor flies from marching flame,
Dusk-healer plays the Shadow's game.
Scribe's deadly slaves both men shall fight
to wake the world from endless night.
Wither they go, Heir shall follow
and Garden's Key they will find, lo!
Night's pow'r is spent, soon breaks the day.
Seek once bright Innoth-Hyeil Darrë."

Elf and angel stared wide-eyed at one another. "You heard it?" Arwë gasped.

"That was no dream," Tyrith growled, rushing to the edge of the precipice again to look down into the deep gorge. "Clear as a bell and coming from below. Look!" Arwë followed his friend's gauntleted finger. It pointed down into the abyss, at some new shining thing that had not been there when they had looked before.

"*Light springs anew,*" Arwë recited. "*Send Qweieth-Sil on renewed legs ... knight is come without the gift ... bring us shroud, for now's the hou'r.*"

"We've rested too long," Tyrith said, taking up his pack, wincing as he did so.

"We've taken ten minutes," Arwë said flatly. "And we're hardly in any shape to continue at a run."

"Hurry!" Tyrith said and plunged down a path that descended sharply away from the precipice and into deeper gloom. Arwë took up his equipment and rushed after him, despite the pain of his bruises, and the distress of his knee when he burdened it.

Farther, deeper, and for hours, they descended into the dark fissure. Descending ancient stairs and clambering down tunnels of carven stone, Arwë followed his companion, who, in turn, followed the growing light.

Arwë thought of the fabled underground reaches of the world, remembered tales warriors had told of sunken kingdoms and treasures beneath the earth. He and his folk preferred open sky and wind, but Arwë could not help thinking that the cool breaths of air pockets under the earth and the tight winds of his beloved forests shared a kinship. And as a younger, bedridden lad, he had journeyed to more than one deep trove in his dreams.

Innoth-Hyeil Darrë, he thought as they picked their way in the ashy twilight. *I know the name. But from where?*

Arwë could not see clearly, but instead felt the rocky path he and Tyrith tread as they descended farther with each agonizing footfall. The path lay wide enough for the huge man and slender elf to run side by side, but it took many confusing turns, hiding the strange, deep light from their eyes after one turn, then blinding them with brightness at the next. So they plodded along, Arwë with a hand gripping tightly the links of Tyrith's mail. This proved useful more than once, when the path turned sharply and Arwë found himself hanging by aching fingers while his feet dangled out over black nothingness. Always the angel would hold him fast despite his haste and return the elf to solid ground.

Arwë still gripped a handful of his companion's metal

links but now held the fingers of his other hand splayed in front of him should wall, foe, or emptiness leap at him from out of the dark. "The idea of descent into darker-than-black places in hopes of finding knight or light makes my stomach lurch," he blurted in his uneasiness.

"No way but forward and down," Tyrith rumbled. "Even if my wings could carry us back to Qweth-Wëalda, what good would come of it? Wildercrown burns, and the forest is invaded."

"I know!" Arwë hissed. "Still doesn't make me less uneasy."

"At any rate," Tyrith said, "our descent shall become easier. Signs of those who lived here long before are unmissable now. The stairs and hallways we came down, cut by tools, were only the beginning."

Arwë looked all around, keen eyes catching half-buried stonework, the ashy remains of trees, and the walls of gardens. "What do you know of this place, Tyrith?"

"Once a great place, my people thought," the angel's voice thrummed in the quiet dark. "Filled with light, laughter, music, and love. But it was long abandoned, even when we and your oldest elders arrived."

"Your people didn't settle it?"

"No," Tyrith said. "We took land, both empty and inhabited, if it served our interests. But this valley has never been more than a black pit. Something terrible happened here before ever we came."

"If not the Nephtyr," Arwë breathed, "then who lived here?"

DEADLY MESSAGES

Tyrith heaved a sigh. "Your conversations with the Nokleth—you wrote them down, yes?"

"Yes," Arwë said.

"And they mentioned a terrible betrayal by the hands of *friends-light-the-highest*?"

"Atrellarrath," Arwë breathed. "You think they once lived down here?"

"Once lived," Tyrith said, "and live still."

"Hidden?" Arwë asked in wonder.

"Enslaved," Tyrith said. "All that they did, they did wielding light brighter than the day. And it was taken from them."

"How do you know this?" Arwë asked.

A sudden horn blast roared in the murk above, startling them out of their conversation. The trumpet wail echoed off the gorge's slopes, growing louder and louder until it was a tempest. Then fomori voices and those of other dark-dwelling creatures howled in response.

"You see? A thousand-foot fall, and still they pursue us!" Tyrith cried amidst the chatter of voices descending from above. "Come, Arwë! Things aren't so dark now. The bottom is close." He took off at a rattling run.

Arwë followed Tyrith at a painfully slow pace. He soon heard his clumsy steps blend with the tapping of water as it trickled down in staccato rhythms over rock. It dripped and spattered off hard surfaces, the sound echoing all around him to form lurid music with the dark keening of chasing fomori. Tyrith pulled ahead of him, so Arwë did his best to speed down a narrow tunnel, following the angel.

The light burning brighter at the tunnel's end became his goal.

Arwë looked back, seeing no sign of their foes. Looking forward again, he met the abrupt end of the tunnel, and his foot slipped out over empty air. He hollered, plunging end over end into darkness and light. His travel pack broke the fall more than once as he crashed down a flight of carven steps. He landed on his back and saw light dancing golden-red behind clenched eyelids. He moved gloved fingers to a hot spot on the back of his head. He opened his eyes to the glare, and his fingers came back red and sticky.

The low voice of Tyrith came wafting down to him, rumbling low under the voices of monsters. "Nephtyri wings may not be made for flying, but elvish eyes should certainly have seen that missing step."

"My head," Arwë mumbled as the big man eased him to a sitting position. Arwë stared at the blood on his glove. "Red blood—I can see red blood. I can *see*. Clear as daylight!" He blinked hard, the pain searing at the base of his skull. But light, dancing both in his head and off wet rock and in flickering pools, chased away the pain. "True, golden daylight."

"Still below," Tyrith rumbled. "But closer and brighter than ever."

Arwë made to stand. His rising was slow, and all the world spun with the aching of his head. But his eyes drew upward, his mouth falling open. The loud, falling waters flared with the light below, and he looked into a world showered by silver crystals. The shining water cast riots of light up the uneven stairs he had fallen down and up the implacable wall of rock that stretched away upward into impossible heights. In these, he saw the skeletons of broken latticework, once wrought by ancient hands.

"Stairways, bridges, and trellises above," he murmured. "All carved into the gorge's slopes, spanning the gap between a city and Eternity-knows-where. We must have ventured down some great thoroughfare during our descent. This must be where all roads once met. We must be buried under entire kingdoms."

Tyrith lay colossal hands on Arwë's shoulders and studied the elf's eyes.

"And aqueducts," Arwë continued, speaking clearly so as to reassure his friend of his mind and body's soundness. "Sturdy construction, shorn by immense tools. But neither by Nephtyr nor Man nor Qweieth-Sil."

"Giants," Tyrith said, his concerned gaze sliding from his friend's face upward to the dark heights.

"Same hands that wrought Mithweileth-Nal?" Arwë asked.

"Perhaps," Tyrith said.

Arwë's eyes fluttered as he cleared away the pain. He looked up one last time, picking out scaffolds, fastened with the remains of rotted cord. Ladders secured by rusted chains extended to otherwise unreachable mouths in the stone wall. Chains also hung from high overhead, suspending crates and buckets in the air. Chains also secured great wooden platforms in upright positions, blocking whole passageways.

"Drawbridges too," Arwë said. But the renewed tumult of dashing feet and cries cut short his reverie. Looking ahead and taking ginger but deliberate steps, Arwë journeyed downward toward the light. Tyrith followed closely. The screams of beasts propelled them down switchback steps. The light shone gloriously below them, gleaming brighter than ever from across a bridge that crossed a wide gulf.

"My head," Arwë suddenly said again. This time, his long fingers quested up and down the length of his neck, then his cheek. They found nothing. "The pain is gone, as if I'd never fought or fallen."

"Farther down," Tyrith murmured, passing him. They descended to a rough landing across from the light. The great bridge, formed by the slow crush of water against stone over thousands of years, spanned a gap over pure emptiness. Tyrith froze, engulfed in light.

"What is it?" Arwë said, now shielding his eyes against the brilliance.

"Power we were never meant to hold," Tyrith said, his voice quaking.

"Please, Tyrith," Arwë said, approaching his companion, "no riddles." But he saw Tyrith raise his hand, pointing a finger. Beyond the blaze of light, the elf could see a set of clockwork doors, fixed all about with gears, locks, and pulleys.

"You know this secret?" Arwë asked in awe.

"No," Tyrith said, staring straight on. A fierce change came upon the angel, his azure eyes blazing. "But I knew a Nephtyr who once kept a Key, then lost it. Could this be its door?"

"The champion lost his Key to *me*, Nephtyr Ithar-fel!" cried a voice from across the bridge.

Tyrith's face contorted with recognition and rage, and he stormed across the bridge, tearing his sword from its sheath at his side.

"Tyrith!" Arwë shouted, making to follow his companion. But no sooner had he mounted the bridge, against his better judgment, than Arwë looked down. To his horror, not even the farthest-reaching beam of the shining brilliance ahead could reach into the blackness below. The need to drop to his knees for stability lest he fall into such terrible depths clawed at him. Allowing the fear only a moment as his pulse hammered in his ears, Arwë dashed after his friend, drawing his own sword.

"You!" Tyrith's voice roared like a hurricane over the span.

Crossing the bridge and coming fully into the light, Arwë heard a crash of steel. His eyes separated shapes from the glare, and he saw three bodies. First was Tyrith, the Nephtyr's whole weight behind his sword as he bore down on a bright figure. Second was the source of dazzling light: a bundle held fast in the figure's arm. Finally, the figure himself stood, tall and mighty, wielding in his other hand a sword whose blade held against Tyrith's assault, bearing the angel's crushing weight as if with no effort at all.

Arwë stood aghast on the bridge, then whispered, "*Atrellarrath*."

7
AT A LOSS AND INTO LIGHT

Dusk the healer sat under a roiling sky that threatened rain. He warmed his hands by a fire he had built into the lee of a rocky ridge an hour or so after light had gone down for the night. Defeated again, this time by the impossible steepness of the ridge that rose like a spike hundreds of feet above, Dusk flung a rock into the blaze.

"Done t-t-trekking for the d-d-day," he muttered to himself. "T-t-time to let dreams p-p-provide a new path to m-m-mill over tomorrow."

Three weeks' foot travel had brought him down out of the Sunreach Mountains and into the rough country of the Lower-world. Knowing the way through forest, glen, and stony Downs, Dusk had struck the road he and his father had taken a handful of times to the Hidden City in years past. This newest adventure had brought him to the well-tended lane a week before. The journey went faster then, and what few people he had met, he greeted politely. As was the custom of traveling medicine men and women, Dusk offered folk tonic, poultice, potion, and splinting in exchange for news of the wider world. Tidings were strange and did not disappoint.

"Aye, lad, fey folk move along the far-north borders of T'Rhonossarc!" a traveling Midlothean peddler pushing a hand cart had told him five days ago. "The Elf-wood is burned, and no longer safe for anyone to walk!"

"News, boy?" said a rugged Suthesturri widow who bounced along in a wagon pulled by a pair of what Dusk thought were dragons. When the old woman called him back after he had run a hundred yards up the road for his life at first sight of the serpents, she turned out to be friendly, albeit a bit gruff. "Giant perentie lizards, boy!" She laughed after Dusk had mastered his racing heart. He approached slowly, this time with his staff poised to strike. "These beauties come from the lush islands in the sea, far south of the ruined desert. My man captured 'em himself with spear and net. The greatest treasures I have from him, and they'll be in mating-shape for another thirty years! Don't you mind 'em. They've eaten their fill on carrion and won't feed again for a month or so.

"Anyhow, it's news as what drew me westward out of the desert with all that I own, but no longer!" she had said, changing the subject from family matters to travel plans. "I was looking for a bit of peace in the Westreach, what with the wars raging in the deserts. But now folk say the Anglorean King away west is all in a fury over something precious stolen from him; a key or locket or some such fancy. And to have something that trifling stolen right out from under his nose? Only one answer suffices: There was a traitor in his midst!

"But *then* folk said the king could pay the theft no mind, as hosts of evil Men began marching straight down from the snows of the North. The Anglorean country's all ablaze with war now too! So, instead of west, I try to find this Hidden City, as folk have been calling it. Maybe I'll set my household on a good bit of land and get 'em tilling again, just the way my man did before he went away and got himself killed in the desert battles. Fare ye well, boy, and may Eternity bless ye in this present darkness!"

Two days after his encounter with the Suthesturri woman and her cart pulled by dragons, Dusk had crossed the once-amiable soldiers of the Hidden City along the road. Hoping for a game and friendly chat with patrols who respected the reputation his father had built for himself years back, Dusk instead found hard-eyed men bearing sharp spears and heavy shields. Their armor was scoured, scratched and polished again, ready for battle. Apart from grunting something about a mustering of Men by order of the prince, the soldiers had few words for a stuttering boy of sixteen years, fresh out of a country they had never heard of.

Then, two nights ago, Dusk had left the road, striking northward through the wilderness just as the helm had shown him.

"And that's where the troubles began," he muttered to himself, staring into his fire. He considered the weight of the walking stick that rested on his shoulder while he sat, and the wolves he'd had to shoo away. The country had become strange and harsh without the constant vigilance of the Men of Ephtar-Malas. So, Dusk had decided to keep the Great East Sea on his right side, ever in his sight. But he had quickly gotten lost in thickets of trees while trying to follow a little river that cut through them when the land refused to rise and let him see ahead. When he had come out of the woods, he had traveled a twisted path that led him back to the same labyrinth of rocks three times in a single day. He had lit his fire in the highest place he could find to think, eat, and rest.

"And here now I s-s-sit," he grumbled. Lightning flashed far above. He stood and watched the horizon. The storm crashed away over the sea, began wafting its way inland, toward his confounding campsite and little fire. The thought of surviving a night in the open, blasted by thunder and lightning, sent his shoulders bowing forward. Then he thought of the helm, the wonders it had worked and shown, and pondered whether it would do him just one more favor.

"Alright, helm," Dusk said, digging the helm out of his pack and pressing the cool, scarred metal to his forehead. "You sh-sh-showed me p-p-power that would help me s-s-save my mother. Now sh-sh-show me how to g-g-get there from this m-m-maze, to the place that h-h-holds the healing p-p-power I s-s-seek." He turned the helm in his hands, raised it, and placed it on his head.

His head stung with cold, then Dusk's mind fled with terrible speed, away from his little fire under the stony ridge. The vision flung his thoughts far out, under a dark sky filled to the brim with cold, flickering lights, the likeness of which he had never seen. One light grew among the others, burning brighter and brighter until it ate the sky and filled all the world to bursting with golden incandescence. He thought to scream, but instead he sang, for joy came from the highest places, and voices innumerable took up the song. He heard the chorus but could not understand it. Then the light shrank in size but not in glory, retreating into a deep, hidden place. It drew his mind down, under stone and water. The light traveled behind a pair of tall, stone doors. Then the doors clanged, shutting away the light completely. But there stood the doors, ablaze with silver runes. Sigils and carvings of ancient stories also decorated their clockwork faces. The doors shone a deep blue, specked all over with discs and pinpricks of light. Dusk knew somehow that hope, purest light of the world, lay behind them.

He felt the long passage of many years blur past in seconds as the doors glowed gently at the bottom of a lightless shaft. Always the neat inlay of symbols remained constant, but he did not understand what they meant, nor even in which language they could have possibly been written. Time raced like a book's pages wheeling under an incessant wind. Up from the pages walked kings made of light, and the story told of evil deeds, wars, and death in the skies beyond the reach of power. Angels came then, supplanting the kings, and ever the angels kept watch over the door, keeping it shut. Time and its pages passed once more, then the book fell open once more, opening to reveal a man Dusk knew. Dusk cried out, spying him, armed and armored. At long last, one among Men had found the doors in the deep mine. The man stood before their unyielding threshold. In his hand was a key.

Traitor! Thief of Keys! The thought was not Dusk's but was instead shouted by mighty voices from faraway West, in recent memory. Then, a strange compulsion forced Dusk to look down, and he saw that it was *his* hand holding the key, releasing the marvelous lock.

His eyes are mine, Dusk thought. And at Dusk's touch, latches clacked apart, gears shifted, and the doors separated. The light that poured through the crack made the gleam of the runes seem little more than candle flame guttering before the full brightness of noon. He heard howling and teeth gnashing and could not be sure they were not his own. He pushed the doors fully open and stepped through. The deep bang at his back signaled their closure behind him, then all was peace and silence. He stood for a moment in the warmth of the light as it shone scarlet orange through his closed eyelids. Then someone called, and his eyes snapped open to the brilliance.

"Treiarn," whispered the rich voice of a woman.

His heart skipped, panic and courage battling. It was not his name, though it belonged to one dearest to him. He had not heard it in over two years, since the man it belonged to left him and his mother with no explanation. He stepped forward, ignoring fear. "I am here."

Dusk stood awash in astral fire. Pain and weariness of his travels fled, along with his anxiety. His mind was alert, though it did not seem to be fully his own. He could not escape the suspicion of having died and left the dark earth behind. All was too bright here. But he had stepped through the door, felt himself standing, so he was not dead. But he was not himself.

"Long have you journeyed," said the voice that had called him so many times and from so far. It was real enough. So, no, he concluded: He was not dead. "And through such devouring dark. We knew you would come to help."

"Yes," he said. His voice was familiar, but deeper, and not his own.

"We knew you'd return!" said someone else.

"Our Door was locked, but you took the Key," said another. "Though the time was not right."

"Who are you?" Dusk whispered, peering in all directions. He stood in a chamber of glimmering crystal. Singular tongues of argent flame licked the air all around him. They gathered to him on all sides, cool and calming. Then their shapes changed, and before him stood people by the dozen, then by the hundred. Their hair was long and gold or white as snow, standing on end. Their eyes sparkled like the caps of sea waves. Pointed ears flexed and shifted, seeking sounds like an animal's.

"Elvish?" he blurted.

A woman, slender and pale, stepped up from among them, smiling sadly. "In shape and voice, perhaps," she said. The voice he had heard, over land and water and through dreams, had belonged to her. "We, you, your

Kindreds—all are Image Bearers formed to different purpose. My name was Illariu. And we are no elves, but the dying coals of the fire we once were."

"Fuel for a dying world," said a man behind her. "Long held captive."

"Captive?" Dusk asked.

"To those whom we betrayed, then later to others who betrayed us," a child whispered.

"We were created," Illariu said, taking another step toward him. "Created, as your Kindreds were, but our purpose was singular and beautiful. We were the Tryllyë."

"Tryllyë," Dusk said, the word strange in his mouth.

"Eternity's light made flesh," said a man regal and tall. "Our purpose was to yield our light to the Outer-dark, spreading life and wonder to all things beyond our world. The Creator made us, named us, and called us 'good.' He made for us a Garden of imperishable beauty and set us down in its midst. He taught us many good things, and we walked with Him under trees that bore golden fruit and gave to us long life. All too soon, the Creator left, saying there was so, so much more for Him to do in the new heavens. He blessed us, saying He would return to see our progress."

"We did His bidding for ages," said another woman, wheat-gold hair trailing down the front of her shoulders. "And our Garden shone like a beacon in the storm of this world. The Creator left the naming of things on and of the earth to us, taking joy in our learning of the words He taught us. But greater was His joy in the words we fashioned for ourselves. So, the world, covered in wretched darkness save for the place He had made for us, we named Leóhteness-Fal. And our Garden, we called Innoth-Hyeil Darrë."

"Shining home of the Highest," Dusk whispered without knowing how he knew the words' meaning.

The old woman nodded, a dark look crossing her shining face. "Quickly we found that our light on this dark earth was the same as purest power. From Innoth-Hyeil Darrë, ours was the power to give and cultivate, to withhold and let wither. By our whim, the lesser peoples of the World-without bowed low and begged often."

"The only time we sent our light beyond the Garden, to the skies above," said another child, stepping forward, making to touch Dusk's arm, "we felt power go out from us, as though it had been ripped from our very souls, never to be returned."

"So our power never again went to the heavens, nor even into the wider world beyond our garden home," said a woman, bent by extreme age. "We turned our backs to all the sky and dug into the earth, burying and preserving our gift. Oh, the beauty we built and the monuments we made in those ancient days. Rivers of silver and life-giving water poured forth from the Garden. The sky shone with gold and sapphire above our home only, and we built great shields to keep the light from escaping the bounds of Leóhteness-Fal. Our light was the shining envy of all the earth! Cities under the Garden's roots sprawled for endless miles, and our joy knew no limit, save those times we were bothered by the beggars from beyond our borders. Knowledge of all things bloomed with our power, and there was no problem we could not solve, for ourselves or others. We were the masters, knowing ourselves to be the best judges of our power's uses. Soon, we found ourselves *knowing* we were better than all those others whom we saw as beneath us. Then we knew ourselves to be better even than our Creator. When He returned, we found we were wrong. Oh so very wrong."

"He asked us why there was no light in the Outerdark," said a man with a soldier's bearing. His iron jaw and broad shoulders set him far apart from the serenity of the others. "He told us of all the things He had made in His image and in His wake, promising that the light of the holy Tryllyë would be along shortly to bring flourishing warmth. But it never came. It remained here, hoarded by us in our decadence. His creations on this world and beyond it died in devouring darkness. He was angry."

"Our punishment began," said Illariu. All at once, the people encircling Dusk faded back into quivering fires, as if a baleful gust wracked the chamber. "He broke Innoth-Hyeil Darrë, spread its hoarded light to the corners of the world. He said to us, *'I made you long ago, and I do not regret it. You were good, and I saw you carry my light in this world, even if only in the place I made for you. I told you to share it with your brothers and sisters, visit it upon others when I left you to your own choices. These things you did not understand, and were not yet meant to, for I had greater things planned for you. You were not meant to understand, but to trust in me. Now, so much lies in ruin because of what* you have done. Because of this, you now will know the bite of cold, fear of dark, and pain of betrayal. Know that all these things will be visited upon you in repayment for your pride.'"

"We fell on our faces," said the soldier. His voice was low with the edge of command, that of a general after a grave defeat. "We begged for our lives, for any punishment except being disconnected from our light, His light. And He had mercy."

"'You were good, once,' He told us," Illariu continued. "'And you shall be again. But your keeping of my light from creation, storing it up in order to glut yourselves on power and pride, has done terrible damage. You betrayed your brothers and sisters in this world, and so, so many more beyond it. It is fitting that you shall live in the dark, as you forced my beloved ones far away to do. I shall let you remember your glory as it was when I walked with you under the trees of Innoth-Hyeil Darrë. But you will not remember where to find your treasured Garden. You declared yourselves greater than all my creation, but your depravity did not stop there. You thought the light I had given you made you better even than me. I tell you now: My light has no limit and cannot be contained by all the heavens I have made.'"

The soldier put a hand to Illariu's shoulder as crystal tears fell from her fiery eyes. He continued her story. "The Creator told us, 'Your punishment is this: For this First Generation, your light, for all the power you thought it brought you, shall be poured out of Innoth-Hyeil Darrë and spread across Leóhteness-Fal, but it will not be enough. You Tryllyë were indeed mighty, for you were made by me. But the light of this world, given by you and poured out from your Garden, will fade with time. And you shall watch this failing, to remind you that you are limited, while I am not. You shall walk the earth with lightless eyes, knowing the struggle for survival just as those whom you deprived of your light.

'When the right time comes, light shall spring forth anew in your Second Generation. Glory shall once more be kindled in their eyes, for light shall well up in them, and they shall become powerful. But as the light of the First Generation dies on this earth and the Second form a plan with their great power to set things right, judgment shall once again visit. And the power of the Second shall be twisted to other purposes at the hands of those who would call themselves heroes. The overflowing light of the Second Generation shall not repair the damage done by the First to the heavens. It shall instead be poured out once more, not to spread light, but to restrain a terrible evil.

'Doom greatest of all falls upon your Third Generation. A mere fraction of my light is far greater than any fire you and yours have ever kindled. This I will set in the deep heart of Innoth-Hyeil Darrë. You will find that place again one day, but beware: I will set guardians in the deep places, nameless and watchful. By my fire, they will be waiting. And this is not all. You have made servants of others, so you, too, will be made servants. You shall be humbled and know what it means not just to give away your power, but to give it to those whom you ruled with such contempt. The Weileth will not forget. But they will help you.

'You are my children, and with love, you shall have your discipline. But fear not, for I am with you, and I swear your pain will not last forever. All will be made right again if you keep my commands. Forth! Begone from this place of light.'"

Dusk swatted away his tears. The people made of fire stood all about him, heads bowed in sadness and shame. He came near to them, looking into their crystalline eyes, seeing the hurt there. "You are the Second," he said after some time. "You tried with your great power to make things right, just as was told. But it didn't work."

"Even now we are bound," the soldier said, "by peril and duty. We of the Second are nearly spent, and our power sorely diminished."

"Diminished as we are," Illariu said, "our name remains: *Friends of Light Most High*."

"Atrellarrath," Dusk said. He had never spoken the word before but knew it belonged to them.

"The very same," she said. "And as dusk pervades all that once was bright, evil rises again in the world. But the Garden remains. And a child is born to us: the first of the Third."

"Rejoice, rejoice, rejoice!" shouted the gathered Atrellarrath. "A child is born! So ends our exile. Hope is restored!"

"Rejoice in the trial, knight from beyond the Dark-sea!" she said. "For we, and you, still live to see the beginnings of redemption."

"My name is Treiarn," Dusk said, brow furrowing. "And the true home of Midlotheans, my people, lies over the *Great East Sea*, not the Outer-dark."

"So, the Qwei-Sillar did not tell you," Illariu said

sadly. "We knew the Elder Kindred only for a little while, after the war was ended. We remember them bloody and terrible, but increasing in gentleness as the absence of war assuaged their wrath. They were so few in number ... Men will never know how much, how many, they gave to keep your world beyond the Outer-dark safe."

"World?" Dusk asked. "And a war? Do you mean the war that broke the Hegemony fifteen years ago?"

She shook her head. "So much has been lost to you and your peoples since first you came here. I mean only that we and the Qwei-Sillar are similar. Their sorrow runs as deep as ours, their wisdom every bit as hard-earned. And there had been a plan in place, though the battle that soaked the coasts nearly put an end to it. The Winged Ones tore a rift. The tear brought you and your Kindreds to this place. The Winged Ones sought to use the last vestiges of their power, and what little was still stored up in the blood of the Qwei-Sillar, to keep closed the Coffin. But the Qwei-Sillar were too haggard, too few in number."

"Winged Ones?" Dusk said, shaking his head. "You must mean the Nephtyr. They are no more. And a Coffin? What was in it?"

"All we knew was that it was the sole reason for your Kindreds having sacrificed everything to come here. They had brought with them a great evil, tricked it into a trap. They sought to bury it deep and in darkness forever but needed power to keep it shut. They did not expect to find our world inhabited, and with people whose powers were akin to that of the Qwei-Sillar."

"What are you saying?" Dusk asked. "That elves walk free today because of the Atrellarrath?"

"And the Winged Ones," the soldier boomed.

"Tyrants," Dusk spat, unsure of where his sudden anger had come from.

"Perhaps," said a boy, stepping forward. "But the Winged Ones are not rotten to the core, and they are sorely humbled. Who did the humbling, I wonder?"

Dusk felt fire and shame battle in his chest. "I would have done worse, given what they did. But in the end, they showed a sliver of wisdom. And only one more, not all, needed to die by my hand."

"All the same," the boy replied. "They may yet have a part to play in the redemption of all."

"What is my part, then?" Dusk said.

"To guide our Star Under-earth," Illariu said.

"Rejoice!" the gathered Atrellarrath cried. "Rejoice! Rejoice!"

"I don't understand," Dusk said, staring at them. "The only stars I know burn far away in legends."

"All shall be revealed in time," Illariu said. "For there is a little left. This is all we can show you for now, and all you shall be able to understand. You have journeyed far and away from those whom you love. Be our guest for a time, and learn! We shall send you away soon with a burden heavier than stone. So, rest for now, and know that Dusk sets upon the Dread Coast. The Storm guides. Go now!"

"Da!" Dusk cried, flailing awake. "More than a dream; it was him! He stood before the clockwork door, in a land far away, under the earth." He had not noticed the clear cadence of his voice as he went on. "He's alive, but he's alone and looked hurt. They were talking to you, Da, but I heard them too, because of your helm! I heard the message. I'm to make for—"

"Find me," a voice whispered to him. It was haggard but not unkind. It called from far away, just like the voices from his dream of the door. "Light rises from Galataeum but must walk the deep once more to find Innoth-Hyeil Darrë. Walk with the light. Bring it to me, for the good of—"

Lashing winds gusted, buffeting him and scattering the strange voice to the dark of night. Dusk stabbed the ground with his walking stick, regaining his balance. Looking about, he became acutely aware of his surroundings, then froze in sudden fear. He was not where he had been before falling asleep. The rainclouds had been shoved away westward by fierce winds. And where earlier he had sat in relative shelter at the bottom of the steep ridge of rough stone and grass, he now stood three hundred feet higher, having by might or magery climbed all the way up to the top of the ridge line.

"A regular mountain goat am I!" he laughed nervously into the slashing wind. "Who'd have thought the sh-sh-shepherd'd be a better shambler than the sheep?" He looked down on the ruffled countryside, amber eyes scanning the horizon. When he spotted webs of lightning tracing fire-white paths through the sky northward, he smiled. "*The St-St-Storm guides,*" he said. "I heard it, Da: the st-st-stories those Light-folk told you. I'll remember them. Do what you n-n-need to do. I'll t-t-take care of Ma."

Dusk set off once more through the night, forgetting sleep. He removed the helm from his head, stowing it away. He then began the work of navigating the crooked, stony hills of T'Rhonossarc's northern reaches, aided by his trusty stick. As he went, quiet flashes lit the horizon, guiding him toward a distant coast that filled Men's hearts with dread.

8
FLIGHT TO THE FRINGE

Sojourner slept through an entire day. When he awoke, he had been thrown to the mercy of elvish physicians and their prodding. When he had escaped their scrutiny, the sense that something bad approaching hung about glimmering Wildercrown. His escort to the Elf-lord's house had been swift and brusque. There had been no song in the high, pale trees. The Giant's Ring had shone bloody with the dawn, casting all the city in fiery light. And before him the lords of the Qwei-Sillar spoke hurriedly. Sojourner stood before the Council of Twelve, and what words he caught were frantic and anxious. He brought his focus to Lohrë, Cyrwedh, and Cailus at his side. The tall, night-haired elf spoke openly with the Elf-lord.

"This business with the Hegemony and what stirs behind the gates of Galataeum," said the Elf-lord. "I feel it is connected to Sojourner's waking. And both my sons seem to take part in the world's turning."

"What are you not telling me of my brother?" Lohrë asked, eyes narrowing.

"That he shall come into the keeping of a treasure most precious," the Elf-lord said. "And it falls to us to distract all eyes away from him, whatever the cost." Silence fell upon the lords. Both Elf-lord and Lohrë stared beyond the deep chamber to an uncertain future. Sojourner saw them draw breath in the same manner, squint in the same haunted way.

"Where is he now?" Lohrë asked.

"Making his way through dangers we have yet to comprehend," answered the Elf-lord. "Alongside an angel who betrayed his folk, to our advantage."

"Arwë travels with one of the Nephtyr?" Lohrë asked, incredulous.

"To the anger of all assembled," the Elf-lord said, glancing around expectantly at a dozen darkening faces. "And to what end, we know not. But the Nephtyr marched into our woods, out from the fires of his people's war, haunted and bloody. Then he pledged his service to Wildercrown, begging for the redemption of his lost brethren. I paired him with our Messenger, since the lad was slow in growing, even after the restoring gift you gave him."

Lohrë gave the Elf-lord a meaningful look. "You only need ask, and I will protect him."

"It may come to that before long," the Elf-lord mused. "For now, tell us of Sojourner, and be swift!"

All eyes turned to Sojourner, who stood garbed in the golden mail and heavy, gray cloak of the Qwei-Sillar once more. "He has no memory of any day before his waking,"

Lohrë said. "Though his martial skill and speed over long distances prove the match of any Qweieth-Sil."

The Elf-lord nodded. "I sent Wildercrown's best scholars to all corners of the world in search of any record regarding the fallen light that ignited the Fomori War. Pursuing that goal, they found mention of *one who sleeps*, who may be connected to stories of that which brought our people here, long ago. The task has proven ... frustrating. But a few details have emerged, both from within Wildercrown and from the libraries of our friends: Men of the South and West."

"What have they found?" Lohrë asked.

"Precious little," the Elf-lord said, golden eyes falling to reflect his disappointment. "Nearly all we've collected remains to be translated. The Anglorean, Midlothean, Suthesturri, and even Nephtyri tongues have shifted since the days when the Kindreds broke company. Our scholars are hard-pressed, and the translations are not yet finished. For now, know that your convictions have not led you astray."

"Meaning?" Lohrë asked.

"We believe the Sojourner is Thalassean," the Elf-Lord said.

The word hung in the earthy air, lanterns of floating light casting yellow fire upon Lohrë's shocked face. "Hunters of the Dark Six," he breathed. "The warrior who slew the fomori king was right."

Fierce whispers crescendoed in the hall, not the least of which was Sojourner's. "Six?" he said.

"A lie," one of the lords sneered.

"A promise," Cyrwedh snapped.

The Elf-lord held up a hand. "Seven Scribes of Elderlight," he said directly to Sojourner, who flushed at the attention. "Writers of worlds and wonders into being, if the oldest tales are to be believed. Until, instead of writers, they became erasers, and countless multitudes burned. It was the forbears of the Qwei-Sillar who paid most dearly, dying to the last to extract their revenge out of the Scribes' very perfection: So, the Seven became Six. And Six were hunted across all the Outer-dark. When the hunt became frustrated, unable to find the *last* of the Six, and we Kindreds were dashed upon the shores of this dark world, the Thalasseans swore their oath to the Qwei-Sillar. We are long-lived, patient, and wise. We were hurt most deeply, and the Thalasseans knew we would hold them to their oath: end the War of Scribes, imprison the *last*."

"The Thalasseans were barely strong enough in number to crew a ship when we arrived on Leóhteness-Fal," Cyrwedh said. "Yet, the power that flowed in the veins of just those few was enough to help end those ancient wars."

The Elf-lord nodded to her, his eyes bright behind locks of silver hair. "The Thalasseans told our fathers that, if they still have not found the one whom they hunt by the time the *power of the Six* descends upon Leóhteness-Fal, the Thalasseans would send a son of their choosing to help in our greatest need. They departed then, for the *Star-sea*." He grew severe, and the wandering lights of his oaken hall seemed to dim. "Their ship was said to have leaped up and away from earth on a ball of fire. Sojourner's leaped *down* to us in just such a way."

All eyes in the hall returned to Sojourner, who cast about, growing dizzy, looking for anyone who would explain to him what the Elf-lord's words meant. But as Cailus caught his elbow with a steadying hand, trumpets blasted from without. The long, clear notes echoed down into the chamber of roots.

Sojourner felt Cailus release his arm, heard the lad's footfalls clatter away, up steps of the Elf-lord's house.

"You must leave the city," the Elf-lord snapped.

"You're coming with us," Lohrë replied sternly.

"No. If this army is as terrible as you say, then Wildercrown must be the rock that slows their tide, if we cannot stem it altogether. Take Sojourner from here. Gather your strength, Lohrë. Lead as many of our people away. Wildercrown may be lost, but we will defend her! With my command, and a Thalassean with you, the Qwei-Sillar will listen to you and come out of their exile. Our deadliest foe, worse than fomori, goblins, or cataclysms, reawakens. And it may not be just one. Unite the Qwei-Sillar, Lohrë."

"We would protect our city," Lohrë declared, Cyrwedh grasping his hand.

"You have served her, my son and daughter, from far away," the Elf-lord said. "It is not yet time for your greatest stand." He fixed Lohrë with his eyes, now ablaze with gold fire. "Your hosts will be needed elsewhere, when battle comes to the doorstep of Last-Hope."

"You've seen battle before the walls of the Hidden City?" Lohrë asked.

"No time to show you," the Elf-lord said. "Remember Innoth-Hyeil Darrë! The name was oft repeated in writings from the founding days of Last-Hope, when the Rhonoss Lords and Midlotheans laid the first stones. The voices we've heard mention a Key. And writings suggest the Nephtyr and Rhonoss swore an oath of their own upon their arrival on Leóhteness-Fal."

"Lord!" cried Cailus, racing back into the council chamber to stand before the throne of thorn and oak. "The city is breached. Mithweileth-Nal is broken by the same hand that shattered the Tomb. Thousands, lord; Fomori, goblins, and fell Men pour through the gap, and all our arrows are not enough to stop them!"

"Forth to the fight, lords of the Qwei-Sillar!" cried the Elf-lord, drawing his sword. The eleven elves surrounding him revealed sword, bow, axe, and spear, bright mail shining beneath their robes.

Sojourner watched them depart the chamber as Lohrë asked frantically, "What else of oaths sworn by angels and Men?"

"The Nephtyr are crushed," the Elf-lord said as they all gathered to ascend from the roots of tree and house. "They are shut up in their mountain city, so Arwë seeks answers at Golden-mount, as well as news of the Heir spoken of by the chants. And while the Rhonoss are all but dust, the Midlotheans flourish behind the high walls of Last-Hope. Go there, and take with you the Thalassean.

FLIGHT TO THE FRINGE

Their prince lies infirm, but he may know more of Keys, Gardens, and Doors. Go now! And do not rest until you pass under the Sable Gate of Last-Hope. Though, you and our kin may at needs come to it by a secret way, revealed by broken words. Before that time comes, beware: Some ill fate awaits you 'ere you come to the edge of Qweth-Wëalda."

"Father, I cannot leave you to fight alone!" Lohrë snarled as mail-clad guards gathered about them and their march brought them under the house's windows, filled with fire.

"You must," the Elf-lord said as they cleared the halls of the hollow tree, coming to the Elf-lord's door. "Though you need not go alone. I knew of the coming of a deadly host and have prepared Wildercrown and our people. Flee the city! All my hosts are armed, ready to depart. They will follow, protecting you as you go."

"But what of the city's defenses?" Cyrwedh asked. They marched from the Elf-lord's house now with a hundred elves, emerging onto the high, cobbled streets. Sojourner looked up to see fire licking the night sky, the feet of the shining wall in flames where fomori and elves battled below. He saw thousands of fomori gush from a gulf that had been punched straight through Mithweileth-Nal, like blood flowing in rivulets from a grievous wound.

Golden leaves fell upon their group as they departed the city square, the very air dancing with glassy waves of heat. "Leave the city to me," said the Elf-lord. "There will be enough of us left amongst the walls and trees to check the progress of fomori and goblins. Besides the city, my scholars must be protected while they work, then escorted out when they are finished. Go now, Cyrwedh and Lohrë, my children, with all our blessings. Know that you were right all along, in all things. Know that I was a foolish old man, who works now to put things to rights. I will send you Arwë if he returns and we are still alive to give him tidings of our findings. Go!"

Angry tears fell, but Lohrë bowed and guided Cyrwedh, Cailus, and Sojourner down a stone corridor that led up and away from the crash of battle. Sojourner looked back to see the Elf-lord cast aside his cloak, standing tall in his bright mail before a hundred bright-eyed elves. At his nod, every elf of his household, standing close in height and garbed in similar fashion to their lord, readied weapons and marched serenely with him to fight, singing as they went.

Turning back to follow Lohrë, Cyrwedh, and Cailus, Sojourner saw, like clouds of smoke roiling around his companions, a gathering of what must have been more than a thousand tall shadows. Hoods hung low over their lean faces, but the gleam of their eyes could not be fully concealed. They stood erect, laid all about with bows as tall as Men and weapons of greater size and weight than Sojourner had yet seen.

"One hundred," Lohrë ordered them. "Forward." A column of grim Qwei-Sillar took a single, simultaneous step toward him, making no sound. "Protect the Elf-lord.

FLIGHT TO THE FRINGE

Whatever fire he marches into, there you will be also. Go now." They passed by like ghosts in the wind, melting into the shadows cast by besieging fire. Lohrë turned to Cyrwedh. "The rest of our host?"

"A thousand stand at the southern edge of the Ring, awaiting your order," Cyrwedh said with a smile, pulling her own smoke-gray hood over her head so that her likeness matched her brothers and sisters. "A thousand more march to the gathering point already, as you commanded."

"Good," Lohrë said, turning to his umbrous host. "Captains, with me while we march within the city. Away!"

The battalion of dark figures followed the four companions as they dashed through the brilliant streets of Wildercrown, all pretense of secrecy abandoned. With every glance backward, Sojourner saw another score of cloaked warriors join the one before; a gathering tide, following silently. Sojourner then became aware of a cadre of elves who marched close to Lohrë. By light of the Giant's Ring, each of their cloaks was dyed a different color, and they all bore clasps and badges of differentiating shape and size, denoting rank, Sojourner guessed. Fierce whispers encircled the small group, and Sojourner caught words of elvish and the common tongue.

"Have others survived, lord?" asked a broad-shouldered elf. His hair was a perfect icy stream that ran over the top of his forehead. It flowed gently over his pointed ears, then cascaded down into the folds of his hood. "The Sithar or Fir Bolg?"

"The Gray Masks, Captain Nythroel, have all but fled the Qweth-Wëalda," said a woman clad in green and blue. She was slighter than all the rest gathered about their general but stood as tall as any normal man. "I can no longer hear their singing, nor their laughter. Seems they've taken up the calling of their Matriarchs, marched away to the Tree-the-Lies-Dead at the end of the world."

"Some came to Wildercrown, Vala," Lohrë said. "The Sithari Matriarch attended the Council of Twelve, said she and the sisters put up a good fight against the fomori. I know not whether they defend the city, retreat to the gathering point, or simply return to Dead-tree."

"I hope they travel with us to the mustering," Nythroel said, silver hair gleaming in the fey light. "It would be good to see the Gray Ladies in action once more, defending all elfdom. What of the the Bolg?"

"Some of the beast men remain docile and friendly as ever," said an elf who carried heavy swords on his back, marching in full garb of war. Chain and plate chimed in the empty courtyards with each shift of his weight. "Others are feral, wandering the deepest places, and violent if provoked."

"Others still have joined with the Fomori," added a petite woman with an ugly weal where her left ear should have been. "An endless tide marching to unknown purpose. And at their head, someone new."

"New?" asked Nythroel.

"One of the Masked Ones," the scarred woman said, "We've spied on this host since leaving the Tomb, and one of them walks among the fomori in the shape of a man but fights like a nightmare. Are we of the Qwei-Sillar not the stronger, faster, and the smarter when compared to our manling brothers?"

General laughs and murmurs of acquiescence passed through the marching assembly. "The strength of one of these masked things was the match of any ten of us," the petite elf said, quieting them all.

The group exchanged glances of despair. "What proof?" asked Cyrwedh, clearly troubled. Her eyes were fierce, nearly the color of blood.

"That I myself set a trap for this *man*," the small woman said. "And with ten of my cadre, we attacked him in the night when he was away from his captains, pursuing some evil purpose. I escaped, but at great cost." She gestured to her missing ear. It shone white, pink, and ugly in the flickering crimson hues that overpowered the shine of the Giant's Ring. Sojourner guessed the wound had only days ago been tended.

An alarmed silence followed as the company hurried on. For just as all eyes of the assembly took in the ruin of her face, Cailus, with his sharp ears, cocked his head to the treetops above the houses and halls of their kin. Seeing his eyes go wide, the scarred woman whispered to the whole assembly, "They are here!"

"Flanks!" bellowed Lohrë, donning a heavy, steel helm.

Green, gray, and black-skinned gangling things howled from everywhere all at once, pouring over walls and rooftops and around corners. Arrows sang and thudded down from above, striking box, barrel, cobblestone, and flesh. Then all the street exploded with battle.

"Goblins!" someone hollered. "Close in on archers and captains!" Sojourner drew his blades as steel rang all about him. A hundred bows bent as elves in the center of the marching column fitted deadly shafts to their strings. There was a chorus of cracks, a whistle of wind, then heavy elvish arrows sailed high, delivering death. Goblins fell dead from their perches above, their bodies toppling off roof and ledge, into the chaos of the street. The cloaked Qwei-Sillar abandoned spears for side swords, the battle growing intimately close in its brutality.

Sojourner watched elves hew limb and life from their enemies, their ferocity falling upon the chattering goblins like a river's rage when the dam breaks. An elf beside him fell screaming, black arrow protruding from his shattered collarbone. Fear struck him then, and Sojourner cast about, seeking his friends. Goblins instead hemmed him in, as all the elves engaged in other fights. All he could do was point his blades at the oncoming beasts, hoping their sharpness would be enough to keep them back. The goblins were hideous, and they spat and laughed, lustful hate plain in their black eyes. Horror and bile grew in Sojourner's throat. Then one of their pack charged him, screaming as it stabbed a blade toward his heart. Sojourner roared his fear and fury, thrusting with one sword, swinging the other. His stabbing arm outreached the goblin's, his blade passing swiftly through its throat. Without thought, in slashed his other sword, sweeping the goblin's head from its shoulders. It landed with a crunch at the feet of his gang. The goblins' maniacal confidence turned to terror, and before their eyes, Sojourner turned suddenly from cowering victim to towering menace.

Unsure whether to challenge this new foe or flee, the goblins faced one another, grunting in a strange, hacking language. But the conversation died as two fell on their faces, each struck dead by an arrow shot from Cailus' bow. The elf bound up his weapon on his back, drew out a broad, keen blade, and clove a bloody path through to Sojourner. When he stood face to face with the gore-caked elf, Sojourner could not hear what his friend was yelling at him. Instead, a name rang in his ears with a memory, and all he could do was make Cailus understand.

"Kel—" Sojourner said, eyes wide.

"—off the street!" Cailus hollered into his face.

Sojourner grabbed the elf by his biceps, anchoring him to the earth with a grip stronger than iron. "You will listen," Sojourner said. His voice, spoken so softly, struck the elf like a commandment.

"Speak," Cailus said, staring calmly into Sojourner's frantic face.

"Kel—if-f-ful," Sojourner said, struggling as if with a thought his mind would not allow him to complete. Goblins and elves battled all about them, the carnage coating the street in blood, metal, and filth.

"Careful?" Cailus asked.

Sojourner crushed the elf's arms tighter in his adamant grip, and anger blazed in Cailus' eyes.

"Name!" Sojourner hissed, his mind working to force his hands to ease his hold. "Mine ... it's Kay—Kel—Kay—iff—fail. Morn. Sail."

"Your name," Cailus said, gripping the sides of Sojourner's face with both hands. "Keiphral?"

The sound only confused Sojourner, and he looked away in despair. "No," he whispered. "But close."

Two goblins fell dead beside them as Cyrwedh, her face stained with black blood, spun a protective web of steel around them with her slashing sword.

"Then Keiphral will be your name for now, until you remember your better one!" Cailus shouted at Sojourner in the turmoil. "And if you're trying to tell me you once sailed under morning light in another life, then you'll owe me a quiet trip across a lake of glass when we get out of this. Your name shall be Keiphral Morne while we travel together. Suits you better than *Sojourner*. Come away now, though! The battle here is over and won."

His weapons dripping, Keiphral Morne and Cailus joined Cyrwedh, and the three of them dashed through the stained streets to catch the dark company of their companions.

"They were supposed to be miles away on the other side of the city!" Cyrwedh hissed. "How could they have crossed all the way to the south side without our knowing?"

"The one who leads them," said Vala, appearing in a flourish of blue and green. "The Masked Ones exploit the weak fears of Men, but since Qwei-Sillar are made of stuff hidden deeper, the Masked Ones must find weakness in our walls and outer defenses."

"Swords out," came the deep voice of Lohrë. The elf general passed among the ranks of rushing shadow-folk. "No weapon goes sheathed until we've cleared the Giant's Ring. Captains?"

"All here, lord," broad Nythroel said in a low voice. "Athra took a wound in the shoulder, but her wound is dressed, and she will recover quickly."

"Good," Lohrë said. "What of Cyrwedh, Cailus, and Sojourner?"

"Here, lord," Cailus whispered sharply. "With Sojourner and Cyrwedh, our protector. She slew our foes while some spell, maybe thrown by the masked man, came over him. It made him tell me part of his name. Until he remembers it all, he's Keiphral Morne."

"A better fit, I think," Lohrë said, drawing up to them. His glittering silver helm, set about with leaves and blades, made him look every bit the commander of armies. "If the enemy has infiltrated Wildercrown's streets, then I fear the Elf-lord will need more help than just the hundred I sent with him."

"We cannot hope to hold the city, lord," the elf with the missing ear said, coming up from out of the ranks of regrouping elves.

"No," Lohrë agreed. "But I *can* see the Elf-lord safe, no matter what martyrdom he seeks for his not having struck an end to the Fomori War when the iron was hot. This was not his fault."

"It was not," Vala agreed. "But he is responsible for the good of us all, so he leads from the front, throwing himself in with the common soldier. He's a good leader, your father. Such men are a rarity."

Lohrë nodded, then asked, "The perimeter?"

"Clear during our last sweep, not an hour ago," came Cyrwedh's voice. She had climbed high into the branches of a tree that bore small, golden pears. "Clear still."

Lohrë nodded up to her, a fervent glance passing between them. "Stay alert," he hissed, turning back to the assembly. "We near the city's edge, and under Mithweileth-Nal's light, even our cloaks will not conceal us. Be ready."

With the city's center farther and farther behind, the dark company soon drew nearer the towering wall from the north. Keiphral felt tension grow within the ranks of the Qwei-Sillar as they approached the edge of the city. He noted a change in Lohrë as well. Their general walked alone, hissing frantic commands to his captains when they came close to him. He often looked back to the flames that grew taller and brighter in the direction of the Elf-lord's house.

"We approach the southern gate," Cailus murmured at Keiphral's side. "You and I will stay toward the rear of the column, close to Lohrë, but far enough from the center so as not to stand out. I'm sure you've felt our uneasiness. Too quiet here. I dashed through these southern streets in the summers centuries ago. This was the most bustling part of Wildercrown. Its gate and lower market face the kingdoms of Men to the south. Surely neither centuries nor even a siege would eliminate every soul from this part of the city. Something either caused them to flee, or they've been—"

Crashes like falling mountains echoed through the city. The elves looked southward to see a fist of stone bursting from a colossal hole in the Giant's Ring.

"The same as at the northern gate," Cailus hissed, eyes going wild.

The mammoth hand pulled back from the chasm it had rent with a crash of crumbling rock. Keiphral watched hundreds of sharp-nosed goblins and flat-faced fomori surge through this newest breach. And seeing a host of their dreaded elvish foes clad for war, the gathering throng of murderous creatures bawled their outrage then raced toward the southern gate.

With a shout from Lohrë, hundreds of fomori fell dead to elvish arrows. But still, the gray-skinned beasts surged toward his host, bolstered by hundreds more as rivers of them breached the Giant's Ring. Lohrë leaped in front of his vanguard, slaying a goblin wielding a heavy axe. The rest of the Qwei-Sillar joined him, crashing into the clumsy fomori line like a scouring wave.

Keiphral slew a goblin who made to stab at Cailus. Cailus, in return, struck a blow that cut off a fomori's arm at the shoulder before it had managed to take Keiphral's head. Two more goblins came on, and Keiphral, mastering fear, cut them down with the skill of a hardened veteran. Another went down behind him, with one of Cyrwedh's arrows protruding from the top of its skull as she kept watch with other archers higher on rooftops.

"Too many!" Keiphral snarled, battering through the guard of a wailing goblin. Then he heard elves screaming as the enemy's sheer numbers overwhelmed them.

"The van!" Cailus roared, and Keiphral and the elves closest him lunged forward, forcing their way to where the fighting was fiercest, killing as they went. Before long, Keiphral and Cailus found a lone, grim figure, surrounded, and slaying every goblin that dared come within reach of his long, deadly arms. "Lohrë!" Cailus cried. Their leader stabbed a goblin through the eye with a knife, then caught up a spear, piercing the heart of another that dashed away in panic. Lohrë then found his sword, and its blade swept through three fomori necks.

"Close on the general!" Cailus cried. He, Keiphral, and some twenty Qwei-Sillar hacked their way through the horde surrounding Lohrë, replacing their general's deadly foes with bloody-faced friends.

The battled still raged on all sides, but the elves who had cut their way to Lohrë cried, "Lord, lord!" trying to calm their general, whose eyes were black with frenzy.

"Lohrë!" Keiphral and Cailus shouted, together grasping the general's forearms. Lohrë reared on them, nearly killing them in his rage.

Quailing as his master towered over him, grim and terrible, Cailus whispered, "I will guide the Sojourner, Keiphral Morne. The Elf-lord needs you, orders be damned! Go help your father!"

Seeming to weigh whether he should slay the lad as he would yet another fomori, Lohrë shook, his jaw clenching. Then the general took a step back, closing his eyes and saying, "Bless you, Cailus." He looked back, northward, to the roots of the tallest trees and the fires that burned below them. "You are right. My head is not here; rather, with my father. I can lead armies, but he leads nations, and we need him! You know the plan and the way?"

Cailus nodded, his familiar smile returning. "Keiphral here heard every word of your council with the lords and can recall the details I missed when I was forced away. I'll take him away from here, force him to use his tongue by telling me all there is to know!"

Lohrë nodded in return. "The power of Wildercrown cannot protect him against this foe, and you saw firsthand whatever thing that broke the glowing wall, Cailus. Find the others. March with them if you can. Remember, though, that Last-Hope is the goal, both for the Sojourner and eventually for our people. The forest cannot hide us. We must fight, and Malice is where the final stroke will fall."

Lohrë turned then, placing a hand on Kepihral's shoulder. "You understand me?"

Keiphral nodded.

"Then this is as far as we go, Sojourner Keiphral Morne. My city and the Qweth-Wëalda burn, our enemies have come at last, and I can no longer keep you safe."

A sob escaped Keiphral's throat as panic overwhelmed him, and he clutched at the elf.

"Now, now, none of that," Lohrë said. "You're braver than you believe; I saw you fighting. You'll be a man soon. Men protect life and face down terror with courage, though they be afraid. You'll do these things for me?"

"I will," Keiphral whispered.

"Good," Lohrë said. "You can do no other. Now run, fast as you can, to the edge of the forest. You will not get lost. The Qweth-Wëalda seek ever to expel those not born to it. From the forest's eaves, run southeast. Follow the storm clouds that never break until you reach the Dread Coast. Once there, do not enter the Storm; it will kill you where you stand. But, looking away south from it reveals the only path to Last-Hope from the North. The land above the Hidden City is a tangled mess of forest, mountain, and valley. When you come there, follow the river, through all its twists and danger, to the city. Raise the alarm. Tell the sentries the elves, and they, are invaded. Take these."

He took the pack off his back and slung it over the boy's shoulders. At Keiphral's throat, the elf fastened a silver clasp, which he had pulled from a pocket in his cloak. Keiphral shifted the pack onto his back, touching two fingers to the clasp. He looked at the elf expectantly.

"Show the badge to any Qweieth-Sil you come across. Its runes are written in our language; its drawings tell of my plan and of your part to play in the world ending. Tell any of my kin that Lohrë lives again, that we face a foe deadlier than any we have seen upon this world. If we are to survive, then we must unite. Cailus will tell you more.

FLIGHT TO THE FRINGE

If I can find the Elf-lord, bring him out of here to safety, and survive all this myself, I'll find you."

"If *we* can find the Elf-lord, you mean," Cyrwedh said, appearing out of the shadows to take Lohrë's hand.

"I'd have no luck trying to turn you away, even if I wanted, love," Lohrë said to her grimly. "But I'd have no other at my side. With or without hope, we will cut our way to the Elf-lord."

She nodded, releasing his hand to draw her vicious blade once more.

With that, they departed. And the last thing Keiphral heard of them was Lohrë's cry of, "Hurry away now!" shouted over the elf's shoulder. Keiphral felt Cailus's strong grip pull him away from Qwei-Sillar and fomori as they tore one another to pieces, and battle joined once more as they fled.

Cailus led Keiphral out of the city by secret streets and sewer ways. They passed fomori, goblins, Men, and some Qwei-Sillar who had either fought their way out or broken free from the battle. These fled the city as the Elf-lord and Lohrë had commanded. Some vestige of Lohrë's shadowy host met the two companions along their secret path, covering their flight. And shortly after midnight, Keiphral and Cailus passed like smoke through fire and falling leaf, going secretly under the Giant's Ring and into the open night. Evidence of their march was marked only by the occasional flash of a bright eye or exposed blade as the remnants of Lohrë's host escorted them.

But just as the small host of elvish warriors flew beyond the reach of the light of Wildercrown's wall with Keiphral and Cailus at their head, the cry of ominous horns rose up from the dying city. Cailus stopped then, listening hard with an ear cocked back toward Wildercrown.

"Veilglorrum!" an elf voice rang from the din of battle. "One of the Veilglorrath is come to taunt us!"

Cailus looked to the shining wall. "I hear a mocking voice shouting from the rampart. It is a man, and his threats force my people to cower. I wonder if this is one of the *Masked*, as was reported by our captains. Even now he taunts Lohrë and all Qwei-Sillar."

As if in answer to Cailus, Keiphral heard a terrible voice scream down from the broken wall. "Why do elflings flee from battle and not toward it? Perhaps they bear some treasure most precious, away from the ruin of their beloved city? No matter! I shall kill you all here, then follow the filthy stragglers who scatter like sparks from the devouring fire!"

Keiphral saw the young elf's fury, even in the pitch-black of night. He lay a hand on Cailus' shoulder, telling him bluntly, "I'm sorry, Cailus. But now, we run."

Cailus swept a hand under his brimming eyes, sniffed, and nodded. Then they were off, running again through the too-dark night.

"Relentless!" Cailus hissed. They had run for an hour or more, fire chasing them as they went. The crash of arms rose all about them. Keiphral saw flashes of silver slash the air; the blades of their hidden companions swung into the necks of pursuing fomori as they all sought a way out of the wood and were waylaid.

"Down!" Cailus cried. Keiphral dropped, watching Cailus' own sword sweep from its sheath and into the throat of some pursuing terror. The dark thing fell with an animal grunt, and the elf hurried over to Keiphral.

At a scream from behind that froze their blood, Cailus grabbed Keiphral's collar, forcing the boy's eyes to meet his own. For the first time, Keiphral saw fear, wild and barely contained, in the elf's gaze. "No coincidence that these beasts were waiting for us in ambush after we left the city!" Cailus said. "No doubt the Masked Ones cut through our friends back home and pursue us now. I should have known. I'm sorry, Keiphral Morne. But I must part your company now too, if only to give you a few more hours' head start on our enemies."

"No!" Keiphral snapped. "I won't leave you. We left Lohrë, Cyrwedh, *and* the Elf-lord. No, not you."

Cailus shoved him away as another goblin came spitting and raving out of the black wood, thrusting a spear at them. Elf and man each took an arm off the creature before piercing its heart with their blades. The air suddenly grew quiet, still, and bitter cold.

"Masked Ones," Cailus whispered, his words freezing in the air as he uttered them. Then his eyes grew shocked and distant, and despite the danger, suddenly he chanted in the same way he had done during the Council of Twelve, saying,

GARDEN OF ASH

*"Sailor from stars flees marching flame,
Dusk-healer plays the Shadow's game.
Scribe's deadly slaves both men shall fight
to wake the world from endless night."*

His haunted gaze then fell on Keiphral. "Sailor," he breathed.

Keiphral shook his head at the elf, taken aback.

Dark shapes loomed in the murk, and Cailus hauled Keiphral to his feet, gazing wild-eyed at him. "Lohrë's command is your next move," Cailus implored. "Get to the Storm above the sea. Find the healer and the Shadow he fights. I'm sorry we've failed you, but I'm glad to have called you my friend. Now go!"

Keiphral ran, propelled by the elf's shove. He looked back for an instant to see Cailus without his cloak, standing as tall as his lord and glowing in his mail. The elf stared down three leering creatures and a man whose golden mask shone with the last light of battle fires. But trees and rocks obscured them all from view as Keiphral turned and ran. Crashes of steel punctuated each footfall, growing ever fainter as he fled certain death by swords into the lurking dangers of the elvish wild.

9
FRIENDLY ENEMY

The Sojourner Keiphral Morne hurt all over but sped from cover to cover. Screams and the carnage both had faded some time ago, but fire still scorched the sky. The smoky glow pursued him no matter how many miles he walked, crawled, or ran.

Get you to the Storm above the sea! Cailus' shouts still echoed in Keiphral's dogged mind. *Find the healer and the Shadow he fights.*

Keep on, Keiphral thought. Every joint and muscle ached with his exertions. He would run until he collapsed, inching under the protective brambles of thorn bushes when his body would give out. Under shields of prickly stems, he would fall into exhausted sleep, the amber-brown of the burning sky northward mingling with the bloody crimson of nightmares. And when a twig snapping or a shriek from within dreams or without would startle him awake, off again he would go, crashing through the elvish wilds.

Keiphral had continued this way for days. But the sun

never came up. The only true lights he saw in that place were the spiraling lapis and violet that danced in what he hoped was the south sky. They would peak through the thick foliage above when he looked up, lost. But when he saw the gentle colors and the fey tapestry they wove above, Keiphral would allow himself a hopeful smile, knowing he ran the path away from smoke and certain death.

Half-mad with memories or dreams, an exhausted Keiphral would stop to drink at the little rivers that were so abundant in that sprawling forest. *Qweth-Wëalde*, the Elder Kindred had called it during their brief council before the Oaken Throne. While he drank, the only time his mind was not captive to escaping the terror that stalked him, he would try to remember the council, his journey to it with Lohrë and the others, and the darkness before the Tomb. Though his attempts at searching his memories often ended in sudden sleep, Keiphral made little stops frequently to preserve the provisions Lohrë had given him.

Whenever he stopped, the forest seemed to look for a new chance to reveal to him just how alien it was. Whether in restless sleep or half-awake, Keiphral would hear creatures of the wood all around him. And when he saw them, they were not the kinds he expected. Packs of feral dogs stalked prey at the edge of his awareness. In their long faces, he saw the bones of leering skulls and eyes that glowed with cold fire. White foxes laughed in the dark, encased in radiant, nine-tail cloaks. Lemurs stared at him with eyes large as lakes. When they had drunk their fill of him, they took flight, ears propelling them from the forest floor to the sky with heaving thrusts. And between his running feet leaped rabbits crested with antlers, never once stepped on.

Once at the bank of a racing river, when Keiphral's throat burned and his lungs heaved like bellows, he plunged his entire head into the sweet, flowing water. When he came up again, the air had grown suddenly thick with silver fireflies. A shining stag with thirty flaming horns appeared from smoke and dark, parting the silver lights as it made its way to the stunned boy. Without a twitch of muscle or prick of ear, the mighty creature inclined its majestic head and drank beside him. Keiphral took in cupped handfuls of water, watching stunned as the beast pulled its own drafts from the river. When it had finished, it turned its crowned head to him as if curious. But no sooner had it turned its black eyes on him than it turned its head and returned into the surrounding thickets, trailing little silver fires in its wake. And only after the stag had left the river's clearing did Keiphral notice the woman walking beside the beast, a pale hand on its haunch. She turned to him, eyes flashing the color of twilight. Then the needle-points of her teeth gleamed white in the dark as she smiled. He ran and ran away until darkness took him once more.

Smoke woke him from dreams of ruins under the earth sometime later. He opened his eyes to a bloody-copper sky once more. Keiphral swore. He rose, securing his pack and tightening the fastenings of his elvish garb. Fear snatched the breath from his lips, and the threat of some skulking thing stalking his steps forced him to look behind. But from a cool place in his mind, Lohrë's words found him again.

You'll be a man soon. Men protect life, face down terror with courage, though they be afraid. Do these things for me?

"I will," Keiphral said, facing forward to see a country overgrown and ascending sharply.

Good, the elf had said. *Run fast to the edge of the forest. Once you cross the fae-stones, you will know you've left. From the forest's eaves, run southeast, to storm clouds that never break.*

Stifling his terror, Keiphral nodded at the memory of the elf who had protected him. Setting jaw and shoulder, he set off toward his goal again, picking his way up and onto paths that would give him a better vantage of what lay below. He ran at a long-distance pace, breathing steadily as the way rose upward. As the terrain took him higher and the forest scrub and brambles thinned, he caught glimpses of verdant vistas stretching out below. Water sources grew more frequent, and with each stop, he drank then bent back the pesky foliage to reveal a deep valley that grew and grew beneath him as he journeyed higher.

The routine became simple: run one hour, walk the next, then run the one after that. During the fourth hour, he would walk, then find some new stream of water running or brook bubbling. He drank and ate, did his best to discern his position in the unfamiliar world, then would try to sleep for an hour. Dreams troubled him less as he followed his running and resting patterns. And while it was hard to gauge time's passage in the twilight of the elvish forest, Keiphral did awaken to find his stomach protesting his neglect of it, and that gave him some indication as to how many hours were passing in that dark place.

His Qweiethi breakfast was to his liking. The elvish food he had found inside Lohrë's pack was light in taste but heavy in sustenance. Traveler's bread was cracker-thin and dry to the touch, but biting it was like chewing into a freshly baked loaf. For every dark berry Keiphral tried, he could have sworn he had swallowed a handful. The dried and salted meats Lohrë had stored in various packages were Keiphral's favorites. There was beef, poultry, and venison, and his mouth watered at the scent of cured strips, spiced with coriander, salt, and vinegar.

Keiphral enjoyed one such bit of biltong by a snapping fire when the wind changed and the smell of rot rode heavy on it. Eyes watering as he tried not to gag, he caught up his pack, spilling food and cooking supplies. A low rumble shook the little glade, and hair stood on end over his arms and neck. The noise gathered, gaining volume until he heard the grunts, screams, and cries of animals. Fear returning, he made to run. But birds and beasts of the wood burst through the encircling hedges, ruining his campsite. He dove aside as a horned boar tore past, nearly gouging him as he tumbled away from its tusks and brutal strength. On his back, Keiphral watched a flight of owls and kestrels shoot through the grove, ignoring the throngs of mice, rats, and locusts that leaped by, wanting nothing but escape from whatever it was that traveled with the charnel-wind.

Keiphral shot to his feet at the sound of a bleating cry. Something immense crashed toward the grove. Before he could master his rising fear, a mountain goat, crest hard as steel and horns sharp as swords, careened into his campsite. It tripped over the little brook Keiphral had drunk from, barreling over with a squeal. Keiphral watched the poor creature. Its chest heaved, the beat of its racing heart thundering under its hide. It frothed at the mouth, but its eyes were fully white with fear. It struggled to its feet and froze when its eyes met Keiphral's. He could only stand, equally petrified. Every muscle in the creature's body tensed, ready to propel it away to perceived safety.

Not knowing what else to do, Keiphral took a small step back, hoping not to frighten the creature further. He raised both hands with glacial slowness. "I'm not—"

The animal's head flew from its shoulders. It struck the trunk of a tree with a resounding thud. A silence like death settled on the grove. Keiphral turned his head to the bloody sight in horror. The beast's head stared in shock. Beating down the scream trying to tear itself from his throat, Keiphral jammed his fist into his mouth, biting down hard on his fingers. He tasted salt and iron, smelled rot. Then came a single footstep, and his fears increased tenfold.

Something had entered the grove with him. It was no fae-creature. It wore the shape of a man, pale and masked. Filthy rags covered his body, the tattered ribbons of his cloak fluttering in the acrid air. He wore no hood, and his hair was short and fair. Blood ran in rivulets down his vicious sword, though how its blade had cut through the goat's spine, Keiphral could not guess. All he could do was stare, hackles raised, as the man stepped forward. Dark things dropped from his body, forming little pools of shadow that writhed at his feet. He shuffled, bucking this way and that. Then, turning from the paralyzed boy, the hideous man turned to his kill. He knelt beside it, as if examining the body. The stench radiating from him grew, sending tears trailing from Keiphral's eyes.

Terror and the visceral stench were enough to drive Keiphral to retching. The masked thing snapped its head in the direction of the sound then went still as stone. The mask, a twisted attempt at a human face, leered at him. Keiphral only saw darkness behind the gaping mouth, and the scream fought its way to the top of his throat once more. But before Keiphral could release it, the man spoke, and Keiphral knew it for the voice that had taunted the Qwei-Sillar from the walls of Wildercrown. Keiphral could not understand what the man said, but to him, the grim syllables croaked from the thing's throat sounded something like, *Thyarrenn feil-ahna, Ephtari.* The language rolled from the man's tongue like ancient boulders freshly dislodged. *Dohr-nu annoii-lei. Fai rei, nah Thyarren. Ichelus-toh Nephar-bithenrei.*

As the man spoke, the face he wore swiveled slowly from side to side. *Fai-reck, illeth-sithar bithnethniphall.* The words were whispered this time, and he cocked a notched ear in Keiphral's direction.

He can't see me, Keiphral thought, releasing a breath he

had been holding without realizing. *But he knows I'm here. And the shadow that drips from him ... not shadow—blood! Cuts made by Qwei-Sillar?* He remained still, arms frozen in the same gesture he had used to placate the headless goat.

Just then, he heard his name called, as if from far off. Keiphral's eyes went wide, darting side to side. It had not been the call of a parent summoning him home. Rather, it was a plea, and the promise of answers. The voice was music and joy, chasing away the dark for the space of a breath. It had not been the name Lohrë had given him, nor the one from Cailus. Just as quickly, it was gone, and the dark hemmed him in once more.

Real, or the Masked One's trick? Keiphral thought. Refusing to be baited, he did not move. After what felt a lifetime of waiting, the creature's head swiveled again, grabbing Keiphral's attention. The mask turned to him as if gazing at its prey.

A chuckle escaped from behind the contorted face as the man said to the air, "You are no elf. Dressed like one and nearly as fast. But not. So, who are you, manling? Though I suppose that is not apt for you, either. I smell no manling blood in you. All the same, who are you? And why do you keep council with elvish filth? Are you the one who slept so long under watch of the Qwei-Sillar? Fools, the lot of them, and so few in number. Most likely dead now that their precious forest is ashes. But if you are the one who slept, where did you come from? You, who came burning down from the black sky on a ball of fire. Hardly unnoticed. The elvish filth were not the first to get at you, whatever you are. Your things were stolen. Though you no doubt know it."

Keiphral's arms shook as he struggled to keep them up in the same warding position. *I will not answer.*

"Nothing to say?" the man croaked. He stuck scabby fingers into the goat's blood and brought them to the lips of the sinister mask. "Did the elves tell you at all of their crime? Deepest blasphemy. They slew my god, *may our bodies be broken for him*, before they fled to this dark hell, escaping the wrath of his peers. Your face tells me they must have misplaced that detail."

He cannot see you.

"Blasphemers cannot go unpunished," the man whispered. Goat's blood decorated his mask, what little shine it had possessed now streaked and dull. "T'was right, then, that nearly all of them died in the act." An awful hacking noise escaped the man's throat. Keiphral recognized the wet sounds not for the coughs of a sick man, but for the laughs of a maniacal one. The masked man stuck both hands deep into the goat's blood, drawing patterns and glyphs in the dirt. Keiphral's head began to spin, and he felt a terrible feeling being called into the little grove. He dared not move. He watched as the man squatted, surveying the ghastly work in the soil. His horror renewed, Keiphral saw glyphs traced in blood and the glow that took root in them. Then the man stood, taking several shuffling steps toward him.

"That tall elf," the Masked One wheezed. "Strong, he was. "Such princely blood in so little a rat, at no mistake."

He came within ten paces of Keiphral, who risked lowering his right arm, putting weight on his back leg. "He was protecting someone, someone who escaped our ambush under Wildercrown's trees—oh, we burned those to the ground, then we burned everything and everyone along with them."

Half a dozen thoughts crossed Keiphral's mind as the man made his bumbling approach. *He's baiting you. It's working. But he'll kill you! Not if you kill him first. Draw weapon! No, run. No! He'll catch you. He's wounded.*

From across the world, Keiphral heard the strange voice whisper a name again. The word beckoned him, breaking his concentration, and he nearly took a step toward it.

"And that she-elf, the tall one's lover," the Masked One chuckled. The words cut into Keiphral's impulses, rooting him in place. A scream almost tore itself loose when he saw the man nearly face-to-face with him. Keiphral's despair turned to abhorrence, and he found himself hating this thing that belittled lives, being itself somehow both living and not. "She put up a fight, she did. But oh were her screams a delight, her blood so sweet!" The Masked One's sword, not simply dripping with beasts' blood, but seemingly forged from it, rose above Keiphral's head.

Keiphral imagined the faces of Lohrë, Cyrwedh, and all his companions contorted in suffering. Rage clenched his hand into a fist, and before he could stop himself, he struck the man's throat. The haymaker crushed cartilage, and the Masked One somersaulted end over end. He crashed to the dirt in a tangle of limbs, smearing his bloody drawings. He did not move. His sword, now just a piece of ordinary folded steel, lay harmless, out of his reach.

Keiphral untied the knot of his fist, eyes wide at the wrath that had roared up in him. Then he looked down at his stricken opponent who twitched and shuddered. The mask lay fastened but upset at a strange angle. The bits of face beneath it were dreadful and pocked. The nose was a dark hole, and the upper lip had been eaten away.

Then, the same hacking cough-laugh bubbled up from behind the mangled lips. Blood spewed from them as it mumbled and raved. The coughing, burbling, and laughing continued, growing louder until the entire copse echoed with the sound. Keiphral felt bile and disgust rise as the thing twitched and shook, inhuman. The bloody sigils brightened, a sickly green glow emanating from them. Keiphral felt death draw near once more. Finding his will, he left the crippled, man-shaped thing to bleed and splutter on the ground, to what end he cared not. He dashed away madly in the direction of the fey creatures. Leaf, rock, and bramble blurred in a tunnel of rushing shadow. His body refused to stop, tearing through the wood even after his mind, numb from terror and loathing, fell into blackness.

Keiphral awoke to the heavy sound of water falling. Gulls, white-winged and chattering, arced overhead, telling him he had collapsed near a great deal of it. Swallowing hard, his throat felt as if he had drunk sand the night before. What he had truly done then, or even the night before that, he did not know. His pack, lying a few feet from him, was still intact. It had suffered damage, scraped and slashed by reaching thorns or rocks as he had run. But it was still whole, and nothing seemed to have fallen from it. He breathed, filling his lungs with fresh wind, his memories of burning thickets far off in dreams.

Just then, the wheeling gulls and flecks of waterfall spray drove him to speak. "Light. I see light—real, golden light again. I'm out, past the eaves. Escaped!" But he would not let himself forget. The ones who had protected him had trusted him with their message to the city they had called *Last-Hope*.

Lohrë's command is your next move, Cailus had told him.

Keiphral lay on his back, staring upward. Part of his view lay blocked under a rocky overhang, but his eyes drank in the honey-gold sky, even as the violets of dusk swirled, beginning their invasion. He blinked after a long while, then ran a hand over his salt-stricken face, removing grit from his eyes. Sitting up, every muscle protested, little pains panging everywhere. Upon swift inspection, he found no injury, relieved to know he had not run headlong into a tree or scraped flesh on some bramble. Making to stand, Keiphral's tongue begged for water. He went to the pack and pulled out an empty glass bottle. Some scrutiny of his surroundings revealed he had escaped the Qweth-Wëalda by river. But whether he had jumped or fallen into the racing waters, he could not guess. They had rushed him out of the woods, spitting him onto a craggy escarpment that hung a hundred or so feet over a fair, green country that stretched away southward.

He sat in a bowl of rock, water spluttering down from half a dozen falls to fill a clear, stony pool. He stoppered his bottle after filling it to the brim, nearly succumbing to the urge to douse his whole head in the pool's waters. But the thought of sour bowels after the simple mistake of drinking unfamiliar water was enough for his patience to hold. Looking around from his high place, he saw no person or beast for miles in any direction, only a lake in the deep valley below.

Keiphral walked a little, finding a spot that hid him from all directions if roaming eyes chanced to look up at him. In the misshapen rocks was enough free space overhead to allow smoke to escape. He gathered fallen sticks from the oaks, ashes, and rowans of the Qweth-Wëalde that formed a dark wall above the crag. Then he built and struck to life a small fire. After boiling his water, he drank down the contents of his bottle twice over to satiate his thirst, then a third time for good measure. Lunch was a meager assortment of berries and dried strips of meat. But upon further inspection of his pack, he discovered a wheel of hard, dry cheese. It had been coated in a strange sealant that preserved all but a small edge where it looked to have been cracked during Keiphral's flight. He removed the sealant, broke off the bluish bit, then threw it into the little tarn, the splash luring curious silver fish. The cheese was hard and pungent, exactly what his tongue needed after the monotony of his travel food. But memory of the masked man, and the face under it, made him pack up cheese and rind before he was finished, his stomach cramping.

Removing the elvish travel garb, he jumped into the pool. The chill water relieved so many of the little pains he had sustained. When he came back ashore, he sat in a shaft of warm light amidst the rock, letting the wind dry him. It was the only time he took, for soon enough, the strange thing he had felt in that grove haunted by the Masked One nagged at him. He thought of bloody sigils traced in the earth, then made ready to depart. His clothing cleaned of crust and salt, Keiphral dressed, donning cloth and armor once more.

The voice that murmured names had not called since before he had left the fey woods. But he felt drawn toward the sea, away east. Eager to be off, he scattered his fire with a kick and studied the horizon. Hill and tree abounded, spreading leafy and green in all directions under him. The deep valley fell away down from where he stood, high up in the crags just under the forest escarpment. One edge of the valley's bowl climbed steadily, hills marching away until they were obscured by larger ones. Eventually they gave way to the purple haze of jagged peaks.

Those would be the smaller siblings of Golden-mount, where Galataeum sits above the clouds, or so said the Qwei-Sillar, Keiphral thought. *If that's true, then that way to the mountains is west, and I must go opposite to find the sea. When I do, I'll follow the shoreline south until I find Lohrë's people or reach the Hidden City, Last-Hope.*

Turning away from the hazy mountains, Keiphral surveyed the other edge of the valley. The land that spread beyond the dip of the valley was vast and hilly but manageable with the gear he had. The hilltops would provide better ground for gaining his surroundings as he went, and he knew he could cover twenty miles in a day's hard march. Satisfied with the small plan, Keiphral began his descent from the escarpment.

Climbing down the stony shelves and into the valley that day, Keiphral gathered more water from the lake at its bottom. Then leaving the lake behind, and heavier with the weight of water, boiled and bottled, Keiphral prepared to plunge once more into wild country. Sight of the horizon sent a chill through him as he saw storm clouds gathering high above the eastern horizon. But for the gloom those clouds brought, they were nothing compared to the memory of his Tomb under the earth. And the gift of light, as it shone weakly overhead and all around, was enough to send Keiphral Morne forward, humming a song whose tune he remembered, but whose words he had forgotten.

Rain slashed at Keiphral's face while frigid wind quested into every fold of his elvish cloak. He had hiked eastward for days, following the cliff line that separated the hilly country from the dark eaves of Qweth-Wëalda, keeping millions of fey acreage to his left. He saw the escarpment diminish over the miles until both it and the tree line had disappeared and both pieces of land met once more, the land flattening as it struck seaward. The Storm grew monstrous on the dull horizon as he marched. Its gray darkness had overtaken the twilit sky more than a day before, and the rain had begun at dawn. Its icy fall forced Keiphral to throw his hood over his head. Memories of masks and bloody swords hounded him. But his purpose, and a strange, new music, drove him toward the tempest, step after plodding step.

He had struggled against the Storm for hours, rain stinging his eyes as wind tore open the weakened seam of one his pack pockets. He had not seen the contents fly, but Keiphral knew which pocket had torn, picturing his tinderbox and rope tossed away in the squall. His limbs burned with the exertion of trudging through the Storm, no longer protected by hill or rock. Eventually he crawled, clawing his way forward, toward the music. Its melody had been taken up by two voices. And they sang ever louder the closer he came to the beleaguered coastline. Fears of marching fomori and the haunting laughs of Masked Ones were his only driver after determination had failed.

Whether days or weeks had passed, Keiphral could not guess. But when all had been blasted to sudden stillness, the silence that enfolded him was enough to make him clasp his hands to his ears and curl into a ball on the sand. Beyond his ears that screamed in the deafening quiet left in the storm's absence, Keiphral heard only the tune. It had grown strange and dark, sung back and forth in discordant melodies. The voices, Keiphral's scoured mind had determined, hated one another. He lay face down, head pressed to the damp sand, listening. But a wild scream cut the music from the air. Its frenzied pitch forced him up to all fours, then to his feet.

On wobbly knees, Keiphral released his pack, drew one of his swords, and cast about. Just beyond the eye of the Storm, Keiphral spied a new figure, shirtless, arms raised to the blasting wind. Keiphral only then realized he had not been crawling on a beach, but along the sea floor, surrounded by seaweed, rock, and flopping fish. The Storm had blasted the ocean's waves more than a mile out from shore. In wonder, Keiphral watched the figure stand in the midst of the surge. Whoever the figure was, the Storm roared down on him, forcing him to his knees. Then Keiphral saw two orbs of burning lamplight blaze to life in the figure's head. The eyes raged as the figure writhed under some terrible power.

Images of masked leper-men swarmed his mind, and Keiphral, barely able to lift his blade a moment before, stood fast. Losing Lohrë, and his cowardice during his flight from the elvish wood, ignited his fury. But a thought stayed Keiphral's blade.

"Not the eye of a hurricane," he whispered, seeing the figure not for another masked man but a normal boy. "You fought the Storm to a standstill."

But the tempest whipped itself into a frenzy once more. Keiphral stood dumbfounded as the sea rushed back to ravage the shore, thrashing under lightning and wind. Sea and gale smashed down on the shirtless figure, who stood like a rock in the flood. And he brought them both to heel, ripping power away from them. But a terrible shadow rose from the deluge, then something ancient and malicious glared down at the man, as if to devour him. Paralyzed and consumed by goose flesh at the sight of the monstrous shadow, Keiphral could only watch as the boy disappeared under its weight, and the screams started anew.

Face down terror with courage! Lohrë's words snapped Keiphral into action. He charged the Storm and shadow, not quite knowing what he was doing. He entered the murk, the world going as dark as his living-tomb. But a blast of wind and fire threw him backward, into the air. He landed on his back, all air driven from his lungs. As blackness threatened the edges of his vision, another scream brought Keiphral to his senses. Swordless, he rose to see the figure crushed and mortally wounded, sable-crimson pouring from his shoulder to soak the sand. But just as Keiphral gained his feet to charge at the devouring clouds, the figure stood again. Darkness and light gathered to battle for the figure's armless shoulder, rising in power until Keiphral thought all the world would shake apart under their wrath.

A new scream tore from the Storm, mingled with a cry from the figure. To his horror, Keiphral thought he heard the word, "*Eshra!*" shouted in the tempest. Thinking of burning hosts trailing ruin across the elvish lands, Keiphral watched a vortex of power pull something terrible out of the world and into the prone figure. Then all was calm again.

Every hair stood on end as Keiphral rushed to the dark figure, whether ready to fight or help. When he reached the boy, Keiphral dropped to hands and knees, finding that the dark figure, having just fought a storm and won, was only a lad of sixteen or so. Then the lad laughed, half-crazed from his fight. His face was pale and angled, worn with ceaseless toil. His hair, a dark shade of blond, lay disheveled and soaked under a battle helm. But the lad's smoldering arm blotted all other things from Keiphral's mind. The lad held it skyward, and it smoked from the wound dealt by lightning and that hateful power. But the blackness that lay about it was more than charred skin. Shadow itself filled the blisters as they burst.

Terror bubbled up again in Keiphral's throat at a dark realization: The lad had *lost* his arm; this shadowy one was not his, but part of something sinister. Keiphral groped for a sword, but the stricken lad's eyes snapped open, and their molten light drew out the scream Keiphral had been nursing. He flung himself back, crawling away from the shadow of the arm and the burning eyes.

"Gauze," the lad croaked.

"What?" Keiphral gasped, looking back.

"Linen gauze," the lad said. "Wrappings for w-w-wounds in my p-p-pack. And whatever s-s-salve you can find there. Hurry. I've only j-j-just c-c-contained it."

Dazed by fear and exhaustion, Keiphral hauled himself in the direction the lad pointed with his good arm. Keiphral found a scarred leather pack half buried in the sand with a cloak rolled neatly in amongst the straps. He dug through the contents, fished out linens and a jar of smearing gel, and brought them to the wounded lad.

"I thought you'd died," Keiphral said, removing the jar's lid. "Thought it would come for me next."

"Help me wrap," the lad said, showing Keiphral how he needed to wrap the fey arm. At Keiphral's disgust, the lad rolled his amber eyes and said, "It took my arm, so I took its head! And its p-p-power! I've d-d-done the world a g-g-great s-s-service just now by r-r-removing the curse from the Blood-drenched Shore. You've n-n-nothing to fear from me, so l-l-long as you don't stop me from going about my b-b-business."

"I just saw a lad lose an arm to a hurricane," Keiphral snapped. "Then blast that hurricane to pieces with powers from the Outer-dark. What, pray tell, *is* your business?"

"Healing," the lad said, "as you can s-s-see." He nodded toward his pack, out of which spilled spools of gut thread, stoppered flasks containing a dozen-colored liquids, roots, leaves, and medicinal sprigs.

Keiphral eyed the lad sidelong then nodded. He began wrapping the lad's arm as instructed, smearing a healthy amount of the clear salve over the smoldering skin as he went. Every now and then, Keiphral met the lad's eyes, which were huge and bright as lanterns in the murky noon light. He considered their strangeness, but then considered the strangeness of all things in this world. He shrugged and kept on with the wraps, seeing no evil in the lad's face.

Once finished, the lad flexed his fingers, wrapped individually by Keiphral's strong hand and the lad's instruction. "Well d-d-done," he said. "Now, I think it's t-t-time I—" He tried gaining his feet but rolled onto his back at the effort. "Maybe I should s-s-s—"

"Sleep," Keiphral said as the lad's eyes shut. "I'll look after you. You seem friendly enough, though there'll be questions to answer when you wake. For now, you rest in the care of one trained by the Qwei-Sillar. You have nothing to fear from me either, so long as you don't try to stop me in *my* business." *I'll take time to catch my breath too*, he thought as he stood. *Just in case it really was the Enemy's name I heard you shout in the middle of that fight. If you attack me, at least I'll be rested and ready for it.* He found his discarded sword then returned, sitting by the boy and laying it across his lap. He stood watch for a while, the lad having fallen fast asleep. Keiphral looked at him a moment. This boy was easily three years Keiphral's junior.

"But you fought like a warrior twice your age," Keiphral whispered. "And you bear a warrior's helm. It's the only bit of raiment about you that seems out of place. You never took it off. Might help your head to remove it while you sleep." He went over to the lad, realizing also just how small he was for the colossal deed he had just committed. "Who are you?" he demanded.

Keiphral set his fingertips on the lid of the lad's helm.

Kel. The voice struck his mind like a crashing wave. He recoiled as if bitten, grasping at the fingers that had touched the helm. No damage had been done, but the woman's face would not leave his mind. He saw her without seeing her, just as he had heard her voice without hearing it. She was lovely, regaled in armor that shone like fish scales. Her smile was like the dawn, and she gave her command again. *Kel.* Journeys, fears, storms, and now voices proved too much for Keiphral, and he dropped to the sand. The boy who had awakened in the Tomb fell fast asleep to the roar of the returning ocean.

The boys awoke to a dark sky as eventide rushed in, drenching their hair. They spluttered and laughed, escaping the frigid waters at a run as dark breakers swept in over the sand. Gathering their things, they made their way to a higher part of the beach. When the idea of a fire in the open came up, neither tried to stop the other. And beside a merry blaze, both boys shared a banquet of stale travel food and boiled river water. And when they had finished their feast, they each fell asleep by the perceived protection of their new fire.

"What's your name?" Keiphral asked when they had both awakened and the sky had grown gray.

The battered boy lay on his back, arm held to the sky. He flexed his bandaged fingers in the weak morning light. "I g-g-give a travel-name to strangers," he began. "But s-s-seeing as how you've s-s-saved my life, I would call you friend, and you may call me by m-m-my real name, Treijan, son of Treiarn."

"Treijan," Keiphral said, considering. "Not elvish."

"It's Midlothean," Treijan said, sitting up. "Though my h-h-home was m-m-moved to the mountains after I was b-b-born."

"Well, friend Treijan," Keiphral said. "I'll add the riddles of your misplaced name and storm-contesting power to the collection I've been building since arriving in this strange place! As for me, I was given the name *Sojourner* by my rescuers to keep me out of danger. But *my* real name, or at least the closest thing to it, is Keiphral Morne."

"Well, f-f-friend Keiphral," Treijan replied. "You've done me a g-g-great service. I would have d-d-died had you not arrived in t-t-time."

"I only arrived in time to wrap your arm," Keiphral said dryly.

"No," Treijan said. "Out of the Elf-wood and onto the sh-sh-shores with your s-s-sword. You d-d-distracted it."

"It?" Keiphral asked. His smile dropped away as his hand found the hilt of his sword. "Eshra?"

"I d-d-don't know w-w-what that is," Treijan said, raising both hands in a placating gesture.

"The name you cried before you slew the Storm," Keiphral said. "The name on the lips of the armies that burned Wildercrown."

Treijan frowned, considering. "I know n-n-nothing of the t-t-troubles in the Lower-world. I only came here s-s-seeking power to heal my m-m-mother. I d-d-didn't think I would actually f-f-find it."

"Yet here you are," Keiphral said, eyes narrowing. "Knowing enough off this Lower-world to come to this exact spot, find the exact power you sought, with just enough strength to harness it."

"I-I-I was g-g-given a vision," Treijan whispered.

"By whom?" Keiphral asked.

"This," Treijan said, removing his helm for the first time. He held it out to Keiphral, who cursed himself for flinching. He saw Treijan's eyes narrow slightly at the reaction.

"And someone gave you this thing?" Keiphral said, plodding on despite his slip-up.

"You're v-v-very curious, Keiphral Morne of the elves," Treijan said, a sharp edge entering his timid voice. "My helm is m-m-my property, having come to me honestly. What of you? Why did you c-c-come to this awful place? If you're s-s-so close with the Qwei-Sillar, sh-sh-shouldn't you be h-h-helping with the war you claim they're f-f-fighting?"

"I am," Keiphral said. "I traveled with a great warrior among them. I bear his message and badge, see?" He tugged at Lohrë's clasp, shifting it closer so Treijan could see. "He told me to come this way. Then from here, he said to find the way to a place called Last-Hope."

"Well, there I can h-h-help!" Treijan said, standing. "I may n-n-not know much about the Lower-world, b-b-but I do know where Last-Hope is." He turned, pointing southward across rough-hewn country. "Find River Dethrai'ar a few d-d-days over the h-h-hills. F-f-follow the r-r-river southwest as it m-m-makes its way into the hills. The river plunges underground and into d-d-deep valleys of sharp rocks and f-f-forest. But follow it true, and you'll f-f-find the city. You'll know you've d-d-done it when you see white towers."

"You've been there?" Keiphral asked, rising to stand beside him.

"No, but I've t-t-traveled the road that l-l-leads close to it," Treijan said. Agitation sneaked into his voice then, worsening his stammer. "But I've s-s-stayed too long, and n-n-now I have to g-g-go. Thank you again for your h-h-help, and f-f-for not w-w-waylaying me in my t-t-task, Keiphral."

"Thank you for your help in my finding the city, Treijan," Keiphral said, eyeing the strange lad whose irises glowed with more than firelight. He knew he was letting information escape but couldn't come up with a plan to keep the lad any longer. "And for acting a friend, though you look an enemy."

"New f-f-friends are welcome, but n-n-not enemies," Treijan replied, drawing a long breath. "My only foe is d-d-disease, and it will f-f-flee before my new p-p-power. Now I must g-g-go and use it."

Keiphral only nodded, began gathering his gear, and made ready to depart.

After a few minutes, the boys shook hands. "Good luck with your healing arts," Keiphral said.

"And you in the war," Treijan said. "I've n-n-never seen an elf before. B-b-but when you reunite with them, m-m-make sure to write d-d-down some of their cures in the common t-t-tongue, yeah?"

"Yeah," Keiphral laughed. "Farewell, Surgeon."

"F-f-farewell, elf-warrior." Treijan said, donning his helm. He touched his fingers to the visor in salute.

As Keiphral turned to leave, Treijan's voice, suddenly low and menacing, rumbled to him from across the sand. "Kel. Seek Arwë," he said. "*He and the angel guard a treasure most precious. If Arwë has failed, seek the prince. Malice hides a deadly secret.*"

Keiphral looked back to see Treijan's eyes burning bright, staring straight at him. Then, even as they dimmed, growing foggy and confused, morning's full light burst onto the shore and out to sea. Treijan stood, if a little wobbly, like a shadow framed in golden glory.

Dusk-healer plays the Shadow's game. Cailus' chants echoed in Keiphral's mind.

"Healer," Keiphral said, curiosity overflowing.

"W-w-what is it?" Treijan asked, holding a hand to his head as if pained and ready to topple.

"The name you said you give strangers. What is it?"

"Dusk," the lad said, the word seeming to ground him a little.

"Treijan Dusk," Keiphral said, taking an eager step forward. "Dusk-healer. I've found you."

Taken aback, Dusk said, "I d-d-don't—"

"I think, rather, *I've* found you," a new, grizzled voice boomed in the morning glare. "And you shall both now come with me."

10
A GIFT IN THE DARK

Arwë shielded his eyes from the light with his arm.

"I am not of the Atrellarrath, but I am the knight, and now the runner," said the man who held the radiant bundle in one arm while enduring Tyrith's full might with the other. The blade of his sword grated against Tyrith's, and both weapons threatened to snap under the strain. But the knight seemed untroubled as he stood under the wrath of an angel and looked to Arwë.

Arwë studied the knight's garb and mail, the winged helm he wore, and the sigils of his cloak. "Midlothean," he said. The knight smiled beneath his helm.

"*Wing-ripper!*" Tyrith thundered, pulling back his blade, then striking with force enough to shatter stone.

"You Nephtyri Tyrants were in sore need of a lesson in humility and consequence," the knight cried between each crash of their swords. They hacked, cut, and cleaved, the knight retreating as he turned away each stroke delivered by Tyrith. "Your master by far the most!"

"I'll kill you for what you did to him!" Tyrith roared in a froth, swinging wildly.

"You have neither the strength," the knight snapped, slashing Tyrith's blade away with a shower of sparks, "nor the time." With one hand, the armored man who glowed in the brilliance of his burden checked Tyrith's assault. Then, to Arwë's disbelief, the knight turned the fight's momentum against the massive warrior. With a flurry of blows that sent bursts of light into the black above and below, the knight fought Tyrith all the way back to the bridge. The Nephtyr's back foot struck the span.

"Tyrith!" Arwë cried, making to part the storm of whirling steel, then stopping, thinking better. "Who is this man to you?"

The knight countered every desperate attack Tyrith threw at him. His keen blade struck the angel's wrist, shoulder, and neck, tearing Tyrith's armor. He cut away Tyrith's sword, then smashed the back of his armored knee, forcing the Nephtyr to kneel, ending the fight. "I humbled the Nephtyr," the knight heaved, "and slew their greatest champion before the gates of Galataeum. I took his Key, used it to find the treasure. Seems the master's foolish death taught the apprentice nothing. Stay there on your knees, where you belong, and I'll instruct you further."

Tyrith lunged forward, white-hot fire blazing in his hand.

"Tyrith, stop!" snapped Arwë. "You're the one who advises bridled strength. You attacked this man as soon as you saw him. Set aside whatever grudge you have for now, then fight after we've heard him out."

"Wise words, Prince of Wildercrown," the knight said, fierce eyes still fixed on the Nephtyr. "But will your wisdom guide you rightly to our redemption, or our destruction, I wonder?"

"I am Wildercrown's Messenger, not her prince," Arwë replied. "That role went to one greater than I. As for the first half of wisdom, my companion and I were guided safely by it. We fled my city when we drew near. She was dying before the onslaught of ravaging hosts."

"Then things are worse and farther along than I had feared," the knight whispered, more to himself than to the elf and angel. "They kept me too long, and now I must hurry west."

"For the second part," Arwë continued. "Am I wise to trust you?"

"What have you heard of me?" The knight said, blade still poised at Tyrith's throat.

"*By order of Elf-lord, Messenger and Midlothean make for Ephtar-a-Tyrian Feilleth.*" Arwë recited the Elf-lord's missive by memory, then chanted the strange words that had so completely infiltrated the minds of him and his people. "*Here is the knight, returned with might ... the Heir comes forth but cannot hide, through dark and danger she must ride ... but man and Heir cannot be swift, for knight is come without the gift.*"

"Have you brought it?" the knight asked. An eager light came into his shaded eyes.

"Tell us who you are," Arwë replied. Then he leveled the point of his blade at the knight's heart. "And let him up."

"I am the knight," the man said again, his face barely visible in the glare. "Set to my path by many voices and much counsel, but the road I walk is my own. Your father knew this, Arwë of Wildercrown. As for the winged miscreant here, he is free to get up and go wherever he pleases. But he should know that Midlothean blood is still potent and will break the power of the Nephtyr as it always has, despite their meddling." Arwë thought he saw Tyrith blanch. But his companion rose calmly to his feet. The Nephtyr set his jaw, and the cool fire of his eyes smoldered, but he remained silent.

Feeling the furnace of Tyrith's anger radiating beneath his dispassion, Arwë spoke sternly. "My companion is no miscreant and seeks vengeance upon you for old deeds done in war, whatever they may be. Despite the wickedness that once took root in the hearts of his people, and whatever splinter of it may or may not lie in his own, he is my friend. And I am willing to avenge him upon you." His bright eyes narrowed then. "For my power cares little for the makeup of your blood."

The knight sighed, sheathing his sword and easing his radiant burden down from his shoulder so that he cradled it in both arms. "Insult was not my intent for either of you," he said. "I beg your forgiveness, master Nephtyr."

He bowed his head to Tyrith, whose lip curled into a sneer. "Peace for now," Tyrith said through gritted teeth.

"But beyond the walls of this dark place, and whatever duty we may share, there will be a score to settle, Knight Treiarn, Ripper of Wings."

Another sigh escaped the knight's mouth as his shoulders sagged. "So be it. For now, there is no time! I am come from the hall of my hosts, ill-equipped for the task they've appointed me."

"The hall behind the door?" Tyrith asked. "What was behind it? It was locked."

"Locked by the Key of your master, and guarded by power beyond mortal ken," Treiarn replied. "I can only guess the Nephtyr swore some secret oath to guard the door forever, passing down the Key through the line of their greatest warriors for safekeeping. But I took it when he died, and I hid it, knowing somehow that the time for its use was not the day we ended Galataeum's war. But here I am now, against my selfish hope that I would die an old man before being forced back into the world's turnings again."

For a moment, Arwë and Tyrith stood quiet in the warmth of light under the earth. They forgot for that instant the cold of the black shaft they had fallen down, the hacking cries of monsters pursuing them.

"Forced," Arwë said, drawing back to himself. "By whom?"

The knight's eyes shone like summer grass through his helm's visor as the light of the burden he held bathed them all. "My hosts, the Atrellarrath," he said. "When Galataeum's doors were shut at the Hegemony's surrender,

I stayed at Golden-mount. Your friend's wrath is stirred at my having girt myself in the arms and armor his master, for the Nephtyri champion was dead by my hand, and his spoils were mine. My amusement was to mock the Nephtyri tyrants, parading myself before their walls, daring them to stop me."

"You wore his wings like a cloak," Tyrith said, seething.

Treiarn nodded solemnly but without remorse. "And when I put on his helm, I saw suddenly as if through another's eyes, people innumerable, tortured, brutalized, and worse. They were buried under Golden-mount, in deep, horrid chambers beyond count ... *my* people. With the eyes of the champion's helm, I found the secret ways under Golden-mount. And with the champion's Key, I freed them all, calling my legions underground to help retrieve those bodies too mangled to walk out of their prisons on their own.

"After these mines were devoid of Midlothean screams, there came one final cry for help. But the voices were not the same as the men and women of my blood. These were shrill and powerful, and pulled me under the city, down all the way, to this door. A people, ancient and sorrowful, were trapped, with no chance of escape, though the jailor's Key be in my hand. I could not find the lock, and they told me their greatest light was not yet born. So, they sent me away then and spoke no word to me in more than fifteen years. Now I am come again, reluctantly, by their summons."

"And when you returned," Arwë ventured. "Things were not the same."

A GIFT IN THE DARK

Treiarn shook his head slowly. "They called me from across the world: 'A child is born. And into this child our power is poured.' Because of that overflowing power, and the light that blazed forth from it, I found the keyhole, and opened the door. I entered their heavenly presence and have been their guest for a year and a little more."

"You said you were out of time," Arwë said. "My companion and I are trailed by a host of fomori and someone worse, bearing a mask. What is this business you're on? Do we fight alongside you, or do we run together with you into other dangers?"

"We all go into the greatest dangers of our time, I fear," said Treiarn. "Though we cannot go together, as your father and the Atrellarrath wished. Things have changed, and I am out of time! I fear I must leave many tasks to you both, for there is much I, too, must do. And your speed and strength together will prove greater than my own. So, maybe there is hope ... I see far but not as far as this."

"You speak in riddles, friend," Arwë said, eyes narrowing.

"Then let me speak plainly, Messenger," Treiarn said, shifting the bundle he held as if it were quite fragile. It spanned some five feet across, bending in the middle, like a body. "The masked thing you fought was one of the Veilglorrath: crazed fighters who don metal faces in mimicry of the dark goddess they serve. They seek to uproot a power long since buried and forgotten. Your Elf-lord gave me what provision and counsel he could when I told him of such things. I spoke to him of visions I had seen through the Nephtyri champion's helm, which coincide with the voices heard by the Qwei-Sillar: *A great people, twice betrayed, lay trapped under Golden-mount. They covet help, for the time has come for them to walk freely under a sky that never darkens.*

"Once the rulers of this world, it was by Atrellarrathi will that Men lived and died. Crawling things went about earthly business with their permission. Kingdoms were delved, lights were set in deep places, and wars were fought, and—" He paused, breathed. "Forgive me. I have spent much time with them and have come to know much. Through their eyes, I see the world differently and know more truth, beyond the squabbles of lords in high towers who send Men to die for nothing in faraway lands. You have seen the work of my hosts. Theirs is the light, not the Nephtyr's, that fills the sky. Theirs is the light we name *the day*. And it dies even now as the last of their power is poured out to protect us all."

"But you spoke of daylight in perpetuity, under a sky that never darkens," Arwë said. "Does this thing you carry have ought to do with that?"

"She does," Treiarn said.

"She?" Arwë asked.

Treiarn chanted the words Arwë knew too well. "*First Children paid and were poured out. The Second saved but were enslaved.*" He then held the glowing bundle out, and Arwë saw that it was not wrapped, but clothed, in the knight's arms. He spied a pair of leather boots in the glow, which covered a pair of slender legs. "*Light springs anew.*" He looked Arwë in both eyes, as he said, "*Third take to path.*"

"The answer to the riddle of voices," Arwë said in astonishment. "The *Third* is a person?"

Treiarn nodded. "Hope and light of the Atrellarrath. She has never known darkness, and dropped the moment she first lay her adamant eyes on the oppressive black under Leóhteness-Fal. She is firstborn of their Third Generation, prophesied by the Creator Himself, to arrive after the Atrellarrath long endured their punishment."

"What else do you know?" Arwë said, stepping forward. "There was more to the verse. More voices, speaking of what must be *this* gorge, of things called Weileth-Zhul, two Keys, and a Garden—"

"Innoth-Hyeil Darrë," the knight said.

"Innoth-Hyeil Darrë!" Tyrith and Arwë gasped together. Elf and angel looked to one another, then back to the strange man standing before them as he held a person who glowed brighter than daylight. "What do you know of the Garden?"

"Much as it once was, long ago at the height of its majesty," Treiarn said. "Though where or *what* it is now, I know little; only that it is bound up with Last-Hope, the Hidden City."

"Ephtar-Malas," Arwë said. "The Qwei-Sillar named it long ago."

"The very same, and perhaps rightly named," Treiarn said. "Its cloven mountain, high walls, and towers were my home once, but that was before Galataeum's war. Sunreach is my home now, with my wife and boy. But hear me a moment: the Queen of Light bade me bring the Heir of her people through the doors. I'm sure she thought I was set aside as special, after slaying—er, winning the key—if you follow me."

A rumble bubbled up from Tyrith's throat as Arwë glanced over to see the Nephtyr's lip curling.

"I tell you, I am not special," Treiarn said. "Just a man with skill in war, whose luck won him a prize. Now, that prize has turned out to be a burden, heavier than any I have ever wanted. All I want is to go back to my life in the mountains faraway south. But I cannot, for there are other oaths that need fulfilling, and my business away West is in some way connected to the Heir. It is a thing only I can do, and it may guide the fates of many, should I succeed or fail."

"You charge us with your duty," Tyrith said flatly.

"Not my duty, but *his*," Treiarn asserted, motioning to Arwë. He then recited, "*Come Qwei-Sillar, O Ephtarrath! Remember oaths to ancient friends ... in Golden-mount is born an Heir, who seeks the Garden, with our prayer ... but man and Heir cannot be swift, for knight is come without the gift. O Weileth-Zhul, mercy we beg! Send Qweieth-Sil on renewed legs.*"

"Arwë of Wildercrown, whose ruined legs were restored by magic from the Outer-dark after the Fomori War, has come north bearing a gift from the Stone-folk."

"From the *Nokleth*," Arwë insisted. "The Weileth-Zhul, if ever the giants existed, are dead."

A GIFT IN THE DARK

"The Atrellarrath, who knew the forbears of the Nokleth, saw you long before you were knit in your mother's womb," Treiarn said, growing impatient. "They—we—beg you to take part in a task laid down by a people who are Light Incarnate, and by the Lord of the Qwei-Sillar."

Arwë could only stare at the knight, frowning his misunderstanding as his eyes flitted back and forth from dark to light, to his tall, battered friend, then to the stranger and the glowing burden swooning in his arms. "I bear no such gift," were the only words he could think to speak.

"You must," Treiarn insisted, grass-green eyes turning fey. "You have come too far. The Elf-lord told me of your journey up from the Southlands, from the Quarries. You bear a thing given you by those little ones who hosted you there. You will remember it ere long. No more time," Treiarn said, frustrated. "My hosts spoke of many things, not least of which was this: 'The Second are near to dying. Light will fall, the Coffin will open, and the Garden will be laid a second waste.' You must go, Arwë, and Nephtyr Ithar-fel. The faith of the Atrellarrath is in you now."

Treiarn thrust the radiant bundle into the arms of a surprised Tyrith. The moment the light touched the Nephtyr's arms, he roared into the surrounding dark. The brilliance of the knight's burden bent Tyrith double when he accepted it, and Arwë watched his companion burn. As if a cleansing fire had just been set in the Nephtyr's soul, Tyrith's arms, armor, and his very shadow burst into flame. Gone from them was the quiet, cloaked man. Now stood an angel out of legends, tall and many-winged. His face was bright and terrible to behold.

Arwë and Treiarn flung hands over their eyes, fearing death for simply looking upon the countenance of one so hallowed. They cast about for anything that would let them escape the searing brilliance, finding nothing. Tyrith screamed again. The earth itself shook with his pain, and the bridge shivered under them.

"*Power!*" Tyrith cried. His voice, once deep and implacable, was a maelstrom strong enough to rend mountains. "*With light and power, Nephtyr Ithar-fel shall be king of angels, ruler of Leóhteness-Fal. I will destroy the Sickness that rots the bodies of my people. I shall find the Dark Seed and crush her in her foul Coffin! All the Six shall kneel before me. Galataeum shall be torn open, and in its place will be set a greater kingdom, in my name!*" Lightning exploded overhead.

"No, Tyrith!" Arwë called, gaining some measure of his sense. "With power such as this, you would overwhelm and destroy, not heal the world or your people. No more tyrants. We need men willing to fight, to sacrifice for the innocent. Come, we have a gift to find. This may be a new chance to redeem your people!"

"I would slay him to redeem the Nephtyr," Treiarn said, his voice barely audible over the rising tempest. He stared at the figure bursting with light and power, drawing his bright blade.

Tyrith, with lava-bright feet, took a step, melting the stone of the bridge. He flung out his six metal wings, now molten-bright, and flailed them fiercely. Their beating blasted the dark place with peels of thunder.

Arwë lay a hand on the knight's hilt, shouting into the wind, "Come with me, Tyrith! Away from the lust for power that so ruined your people." He sensed hesitation from his friend, some weakness in the limitless power pouring from his winged body.

The walls of the gorge shook, and the ancient architecture of those who came before crumbled, caught in the storm. "Go now," Arwë bid Treiarn. "Whatever business you have in the West, be about it." Treiarn nodded. But as he turned to leave, Arwë caught him by the arm. The man turned back to the elf, whose gold-latticed face shone stern and proud in the burning light cast by Tyrith. "Be ready to explain all your wild tales when we meet again in the Hidden City."

The knight smiled, producing a piece of vellum. He slapped it to the elf's chest and held it there. "This will explain some," he said. "Don't lose your Nephtyri friend, or the girl. Farewell!" He bounded off, lost down some hall or hole Arwë hadn't seen when they had arrived at the bridge.

"More secret messages," Arwë grumbled, stowing away the sheet. He turned back to Tyrith. The Nephtyr's feet had returned to stand at the center of the bridge. "What is it you always told me, Tyrith?" the elf called. "Though we walk not in the world of Men, we are *men* nonetheless. Face fear and devil head on, for you are not alone! Stand bravely to the last, for it is what we do, and have done, forever!" Arwë saw Tyrith's armor glowing red, the tatters of his ruined cloak charring away in the stifling wind.

"Cloak!" Arwë cried, remembering the garment that lay wrapped at the bottom of his pack.

A gift, but not for the Qwei-Sillar. The Nokleth's gravelly voices rang in Arwë's mind as he tore open his pack. *Take it to those who dwell under Golden-mount. With them it shall find its purpose.*

"Tyrith," Arwë called, spreading the cloak in his long arms. "I've found the gift of the Nokleth, packed away with our gear! It's alright, though. *You* are alright! Come back now, across the bridge to me. I think it would wrap nicely around that bundle of yours. Hurry now!"

"Arwë," groaned Tyrith, radiant and scorched.

"No harm done, Tyrith," Arwë said. "You've not hurt me, nor our things, nor our new burden given by our knightly friend. Bring it here now, my lad! Let's see what Treiarn has given us. *Hurry.* He handed me a new scrap of secret messaging too, which I'm sure you won't be able to resist. He said it would give us at least a few answers as we leave. And we *will* leave, Tyrith. You, me, and that bundle in your arms. All that, and we'll forget any and all talk of destruction and ruling the world, yes?"

"Men," the Nephtyr growled. His voice was a breaker on an angry ocean.

"Men indeed!" Arwë said with more confidence than he felt. "You certainly showed it, giving that masked fellow what-for earlier, eh? Come on, now. Come over and pack up. We've a long road down to Last-Hope."

A Gift in the Dark

Blinding light faded to the glow of a bonfire, and it rested in Tyrith's arms. The Nephtyr's eyes returned to their striking blue. He looked as if he had just awakened from a terrible dream, his breath coming in shocked spurts. "Arwë, you—"

"I did nothing," Arwë said, still holding the cloak outstretched. "Only gave you a bit of a reminder. Your calling is higher than becoming another stooge of the Hegemony. I fear our knight has passed off a burden that would become unyielding power and inescapable shackle both at once, should it be mishandled. Give us that odd thing now, for safekeeping in this cloak."

Tyrith, staring aghast as if he had just committed some awful crime for all to see, nodded. He set the glowing bundle in Arwë's arms, where the elf wrapped it in the cloak of the Nokleth. He set the burden on the ground, and it stood upright on two bright feet. With hood and cloak drawn tight around her, the bright bundle, as the knight had revealed, was a girl.

Bits of broken rock and masonry fell like sharp hail. All the Sable Gorge was settling in the wake of Tyrith's brush with purest power. Despite the choked, stifling air, Arwë and Tyrith stared, transfixed by the girl, whose quiet gaze pierced their hearts. She was slim and fair, with a curious beauty that stole their breath. The Noklethi cloak, concealing her radiance by some power, hung elegantly about her shoulders, and only a gentle glow emanated from her alabaster flesh.

But before any of them could speak, screams raged down from above. Out of every crag, crack, and doorway graven into the dark gorge above clambered beastly things with yellow eyes and grisly tusks. Their horns hung about with scraps of cloth, leather, and root, and their skin was every color of earth, knotted, pocked, and scabbed. Their muscles bulged, and in thick, stubby hands, they bore axes and cleavers, chipped and tarnished with misuse. Hulking legs pumped, hurling the creatures down the stone steps toward the three figures who stood bright-eyed on the bridge.

"*Fomori*," grunted Arwë, casting about for the door through which the knight had disappeared. Shattered rock lay heaped in all directions, and he could spy no escape.

Goblins and fomori scrambled to the bottom of the valley, crossing the bridge to the Door and their prey, hollering obscenities in their hideous language. But when they drew up to the group of three, the girl's eyes flashed, and she seemed to tower over them. The angles of her face shaped a deadly promise that stopped them where they stood. Arwë and Tyrith lunged forward. The elf had strung his bow in an instant, aimed an arrow between a goblin's eyes. Tyrith's wings, uncloaked and deadly-sharp, pointed at the throats of six fomori.

"Leave us," the elf commanded. The beasts poured in from behind in a nearly endless tide. Those above who had heard him, laughed. But the ones facing the three strangers quaked, pulling back from the girl's mysterious eyes and the weapons of her companions. When so many of the beasts had flooded into the great chamber above the mineshaft that it seemed fit to bursting, they began murmuring to one another. Confusion seemed to be the only thing these creatures agreed upon. They looked to have expected tender prey in such tunnels, waiting to be taken without a fight. Warriors stood before them instead, tall and defiant. Discussion consumed the fomori, but one of them from above laughed again, and the rest joined. They pressed forward, drawing sword, axe, cleaver, and knife, and hobbled over the bridge.

The hands of the first ranks of fomori reached out to grab at Arwë and Tyrith. The Nephtyr made to thrust his wings forward, but a sound like an iron bar striking stone rang in the darkness above. The grabbing hands, some knotted with muscle, others emaciated and weak, fell away. All the creatures looked upward. The iron boomed again from above, and all the beasts on the bridge and above it went quiet.

"You will leave *with* us," croaked a cold voice. The very sound of it sent shivers running the lengths of Arwë's arms and neck. It sounded just like the masked thing that had attacked Tyrith under the Qweth-Wëalde's eaves. The half-dead thing had marched itself all the way down into the mines to stop these creatures from murdering the three companions.

Only to do it himself, Arwë thought.

"Choose your next act wisely, elf-runner," it whispered. "Yes, yes, we know all about you. For you have tokens—or knowledge of them, at least—that I want. And

I will have them from you. Come with us, and you shall be rewarded beyond avarice." At the promise, the fomori eyed one another, snickers and laughs bubbling up from wide, jagged-toothed mouths.

"I carry nothing," Arwë replied, looking up into the mass of gloomy figures standing in dark doorways. "And as much as I'd love to settle up on our little scuffle in the woods and would be happy to educate you in the finer arts of combat, my companions and I must be going. We've no time to play with you or your ilk."

The shadow-skinned beasts snarled and spat short, angry words from their foul mouths. They made to advance on Arwë, Tyrith, and the cloaked girl again when the ghoulish laugh wafted down once more. Arwë fought every urge to cover his broad ears.

"Oh, but you will be fun to play with, *boy*," the voice, colored by amusement, whispered. "I've been waiting for this, for *you*, for so long a time." The nightmare sound came from every angle, down every hall, and through every seam in the rock. Then, to Arwë's dismay, a small light came from a doorway above, illuminating the bent forms of the fomori who stood there. The beasts looked at one another, apprehension in their sickly yellow eyes. Then they parted, forming a fidgeting hallway of sorts, down which shuffled a figure draped in rags. Its face lay obscured behind a metal mask twisted into a visage of sorrow, the mouth a black hole beneath iron eyes.

"The fool elvish filth thinks to resist me, does he?" the voice said, emanating from the masked figure. "Oh,

A GIFT IN THE DARK

the vaunted righteousness of the *Elder Kindred*. Ever they saw themselves so lofty, so set apart. Yet, when freedom was handed to you, you slunk away into your woods into primitive diaspora, never to perform deeds of any renown. Your foul babes suckle in the dark of the Qweth-Wëalda, and you hope none will ever find you. Find you we have, elf-prince. Wildercrown is *ours*.

"Such is elf wisdom: You obliterated your own kin to win a battle in a war you will have lost in the end. And so, you and yours subsist here in the void, hoping to be kings of ash yourselves. You crawl out of your hiding places too late, now that the First-lights have burnt out, and the Winged Ones have fallen from the sky. No matter. We shattered your Giant's Ring. The Oaken Throne will burn. Then, when all the elf-lands lie parched, when my boot treads the necks of weakling-Men, and after I alone sit upon the throne of the Black Citadel, I will slowly flay the last contagion of the Qwei-Sillar from your very skin. You will be my slave, and I will rule over you for as many long, slow nights as I wish."

"You certainly paint me a merry picture," Arwë said flatly, though resisting the urge to retch. Keeping the grip on his bow iron-tight, Arwë imagined splitting the space between the brows of the mask with a barbed arrowhead. He would die on his feet, living as no one's slave. But that death would not come here.

"It makes no difference to me whether you come along or die," the masked man said. "I will have my answers and my prizes one way or another. And your filthy Kindred will all die before long. What is your choice?"

"My choice," Arwë said, looking up at the grief-stricken mask, "is to name you coward and liar. The White trees of the Qwei-Sillar cannot be burned so long as the world endures, and the soul of Wildercrown remains, even if Mithweileth-Nal is thrown down. King of Ash is the title *you* seek, else you would quest openly over land with these creatures, your *armies*. A true ruler would not cower under the concealing cover of elvish leaves he hates so. He would gather strength, march against his foes. Your power is not half so great as you claim."

"Kill him!" roared the voice behind the mask. The fomori stampeded across the bridge.

Arwë loosed a shaft at the masked man, but the arrow struck a goblin who had leaped in front of its master in a frenzy. At his back, Arwë heard Tyrith chant, *"Grant me fire once more, holy light; not for dominion but for rescue!"*

Arwë whirled to see Tyrith tear the Noklethi cloak from the girl's shoulders, and they both caught fire once more. Glorious light blazed in the mineshaft. Fomori wailed, flailing about with their crude weapons. Limbs and flesh bled as they hacked one another. In blindness and confusion, they slew themselves, dozens of them falling from the bridge, screaming into the hungry dark below.

Arwë caught sight of the masked man. The figure leaped down the valley walls like an acrobat, sword poised to cut him to pieces. But Arwë lost sight of the mask as it disappeared into the tide of roaring beasts, hidden even from the light that shone from the day-bright fire. Then the masked man burst from the morass, a handful of fomori falling before him. He swung his blade at Arwë's neck. The elf swept a dagger out of its sheath and slashed away the cutting edge. He then swung his bow like a club into the mask. The metal face jerked at an odd angle, still hanging about the ruined face, exposing an eye and ugly scars beneath. Rage filled that single eye, but before the man could regroup, a dozen flash-blind fomori seethed forward, grasping at anything that stood in their way.

Some of them latched themselves to Arwë's arms, others to his legs and waist. He went down with a crash before he could swing his dagger to fend them off. He felt them claw and bite, but his armor was tough, holding against the onslaught of tooth and nail. As he felt the breath beaten out of him with each biting beast that piled on, the last thing Arwë saw was a man whose wings burned white-hot. And with a girl clutched to his chest, the winged man struck the bridge with a fist of fire. Arwë heard an overwhelming groan then a crash as the stones beneath his feet splintered away and into the black horror below.

Roaring winds tore tears from Arwë's eyes. He clamped them shut, and the blackness behind his eyelids was no different from the blackness without. He could not breathe. Two or three fomori still clung to him, while others screamed in free fall. He clutched his bow in the aching fingers of one hand, his dagger in the other. Then through closed eyelids, Arwë saw a fiery red light approaching. He opened them to see searing radiance burn down through the dark. Flaming wings enfolded him. For an instant,

Arwë touched power so great that the seemingly incalculable force that had healed his legs and lungs two centuries ago felt little more than a rain puddle beside the sea in a storm.

But death approaching at blinding speed drew his attention away from the ocean of power, and louder than the howling of stale wind and biting beasts, Arwë heard a heavy boom gathering in intensity. *Downward*, he thought as he and the veiling wings tumbled end over end. *Whatever the sound is, we're falling toward it.* He heard a sudden, sickening crunch a few feet from his head, cutting short the cries of one of the fomori.

Not falling in open space! he thought. *Down another mineshaft. And our fomori friends are finding its stops and turns. How well will these iron wings hold if we hit the sides or bottom? First thing's first: Away with uninvited guests!*

With dagger firmly in hand, Arwë clubbed the fomori tearing at his leg with its steel pommel. Feeling the fomori's grip release, he jabbed at the eye of the one clinging to his chest with his thumb. It only gripped tighter, restricting his already short air supply. The blaze of encircling wings faded gray, then black, as the pain in his chest began cutting short his air. He stabbed his dagger fully into the mass of thick muscle between the beast's neck and shoulder. A gurgling shriek assaulted his pointed ears, but the pain in his chest subsided. The burning wings released the fomori, and Arwë saw the bodies catch fire and scatter like ash on the blasting wind. As they fell, the cacophonous rumble below them grew louder. He drew a deep, cold breath, only to have it snatched from his lips when a sudden gust flung him end over end, down into the clamorous abyss.

Just as he righted himself, another jolt sent a wash of pain lancing through Arwë's back. A glottal grunt told him another fomori still clutched at his shoulders. The beast still pounded away at the elf, despite their impending death. Arwë spun the beast and himself so that the fomori now faced the direction they fell. The close air suddenly rushed away, and a blast of frigid wind struck them.

Out of mine and under mountain! Arwë thought. *And from that shimmering I see below, I'd say we're about to hit a river!* Whispering a prayer as he pummeled the thrashing fomori, Arwë closed his eyes once more. The roar of the underground river thundered all around them as it raced up at breakneck speed. The beast in his clutches bellowed one last time. Then, with an icy crash and pain that obliterated thought, Arwë collided with endless dark.

11
FIRE IN THE HIGHEST

"*Awake, awake!*" someone hollered into his icy dreams.

Wildercrown's Messenger opened his eyes, not knowing his name. All was frigid dark, and he could not breathe. *Buried alive*, he thought. *No, drowned! I fell through the dark, then into ... water. I'm underwater!*

The subterranean river flung him down ancient tracks of rock on the back of millions of tons of cascading water. He surfaced from the black chaos for an instant, clawing for breath. He struck his head on a stone, and white sparks exploded behind his eyes. But fear kept him awake, forced him to fill his lungs just before being thrown back under, sucked down by a sluicing vortex whose fury threatened to burst his eardrums. It spat him into a frothing bowl of rock whose edge he rode in spiraling circles as he gathered precious air. He tried and failed to grab hold of any surface that would slow his slide into the maw at its center. Walls encrusted with crystal, lit gently by mushroom or glowing worm, spun by. His throat could not contain the scream he had been holding. He hollered it aloft for none to hear as the bowl emptied him into another seething stream, which drove him for a while on the water's angry surface before casting him over a terrifying drop. The waterfall pitched him into a swirling pool that pulled him under once more. But he surfaced again, this time to the rush of a new river.

As he rode the rapids, the Messenger found through blurry eyes that he could see jagged walls and the stony ceiling under which the river drove him. *Light*, he thought. *Gold, white, and pure. Shining far away. Water's carrying me straight to it.*

The water's course dragged him under a hollow dome of rock then threw him out under a cold, open sky. The rushing river sprayed him with foam and a thousand colors of daylight. The water released him, and he hauled himself up onto dry land, retching brackish water onto the sand, fingers digging into soil. His arms gave way beneath him, and he collapsed. He turned onto his side, unable to roll to his back for the bleeding pain left there by fomori claws.

Sleep, he thought. His chest swelled and contracted with short, shocked breaths, as if at any moment, the fierce water could snatch him away once more and the tiniest intake would be all he would get. Releasing the broken bits of the weapons he still clung to, the Messenger fell near to sleep, smiling his relief under the honey-hued sky.

"Awake, prince!"

His eyes fluttered open, brightness searing his vision. "Arwë," he groaned at the air. "Arwë the *Messenger* is my name. I am no prince." He turned his head, happy his neck had not been broken. He stared up at the clouded glory above, reveling in the golden light of late afternoon.

"Help me then, *Arwë the Messenger*," shouted the same voice that had commanded him awake.

"The sky's brighter, somehow," he whispered. "Unless some trick has been cast over my eyes. The wind here is cool and fresh."

"Arwë! I don't think he's dead, but he will be if we don't pull him up."

"Tyrith!" Arwë hissed, eyes widening. He tried sitting up and cried out as agony lanced through the wrist he had burdened with his weight. "Broken," he grunted. "Though a miracle I didn't lose the hand." He examined his vambrace. It was mangled and torn, having taken the worst of whatever blow either the fall or the river had dealt in the dark. Bracing the wrist with his other hand, he elbowed himself up, looking over his body for other wounds. Blood ran bright red under what scraps of elvish armor still clung to him. What was left of his bow lay beside him in two pieces. "I'll put you to use later," he said, gaining his feet with more than a few grunts.

Warmth ran in sticky tracks down his neck from a pain at the back of his skull. But the Atrellarrathi girl, hooded, cloaked, and struggling, drew his full attention. She bent double, working to haul an unconscious Nephtyr Ithar-fel onto the rocky shore. The angel lay pale and cold, his armor nearly destroyed by the fierceness of his battles, and no doubt their fall from impossible heights under the earth. His iron wings lay exposed, broken, and spread wide across the ground. His lower half lay submerged in the river, which threatened to pull the rest of him away into its cascading rush. Arwë stumbled over. Clutching his broken wrist to his chest, he lay the fingers of his good hand in Tyrith's wild spread of night-black hair. Expelling the last of their strength, elf and maid dragged the huge man almost fully ashore. They rested once his booted feet were all that touched the water's edge.

Arwë ran his good hand over Tyrith's forehead and chanted a few Qwei-Sillari words. He noticed the girl's stare as he checked Tyrith's vitals with practiced fingers. He opened Tyrith's eyelids, seeing no sign of the cobalt fires that burned so doggedly in those ancient eyes. "Well, he'll survive," the elf said. "Though I think he'll be asleep for some time with those injuries. He also seems to have burned himself out. The source of his light was taken from him long before we met, and now it's out completely. Remind me to tell him that his debt is now paid in kind, not that there was ever any debt between us, the oaf."

"You're injured as much as he," the girl said, approaching him. The treacherous river wind shifted the Noklethi hood, revealing a shock of her hair. Arwë saw strands golder than the sky. She guided him to sit on a withered stump. When he sat, she examined the places where blood ran freely out from the gashes in his armor. Her touch was light, her temper calming. She knelt and took his injured wrist in her hand. The motion parted her new cloak. Inside, Arwë spied a tunic, thin and gray, belted around her slim waist with scales of gold. A length of pale, slender leg stuck out from the cloak's cover, her knee bending at the top of a leather boot, which was finely crafted for long travel.

"Are you sure so scant an outfit is cut out for this kind of adventure?" he asked.

She set the bone in his wrist, forcing a gasp from him. "My garb and gear are made for running," she said with a knowing smile. Using the broken halves of his bow to splint his wrist, she continued. "They will endure the journey, and I myself may surprise you. Besides, I have the cloak of the Craftsmen, bestowed by an elvish prince! It will keep me safe from weather and spying eye. I also possess two of the finest warriors Leóhteness-Fal has seen at my beck and call. They survived a fall from the heights of Golden-mount itself after battling a legion of deadly foes!"

"Two warriors who were *defeated* by only a small part of that legion of deadly foes," Arwë corrected. "Before they fell *off* the aforementioned mountain."

She laughed then, and to Arwë, the world seemed to slow, peace reigning for a little. Her high, bright voice promised the new growth of spring too long in coming. With the song of her laughter, he felt the withering pain of bruise and broken bone dissipate. His cuts, many, jagged, and deep, closed at the command of her sweet smile. A light was on her, *in* her. And Arwë saw that it was only by some woven enchantment of the Noklethi cloak ensconcing her that this girl's power was kept from outshining the sky. For without it, she had done just that in the mines of Golden-mount. Arwë found himself staring until she went quiet. The waning of her voice was brightest daylight shrouded by a roil of cloud.

"What is your name?" he whispered.

"Ithyeil Stëorra," she said solemnly, continuing her ministrations.

"Then you are our *Star Under-earth*," Arwë said as she examined the skinned knuckles of his opposite hand. "Though the word holds no picture for me, or any of my kin who now live. We have only heard stories of starlight and the faraway wonder contained within it."

"I've not seen it with my own eyes," Ithyeil Stëorra said, staring skyward with his hand in hers. "But faith has shown that the heart of the Outer-dark so far away is not so dark as we think, Arwë. We've yet to see true light and joy above. But believe me, it descends."

"Joy is seldom found," Arwë said. "Wars and endless toil are the vellum of this world, and our blood the ink. As a crippled lad I spent centuries dreaming of taking part in tales of heroic courage, slaying fell beasts, and rescuing my people as I became lord of the hunt."

"And now?" Ithyeil asked.

"Now I'm a young elf grown old with cynicism," Arwë sighed. "Even after I was given a new chance at life. With new legs to run, instead of seeking glory in the world, I ran into fear, doubt, and the depravity of all peoples, great and small. I've lived a fuller life than I had been promised, and seen many things, good and bad. And that dreaming part of me still wishes I would be the hunter, ever providing.

But I couldn't help but grow more and more frustrated with each passing year as duty and war pulled me away. And with each thankless task came another betrayal of my trust."

"Fear not," said Ithyeil Stëorra, releasing his hand and moving on to touch a cut on his long ear. "So long as you are with me, I will protect you."

Arwë glanced down at the fingers she had held. Instead of the painful abrasions that had laid bare his knuckle bones, a pale, yellow light shined now from them. The flickering faded like candle flame, and its departure left his hand wholly renewed. He flexed the fingers, then brought them up to touch his ear, which was cool and smooth, where a moment before it had burned and stung.

"You *would* protect me," Arwë breathed, hand still pressed to his ear. "Better than armor, wings, or walls. Though I don't deserve such a gift."

"None do." Ithyeil giggled as if trying not to laugh at a joke made at his expense. "The beauty in such grace is simple: It is a gift!"

"To whom?"

"To all those who would receive it," she said, smiling as she examined others of the elf's wounds. "Such was our purpose, even before the forming of the world. And though we failed in the task, to terrible sorrow, hope springs anew."

"And with that hope ignites light-imperishable: The Heir of the Atrellarrath has come forth," Arwë said, calling to mind the omens of elf scholars, Noklethi messengers and a head filled to brimming with the earnest chants of a people eternally imprisoned.

She gave a distracted nod as she sought more of his injuries.

"Well then, being a clever keeper of such messages, and, I hope, a faithful servant for the good of all elfdom, my mission at least has become somewhat clearer. I must escort the Heir to her Garden, whatever, wherever it may be."

"Innoth-Hyeil Darrë," she laughed. To Arwë, all the world seemed suddenly bright and full of promise, the way it had years ago upon the mending of his limbs that changed his life forever. "We will find it. And good things will grow once more in the world. No more for this passing dark, for the light shines in it, small but fierce!"

"You almost make me believe it," Arwë said, unable to keep himself from smiling back.

"All things in time," she said, growing somber. "Now onto business with your winged friend."

"By all means," Arwë said, watching her. He felt a swift, cold change in her, as if night had blanketed all the world, with no evening or twilight to ease the light's passing. "Healing should prove a small task, since your mere touch gave him enough power to light up all the world. Although I suppose that's exactly what got his angelic ilk into so much trouble in the first place. What was all that back there?"

"As one of the Qwei-Sillar," Ithyeil said, standing straight and rigid, "you will have learned that light in this place is different from the place whence you and yours came." She then strode to the fallen Tyrith.

"I know nearly nothing of the World-before," he said to her back. "Only legends concerning Six Fallen Ones and the war against them that brought us here."

"But you do know that light is power on Leóhteness-Fal," she said, reaching Tyrith. "And my people, trusting foolish hope, revealed this to the Nephtyr." She hesitated over the warrior's prostrate form.

"The Kindreds gave much in trusting them," Arwë said quietly. "That trust ended in utter ruin. But some good came too. We cannot forget that."

"His people, the Winged Ones, so full of power and ambition," she said, holding a hand out over Tyrith. "There was an oath they had come to fulfill, some sacrifice they were sworn to make. From what little I know of those times, I'd say your Fallen Six had ought to do with it. But instead of holding to their oath, the Nephtyr saw light overflowing from our mothers and fathers of the Second Generation. The Winged Ones saw quickly the connection between light and power here, and so hatched a new scheme. They demanded our ancestors use their light for greater good. When my ancestors, thinking they were beginning upon the path toward redeeming us all, agreed to help, the Nephtyr enslaved them. They sidestepped their oath and used us, our power, and light to keep locked up some terror they and your ancestors had brought to our shores from across the Dark-sea above. By our power, not that of the Nephtyr, are you kept safe from your nightmare, Arwë."

"Ithyeil," Arwë said, rising slowly. A warning, and the very air surrounding them pulsing with sudden power, made him feel as if he were speaking through a storm. "Better to make the choice Tyrith did: protection over power, healing over harm. Can you do that for him?"

"With light and power, Nephtyr Ithar-fel shall be king of angels, ruler of Leóhteness-Fal," she intoned, a white-gold globe bursting to life in her palm. She stretched her shining hand toward the stricken Nephtyr. "Power, ambition, and betrayal: tools of all Nephtyr."

"He is not them," Arwë said, his own mended hand reaching for her. "He proved it on the bridge."

"He could have taken me, Arwë, drained me of my light and power, made himself king of a new world with it." The sphere in Ithyeil's hand doubled in size and brightness, turning all the rocky shore about them gold, the rocks reflecting her power.

"I felt it," Arwë snapped. "So did you: He *could* have taken your light, though maybe not all of it, for his own. He could have built a new Hegemony with the strength of his arms alone. But with a little reminding from his git of a friend, Tyrith remembered himself. He overcame his own will and saved us all."

"He did," she said, cocking her head as she stared at Tyrith. "I just hope he continues rising above his nature. And in that rise, I hope not to see his wings broken in black chasms again, no matter his act of selflessness."

"If we're to fight our natures," Arwë said, "then grim battles await us indeed."

"We have sinned greatly," she whispered. For the first time, Ithyeil bowed her head in sorrow, and the fire in her hand disappeared as if doused.

"We all have," Arwë said. "But grace and redemption both are freely offered, as you said. We need only accept it, turn from our evils, old and recent, and make the world just that much better for those who come after."

Lips pursed, Ithyeil looked back at Arwë, her eyes aglow with sorrow and the color of smoldering coals. She looked away, taking a breath. Then she thrust her arm at the angel, the light in her hand blazing up as bright and fierce as before. Her orb struck Tyrith.

Arwë cried out, charging the girl with his splinted wrist. But an indomitable will forced him to stop, then to kneel. He dropped to his knees, wide-eyed, his mind screaming at his limbs to lift. They did not listen. He could only watch in horror as Ithyeil herself knelt down over Tyrith's burning body. She lay both hands on his chest. Then, to Arwë's shock, she began to sing.

To Arwë's ears, the melody sounded sad and longing. But in Ithyeil's song, he heard power enough to call summer back in the dead of winter night. The chorus made ancient memory as new and clear as the day it had been seen. The song spoke of an eternal place far greater than the painful world in which they found themselves. Arwë trembled at the images of such things, then saw what he had mistaken for ruining fire all over Tyrith's body instead turn to gentle, healing light. He saw his battered companion renewed.

"Almost young again," Arwë choked, looking at Tyrith's sleeping face. "Would that an angel could ever be young, or be born at all, for that matter." He watched until Tyrith sighed with relief. Arwë turned away. Wiping at irksome tears drawn by the girl's song and his friend set aright, Arwë found himself able to move with no restraint. He watched in awe and fear of Ithyeil's work a moment longer, then stood. Busying his mind with plans for their trio's survival, Arwë began rummaging through what provisions were left to them.

After Arwë's careful examination of their supplies, Ithyeil Stëorra's tired voice whispered to keen ears. "What food have we?" she said.

"No game in this country," Arwë said, having emptied and spread the contents of their packs. "Although a travel pack seems to have weathered both our fall and watery journey. Most pouches and pockets are torn, cut, or empty. But a little food is still stored and dry at the center of it: nuts, berries, and venison sausage. Have it all for now."

She nodded her thanks as he handed three packages to her. The leather of the bundles was scratched but well-wrapped, and each still lay bound with strong cording. Before she had fully untied them, Ithyeil stopped, asking, "What of you and Tyrith?"

"I'll catch us some fish with traps, seeing as how my bow arm is no good to us now," he replied, shuffling out of her reach. "A shame. Would that I could find and hunt another doe. The meat would serve our mending far better than dry rations, alas! I'll make the traps, catch our fish that way, then cook us a meal."

He glanced over, surprised to see astonishment in her face. "What is it?" he asked, frowning.

"You seem so sure," she replied, chewing a handful of dried berries. "I was taught how to sing flowers into blooming, then eat the petals, surviving that way. I know nothing of hunting. Taking care of yourself seems a daunting task."

"A woman who binds wounds with song and light sits in awe of a *hunter*?" he asked, incredulous. At another nod from her, he continued, "Ithyeil Stëorra, when I saw what I thought you were doing to Tyrith, when you bound me, I feared you."

"I'm sorry," she whispered. "I didn't want you to hurt him or yourself in your misunderstanding."

"When I saw you healing him instead of hurting him," he continued, "I feared you all the more."

She stayed silent at that.

"I have seen the power you bear, its benevolence, as well as the terror it would bring should the wrong hands take it from you."

Her back went stiff. "Only benevolence while it remains in my keeping," she said.

"It *was* wrested for your keeping," Arwë said. "On the bridge. Or at least it could have been, had a lesser man been shown the depth of it."

"It will not happen again," Ithyeil replied. "Now that I've had more than a few simple minutes in the world."

"It must not happen again," Arwë snapped. "And you must hide your light, for now, under the Noklethi cloak, until we find a better way to deliver you."

Ithyeil, with a small voice, asked him, "What must I do?"

"Keep your promise to protect Tyrith and me," Arwë said. "Without use of powers handed down by the Atrellarrath. I shall, in return, teach you things of the hunt and of mending without light or magic on this journey we've found ourselves on."

"Companions," she said, smile returning like the dawn reaching over the dark earth.

"The three Messengers." Arwë chuckled, kneeling to retrieve some soaked linen gauze from the pack. He unraveled it and used it to form a makeshift sling for his arm. He then offered the lion's share of wrappings to Ithyeil, showing her how to dress what of Tyrith's wounds her power had not fully closed. The angel's face no longer shone with deathly paleness, but he slept deeply and did not stir.

"I wonder," Ithyeil said after forming a cushion for Tyrith's head out of a spare cloak from the pack and laying it under him. "If your shouts of honor and courage while the Nephtyr threatened to seize my power, were what you called *gentle*, then what would have been your more contentious method for catching the Nephtyr's attention had he decided to take the power of my light for himself?"

"Two or three elf-steel arrowheads to his heart would

have proved convincing," Arwë replied, mouth curling upward at one side.

"You would slay a friend?" she whispered, the gaze of her opal eyes piercing his levity.

"To *save* a friend, and the world from a new tyrant, yes," he said, all humor gone out of him. "This world can ill afford more bloodshed, even if the one ready to meet it out upon those who are truly evil, as the fomori are, professes goodness. For none are truly good, no matter the count of their deeds."

"How would he feel were he to hear you speak of him in such ways?" she asked.

"Oh, after falling under the healing skill of Light's Heir herself, I think Tyrith can hear me just fine, though his eyes be closed." Arwë chuckled. But the smile suddenly dropped once more. "He knows where he's to stand, and that's right in the gap between tyrants and the weak. Though subtle reminders are nice now and then."

"*For none are truly good*," she repeated.

Arwë nodded. "All power turns to darkness, no matter how bright it first may be."

"And that," Ithyeil Stëorra said, smile shining once more, "is why we must give it away!"

"Quite so," Arwë mused. "Though how we go about that task I fear will have to be revealed by time, travel, and our dear knight's musings." He revealed the small, leather pouch he had used to carry the Noklethi cloak before giving it to Ithyeil. "He gave me this before he left, saying it would help some."

"That is good," she said. "My family revealed much to him during his time with us. We feared his mind would bend, or even break, if shown too much. It may be a record of our stories, written to help him sort it all out."

"Wise of your folk," Arwë said. "And of him. For now, we care for ourselves. Along our way, we may gain some answers from Knight Treiarn." He stowed the pouch with his collection of documents, then set to removing bits of armor. He did his best not to rub freshly healed wounds with wet cloth, steel, or leather. Sitting shirtless, Arwë wrapped and salved all manner of cut, bruise, and abrasion, anything the Heir's healing light had missed. He whispered his thanks to Eternity, having broken only his wrist, given their fall from the near-impossible height of the bridge under the aqueduct way. Their trip into that raging, watery hell under the mountain had done no good for his bones, either. It was a wonder they had not all been brained a dozen times over on the scores of jagged rocks that had lashed out at them from within the water and without.

"Suppose we have Tyrith to thank for all that," he mused.

"For what?" asked Ithyeil, who had already gathered what scarce wood could be found from their rocky surroundings. As she asked the question, she waved a hand at the kindling, and a merry blaze sprang forth from it.

Arwë considered her a moment, again not with a little fear. "His wings shielded us all. Through the fall, the river, all of it. Until I fell out of their protection and went on my own, awful ride toward the end of it!"

"Yes," she said, giggling at the fire she'd made as if its warmth were a delightful thing she'd only just then felt for the first time. "He was brave and strong under the mountain. We were there, you know."

"Where, pray tell?"

"Galataeum," she said lowly. "Under it."

"Yes, the Nephtyri Hegemony once began at the western edge of the Qweth-Wëalda," Arwë said. "I had some vague idea where we were in relation to the High-city, from what Tyrith had told me. But I'd never seen it from the forest side and would have been lost without him. Golden-mount's brothers must have obscured the city from our view. If not, still I don't think we would have seen it had the mountain had no siblings at all, given our flight from the fomori and goblins. And never have I sensed the foreboding I felt as we descended into that black valley. I had only heard tales of Galataeum in my youth, centuries ago. The world is much changed since then."

"I have never escaped it," she said, her long, pale fingers stretching out to the fire. "Until now. This country is as barren and dull as my parents told me it would be. And still its shadow presses on my heart, though I am better now than when my parents sent me out with the knight."

"Bleak indeed," Arwë said, gazing at the river, islets, and barren crags surrounding them. "But some good remains."

"You and your friends make that much clear," Ithyeil said, smiling.

"We try!" Arwë laughed, drinking from his scuffed

water bottle. The last of his water was a blessing to his parched throat. And the berries and strip of meat Ithyeil had offered him brought some feeling back into his gut and limbs. Then, looking about once more, Arwë saw they had ridden the hidden rivers out into a somber, stony country. The surrounding faces of cliffs stared down stoically at them, and near-barren islands formed a chain of sorts in the racing river. One such island lay beneath their aching feet. He watched glacial rivers thunder down from mountains northward whose peaks disappeared into the clouds above. And for all the grayness that surrounded them, Arwë smiled as the foaming spray shone in the daylight—a burst of silver shards turning the gray heights into a shimmering glory.

"What is the cause of this light?" he suddenly asked of their surroundings. "Light should have gone down for the evening by now. Is it always so bright in these lands? Ever the forest of the elves lies in utter darkness, and even beyond the reach of its eaves, the light of day has never shone so piercing bright."

The motion of the girl's arm drew his attention. Her smile had fled, wide-eyed fear replacing joy. She pointed a trembling finger north to a distant horizon.

Following her gesture, Arwë's eyes were drawn up into the mountains. The summits piled onto one another as they marched northward until he spotted one unlike the others. Behind and above them rose a titan of ash and glass. It was mountain and menace both, black as jet, and older than dark. It rose out of some great depression, its gray brothers seeming to bend away from its tyrannical presence. From down and out of some forgotten, calamitous age, the mountain looked to have dropped from clear out of the sky and landed square in their midst, followed by the explosion and hail of violence that would have made this land so desolate long ago.

Arwë could not be sure why, but something about the monstrous mountain compelled him to stand. The brightest daylight he had ever seen glared above it. Filling the sky, the mountain seemed somehow to be the light's source. Then, for the space of a deeply drawn breath, all light died in the surrounding world, all things turning to sudden twilight. Arwë then saw in the dark, a pinpoint of light that ignited in the blackness above the mountain. Up from the small point sprung other points of bright light. They grew and gathered until their shapes changed and each light reached skyward. A dozen squirming tendrils of gold-white brilliance set the broken summit ablaze once more. The pillars of light struck skyward then swayed like saplings in the wind.

Then, as fast as he had seen them, the white-hot threads broke, and light raced across the sky from the north away south. And with the tendrils' tearing and the light's departure, the world was suddenly plunged into evening dark. Arwë rubbed at his eyes, blinking incessantly in the gloom. He gazed back to the heights, now pitch dark, but outlined by a decaying radiance. A shiver ran through him as he spied the hint of turrets and battlements silhouetted against the darkling sky.

He turned to Ithyeil. "Night had nothing to do with

the darkness Tyrith and I walked through in that valley," he breathed. "We traveled by day and night. But the dark we descended into was the absence of power. Because it is running out. There was dread in that darkness."

She nodded, meeting his gaze. Her crystal eyes brimmed with tears.

"And that which shines above the mountain's crest bathes the world in warmth and light," Arwë continued. "It is uprooted from the Sable Gorge, torn away from *your* people ... who draw it from a deep well, only to expend it, then die."

"The same," she whispered, the hand that had pointed now covering her mouth. "One of our many punishments, achieving dual purpose: to keep shut the Coffin with steadfast light, but also to hold light aloft in cycles, as the Creator taught us. We cast what little is left of our power as high in the sky as we can manage, forming the daylight. Then, when the day is done, last-light falls, then the dark buries all."

"And nights are all the blacker of late because of the waning strength of your Second Generation?" he asked.

She gave a solemn nod. "The Second wane and die. But their power is born again in the Third, growing with each of them that passes away."

"And you grow stronger, brighter every day. That is why your parents entrusted you to the knight. Your light and power have waxed so much so that the time is right to set you on your path to this Garden. But you're short on time, for the moment the Second pass fully away, and your power reaches its zenith—"

"No living power in Galataeum will be present in that moment to keep the Terror in check," she said, as if reciting something impressed upon her since youth.

"Terror?" Arwë asked. "Is it some devilry out of ancient days? Is it locked up in Galataeum? Is that why the Nephtyr, with the last of their strength, shut themselves behind their towering gates?"

"I do not think the mountain-city contains it," Ithyeil said. "Whatever the Winged Ones concoct behind their gates is of their own making. And I know very little of the Terror; only that we keep it in check with our waning strength. And since the Winged Ones only told our ancestors of its nature when they came here, before you and your Kindreds, much that was known has passed on. All we have now is a name."

"Eshra," Arwë whispered.

Ithyeil nodded, darkness somehow passing over her softly glowing face. She fell silent in sudden sadness, and Arwë did not press her any further.

A short time later, Arwë came to Tyrith in the firelight. He checked every vital as could be possessed by angels. And seeing his companion was still far from waking, he thought to busy Ithyeil, hoping to bring the girl out of her melancholy. "Ithyeil," he said in a gentle voice. "I think a few hours' rest will be best for us all. See if you can make Tyrith comfortable. I'll catch those fish and make us some supper. After that, you should sleep."

"What of you?" she asked.

FIRE IN THE HIGHEST

He pointed down at the mess of his wrecked mail and livery. "After we're all fed, I'll mend my gear on first watch. Let's be about it."

Ithyeil pulled Tyrith close to their cooking fire. She did what she could to ease his pains, erasing little wounds here and there with a touch. She covered him with spare cloaks dried by their fire and the wind, which had kicked up out of the west with the coming of night.

Arwë snared a few small, silvery fish as they leaped up the rushing river and cooked a fragrant meal for the three of them, taking care not to jar his wrist in his efforts. After they had supped, Ithyeil went down for rest, laying her head on Arwë's pack. After she had turned her back in sleep, Arwë gathered up his mail, shirts, and belts. Setting his scarred back to the wind, he set about mending his gear by the fire. He sewed back the cloth and leather pieces with thread and gut. His work was slow going with his wrist throbbing and immobile. Eventually he gave up on his armor with a snarl, jamming his head back through his mangled shirt of elf-steel rings. He slapped into place what bits of plate and leather as would stay. An elated sigh escaped his lips when he donned his boots, finding them fully intact and somewhat dry with their exposure to wind and warmth after his swim under mountain rivers. Lastly, he mended the few holes in his heavy cloak, then wrapped himself in it, drawing its hood over his head.

Dressed fully once more, Arwë jumped up on the islet's only boulder, and sat to keep watch over his companions. He looked this way and that, trying to see if anyone, be they fomori, goblin, or masked menace, would come screaming down on them from the cliffs above.

No sooner had the burden of his eyelids grown unbearably heavy after a minute or two than from faraway upon dream-like heights, he saw a seething tide of blackness. Thousands upon thousands of chanting creatures and Men burned all the earth as they surged toward a beleaguered wall. Men screamed and died, and the ravaging hosts gained the wall, turning yellow eyes to the city below. They grinned, licking lips as they made to ravish all they saw. Then, from on the wall, and in their midst, rose a great shadow, black as ink and voracious. The frenzied creatures shouted their victory, thinking they had been further reinforced by some power of their dark master. But their cries rang hollow, blunted by the dark that gathered about them. The hungry shadow reared up before them and ate them, crunching down on a hundred fomori necks. Victory turned to a screaming route, and the shadow whipped itself into a rage. A dark blast carved a wide gulf in the earth, out from the wall, killing thousands in its savage wake. But just as the shadow faded, giving way to a small fire-eyed figure at its center, a deep, powerful voice cut through the dream.

"Arwë." He startled awake, grasping at his sword and wrenching his wrist as he did so.

"Tyrith?" Arwë gasped. "Alright?"

"Alright," Tyrith rumbled. The Nephtyr stood upright, clothed in spare garb but without his plate. He stood straight, just taller than the boulder on which Arwë sat.

FIRE IN THE HIGHEST

Tyrith's eyes were nearly level with Arwë's as the elf sat on the rock, nearly ten feet above their fire. Arwë saw no brightness in his friend's eyes, only sea-gray irises betraying concern. "You were restless, nearly cried out. I awoke you before you could."

"I'm fine," Arwë said. "What of you? Any new desires to conquer all the world?"

"I refused the power," Tyrith growled. "Chose to save your hide instead."

"That you did," Arwë said. "And I've never been prouder in all my days."

"We should leave," Tyrith said, grabbing up a few pieces of stowed fish and gathering his armor and weapons.

"What of the girl?" Arwë asked, gaining his feet.

Tyrith motioned to a figure standing by the cascading water, nearly matching the sky for darkness.

Arwë jumped down and came to Ithyeil's side as she stared out over river and cliff. "Seems I'm the only one to have gotten any sleep," he mused. "Shame on me."

"You were hurt," Ithyeil said.

"Mine was the watch."

"Bigger things to worry over," she said, glowering at the horizon. "Seems Galataeum's was not the only light to fill the broken sky tonight. See yonder!" She threw her hand southwestward, pointing to a red light rising high in the gloaming.

Arwë followed her gesture and gazed away to a ghoulish sky over the mists of Anglorost. He had not seen it in daylight's brilliance. "Fire and smoke," he whispered.

"Eth Gathilin burns, the same as Wildercrown. The hammer falls. And Qwei-Sillar, and now Angloreans, are the anvil. If it has so ravaged all the North and Westlands, then war marches toward Ephtar-Malas. It is all that is left. There will be no help from the West, nor from ruined Belrath'ir away southward. If Malas truly is *Last-Hope*, from where shall it come afterward?"

"Innoth-Hyeil Darrë," whispered Ithyeil Stëorra, taking his hand. "If you would listen to the knight's story and you believe my people, Arwë of Wildercrown, then come away with me to find a city and a Key, both hidden."

"*Answers* may be hidden there too," Arwë said, gazing at the gentle glow of her hand. "We seek Ephtar-Malas, the Hidden City, to protect its people and ourselves from this dark torrent. If we cannot protect it, then we will fight for it all the same, and die trying. If we are to avoid the latter, we must hurry. Tyrith?"

"Aye," Tyrith said, standing rearmed and armored before his companions.

"We go south."

12

SORROW
AND SALVATION

"Explain yourself," Dusk snapped at the tall, cloaked man. Though ragged and tired, he readied a command to his newly won power. It would strike down the visitor should he be a bandit or one of the elf-slayers Keiphral Morne had warned of.

"There is little time," the man said, pulling back the cowl of his hood to reveal olive skin and a head of neat black hair flecked with gray at the temples and in his beard. A pair of icy eyes sat atop sharp cheek bones and a large nose. "But I am the surgeon, charged by the prince of my city to fight the Wasting Sickness."

"Surgeon?" Keiphral said.

"You know h-h-him?" Dusk hissed, snapping his head to look at the bigger boy.

Keiphral hesitated, his expression vaguely haunted and a little fearful. "No," he whispered finally. "No, I don't."

The man nodded as if he had heard Keiphral's whisper. He then turned to Dusk. "Elijah is my name, and I've heard of you both. News of a lad with power and knowledge beyond any doctor traveled down from high places to my city, Last-Hope. And, seeking a surgeon of equal skill to bring minds together for curing, I traveled to your mountain. I arrived too late to find the healer named Dusk. So I chased rumor of him back down the mountain and across the Ephtari Downs. The tracking was not difficult, as men and women of the country below the Hidden City couldn't help but sing your praises on the road, having been healed by one whom they said was, 'possessed of molten eyes and miraculous hands.' With stories of the Sunreach Healer very nearly shouted from every hilltop, your reputation made for easy tracking."

"And what does your tracking of a healer have to do with us, sir?" Keiphral asked.

"I was getting there," the man said. "After I had crossed the Downs, forded the rivers Aleph'ar and Dethrai'ar and gone into the hills of T'Rhonossarc above the Hidden City, a messenger came to me. You may recognize his name, Keiphral Morne. He was Cailus Tombguard, Keen-Eyed of Argentleaf."

"Cailus is alive?" Keiphral blurted, practically dancing with delight.

"Ah, so a friend's name is all it takes to break the lock on your secrets." The man chuckled.

Dusk gave Keiphral a withering glare, and the taller boy blushed.

"Caution is best these days, and in such strange parts," Elijah said. "But I am only here to help, not to rob or hurt you. When last we parted, yes, Cailus told me to look for the arrival of one whom the elves had named Sojourner. He was to be a dark-haired lad dressed in elvish garb. Cailus then helped me spot a change in the ever-raging Storm over the Dread Coast. I couldn't see why he was so concerned with clouds and told him I had no time to study the weather. But when the tempest blasted itself to a standstill before our very eyes, I knew then that my path had set me to tracking more than a mere healer."

"Where is Cailus now?" Keiphral asked, looking beyond the old man as if to see his friend standing somewhere behind.

Elijah turned back to Keiphral. "He departed northward, seeking a secret place known only to the Qwei-Sillar. His path, and the paths of many, are hidden."

"No more than that?" Keiphral asked.

"He was out of time," Elijah said. "But his message for you was to continue on to the Hidden-City."

Dusk felt a line of tension drawn suddenly between Keiphral and the tall man. "And among his messages," Keiphral began. "What other name did Cailus give the Sojourner?"

"If you're trying to test me, Keiphral Morne, Sojourner from the Outer-dark," Elijah snapped, "know that I am who I say I am, I am not lying to you, and that Cailus also named you Sailor. And if you both wish to get to the Hidden City unharmed, we should start by curing you of your recklessness."

Dusk looked over as Keiphral turned to him. The bigger boy gave him a sheepish shrug.

Elijah rolled his gray eyes. "You silenced a hurricane that had been blowing for two hundred years. Then you celebrated by building a bonfire in the dead of night, *and* in the open. This makes evident the fact that you both need concealing and protecting. And my city's walls are best for that."

"We've both made it this far without protection," Keiphral said flimsily.

Elijah snorted. "You were lucky that I arrived here first, ahead of those who would do you harm."

"Who?" Dusk asked. "I have s-s-seen no bandits on my way here. And the s-s-soldiers of Last-Hope are well armed and armored, p-p-protecting the road."

"You came down, out of your mountains, whose heights and nigh unreachable places of refuge have so far seen little need for guarding, Dusk of Sunreach," Elijah said, eyes flashing. "But war will come to the foot of your mountains ere your people are prepared. And what soldiers you would have seen are already called away to defend T'Rhonossarc from the same fomori that march down out of the North. If you do not know of whom I speak, Healer, the Sojourner does. He escaped the burning wrath of our Enemy's hosts."

"Fomori with horns and yellow eyes," Keiphral said. "Goblins with skin all the colors of earth, pointed teeth, and poisoned arrows. There were the evil men too, armored like knights but cruel and fierce. Then there was one man who was worse than all the others."

Dusk looked to Keiphral, thinking the older boy would say more, but he said nothing.

"One of the Veilglorrath," Elijah said, breaking the silence. The strange name sent a chill down Dusk's back. "That will be the only time I mention the name, even under daylight. Cailus told me of the one he had seen on the walls of Wildercrown."

"It came after me," Keiphral whispered. Dusk cocked his head to see his companion staring with wide eyes into Elijah's.

"If you have seen one," Elijah said quietly, "then more will come. Already I fear they have taken interest in Healer Dusk, here. That they should know already of your awakening, Keiphral Morne, and pursue you when there are more important battles that require their tending, is troubling news indeed."

"Why?" Dusk asked. "I h-h-have no enemies. I only s-s-sought knowledge and p-p-power enough to heal m-m-my mother."

"And that's just it," the man said, taking a step toward them. "You've just pulled a great and terrible power out of the world, Healer. Many watchers, both honest and unsavory, have considered the Storm over the Dread Coast for ages. Now that it is snuffed out, and its power taken, those watchers will be looking for the one who took it. My city calls all strength behind its walls, and I fear the hammer blow is soon coming. But already it is beleaguered in other ways and could use your help while it yet stands. There will be ample time to hone your skill at healing before putting your new powers to their ultimate test on Eissyr."

"You know m-m-my mother?" Dusk said, frowning.

Elijah reached inside his cloak. Keiphral drew out one of his dueling swords. "Stay your blade just a moment," Elijah snapped. "I bear a letter, not a knife. Here." He proffered a folded sheet of sheep skin wrapped with leather cording. "It is cut from Sunreach sheep and addressed to one Dusk of Sunreach, from a young woman named Aryka. Does that interest you?"

Dusk's blood froze. Each word came sharp and clear, like chips of ice from his throat. "What had you to do with Aryka?"

"For Eternity's sake, there is no time to explain it to you on a beach in the wide-open air!" Elijah said.

"Aryka," Dusk growled. "Tell me."

Elijah sighed. "Despite what you said, you *do* have enemies, Dusk. A guard has been set upon your mountain, though no real danger assails it yet. Your reputation for calling forth power to heal people, plants, and animals attracted guests, both welcome and less so. Your friends and family are safe for now, but to return to them with Eshra's servants sniffing about for you would be most unwise."

"Eshra?" Keiphral asked, wide-eyed.

"You've heard the name?" Elijah asked, turning to the boy dressed as a warrior of the elves.

"Underground, and in battle," Keiphral whispered. He then pointed to Dusk. "From his mouth in the center of the Storm."

"Then things are farther along and perhaps worse than I had thought," Elijah muttered to himself.

"I m-m-must help m-m-my mother," Dusk said, his agitation returning. "The curative I g-g-gave her will r-r-run out if I am g-g-gone too long, and she will d-d-d—"

"Your friend's letter may mention some happy news regarding your mother's ailment," Elijah said. "As I told you before, I am charged by the Lord of Last-Hope to treat the Wasting Sickness and have had some success in my journeys, as *you* clearly have. I applied my craft to your mother's sickness when I found your house, with permission from your neighbors, whom I spoke with openly. I told them I was a healer in similar fashion to you and that I was there pursuing my task as I told it to you just a moment ago. I spent two days treating the sick and wounded before asking to be shown any others who needed tending to. So, it was your neighbors who brought me to your house, and under Aryka's watchful eye, I treated your mother with medicine similar to the stuff you gave her, only of a more concentrated dosage.

"I mean to say that I left your mother in better health than you had left her weeks ago, and you left her in a better state than even my finest apprentice surgeon would have. Read the letter as we walk to prove my story. But know that your mother is safe and that I gave many doses of my cure to Aryka for administration to your mother. If your friend applies my medicine as I instructed, your mother will remain stable for a year or more."

"I will n-n-not be away from my m-m-mother for a year," Dusk said, resolute.

"Certainly not," Elijah said with a placating hand. "I'm

simply saying that she will be well tended in her condition while you are gone away with me to my city. Cailus also said the Sojourner will want to come there, given tasks laid upon him by the lord, Lohrë. So please, Dusk: Come with me. If not for defending the last great city of the world, and healing its good people, then at least to help me escort the Sojourner there! Thence you can strike off home again, once you are resupplied and advanced in your arts, should you choose to turn your back to us."

Dusk looked to Keiphral, who shrugged. "If what this Elijah says is true," Keiphral said, "then he's left your mother and friends in good care. And since he claims to know all about Last-Hope, I'd say he's my best chance to get to the city in one piece with time to spare for puzzling out just where I fit in. We go with him, you learn new skills, I figure out just what it is I'm supposed to be doing here, then we leave. And if he's lying or tries to lead us into a trap, we kill him. Me with my weapons, you with your powers. Deal?"

Dusk turned back to Elijah, who stared at them flatly. "I will r-r-read Aryka's letter," he said. "Then d-d-decide whether the t-t-trip to the Hidden City will be w-w-worth it for me. I've b-b-been near there before, with my da, and there is n-n-nothing there now that sh-sh-should interest me m-m-more than getting back to my h-h-home to help my m-m-mother."

Elijah nodded, handed over the sheepskin scroll. "As good an answer as I could hope for," he said. "Don your packs. We walk until noon."

The long walk began. Elijah, who had been so irritated at the boys' testing of his motives a moment before, made a point of questioning Keiphral immediately while Dusk, tripping over rock and root, studied the old man's letter as they went.

"You attended a council of lords of the Qwei-Sillar?" Elijah asked Keiphral as they walked side-by-side in front of a quiet Dusk.

"I did," Keiphral hedged.

"How many great lords of the elves attended the meeting?" Elijah said, eyes narrowing.

"There were twelve lords, including the Elf-lord himself. General Lohrë and the lady Cyrwedh attended as well, with me. Cailus was there too, as listener, runner, and my balancer."

"Good," Elijah barked. "And is the Elf-lord of Wildercrown a man my size, with golden hair and eyes?"

Keiphral stopped to look at the robed man, who stopped in return. Dusk ran headlong into the older boy's back, releasing an annoyed grunt.

"Tall, yes," Keiphral said. "But not as tall as you. And with gold eyes, yes. But you're wrong about his hair. It was white and gray, like falling snow."

The man gave a satisfied nod then continued walking at the same brisk pace he had set before.

"Why?" Keiphral asked, running a few steps to keep up.

"You speak the truth of your having been to the Council," Elijah said.

"What do you mean?"

"I spent much time among the Qwei-Sillar," Elijah said. "Being court surgeon of Last-Hope and its mostly Midlothean folk makes me an ambassador of sorts. The Council of Twelve is called only at needs most dire, due to their, shall we say, reclusive nature. The lords of elves only convene such a council if all are present, and you recounted their correct number. Cailus gave me your description, but I needed to make sure you were whom you said you were."

"So, we *were* in the right to question you," Keiphral said triumphantly.

"You were," Elijah grunted.

"Then permit us one more," Keiphral said. "How do we know you are the surgeon you say you are?"

Elijah stopped abruptly and took Keiphral's right hand before the boy could react. Dusk stopped short, ready to attack the tall man if he gave any sign of hurting his new friend. Elijah removed Keiphral's elvish gauntlet and rolled up his mail sleeve with gruff efficiency, saying, "The yellowed contusions on your knuckles suggest you struck something hard several days ago that nearly broke your wrist. These cuts," he said, turning Keiphral's arm to reveal the cross pattern of cuts delivered by the masked man's sword, "were poorly tended to, as though you were forced to wrap them in the field while on the run."

Keiphral had barely formed his answer by the time Elijah had threaded a needle with gut string. Then, before either boy could protest, the tall man stuck the needle into Keiphral's flesh and sowed up the worst of the cuts. He then studied Keiphral's eyes, ears, and throat, saying,

"Healer Dusk. The subject has suffered multiple contusions to the neck, cheek bones, right eye socket, and left ear. He has just now been sewn up, with several deep lacerations delivered by a blade not made for cutting. My prescription is ice or a cold compress to reduce swelling, rinsing the cuts with ash soap, then re-dressing with a paste of turmeric, honey, and olive oil. Are we agreed?"

Dusk nodded, and Elijah went immediately to work, doing exactly as he had said. After Elijah nodded and rolled down the sleeve over Keiphral's freshly salved and bandaged arm, their conversation, and their walk, continued.

"How long were you with them?" Elijah asked.

"The elves?"

"Only two days," Keiphral mumbled. "I slept through one of them completely."

"And what did the Qwei-Sillar tell you of the fomori?"

The word hung in the windy air between the three companions. "That there was a war," Keiphral said darkly. "Fought two hundred years ago. The Qwei-Sillar told me it began soon after I arrived here."

"Two hundred years?" Dusk blurted. "This is n-n-news to me. You're sure you're n-n-no elf, Keiphral?"

"No, I fell," Keiphral said, trailing off. "I crashed to this world. Then the Qwei-Sillar found me in the wreckage. They took me to the Tomb and hid me there while I slept. All I remember from before my awakening is fear and fire."

Elijah nodded. "Your arrival stirred the fomori into a frenzy."

"Who are they, Elijah?" Keiphral asked suddenly. "Why my arrival, of all things?"

"Men, once," the old man grunted.

"Men?" Keiphral asked, incredulous. "They couldn't possibly ... their horns. Their fangs—"

"When they came to this world with our ancestors, they renounced faith in Eternity and all kinship with the Kindreds, falling into hopelessness, and eventually atrocity. Fear drove them to murder, and worse. Although they fought amongst each other as often as against the Kindreds, never forming bonds or fellowships, only loose tribes that warred with one another. But something changed.

"Centuries ago, many fomori, twisted beyond any semblance of what would once have made them recognizable as human, banded together under a single, growing power. They struck villages, towns, then whole cities. As their strength and audacity swelled over generations, Men and elves soon saw armies of fomori marching under one hateful banner, hearing fomori screams to tear down the kingdoms of Men, so as to rule over rubble. And when their numbers, their depravity, and the people they stole and killed grew to overflowing, the fomori claimed, too, the fire that fell from the sky. It was *their* sign to begin a war against all the world. In that sign, they marched upon Eth Gathilin of the Angloreans, Wildercrown of the elves, and even the Nephtyri capital of Galataeum."

"The elves said the battles of that war were fierce and bloody," Keiphral said. "And it took more than half the world to fight the fomori to a stalemate."

Elijah nodded. "The Qwei-Sillar have ever deserved better than what they were given. But they stood strong then, just as they do now. For when all their strength lay spent against the hosts of the fomori, and the king with his baleful eye lay dead, Lohrë gathered the last of the fighting Qwei-Sillar. He struck a blow that should have forever scattered the fomori, but they are as numerous now as they were two centuries past. Some new power, an Enemy, drives them."

"Eshra?" Keiphral asked.

Elijah nodded.

"What—or rather, who—is it?" Keiphral asked. "The name has hounded me since I awoke in the elf-lands."

"It is old," Elijah said. "A name from across the Outerdark. All I know is contained within a title and a place. She is known in the most ancient lore as the Witch-Scribe of Elderlight." The tall man seemed to shiver at his utterance of the words as he walked, then turned to Keiphral. "Ask me not for any further meaning, for I know not! And speak not the name again while we march. We do not know who may be listening."

Keiphral nodded, then asked Elijah a series of questions regarding the lands south of the Qweth-Wëalda, and how they would find their way to Last-Hope, the Hidden City.

As the tall man described their course to Keiphral, Dusk dug in his pack to find a small scrap of parchment. When he found the piece he sought, he studied it thoroughly. It was a list Aryka had made for him months back when he had gone down to the knees of the mountains during market season. It was during this time that Dusk would buy provisions for both their households while Aryka looked after his mother. Her catalog of provisions had proven a useful reminder whenever Dusk ventured out for food or other necessities, but now it helped him doubly so. He held Aryka's list beside the letter Elijah had handed him, comparing the iron-scratch writing.

"It's hers," he whispered. "G-g-good to know this f-f-fellow isn't a liar ... yet." He stowed Aryka's list in his pack, then examined the letter given by Elijah. The skin and cording was skin and leather from Sunreach. Of that, Dusk had no doubt. And the leather strings had been tied in a fashion taught by folk of their village. The reader would be forced to cut or tear them to open the letter. Aryka's cleverness made him smile as he drew out his ram's horn knife and sliced through the leather pieces. He began reading, tripping only a few times as the trio walked.

Dusk,
The runes your da taught me prove useful again! I'm glad this letter will come to you, or so has been promised to me. Anyway, I don't have much space to write, so I'll just say this: The tall man is named Elijah of Last-Hope. He's alright, and he knows a prince! Although his face goes sad all over whenever he speaks about the lord of Last-Hope. Anyway, Elijah arrived in Sunreach a month after you left—I counted the days! He scared away the bad men who came sneaking around asking questions about you. He helped people. He set Èorthel's broken leg and

cleaned Bella's cut so that her arm wouldn't go sour. He helped others too, but your mum most of all! He gave her something similar to what you gave her. I made sure to stick to his side and watch what he did. Know that she's even better than before.

I miss you, and I hope you'll be back soon. Your da too. I'm sure the two of you would scare off any other bad men who come about. So hurry home, but don't worry about your mum or me!

Your friend,
Ary

Dusk folded the letter and set it in the inner pocket of his cloak, close to his chest. He caught up to the two taller men, listening to Elijah's talk of wilderness ways and the walls of his city. While they talked, Dusk made a point to check over his shirt and trousers for damage during his travels and fights. His trousers were only a little more ragged since before his challenging of the power that knit the Storm over the sea. And he whispered his thanks to Eternity for his having thought to remove his shirt, as well as his cloak, boots, and heavy gloves, and stow them in a hole he had dug in the sand before his battle with thunder and lightning. The tight warmth of his people's gifts, all back in their proper places now, brought on another smile.

A miracle you all lasted me so well for so long, Dusk thought of his garments. *Now, just keep me covered until we reach this city, and I'll be sure to buy new clothing, and provisions for the village too, on the return journey.* He sorted herb from leaf, root from stem, and seed from stone, having had his neatly arranged healing wares jumbled up by his struggle on the coast.

Thinking then of Eissyr and how she must even now be lying in her sickbed inside their little cottage, he looked away southward. There, like a spike of shadow risen to split the weakened light of morning, he spotted Sunreach, tall and ominous. Looking as far as the heights that daylight was not strong enough to touch, Dusk made up his mind. "I will return," he whispered. "I h-h-have my own b-b-battles to f-f-fight. Elves and princes will have s-s-strength of arms enough to make w-w-war in the Lowerworld without me. Perhaps if I can h-h-heal Ma, then I will r-r-return to the Hidden City and offer my new p-p-power in w-w-what ways I can."

No sooner had he uttered the words than a shrill, sharp call riding the wind struck their ears, forcing all three to clap hands to the sides of their heads.

"Pursued," Elijah spat, casting about. "Hurry!" The tall man sprang away, bounding down a rocky slope and disappearing behind pine, bush, and stone as he ran.

"Dusk, come on!" Keiphral hissed, looking back as he made to catch the old man.

"Keiphral, I n-n-need to go—"

"To the city!" Keiphral snapped, hauling Dusk up from under his arms and slinging him onto his back. "I hope that helm of yours can fend off a blow as well as it can give secrets." Before Dusk could protest, the dusty ground sped by, and Keiphral's muscled legs drove them both after Elijah at nearly the speed of elves, who were said to be fastest of foot among the Lower-worlders, according to the wise women of Dusk's village. And as Dusk cast his amber gaze back toward Sunreach one last time, a strange glinting smote him from a concealing thicket. For an instant, Dusk spied the source of the flashing. Weak daylight glanced off the polished surface of what seemed to be a twisted, leering face. But before he could be sure, Keiphral rounded a rocky corner, and all Dusk saw then were the overgrown beginnings of the secret path that led to Last-Hope.

The three companions ran beside noisy brooks and passed between vine-wrapped walls of craggy rock. Every now and then, they passed over patches of dark blue grass that burst with white fire with each touch of their feet. Keiphral had set Dusk down after a mile of hard hiking, and Dusk offered to carry the older boy's pack for a while as thanks. Laden with gear enough for three men, Dusk, red-faced and heaving, risked calling upon his new, hard-fought power for support. It obeyed his command, and more of it than he had intended coursed through his burning legs. Running on renewed strength, Dusk marveled as his legs threw him forward, to the sides of the two tall men, with no effort. Knowing he could overtake them should even the smallest thought say he do so, Dusk, covered with cloak and gear and more shadows than daylight should have allowed, forced himself only to keep pace with the strides of Elijah and Keiphral.

"Elijah," Dusk said, his voice strangely low to his ears. "You n-n-never told us how you c-c-came to know Treiarn."

"A friend unlooked for!" Elijah grunted as they ran. "My life has been one of travel and war, and I have been warrior, counselor, and healer. Treiarn appeared, leading his armies out of the South against the Hegemony, long after I had lain aside my sword."

"He f-f-failed to tell me he l-l-led armies!" Dusk said.

"No surprise there," Elijah replied. "Dark, bloody days were those under rule of the Nephtyri Hegemony. And Treiarn's people, descendants of the Midlotheans of old, suffered badly. But when I met him, as I traveled out of Westreach, he seemed the sort that could be trusted."

"He is," Dusk said fondly. "Though I w-w-wish he would have b-b-been more f-f-forthcoming, both about his adventures, then and n-n-now."

"We all have our reasons," Elijah said between measured breaths. "Just as you have yours for knowing exactly where to find an ancient power guarded by the sea and how to subdue it to your will. If nothing else, I'll need to keep an eye on you, just as I did Treiarn."

Ignoring the comment about himself, Dusk pushed forward. "What d-d-did you do for him?"

"I told him the war he fought was a prelude to something greater, worse. I revealed the stories of things hidden in the world and under it, and that he would need to find them before being allowed to rest. I don't think he took kindly to my counsel then, but it seems his mind is changed of late. His journey began anew some years ago. I met with him only after he had traveled beyond the Westreach and reminded the Angloreans of their causes for war."

"A bitter war," huffed Keiphral, "the damage it wrought and lives it took, paling in comparison to what's coming. A strange warrior who appeared at the direst hour to reveal to the pawns things of far greater consequence. This story is familiar."

Elijah arched an eyebrow at the tall, armored lad.

"You d-d-don't think Treiarn was the cause of w-w-war st-st-starting in Anglorost?" Dusk asked, refusing to let news of his father be interrupted.

"I don't know," Elijah said, remaining silent as they dashed through tunnels of rock carved by the flowing river that raced beside them. Their course took them along winding paths under cool roofs of rock passages, then out into warm day-shine. "What have *you* heard of late?" Elijah asked after a minute or so.

"T-t-traveling the great road up from the mountain to the Hidden City b-b-brought me into the c-c-care of Suthesturri refugees," Dusk said. "They t-t-told me a knight from the m-m-mountains stole something p-p-precious from the Anglorean King. The king b-b-burned with fury, s-s-sending his armies in pursuit of the knight."

"I heard similar stories along the road and in the wild," Elijah said. "I cannot believe the man I knew would be such a betrayer of trust. Though, in these latter times, who's to say?"

"My father is traitor to no one," Dusk asserted.

"I never said he was," Elijah replied, dodging under a low branch. "But, as a man who slew a storm and stole ancient power, you of all should understand that things are not always as they seem."

Dusk harrumphed at that, then went silent. The lively wind out of the wild lands and the gentle mist of the river that raced beside them soon lulled him into reveries of his parents and what else he did not know about his father as the trio continued at a run from some pursuing fear.

After setting them a steady pace for nearly an hour, Elijah led the two boys under waterfalls, through little caves, and along rivers, before crossing into clearer country. Dusk noticed the land all about them gathering upward into a gentle, green slope. His breaths came quicker, and his legs burned faster as the rise increased. Dusk noticed their strange leader bounding toward the top of what quickly became a great hill, spotted all about with standing stones and little cairns. As they gained the hilltop, Dusk saw on its crown a broken bastion of gray stone. The fortification seemed to grow in size as they approached. Dusk soon saw that it was not the tall, slim build of a watchtower, but the stout construction of a battle turret. In ancient days, it must have stood strong and ready to guard surrounding hills from invaders by sea or northern fields and forests.

When they reached the old ruin, Elijah held up a hand. "Rest here a few minutes, and drink a little," he said between gasping breaths. "But don't eat! We leave down the hill and to a ridge of low cliffs above the hidden North Road to the city at a moment's notice. I'll scout a bit, but I will return before muscle can relax, so don't sit either! We've come nearly twelve miles from the beachhead, and it's another sixty to Last-Hope, though I hope to find an easier road than the one I'm thinking of. I'll return shortly." With that, he rounded a stony corner, and his footsteps, crunching on loose gravel and clacking on flagstones, faded from hearing.

The boys released their packs, each retrieving their water bottle and drinking deeply. With his bottle in one hand, Keiphral ran his other along the neatly constructed stonework of the tower, walking a few paces as he said, "There was a battle here; a great one, not just some border incursion. Look here: The stone was cracked, as if by some huge weapon. And much of it is destroyed and fallen from above, there." He pointed away to the top of the tower where blocks looked to have been blasted away by some unknown force.

Dusk looked at the war scars and could only think of the coastal Storm. He wondered if the tempest had once blustered as far inland as this hilltop, assailing with hail and high wind the Men of old who guarded it. Just then, the strange compulsion that had guided him through his vision of the doors under the earth forced Dusk's hand to rise slowly to his forehead. When his fingers met the metal of his helm there, a memory suddenly struck without warning.

Dusk stood alone on the bloody hill under a black sky that burned. His spear had snapped, his friends were dead, but still he fought on. He tore his golden sword from its sheath and skewered the hearts of his enemies. But his shield soon shattered, and his bright mail broke. He fell under a thousand stomping feet, his blood crushed into mud, but he would not die. With colossal strength, he dragged himself up from the mud, then he cast about. Light burst from below, far away south and west, smiting the sky. It was the last radiance the dying world could offer; one last ember laying a trap for the terrible evil he and his Kindreds had brought. A miracle happened then. The light tore evil in two, then drew its greater part into the Coffin. The lesser part flew out, away over the sea. But even as darkness fled, half-captured in the Coffin, her dark hosts still surrounded the hill, roaring her evil name.

"*Eshra, Eshra, Eshra,*" screamed the wicked.

In answer came the deep cry of, "*Rhonoss!*" And out from the gloom marched tall, cloaked figures whose keen eyes caught the final flash of imprisoning light. Bent by battle, the cloaked Men, overflowing with wrath, slew the last of their dark foes. "*Rhonoss!*" Dusk screamed, and his shattered sword struck anew. The crash of battle redoubled, and a song echoed out from the cloaked ones, sad and filled with dread. Then, all that had been plunged into darkness absolute.

SORROW AND SALVATION

"Dusk!" came the distant cry of Elijah, as if from out of a dream. "Awake, and no more shouting. We will be found again, and so near the end."

Dusk came gasping out of battle, his mind reeling. He forced himself to accept the truth that golden blades and cloaked heroes, not Elijah's voice, had been the dream. He had fallen against the block wall of the tower, and he looked up at his tall companions. They stared back with concern. His bandaged arm burned.

"Up now!" Elijah snapped. "I told you both not to rest, and here I find you napping and thrashing about, wailing like a trapped rabbit. Hurry. I may have found us a safe ride to the Sable Gate of Last-Hope. And I think we've been off-road long enough and maybe overdue for solid stone under our feet instead of soggy soil and loose rock. You agree?"

Dusk gave a grin that showed more confidence than he felt. In truth, he felt sick and groggy. Still, he gave a nod as Keiphral pulled him to his feet.

"Excellent," the man said. "Then convincing you two to run another leg of this venture ought to prove easier than I'd at first thought."

Dusk groaned, rolling honey-colored eyes.

"No time for all that," Elijah boomed. "Besides, I've already done the hard work for us—*good* work, I'd say. Come, we'll make our way to the place where I made my discovery. Neither of you will be disappointed, I promise. An hour or two of hard running, and we'll be off our feet for days—"

"Two hours!" Dusk and Keiphral cried.

"Hurry up!" Elijah said, clapping them each on a shoulder. He sprang over a fallen stone block, then went off down the hill. Half afraid at the thought of being left behind, half angry at the old man and wanting to chase him down and throttle him, Dusk took off at a run. Keiphral was at his side, and both lads tore off down the windy hill. With Dusk's power and Keiphral's strength, they caught up to their guide, and the three passed swiftly down through the high country, leaving the ancient tower behind.

"Nearly there," Elijah hissed more than an hour later. Daylight had been blotted away by invading clouds soon after they had left the tower. Rain fell steadily now, changing the morass of wild grass and rocks the three runners plodded over from a mild irritant to a slippery mess.

"Won't you ... at least tell us what ... you've found in the valley below?" Keiphral begged between breaths.

"A job if nothing else," Elijah said. "Think of this ... as running your race ... toward the chance ... to help those in need and ... to prove yourself to me."

"Helping p-p-people has bec-co-come my life!" Dusk barked.

"All the more reason for haste," Elijah said. "You may be needed in the valley."

"Fine," Dusk growled. "But what have I g-g-got to p-p-prove?"

"Not every day ... that a power older than the earth ... is stolen out of its prison—part of its power at any rate," said Elijah. "Not every day ... that the sky overhead, already gloomy, turns to twilight an hour before noon."

Dusk looked up, having mistook the oppressive darkness overhead for a squall rolling in to buffet them with further wind and rain. "What d-d-does it mean?"

"Light fails," Elijah grunted. "Deeds, both great and terrible ... are set in motion. Keep up the run, Master Dusk. We will your power and attentions ... to the test for the good of all."

"I s-s-seek the good of my mother," Dusk said.

"Which you shall have after ... we hone your skills to a scalpel's edge. Only then will you be ... strong enough to heal her. Hurry!"

Indignant, Dusk huffed then sped forward to run side by side with the taller man, seeing what lay ahead. Drops of icy water pelted the three companions as they leaped over puddle and log. They descended out of the hilly country and came to a deepening valley. And just as the thin line of Dusk's patience readied to snap, Elijah stopped at the edge of a cliff. Keiphral caught Dusk's bandaged arm, keeping the smaller boy from careening over but sending a sheet of pain burning its entire length.

All three of them bent double, panting and overlooking the breathtaking valley sprawled out below them.

"Ah," heaved Elijah. "Got us there. And not. Too. Late."

"What?" Dusk asked of the ground.

"See below. Use those torchlights you have for eyes," Elijah said. He pointed a long, thin finger down into the valley, past a swollen river. Beyond the sparkling thread,

GARDEN OF ASH

Dusk and Keiphral spied a trail of dust rising over treetops. The longer he looked, the more Dusk caught glimpses of firelight and the trundling of wheels passing in and out of view with the surrounding scrub.

"A car-car-a-van?"

"A caravan!" Elijah laughed, clapping the boy on the back. "Some fifty wagons. Far more of late with the Suthesturri coming up from the broken pass between the Glacial Waste and Sunreach. They flee Belrath'ir. This caravan's wains are no doubt laden with salt, dye, spice, and many swords. And they are guarded by men garbed in the scarlets of my city. Down we go!"

Dusk and Keiphral groaned, preparing leg and lung for the next torturous hour. They set off once more at a run.

13

HAMMER, PLAGUE, AND STORM

Not always lightless was our world. For born to it were two great peoples—we the Kindlers, the other the Crafters. Between us was light and an understanding of sorts, for a while. After Creator's punishments came war from farthest heavens. War tore worlds. In the tearing, a conjoining. When ones who called themselves Kindreds came, we Kindlers, having betrayed the Crafters when Belfaerilorn-the-Jewel and Adùnaton-the-Crown fell in ruin, found the Gift in the hands of winged friends. But all was not as it seemed. For the Gift, we were grateful, for a while. But ere long, the menace it visited upon us stirred our wrath. The Gift gave new light and life, or so it seemed. For in the Coffin was that light, and we draw from it. In the drawing, we find sustenance, and in our sustenance, we sustain the world. The more we draw, the tighter the lock turns. Thus is held the One. These things were good, for the One is a thing not of our world, but Theirs, and They guard it. The seal holds for now, but light fades, both from the One and from eyes of the Second. And our friends fear a crippling of wings coming. But when?

—A record of the Atrellarrath,
transcribed by Knight Treiarn the Midlothean,
Under Galataeum—

Many stories have my hosts told me, but the one above seems foundational to their faith in a faraway hope, and to the ways in which their generations understand the history of Leóhteness-Fal. "Kindlers" refers to my hosts, the Atrellarrath. "Crafters," I have learned, refers to giants who walked out of myth and onto this earth in its youngest days. They were named the Weileth-Zhul, alive only in distant memory, even by reckoning of the Atrellarrath. Only the Qwei-Sillar have mentioned a single one, and that is a secret among their people. According to the elves' legends, it was one of these Weileith who pulled their Wall, Mithweileth-Nal, up from under the earth, and set it as a protective ring around them in the farthest depths of the Qweth-Wëalda. It is thus named the Giant's Ring, and I wish one day to see it.

Nephtyr are the "Winged Ones," who found a people betrayed, and so became betrayers themselves, having given some terrible burden to the Atrellarrath. The lifting of that burden gave the Nephtyr such freedom as so they could delve the world and all its depths. Perhaps too much. But the duty they seemingly shackled to the Atrellarrath seems to have given some benefit or renewal of strength. Though it seems as though there were limits. The Nephtyr bear no mention of *such Weileth in all their records either. But my hosts mention "Little Ones" who protect secrets of the Weileth, digging for that which was buried at the foot of the Glacial Waste. A visit to the quarries there may prove useful once I've returned out of Westreach, for the Surgeon said the hammering torments the ears of the Qwei-Sillar. I wonder, could there be some connection between the songs sung of old friendship between the Atrellarrath and the Qwei-Sillar, and the incessant hammering and digging that keep the Qwei-Sillar awake night after night?*

"Yes," growled Arwë, paging through the knight's account with a recently healed wrist. "We know what the Atrellarrath want, but does the knight refer here to the Nokleth? If so, we found no such buried secrets when we stayed with them. And, although we seem to be rid of voices in our minds, the hammering continues."

"*Once you've captured the Garden's prize, come back. The Nokleth will have uncovered a great gift for all. And with the Lathe, we will form it for deeds of this age. So, we dig.*" Tyrith recited the message given to them by the Nokleth from months before, when they had left the Quarries.

"I remember," Arwë said. "And the cloak they gifted to us became the exact thing needed to contain Ithyeil's light. With boons such as that, what is this mightiest of gifts that surprised even the Atrellarrath? And why does it run out? It's all more than enough to give me pause, especially if the Nokleth bear some connection to these Weileth-Zhul Giants. I wish I knew how our Mithweileth-Nal came to be.

Perhaps you and I will find our way back to the Quarries after all this business concerning the Heir is over. Maybe we'll come across our friend the knight again, and he can help me discern some of his own chicken scratch."

"And what of the other coded messages sent by Wildercrown; the ones you collected before we fell into Sable Gorge?" Tyrith asked.

"Nothing," Arwë said, annoyed. "I've had no time to read them since trying to read the knight's account. I am still no nearer to learning anything of relevance to our goal, and we are still quite lost!"

They sat high up on a hilltop in north T'Rhonossarc near the Great East Sea. A crackling bonfire kept them warm after daylight had fallen too quickly, rushing away from its zenith in the northwest. They had watched the sick light smite some place south and west of where they sat before twilight fell. Neither elf nor angel was overconcerned about attracting fomori or goblins. They had both reasoned that, while they were unaware of the Hidden City's whereabouts, they did know a watch would be set on the surrounding hills. Sentinels of Ephtar-Malas, doubtless seeking reinforcements in preparation for the whispered invasion coming down out of the North, would be first to find them. And hearing of the city's want for strong men, Arwë and Tyrith would oblige on the condition that Ithyeil would be given a place within the city's infirmary, her powers at healing being *nearly miraculous*, as he and Tyrith would say.

"Whenever my people would take to the skies of the

Lower-world," Tyrith said, "they would navigate by the Storm over the Dread Coast. It's been blown away now, and not by weather of the world. I'd say we strike toward the Coast itself, rather than be steered by it, see what power was unleashed or lost there."

Arwë sighed. "If my eye finds nothing else in writing or scouting, then the Coast will be our course."

Eyes glittering with irritation, Tyrith said, "My hope is for our knight's tale to illuminate, rather than to trust those keenest eyes of yours, which have missed the mark by so many miles, to this spot."

Arwë threw a clay cup at him, which, had the warrior not caught out of the air, would have broken his handsome nose. "Let that be a lesson to those who doubt the sight of elves," Arwë said, glaring at his companion. "Besides, light is not an easy thing to track, given its race through the sky each sporadic twilight."

Tyrith set the cup down beside the rock he sat upon. "If the sight of elves is not to be questioned," he rumbled, "then perhaps the eyes of our leader would see the benefit in handing over the knight's records for his friend's eyes to consider. Those are written in the common tongue and recognizable to me no matter how badly scrawled. Read the messages given you by your people, Arwë. I cannot decipher Qwei-Sillari code. Besides, we both need any hint as to where Ephtar-Malas is, or what it is we are to do once we get there."

Arwë hesitated and acted as though he were lost in thought as he continued reading.

Tyrith sat for a moment, considering Wildercrown's Messenger. His voice went lower than usual as realization struck. "You don't trust me to be truthful of the knight's words once his records are in my hands."

"The knight's words may concern your people, the things they've done, given his time spent with the Atrellarrath," Arwë said, scowling. "I cannot run the risk of misinterpretation for the sake of erasing old sins."

"My people's sin is great, and I am the bearer of it," Tyrith said, sudden fury kindling in his lightless eyes. "Am I not friend to you and your Kindred? Have I not rescued you from danger, shielded them and their secrets from our enemies? Even with Wildercrown burned, I walk your path, fight alongside you. And you recoil because you think I may lie, or worse, yell, scream, and tear, or burn the knight's letters should I take umbrage with a thing he says against my people? Only fools act thusly. Very well, master Messenger. Continue reading and getting us lost, for all the good knowledge so closely kept has done for you. I will keep on protecting you with no other cause than that of being your friend."

"Leave me be, Tyrith," Arwë said sternly, continuing his inspection of the documents. "I have much to read tonight, since I've clearly failed and overshot the mark of the light's path southward. We set off again at dawn to see if we can do any better in finding our way in this twisted country."

With a clash of mail and wings of broken iron, the angel left the elf to read on the hilltop.

HAMMER, PLAGUE, AND STORM

* * *

Tyrith's mouth curled as withering pain crawled into every muscle and joint of his mighty body. The heated words he had exchanged with Arwë had only made the searing heat worse. He held up a massive hand, cringing as the pain poured in. Then he snarled and let his anger get the better of him for a moment.

"The Nokleth didn't give cloaks only, and you weren't the only one to receive secret tidings, Master Elf," Tyrith whispered downwind, knowing well the Qwei-Sillar and of the acute hearing they possessed. He stalked away from the circle of rocks Arwë sat in, limping toward their camp. "We need more answers than we have, and more than you're willing to divulge. With Light running out, the pain growing, and the last of my strength spent too soon, nothing, not even a hundred of my own kin with flaming swords, would stop me from finding what I need. We of the Nephtyr are depraved indeed, but I will never cease seeking our redemption and healing. And so, I come along for reasons more than friendship, and I will protect Ithyeil Stëorra too. Then, with or without your help, I will seek this healer of Sunreach."

He walked on down the hill, passing under trees and over low stone ramparts crumbling in their ruin. As he went, Tyrith breathed, cooling his temper, and his pain as a result. He brought up his hand again, then rolled his wrist to look at the back of his mailed palm. His face contorted at the sharp, little stab the motion brought. He drew another breath, with less success at calming him than the last. "Anger and angst make it worse," he rumbled to himself. "Take heart, my soul. The world is moving in strange ways these days, and people with it. Which means others suffer, and a cure will be found, if you don't find it yourself."

Tyrith came to an outcrop of the crumbling tower, slowing his pace so as not to further upset his already swollen hands, and, worse, his feet. The ruined overhang jutted far out over the hilltop and countryside below. He lost himself for a moment, staring long into the crepuscular violets and golds of the horizon. His thoughts strayed from pain into memory, losing himself to visions of wind blasting him through a sapphire sky. A woman's face, his master's stern words, and the pleas of his foes melted together in melancholy. The ghost of a smile crossed his lean face. Then it vanished when a flash of light far away southward wrested him out of his reverie. He stood looking for a moment. But sight of his gnarled knuckles drew back his attention, and the usual rising panic threatened again.

"Let's see how well you'll work with me this time, fingers," Tyrith whispered. Setting his jaw, he twisted the fingers of his dominant hand into a fist. His jaw then clenched as he forced the fingers closed, and torment bloomed in every joint. "Worse this time," he grunted. Clamping jaw and fist harder, a bead of sweat started at Tyrith's hairline. Doubt and fear gnawed at him as his snarl at the twinging agony worked its way past his gritted teeth.

"Tyrith," whispered a voice that trailed down from the sloping trees and rocky paths above.

The angel released both his indrawn breath and clenched fist. Relief washed over half his body at the relaxing of sore muscles and joints. He lowered his hand, catching sight of another small flash faraway and below in the darkened forests.

"More than one this time," he whispered. "And in a rough line." Then he turned slowly toward the whisper and saw a gray-clad girl.

"I'm troubled," said Ithyeil Stëorra, who stood on a fallen block of stone a few yards away.

"As am I," Tyrith scoffed, gazing at glittering blades of grass as they swayed in the blowing wind. "My troubles lie with our esteemed elvish leader. He keeps eye ever sky and nose so close to ground that we'll wander the wilderness long enough for fomori armies to march over all the earth and back in the time it took him to find an ocean. Where lie yours?" When no response came, Tyrith looked to her. She stood like a warding statue, carved as if to forever point northward.

"They have found us," she said.

Tyrith snapped his head back to the shadowed world below. The motion startled a gasp out of him. The stinging spasms that had so drained the strength of his hand a moment before now lanced through every muscle of his neck at the movement.

"How long?" Tyrith was half speaking, half-growling at the pain. He scanned the trees that swam with firefly lights below, then beyond to the grass whose vibrant blades covered all the world from hill to northern horizon. He saw no sign of their enemies.

"Hard to say," Ithyeil said, squinting. "They move fast and pursue us through the night without sleep. Light glints off masks and leering faces through the thickets of the lower country. I figured our pace and Arwë's false trails would have kept us weeks ahead."

"And with us stopping for rest?" Tyrith asked, bringing up a hand to rub his aching neck.

"Days only," Ithyeil said. "More with rain, but both Arwë and I figured we'd have more time."

Tyrith made to turn his head back to her. He turned his shoulders instead. As he faced her, he again glimpsed a string of lights flashing over her shoulder, southward. "Our hunch is correct, then," he rumbled, focusing on her eyes. "You draw them to us."

"Moths to flame, given what I am," she said. "All the world is parched for light, and I seem to be satiation for all."

He grunted a laugh at that, regretting what the motion did to his neck.

Ithyeil's eyes narrowed. "You don't seem to have gotten much better, given that weeks have passed since you sustained those injuries."

"Travel has not made the healing easy," he rumbled. "Though I'm thankful for the small bouts of flight my wings allow. They help keep me off my feet at times."

"You're not telling me the whole truth," Ithyeil said, gazing sidelong at him.

"Yeiley," Tyrith replied with a sigh. "You can restore what I lost. But I do not want to take the risk of hoarding your power for myself. I nearly ruined everything when we first met. I will not come that close again."

In a small voice, Ithyeil simply said, "But you need not hide your pain, nor must you suffer alone."

"The Wasting Sickness plagues my people as it does the world of Men," Tyrith rumbled. "Though searing pain is its manifestation for us, for we do not die unless slain. There is little more to be said of it, for there is no cure. Although the Qwei-Sillar spoke of a surgeon who seeks a healer of renown, who, in turn, may have learned how to treat such things. Any treatment would prove a lifting of heavy loads from our backs, even if no cure is ever to be found. I would rather consult him than draw too close to the fount of your power again."

"I don't know how or why," Ithyeil said, seeming to change the subject. "But my heart tells me I know the man of whom you speak. Or at least I knew one close to him."

"The knight?" Tyrith asked.

"Not him," she said. "Treiarn's kind are a rare thing, or so my people say. But perhaps one close to him fights other battles for our benefit. Time will tell, I suppose. For now, we should leave and pursue Galataeum's light southwestward. It would change Arwë's plan to watch tonight then leave at dawn."

"Why?" asked Tyrith.

"I feel the tendrils' course now, somehow, the farther south we go."

"You may be right," Tyrith conceded. "Arwë's plans have led us astray so far. And though they've not led us to disaster, I think you and I should convince him of our need to change tack."

"I won't argue," Arwë's voice trailed down to them as he descended a flight of cracked stone steps half-reclaimed by the earth.

"Glad to see your secrets haven't caused you to sneak away in the night, leaving us to roam leaderless," Tyrith said.

Arwë landed in their midst with a light crunch of gravel. "I've led you both to folly with my lack of knowledge in these lands of Men," he said. "And for my inability to properly track the course and destination of grasping tendrils of ethereal light. For those things, you have my apologies." He then looked Tyrith in the eye. "But as for secrets, I'll reveal them as soon as you tell yours to Yeiley, for your own good."

"I have none," Tyrith snapped.

"In that case, I have *read* none," Arwë retorted. "Until better trust is built between us, what do you advise, Tyrith? Yours is the lead now."

A glaring silence grew between the tall elf and Tyrith. Then the angel, refusing to look away from Arwë, said, "Off you go for now, Yeiley, up the steps that curve away and around the hill. I may have a plan to get us away from our foes and into friendlier arms. But I need Arwë's help. For that, he and I need to come to an understanding. Keep an eye out for masks and fomori. I'll fetch you shortly."

Ithyeil's eyes narrowed at angel and elf. But she nodded. "I suppose there's time to finish the venison cut Arwë shot and cooked," she said, shrugging. "While you two bicker, I'll be enjoying my salted steak!" With that, Ithyeil leaped up the rough-hewn steps, disappearing around the curve of the hill.

Tyrith chuckled. "Once again, your skills at heralding and hunting prove of equal match and worth."

"I aim to please," Arwë said, fighting a grin. "Now, what's our understanding?"

"She must take the easiest way southwestward," Tyrith said. "You and I will avoid the roads completely."

"Will you be able to?" Arwë asked with a little concern.

"I'll be fine," Tyrith barked. He looked away again, catching the bustling flicker of lights down in the valley, far beyond the lowest steps of their hill.

"Who's going to tell our girl she'll no longer be traveling with us?" Arwë asked. A lock of silver-gold hair fell from the confines of his hood. He tucked it back.

"I will," Tyrith said. "Seeing as how you're born of the Fair Folk, I, brawling fool that I am, somehow was gifted the silverer tongue when it comes to Yeiley."

Arwë chuckled at that. "Silver may be a stretch. But how was she before I came down?"

"Agitated," Tyrith replied, taking a moment to pull at his gear, which chafed at the joints of his shoulders.

Arwë grunted. "To be expected. With the way she draws the attention of brigand and beast, she must want to find the city and have done as much as we."

Tyrith nodded and shifted his pack into a less irritating spot on his back. He looked to see Arwë gazing east. The elf's lean face grew severe under the cowl of his cloak. "Things are not right," he said. "You may have been right in wanting us to strike toward the Coast, see what came of the Storm. Though, I'm uneasy at what we may fi—" He gasped suddenly, then gave a small cry.

"What have you seen?" demanded Tyrith, steadying his friend with a broad arm.

"Some far-flung threat is there," Arwë breathed, pointing eastward. "It is become aware of my watching. I knew it was there but turned away to some distraction. So I quested out, both with eye and foresight. But just now I felt the sudden turning of its deadly mind, and it crossed the chasm between us to rear up before me."

"Are we safe?" Tyrith demanded.

"For now," Arwë said, shivering. "Its sight is as clear as any elf's, and it would have seen us. But before it could, I jabbed a finger in both our eyes, cutting short the search. But it will know something it wants is on a hilltop inside a broken tower."

"What of the West?" Tyrith said, worry catching at his voice.

Arwë faced the western horizon, looking far. "Anglorost burns still, just like the Qweth-Wëalda. No relief has come for the Angloreans. But Eth Gathilin will hold long should the Swardha-Menn prove bold enough to challenge its gates of rock."

Arwë then faced southwest and removed his hood, revealing his elongated ears and hair that shone nearly white in the dark. He lay a long-fingered hand over his eyes, and his ears flexed and bent. He listened intently for a moment. When he moved his hand and his eyes opened, Arwë said, "That way lies our road. New hammers have joined the Noklethi dig. The din travels right up the corridor between the Glacial Waste and River Hills. But there is a gap in the sound, as if it is forced to travel around some immense obstruction."

"An obstruction the size of a towering city?" Tyrith asked.

Arwë nodded. "Strange. Whether the Nokleth have begun tunneling into the ice of the Waste or opening some new chamber in their Quarries, I cannot guess. No foe is there, though, to answer your question. If ever it were black-night, and all light truly poured out, I would wager I could see the glow of their forge fires from here!"

"Four-hundred miles?" Tyrith demanded. "Even *you* couldn't make out a glow from that distance. I don't care how great you and yours claim Qwei-Sillari eyes to be!"

"Perhaps not with them injured, having just protected you from some enemy out of the East," Arwë snapped. "Regardless, a frenzy has taken the Nokleth. They've more than enough strength to bring down whole mountains, given motive. We can only hope that motive isn't bent toward doing T'Rhonossarc, or any other Outer-worldly place, harm."

"Surrounded on all sides, then," Tyrith rumbled, gathering packs and provisions. "And you still advise returning to the Quarries?"

"Once this present business with Ithyeil is settled," Arwë confirmed, "we need to find this 'Lathe' the Nokleth spoke of. Knowing what little we do of our Stone-folk friends, I'd say it's a tool of great craftsmanship, and perhaps magic."

Tyrith grunted. "The Wasting Sickness plagues all folk in one form or another. Cities burn under torches of marching hosts screaming an evil name. We find the waning of daylight, and its link to the Atrellarrath. The ever-blasting Storm on the Dread Coast is snuffed out with no warning at all. Our foe searches for us with as much precision as that of the Qwei-Sillar. Then the Stone-folk tell of a tool that can craft machinations beyond the ken of the Kindreds. You think they all may be connected?"

"I do," Arwë said darkly. "Though I fear we may not live long enough to unravel the answers we seek."

"Cut down before we can find them?"

"No, dead of old age, though one of us be immortal," Arwë said with a pained grin.

"Well then," Tyrith said. "After Ithyeil's delivered and our battles are resolved by victory or defeat, you and I can retire from our wandering service to lords and lands. I'll go with you into whatever dark terror you're hell-bent on throwing us into. Then we'll both have our answers, even if the price of knowing is death."

"I'll hold you to that," the elf said, a smile spreading

to the dark angles of his face. But he grew serious again, turning back to the distant sea. "Though I tell you this, Tyrith—of all that passes in the world, have a care for the Storm that rages no longer. Its silencing heralds more than danger. Something bigger."

The angel's eyes narrowed as he stared down at the gray figure of his friend. "Meaning?"

Arwë shook his head. "No time. More questions than answers lie at the heart of the Storm. Hurry, before we are found! Call for Ithyeil. We must be off, and her eyes will be better for the night than mine."

Tyrith turned a surprised gaze at the elf.

"I know," Arwë snapped. "Truth be told, I'm making my best guess, Tyrith."

"Arwë," Tyrith rumbled, placing one giant hand on the elf's shoulder and bowing to meet his gaze. "We've kept Ithyeil under Noklethi cover for weeks now. For all that time we've been hounded over highland, hill, bog, river, and rock. Still we're chased. Our enemies are drawn to her, but your eyes have caught them before ever they find her, and you've led us to the safety of hidden places. And still you've managed to track the path of Galataeum's light to a place within miles of Ephtar-Malas. I spoke too harshly earlier. For that, forgive me."

Taken aback, Arwë gave an awkward smile. "Nothing at all to forgive, friend Nephtyr Ithar-fel."

"Good. Now look!" Tyrith said, shoving at Arwë's shoulder, turning him toward the wandering flash in the valley below. He pointed to it. "It's made a little progress since I left you reading above in the ruined tower. You may have found Ephtar-Malas by use of your ears. But one more thing your *eyes* have failed to catch is perhaps a trail of friends seeking the Hidden City, as we are."

Arwë nodded. "As good a guide as any. You suppose they could be Suthesturri fleeing the desert?"

"As good a *guess* as any," Tyrith said with a wry smile.

"Save me from the humor of angels," Arwë hissed. "Very well. How are we to approach the wain line?"

"You and I stick to cover of shadow. Yeiley goes down as a refugee, fleeing the burning North."

"Is that wise?" Arwë asked.

"As wise a choice as any now," Tyrith rumbled. "We have no time. She has uncanny skill at healing, so she'll be a useful guest. She carries that nightmare-sword in an arm that knows how to use it should the worst happen. She is an Heir to a great people and wants to prove herself. We'll let her. She can go down to whoever travels in the valley and be of service to them."

"So long as you're sure."

"No surer than you," Tyrith said. "But tell me quickly what you see when you look hard at the rolling wains."

Arwë gazed toward the trundling light for the space of two long breaths. "They've women, children, and the old with them. But guards I see too. Many guards."

"Ha!" Tyrith thundered, clapping the elf on the back. "Then should our pursuers decide to get gutsy and attack her, they'll fly headlong into a hundred swords at the least. Then we'll get a feel for their strength and squash them."

"She's the bait, then," Arwë said with a note of accusation.

Tyrith's smile froze. "Maybe," he conceded.

Arwë held Tyrith's gaze for a moment, then sighed. "If an attack were to come," he said, "I would rather her be surrounded by scores of armed men *and* us than be run down like game. It may not be the worst plan."

Tyrith smiled as he turned away. "I suppose that's as close to a compliment as I'll ever get from the likes of you. Very well. I'll find Yeiley and tell her of our plan."

"Tyrith," Arwë said gently.

Tyrith looked back at the elf, drawn by the change in his tone.

"Let Yeiley help you."

Tyrith heaved an annoyed sigh, then nodded.

"Good," Arwë said, taking up a newly carven bow from their supply. He strung it, and, even bent, the weapon stood taller than his six feet. "I'll go down and scout ahead." The elf faded away, a passing shadow in the night as he left the hill for the forests below.

Tyrith put a heavy hand to his neck, and the resounding crack sent startled birds skittering skyward. He let his head roll from side to side, appreciating the small relief brought on by the stretching. He then took a few steps to test his toes. Satisfied with only small aches, he stood to his full, intimidating height, breathed deeply, and walked.

Wind caught at his cloak then. The wool fanned out like a sail, and Tyrith caught it up with one big arm, wrapping it close. Continuing up the winding stair, he soon reached a ring of cracked flagstones set in the circle of another crumbling wall. There, Tyrith found the Heir of the Atrellarrath. She danced in and out of broken pillars, cutting the air with a rapier that blazed like a firebrand in the night.

"Ithyeil," he said, his voice a low roll of the thunder.

"Time to leave, then," snapped Ithyeil Stëorra, panting a little with her exertions.

"Yes," he rumbled, rubbing at his hands. "We've a better idea of where we go next."

"More pain?" she asked. The molten glow sloshed against the containing vessels of her irises.

Tyrith's upper lip curled before he could control it. He looked away, nodding. "I could use your help."

Ithyeil smiled, sheathing her bright blade, then came to him. She took his huge hand in hers. Before he could protest, light welled up from the core of her, flooded from her hands, then onto his. The relief was staggering, and Tyrith felt soothing coolness displace the burning aches in his fingers and wrists. He flexed hand, arm, and ankle, astonished by their easy mobility. And while he basked in his recovery, she touched his brow with a slender hand. The pouring in of new power nearly overwhelmed him as it had at first touch of Ithyeil's power under Galataeum.

Dominate, crush, kill, rule! he thought. Then he screamed to himself from the wiser part of his mind. *No! You will not fall prey to the weakness that ruined your people. Release it!*

Tyrith hauled himself back from Ithyeil, crashing into a wall of loose stone blocks. His body crawled with power, and he worked to master himself. His eyes were shut tightly. But when he opened them again, he knew they blazed with white fire—a window into the deadly power returned to his command. His whole body was tense as a lute string, ready to snap. But he sighed then, celebrating the small joy of a moment without pain, and he returned to himself.

Ithyeil ran to him, knelt beside him. "Do all angels suffer so?" she asked.

"That name," Tyrith growled, "is one thing my people do not deserve. Such titles are for those greater than what we are. We were *once* great; now we are not. The story has ended. Anyone who tells you otherwise lies."

"I'm sorry to say my people say the same," she said, retying her boots just below the knee with lengths of leather cord. "Though I'm glad I could help."

"Don't be sorry," he grumbled. "We deserve every curse. But there may be some redemption left to us. Thank you for your healing hands, Yeiley. Though I can feel in my bones that your gift is a temporary respite, and not a cure to my ailment, I am restored to fighting fitness."

"And you neither hoarded my power nor ruined anything," she said with a smile.

He gave a weary nod. "Not perfect, but not a monster, at least," Tyrith said.

"Precisely!" Ithyeil said. "Now then, where are we off to next?"

"We've changed the plan," he said.

"To what?" she asked, examining her sword once more. Tyrith recognized the rapier as blackened fulgurite. Its straight edges met to form the most ferocious stabbing point he had ever seen. Its guard, housing some fey light at its center, was wrought from warped bone and glass. He stared at the twisted mass, thinking of some creature out of myth, whose bones were diamond, that had somehow swallowed the sword along with a star and burst from the inside. Ithyeil held it by the elegant hilt. After examining it from pommel to tip, she sheathed the sword, then grabbed up her pack. She raised a long, expectant eyebrow at the angel.

Tyrith grunted, shaking the weapon's grim edges from his head. The motion, to his relief, brought no pain. He then prepared himself for what would be her objections. "You won't like it, but it's what's happening. A caravan travels southward. We think it makes for the Hidden City. You will go down to it, offering them gifts of healing in guise of an elf newly escaped from the ravaged North."

"But traveling a road when the fomori have been skilled enough to track us through the wild will draw more of them, and maybe other horrors, right to me," she said. "I won't cause the deaths of innocents if I can help it."

"And that's exactly why innocents will remain safe," Tyrith boomed. "They'll have you, a skilled healer, to mend their hurts and to keep them from harm again." He then arched an eyebrow at the young woman's sword. "You've also a weapon which can sheer through stone, should you wish it, one that once brokered the surrender of entire continents."

"I'm to be the bait," she said flatly.

"Maybe," he growled. "I swear, you and Arwë are more similar than either of your thick heads have the wit to admit."

She gave a small snort, covering her mouth with a delicate hand. "Oh, Tyrith," she said. "You've been the perfect protector up to this point. Very well! It's simple enough. I'll steal Arwë's story: I'm escaped from the war in the North, seeking counsel and shelter in this city, Ephtar-Malas. I look close enough to the Elder Kindred, and it's not as though folk of these parts see them frequently enough to tell the difference between Qwei-Sillar and Atrellarrath."

Tyrith nodded. "Arwë scouts ahead. Let's be off."

"Once I reach the caravan," Ithyeil said, "what will you and Arwë be doing?"

Tyrith hefted his hulking black-metal axe onto his shoulder. The motion was fluid, and the pain he thought it would bring never came. "Oh, don't worry about us." He laughed. "We'll be watching."

14
REFUGEES

Dusk, Keiphral, and Elijah burst out from under bough and onto a road.

"Just in time to strike the wain's end." Elijah laughed, pointing toward torchbearers marching at the caravan's back end.

"No farther!" a male voice shouted. The trio, bent double after their miles-long race down through the jagged countryside, looked up to see a lad of eighteen or so. He was arrayed in scarlet and bronze and held his blade with a master's skill. Its point rested at Elijah's throat. The lad's eyes were stony blue and fierce.

This one would kill if pressed, thought Dusk, too stunned by fatigue and the sight of a sword held in the hand of one who did not look like an enemy. He could only look to Elijah, who towered over the threatening boy, regarding him with fascination and a little annoyance.

"Why draw sword at me, given we are three?" Elijah asked.

"Because you are tallest, old man," the boy spat. "Most powerful in stature and dangerous of eye."

Elijah frowned at that, shifting his gaze to Keiphral Morne, dressed in elvish argent and gold, whose hand lay on the hilt of his own sword. Elijah then looked to Dusk, who hoped his molten-metal eyes betrayed raw danger despite his weariness. Mastering his shock, Dusk prepared to set loose his new, rending power. The sword-bearing lad's steely eyes flicked to either of Elijah's companions. For an instant, he looked unsure.

"Your flattery is well received and will work to bolster your rapport with others, given that awful attitude," Elijah said to the swordsman. "But having run me through the throat, both of these, who are far stronger than me, would have torn you to pieces before you could pull free your sword from my corpse. You still have much to learn in the ways of our enemies, squire."

A tumult of mail and stomping feet clambered toward them. "That is why I am not alone," the lad said, composure returning. A dozen soldiers clad in greens, blues, and golds came up the road. Others blurred into their midst from various places of watch in the forest. The lad, who watched his own companions gather round, returned his attention to Elijah. "What business do three fighters, two of which are beset of deadly danger as you say, have in the Rhonoss Arch? Answer quickly, or show me just how strong these companions of yours are, old man."

"Del!" barked a grizzled voice, accompanied by the clack of hooves. "Well enough done for defending our flank. But a good defender should recognize friend from foe!" A man atop a restless horse, scarred and dressed in the same red and bronze as the grim-eyed lad, rode up to the strange gathering.

"I was finding whether they *were* friend or foe, Sergeant," the lad growled. "We're assailed from all sides, and I'm the only one standing ready for a fight!"

"You're doing just fine, lad, and the tall one may not be friendly," the scarred man said with a wry smile toward Elijah. "But he's one of ours at no mistake. Returned to T'Rhonossarc with fiery words for the masses, no doubt! And hopefully the surgeon bears a little good news to lighten up these dark days?"

"Ethstan," Elijah chuckled. "I've been away a long time indeed, with a better, burning message for the folk of our city. But yes, I think I have some good news before the storm strikes. But I fear we have no time! You and your soldiers, even your youngest here, are right to be suspicious. Architects of the troubles visited upon the elves pursued us even as we made our way here to you from the outer hills. The Hidden City, I fear, is nearly found."

"Seems even the good news you bear is grim," Ethstan said without mirth. "We will bear you thence, for we must hurry. But what of these two? I know your penchant for traveling alongside strange folk, but I see with you an Elf-lord! And beside him, I see a little slip of a lad, but those eyes of his promise more of death than all the swords of the men at my command."

REFUGEES

"You're closer to the mark than you may think, Sergeant," Elijah replied. "These two are strong beyond my ken and have seen more trial and woe than most. Should you welcome them with me, then you will have done the prince a mighty service."

Ethstan stared at Dusk and Keiphral in wonder. "For Healer Elijah, sternest of word and heart, to speak so highly of two lads, then virtue and great dread must follow them indeed. They are welcome, so long as you and your lads pull your weight. I know you will." He arched a knowing brow at Elijah.

Elijah nodded. "Give the lads an hour to rest, then they shall work. The broad one will join the ranks of your guard, and the smaller will treat any travelers here for disease, malady, or injury. Until then, I will ride with you. I have news and dire want of the goings on of Malas."

Sergeant Ethstan looked Dusk and Keiphral up and down as if measuring the surgeon's words against his own standards. The red torchlight gave the man a grim appearance, and Dusk could sense an uneasiness in Keiphral's stiff stance. "Very well!" Ethstan laughed, dispelling the tension in his voice. "Three new protectors prove better than three timid escapees, and far better than brigands." He pointed to Keiphral. "The tall one?"

"Keiphral Morne, sir," Keiphral said, stepping forward, chin held high.

"No doubt," Ethstan said, nodding in approval. "You will join up with Del here when your hour's up. He may not look or act like it, but he's the best sword I have, better even than hardened veterans at my call. Stick close, and learn what you can, even if you have to pry it from him!"

Keiphral nodded.

"Good," Ethstan said. He turned his grim gaze to Dusk. "And your healer-lad?"

"Dusk, s-s-sir," Dusk said. *Blast, I can't control two simple words in the face of these scowling soldiers!*

Ethstan frowned down at him as he fidgeted in frustration. "He shall stick close to you, I guess, Elijah?"

"For a time," Elijah replied. "For as long as it takes me to learn the things he can teach."

"*Teach* the Surgeon of Ephtar-Malas?" the sergeant said, brows rising.

Elijah smiled, nodding.

"If a cure has been found," breathed Ethstan, "and this is the one for whom you've searched, then blessed is this meeting and the news you bring, Surgeon."

"That remains to be seen, Sergeant, and that bit of news is not to be shared," Elijah said, sternness rising in his voice. "But I feel I have made no mistake in choosing the Healer of Sunreach."

Ethstan stared at Dusk with renewed bewilderment. "Elijah," he said. "You have many secrets to keep and divulge. But come away with me to the head of the column now. It will be good to talk with one possessed of a little sense on this journey."

Elijah nodded, making to step forward, but Del's sharp blade at his neck hindered him.

"Del!" Ethstan barked again. "Stay sword, and back to post."

Without looking away from Elijah, the grim lad cut the air then slammed his blade back into its scabbard. He turned and stormed away without a word.

"Glad *you're* on h-h-his team and n-n-not me," Dusk whispered to Keiphral.

"Lovely," Keiphral sighed beneath his elvish helm. "Out from under goblin swords only to be put inside the reach of a fool with a deadlier one."

"With me, the three of you," Ethstan said. The sergeant guided his war charger toward the trundling racket of the caravan, up the road. "We're expecting another attack."

They jogged beside the sergeant's trotting stallion. Ethstan led them past cart, wain, and wagon. Each lay heavy with staring children, blankets, bottles, and dry foods. Some rolled along behind horse and mule. Ox, camel, and lizard tugged others, the last to Keiphral's surprise and Dusk's delight.

"Perenti they are c-c-called," Dusk said to the larger boy. "Not dragons, b-b-but they are fierce, aren't they?"

"The riders are mostly Suthesturri, out of Belrath'ir," Ethstan said as they went. "They seek refuge from war and fire in the South, coming up the cut between Glacial Waste and Sunreach. Most are willing to fight. These and their families we guide to the city under guard. They then bolster our ranks as we prepare for battles of our own. Mountain folk have come down too, and their keen eyes, arrows, and shepherds' staffs have done wonders protecting the roads, both from beast and brigand."

Dusk's chest swelled a little at the mention of his people and the part they were playing in protecting the Lower-world.

"The rules are simple in Malas," Ethstan continued. "Those who don't work don't eat. And those who don't stand ready to defend her walls are given their choice: flee north, into the fires; flee west, into the arms of Swardha-Menn who rape all the Gathilin Reach; or flee south, back to the hell whence they came."

The distaste of such choices lay like ash in Dusk's mouth when the group came to a wagon that bounced along somewhere near what must have been the middle of the traveling line. A grim woman, clad in veils of violet and a patterned mantle of rich oranges, pinks, and blues drove her beast of burden as she sat in front with the reins. Plumes of smoke rose from her lips as she took long drags from her pipe. Dusk saw her eyeing them as the orange glow of her coals lit her face for an instant. Then she turned away. Dusk noticed the woman's cart, empty of all provision except one. In a corner, wrapped and hooded in a heavy cloak, sat a girl whose knees were pulled to her chest.

"You'll rest here," Ethstan said to Dusk and Keiphral. "Bother neither driver nor passenger, and ol' Del won't bother you. Find us at the front of the train after one hour. Understand?"

At Dusk and Keiphral's nods, Elijah and Sergeant

REFUGEES

Ethstan continued onward, the latter standing as tall walking as the former sitting in his charger's saddle. The lads looked forward and backward, up and down the wain line. They walked beside the almost-empty cart a while. The train's ends faded into mist at either direction. Keiphral shrugged, grabbed the side of the wooden wagon, and leaped in with a jangle of mail. Dusk grabbed the lad's outstretched hand and hauled himself into the wagon. They sat with their backs to the wagon's walls, and Dusk, spying the girl who sat opposite them, readied questions for her. But, to his brief dismay, Dusk's vision went dark at the edges, and all curiosity fled from him. Having just now left his feet after such an excruciating pace, exhaustion assuaged all need for news, and he fell fast asleep on Keiphral's shoulder.

Dusk's thoughts swam lightly on clouds of gold and black. The rhythm beating up from below lolled him, and the cloak on his back kept him warm from the windy dark without. Living lights walked in a verdant garden and laughed at the coming dawn. Then came the crash, and the lights suddenly screamed.

"Fomori!" cried a man from some place distant.

"Goblins!" cried another.

"Dusk, up!" an avid voice wrenched him out of dreams. Pain seared every inch of his covered arm, and Dusk's eyes fluttered open. He saw fire in what had been a placid, darkling sky a moment before. An elf, tall, mailed, and glowing, bounded over him, striking the earth. Then the elf offered him a gloved hand. He looked away, to the corner of the wagon.

"She's gone," Dusk whispered.

"Dusk, come on!" the elf said. Another second of bleary staring smoothed the face's sharp edges, and Dusk recognized Keiphral in his elvish mail. A ruckus of splintering thuds smacked the side of the wagon, and he looked to see black arrow shafts firmly embedded in the wood. The driver's beast bellowed, making to dash away in panic, wagon and all. Keiphral heaved Dusk down, drawing an elf-sword. Before they could regroup from the ground, a chilling shriek unlike any from the mouth of fomori or goblin assailed their ears. Head snapping toward the cry, Keiphral bore his teeth then took off at a run as Dusk readied his heavy walking staff for fighting.

"Why this w-w-way?" Dusk asked, trailing the tall boy and rather not wanting to find the source of the baleful voice.

"Del and his men fight at the rear, that way," Keiphral said, pointing a thumb over his shoulder toward the end of the panicking wagon train behind them. "This way is Elijah and the Veilglorrath."

"Veil-wha—?"

"Whatever power it is that you ripped from the heart of the Storm," Keiphral cut in. "You'd better be ready to use it here. Hurry!"

They sped forward, and the din of battle rose at the front of the caravan. Men were screaming, arrows were flying, and deadly flashes lit the night ahead of them. Dusk

REFUGEES

set his staff in his bandaged hand, and his own grip made him wince. With his free hand, he made to loosen some of his arm's wrappings. They were hot to his touch, as if they had been lain on a rack beside a fire. He hoped for even the slightest relief from the tearing, burning soreness under the skin of his arm. But as he fidgeted, he ran headlong into Keiphral's back. From the ground, Dusk looked up to the older boy, who stood rigid beside the front wain, listening. Keiphral was wide-eyed and gripped his sword with a strangling grasp.

Dusk frowned up at him. "Keiph—"

A man exploded out of the brush and onto the empty road before the two boys. The body skidded across gravel and grass, crashing into the thick trunk of a tree off the road. The resounding crunch of splintering wood and maimed steel left a void soon filled by a silent tide that stunned Dusk and Keiphral. They stared at one another, then the wreckage of man and tree. The fallen man's helm looked to have been beaten from his head, the proud face bruised and scarred. His plate was a hacked, twisted ruin, the mail underneath rent asunder in every spot. Although his body lay crumpled, with his back to the tree, they could tell he was tall and broad. One huge hand still clutched the end of a shattered spear. The other gripped the haft of an axe as big as Dusk, its edge bitten and mangled.

Hair stood on end as Dusk and Keiphral shared the same, ghastly thought, then looked to one another.

"What did *that* to a man like *that*?" Keiphral whispered. But against all reason, the man stirred, then he rose.

"Run," the man said, his voice like a peel of faraway thunder as he gained his feet. Blood streamed from every limb as he set his jaw and threw away his broken spear haft. He took up his axe in both hands, then charged back the way he had come.

Before the boys could breathe, a howl tore through the trees. It was the same shriek that had brought Keiphral racing forward to the front of the train. Following the cry, a hooded figure breached the grove, then darted toward the wounded man. They met with a crash that sent the armored man to his knees. But he swept his axe-blade at the figure's feet, regaining his own. The boys watched in awe as the two fought. Their skill was unparalleled, each of them swinging, hacking, wounding, parrying. Neither yielded a single step, the clash of their weapons filling the air as night-creatures fled for nook and den. But the huge man was worn down, the last of his strength ebbing. Still he fought on, growing sluggish. He no longer pressed the attack, but fell into a defensive posture upon which the slender creature rained down blows, cutting his armor to pieces.

Sweat stung from every pore as Dusk stared desperately at the fight. His mind screamed at him to help, but his feet refused his commands, rooted by terror. He stared wide-eyed at Keiphral, who stood stock-still, frozen by what seemed to be the same fear. But just then, a cry tore from Keiphral's throat, and the young man charged the figure, who seemed cloaked in shadow, with its face covered by shining bronze. The sight, Keiphral's outburst, and the glittering of his elf-sword broke something inside Dusk.

"The m-m-mask I saw when we f-f-fled the Endless Shore," Dusk breathed. Keiphral's courage, and the image of his da, who raced ever toward danger, buffeted his mind. With a growl, Dusk leaped after his friend, leaving fear and pain in dust. He uncovered his burning arm.

The creature struck at the armored man with a heavy, straight blade that seemed too broad and long for so small a wielder. Its ferocity dashed the man to his knees under relentless strokes, and his axe fell away, useless. But before another blow came down, Keiphral swung hard, slashing a flaring line at the figure. The figure disengaged, retreated, and to Dusk, seemed for the first time to hesitate. But as Keiphral pressed his attack, the figure deftly cut away his blade. It made to kill an off-balance Keiphral, but the tall man rose again. Heaving a great shield from its place on his back, the bleeding man slammed it down into the earth, raising a wall of steel between boy and blade. Sword and shield met with a ferocious crash that clove the shield fully in two. But the man lunged forward with his broken half, striking the creature off balance. Turning the lunge into an angry haymaker, the man hammered the masked thing's chest with a mailed fist. The figure's body dredged a new trough in the forest floor before crashing into a thorn bush, a sprawled tangle of limbs.

"I told you to run!" the man roared, catching Keiphral by the collar and retrieving his axe.

"No!" Keiphral shouted, shaking free and fixing his

sword with a tighter grip. Before another shouted word, the creature was up and out of the brambles, leaping at the pair. Man and boy broke apart then fought together, each trading a flurry of blows with the masked swordsman. Keiphral engaged, and the tall man pulled a knife as long as a sword from a great sheath at his boot. Keiphral broke away, then the tall man spun webs of silver in the air, bringing both axe and knife blades to bear against his foe.

Steel whistled, sang, and struck. Together, man and boy drove their enemy back. But before long, the figure struck a blow that left an ugly dent in the man's chest plate, driving him down once more. Then, with three clever swipes of its blade, the masked shadow broke Keiphral's guard, sending his sword flying. The back of the figure's fist cracked across the boy's face, and he went down.

The neck underneath the bronze face bent back toward the fallen mass of the man. The figure readied a killing blow. Its huge sword came down, but Dusk leaped into the fight, fire and shadow consuming his wounded arm and burning his bandages to ash. The masked man's sword struck the boy's thrusting hand, and the blade shattered like glass. The might of the blow sent Dusk slamming to the ground, but he got to his feet with little effort. The power crawling the length of his arm burned, and he screamed, both at it and his assailant. He held aloft his hand, light flickering weakly in his palm. It revealed to him the figure who knelt on the spot Dusk had awarded the savage stroke. One clawed hand lay buried in the dirt to steady itself. The other clutched at its gushing side. Plumes of black blood stained the thing's garb a darker shade of gray. The hood of the creature's cloak had fallen from its head, and the light in Dusk's hand revealed trails of cracks in its mask. Its eyes burned like pyres. Shining white air stood out at every angle from the back of its head, writhing back and forth as if under water. The strands, glowing brighter than daylight, rose every hair on Dusk's arms and neck, but he took a step forward.

"Leave," Dusk snarled, his upraised hand catching new fire as he leveled it at his foe. The creature regarded him with deep eyes filled with fury and awe. Dusk stepped forward, his whole arm now bleeding light and shadow. The creature looked him up and down as if observing the behavior of a wild beast both never before seen and deadly in its unpredictability. Dusk glared back, unblinking. Then the creature rose, keeping one hand pressed to its side. With the other, it clawed up a handful of dirt, but then held it out against Dusk in a warding gesture. Dusk did not move, clenching his teeth against the agony that raked his arm.

With slow grace, the masked figure set its hood back over its head, the flame of its hair snuffed out under oiled wool. It then backed away, step by careful step. When it reached the edge of the clearing, the masked thing drew up to its full height, which was taller than Dusk had first thought.

In a distinct tongue, the shadow-man whispered, "Sith-hyeil, Èanval. Astarryei Belfaerilothe illarn. Itchah gescilla weileth-alessindei fýr-leóma ihn-arwei'ras."

Dusk nodded. But before he could reply, an arrow shot from above struck the mask. The steel tip exploded into fragments off the forehead. The figure lurched back, then vanished through the trees.

Dusk stared after it a moment. Then with a thought, he extinguished the fire that had burned his arm and broken a blade. With his good arm, he dug into his travel pouches for new gauze. He made swift work of salving and wrapping his blistered fingers. He covered his melted palm, then tended his arm up to the elbow. He then ran to Keiphral, who lay curled on his side. Dusk turned him face up and saw yellow-black bruises spreading across half his face. But after placing an ear to his chest, Dusk felt the older boy's steady breathing.

"He'll be alright with your help, lad," Dusk heard a voice boom. "Few can stand against one of those Masked Ones and live. He'll pull through."

Dusk looked up to see the tall man in battered harness standing straight, broken axe at his side. He stared for a moment, then the shouts of fighting rose again all around them. Then a deft, silver-green figure dropped from the trees to stand between him and the battered man.

"What must we do to kill one of those things?" the deft man snarled, pulling off his hood to reveal long, pointed ears and far-seeing eyes.

"Where is Yeiley?" boomed the big man, limping as he gathered up his broken shield.

"I lost track of her when you tackled that masked thing to stop it from killing her," the long-eared man said.

REFUGEES

Dusk noted the colossal bow in the newcomer's off hand, the quiver stuffed with arrows at his back.

"Ethstan!" screamed a familiar, arrogant voice from farther back.

"Del!" Dusk hissed, looking up to see fire and smoke in the sky over the rear of the caravan line.

"I'll look after your friend," the big man rumbled in Dusk's direction. Dusk turned to the strange men. At the lithe one's frown, the big one said, "I'm no more use in this fight. You track down that masked bastard. It's wounded, and you're still fresh. I'll look after this lad. He and this one saved me."

The long-eared archer nodded, looked to Dusk, then turned away to leave.

"Arwë," the axe warrior boomed after him. "Show that thing the meaning of the hunt."

Unsure of the conversation's full meaning but satisfied with the big man's promise, Dusk turned to go, arm throbbing beneath its new bandages.

"Young one." Dusk turned back to see the archer, whose dire eyes were locked to his own. "The Veilglorrum in the mask. It spoke to you?"

Dusk nodded.

"And you understood it?"

"Y-yes," Dusk said as dark clouds loomed on the edges of his vision, threatening to invade.

"What did it say?" the archer asked, his face severe under the frame of long brows.

Dusk shook his head. "It greeted m-me as its equal."

"What else?" the man asked, his eyes bright.

"It c-c-called me a strange word ... Èanval ... ancient one," Dusk said, giving a slow lilt to the word. "It t-t-told me that Belfaerilorn's stars fall, that light conceals the shadow."

"Grim," the man said. "But little more to be done here. Go! Help the caravan's protectors. We will guard your friend, hunt that masked thing." And with a blur, the green-and-gray man jumped into the highest tree. He looked back then down at Dusk one final time. "What's your name, lad?"

"Dusk of Sunreach."

"Dusk of Sunreach. I am called Arwë. We shall meet again."

A ravenous gleam stole over Arwë's eyes as he smiled, and Dusk felt a chill as he disappeared into the trees above. Grateful the green man was gone, Dusk turned to leave, but he saw Keiphral's eyes, wide open and filled with awe. His friend, agitated by pain and something more haunting, stirred in the giant's arms. "Lohrë!" cried the gold-clad boy.

* * *

Ithyeil Stëorra swung her rapier forged from spell and lightning glass. With little effort, she caught a slashing fomori blade on the flat of her own. The beast roared into her face, its black fangs dripping with spittle and filth. She raised her other hand and grabbed its neck in an iron grasp. Its battle shout turned to a blunted scream as fire jumped from her palm and scorched the beast from the inside. She looked into the steaming coals that had been the fomori's eye sockets, dropped its lifeless body, then turned to find her next foe.

All the men are dead, she thought, scanning the bodies of cloaked soldiers and the corpses of lanky fomori and stubby goblins. More came on, and their charging ranks flooded the road. *I'm alone with none but cruel foes for comfort. Where are Tyrith and Arwë? They said they would be close at hand should things go amiss for me. Unless things went amiss for them and more masked men assailed them. Could that have been? I heard a shout while I slept in the wagon. Tyrith's voice? I did feel a dreadful thing close by. Then there was rustling, grunting, and a racket of mail links. Maybe my friends were closer than I'd thought. But no time to think now. More fomori come, and need may force me to reveal my secret fire! I should not release it, but there are at least fifty, and I'm surrounded. No one is here to help me fight—*

"Run!" bellowed a fervent voice. Ithyeil felt a rush of air as something broad and dark shot past her. It crashed down onto the heads of the fomori vanguard. Five or six fomori fell and never rose again, for a trained blade swept up into them, tearing leg and ligament. She took her chance to thrust her fulgurite blade into the swarm, piercing the eye of a goblin. She was busy cutting the throat of another when the dark mass burst from under the clump of monsters, causing more of them to fall and shout. As fomori were buried under their stumbling comrades, Ithyeil stabbed down at their open mouths as they screamed with rage. Her thin sword silenced them forever.

Her foes fell back an instant, and the dark shape in their midst became a boy. "Del?" Ithyeil gasped. "I thought you'd died!"

"I'm the best swordsman in Malas!" Del spat, running the point of his sword into an exposed throat. Then, as if trusting a trained pattern of swordplay, the swordsman pulled back to assume a ready position once again. "I don't die here. *They* do." He struck again, and more fomori fell, gurgling and bloody.

"I fight with you!" she shouted, backing up to him so that their backs touched, and she kept at bay any goblins or fomori who sought to flank him.

"No," he grunted, swinging his blade as he spoke. "Away with you, to the front of the wains. Ethstan will protect you."

"His soldiers are dead, and he may be too!" she cried. "You're all that's left, and I won't leave you."

"Then fight, and stop arguing!" he bellowed. Together, they struck their foes, and fear soon replaced the rage that drove the charging fomori. But more of the beasts poured from the forest and onto the road. And those that quailed under the might of the unexpected swordsman and girl whose hands blistered their flesh, were crushed under the weight of fresher, angrier reinforcements. Ithyeil and Del were soon assaulted from all sides. She watched a crooked knife cleave through Del's armor and into his shoulder. The boy's face contorted with fury. Ithyeil set a hand to the gray arm that wielded the wounding knife, and the fomori's body blazed like a torch. Her victim burned every beast it touched as it thrashed and screamed, trying to escape the devouring fire.

But for every beast they slaughtered, two more lunged in, and the fomori drove them back. Blood soon ran hot and sticky as Ithyeil and Del collected cuts and other wounds. Then Ithyeil watched Del fall to one knee as ten fomori piled on him. He clove upward, stabbing through jaw and into brain, then jabbed his finger into the eye of another, who screamed. A goblin bit Ithyeil's ankle. She kicked free then stomped its head into the ground with the steel-clad sole of her boot. Another sliced her arm with rending claws. She cried out, and with the light of her ancestors coursing through her, Ithyeil poured power into her wounded arm. With it, she gripped the goblin's sharp hand and tore it off at the wrist. But still they came on, beating, hacking, and biting. She could no longer see Del, the lad lying buried beneath the hideous mass. Ithyeil then felt a hundred hands yanking at her concealing cloak.

"Not afraid of you fools," she spat. "But afraid to reveal my light too soon and draw those worse than you. No more for it. Die now, churls!" She made to tug the cloak from her shoulders, to reveal the infinite light that would blot them out like a rushing ocean wave.

But then came a cry, not from a beast but from a boy. And a burning shadow turned all the air into a furnace. The screams of goblins and fomori died upon leaving their throats as voices and bodies were eaten by the shadow.

Ithyeil closed her eyes, throwing herself on the prone form of Del, doing what she could to shield him with her shredded cloak and her power. Then all was quiet, and she looked about. Strewn all about her were the charred corpses of her enemies. Charcoal faces were frozen in visages of agony and terror. She felt Del stir, groaning beneath her, and she released him. Rising slowly to her feet, she started. Before her stood a thing of grim horror. The form was small and cloaked, and its charred arm still lay outstretched toward her, Del, and the corpses of their foes. One last tongue of dark flame smoldered in its palm, and smoke rose from the melted skin of its hand. All the figure's garb from shoulder to hand had been burned away.

"Who are you?" Ithyeil whispered, preparing for another fight as she resisted the dire need to reveal her hidden light again.

"Dusk," the shadow-wrapped figure croaked. "You are Yeiley." Then he wavered and struck the ground and said no more.

15
FIGHT IN THE FOREST

The hunter had caught the hare, and all that was left to do was skin it. The rodent was a clever thing, dashing, dodging, leaping, and hiding, but its life belonged to the hunter.

"Oh no," the hunter whispered to the fly in his web. "No, no, no, you can't get away. Oh, no, no, no, no, no!"

Despite having slain fomori and gurgling goblins, the hunter's quiver lay filled to bulging at his back. The rain he let fall upon his quarry was cold and deadly indeed, and he had stolen many of the enemy's foul darts. From tree to tree the hunter leapt, his feral mind bent on one thought: the blood coursing the veins of this most dangerous game that ran in terror from him.

Every now and then, a stray goblin would cross the bronze-faced man's path below. The man would throw the creatures in his wake as he tore through the forest in his flight from the hunter. At this, the hunter would smile wider, thank his prey for such fomori and goblin gifts, then put an arrow in the eye of each.

Leaf and whirling wind sped by, and the hunter found

that this forest in the Outer-world of Men was not so different from his own Qweth-Wëalda, where the leaves always shone summer-silver and green. But before thoughts of home as it was in more innocent days could invade his instincts, the hunter saw a thinning of trees that bothered his tracking mind. "Too close to forest's edge." He laughed. "Can't have you escape to some hole in the hills beyond. Time to change direction once more and for fear to set in!"

He pulled and released his bowstring amid a jump between boughs. Two of his arrows struck earth mere steps in front of the masked man. They halted the thing's advance, changing his course so that he ran wildly in directions he could not trust. Arwë kept up the hunt, hoping to find a bit of unguarded flesh.

"Tyrith mentioned wounds," he whispered to his enemy as both hunter and masked hunted ran through the murk. "Seems your side is what bothers you. But before I can open it further, I have friends of yours to deal with nearby, waiting in ambush! Clever, should you have chanced to steal away with Ithyeil, hoping to cover your tracks with swords as you fled. But no, no, no, my dear, dead friend. Your plan is killed, and so are your servants. And so too, I'm afraid, are you!"

In his blood-drunk dream, Arwë flung himself into another tree and readied his bow for the slaying of three new targets. The first, a muscled fomori with only one glaring eye, nestled into the hollow of a tree northward. It had an ear pressed to the ground, listening for someone's approach. And when it heard the bronze-face's footfalls

FIGHT IN THE FOREST

racing toward it, it poked its head out for a look at what passed. Arwë's arrow put out its eye, pinning the beast to the tree by its head. His second victim was a fat, little goblin possessed of a lust-filled smile. Hiding under a shelf of jutting rock, its yellow eyes glowered this way and that as it lay ready with a notched knife. Arwë ended its grin forever as his next arrow cut off the goblin's nose completely, and it lay bleeding in the dirt.

The last was a man, of all things, and his presence made Arwë stop to gather himself in the high shadows of a drooping willow. The elf's eyes spied a shield of wood and steel, along with a pair of honed battle axes. A heavy chain haubergeon and a hood of chain and plate protected the man's chest and head.

"Swardha-Mann?" Arwë asked quietly, unsure whether the man was friend or enemy. Given the gloom and Arwë's having overheard the caravan's sergeant mention to the surgeon that he had commanded protectors to lie in wait in the woods, he could not be sure. Anxieties rising as his masked quarry seemed near escaping, Arwë drew out an arrow with a round iron cap, took aim at the sentry.

"Forgive me if you were for me when you awaken," Arwë whispered then let fly. The shaft cut the leaves from a handful of branches, then struck the man between the eyes of his hooded helm. He swayed backward, the back of his head cracking on the bole of the tree he stood under. The armored man only let loose a low grunt, and he slumped down the trunk. There he sat, as if taking a short rest under its breezy eaves.

His distractions quelled, Arwë cast about for any sign of his Veilglorri prey. He saw none but held his breath, waiting. Battle clashed dimly away eastward, but this part of the wood lay quiet, and his long ears worked to gather all noise to him. His own heart drummed loudly, and he forced the power of his ears further abroad, listening for little disturbances or the dripping of black blood on leaf or soil.

Just as fears of his having lost the masked man after his promise to Tyrith rose up in his chest, there came a screech in the dark. The snap and beat of wings accompanied a small flock of little black birds as they flew up and away in fear, driven out of sleep. Seeing his masked quarry scramble up and out of cover after the disturbance, Arwë smiled, preparing three shafts with plate-cutter points.

The masked man's heavy sword still shone, unsheathed in his hand, even as he ran. Arwë aimed his first shot just above the creature's wrist. Bending his bow nearly to breaking, Arwë released. The arrow struck just above its mark. The shaft shattered on the blade of the man's sword with a steely crack. The shot, though high, disrupted his prey's motion, throwing him off balance. Arwë aimed his second arrow at the Masked One's heart, but it glanced off the strange armor he wore, skittering away into the brush. Then, Arwë's third struck true, piercing the exposed gap in the knee joint of the masked man's leg plate. The arrow tore through the thick muscle of his prey's thigh, pinning him to the forest floor. The wail that raged up from below forced Arwë to cover his broad ears, the cry rattling his skull.

FIGHT IN THE FOREST

"So," the elf said, hearing his own voice in his head through his muffling hands. "You feel pain just like the rest of us." But suddenly, the slim creature wheeled his body in a full circle, tearing the arrow out of the ground beneath his leg. Gathering speed, the masked man swung his blade in a wide arc. His rage drove the blade into the trunk of a thick, old oak. The masked man's blade shore right through the tree. It shivered and fell with a thunderous crash. Then the mask's face, forever stuck in a visage of haunting sorrow, turned to the tree in which Arwë perched. The hunter saw cold fury flash in his prey's black eyes.

The Veilglorrum took a shambling step toward the elf, but an arrow cut across his path. Arwë's shot thudded into a new tree, barely an inch from his prey's skull. The man looked for a moment at the shivering arrow, then turned. Light glinted off the scoring mark carved by the arrow's path as it had glanced off the mask and into the tree. The haunted sockets met Arwë's eyes.

Arwë the hunter stood laughing in a frenzy high above, defying the anger of his masked foe. "Come then!" he cried. "You and your wretched ilk have proven you can overpower my friend, who is wasted by devouring disease. But you flee in fear at the sight of a single Qweieth-Sil! Come, my prey. I will mount your head on the Giant's Ring!"

The creature shot toward the tree that held Arwë. He ran as if Arwë's arrows hadn't just gored his leg and nearly taken his eye. But Arwë, judging the masked man's speed and distance, drew an arrow for one final shot. He bent his bow with the strength of his shoulders and sighted down the shaft. He made a single count, holding his breath. The figure's foot struck the roots of the tree, then he leaped into the air, ready to slice Arwë in half for the pain the elf had caused. Arwë watched the sword blade slash through the air toward his neck. Releasing the breath he had been holding, Arwë loosed the shaft. His arrowhead exploded into flaring fragments as it struck the creature directly on the bronze crown of his head. The arrow shaft shivered to pieces. The mask flew from the man's head, and he fell. But his reach had barely allowed his blade to slice through Arwë's bowstring. The weapon flew from the elf's hands.

Arwë drew a pair of razor-sharp daggers, then arced down to the forest floor where the creature fell with a crash. Arwë struck at the man with one dagger, using the weight of his fall for a killing stab. The man heaved his slender form out of the way just in time to avoid being skewered. Arwë's knife stabbed dirt. But the elf's second dagger lashed out, breaking the creature's haphazard guard. But the Veilglorrum, whose gaunt face lay shadowed under the cowl of his hood, used the force of the elf's stroke to push himself away, falling too far back for Arwë to land another stroke with his knife. Instead, the elf snapped out a long leg and his botted foot smashed into the sharp outline of the man's chin, sending him tumbling.

Arwë pursued his foe with blinding speed. He struck and struck, hammering his prey's guard with one dagger, slicing at the exposed throat and stabbing at an eye socket with the other. Arwë possessed the tireless speed

FIGHT IN THE FOREST

and strength of the Qwei-Sillar, honed by two centuries of travel and war. But this thing, unmasked and desperate, regained its footing, threw off Arwë's assault, and pressed him back. Arwë could not understand the source of the creature's power, guarding a stroke that would have taken his head had his dagger not intercepted the whirling blade in time. Arwë heaved himself away from a stab aimed to take his heart. Then his eyes grew wide as the maskless creature turned away his every attack. Anger and fury replaced Arwë's hunting savagery as the creature's blade cut one of his daggers in half, the blade spinning away into the dark. Still Arwë's prey pressed the attack, stabbing and slashing, forcing Arwë to use every limb, muscle, and trick just to stay alive.

Arwë parried a blow, but the creature swung wide and cut the damaged knife out of his hand entirely. Hand now free, Arwë caught the wrist of the man's off-hand in a crushing grip as he overswung and fell past the elf. Arwë bent the joint until it creaked. The man with no mask snarled. Arwë wrenched the wrist, and the figure bent double, exposing his torn side to the elf. But just as Arwë made to drive his good dagger down into the wound, his prey lashed his blade upward, leaving a burning, bleeding line down the side of Arwë's face.

Arwë broke his prey's wrist.

Outrage roared in the amalgam of shadows that was the man's naked face, forcing Arwë to release his grip and cover his ears once more. In a rage, the shambling man threw a kick of his own at the elf's solar plexus to end their entanglement. But by a trick of shadows, Arwë vanished, and in his place hung one of his vicious war arrows. The man's momentum drove his foot onto the bodkin point, impaling it through what the elf assumed to be skin, nerve, and sinew. New howls tore through the fey wood, scattering silver fireflies.

"You lose," Arwë, whispered from behind the trunk of a new tree. The man without his mask writhed on the ground, clutching his foot and screaming his rage at having been bested and wholly abandoned.

His smile now gone with his lust for the chase, Arwë the hunter, grim and tired, drew out his sword. He stepped toward the pitiable, suffering man. Letting his sword fall, Arwë made good on the first part of his promise to let hang a new trophy from the ruined walls of Wildercrown.

* * *

"Lohrë!" Keiphral shouted into the trees, seeing his master flee into the dark beyond.

"Alright, lad," murmured a voice that sounded like the incoming tide.

Keiphral sat up, suddenly noticing the man who knelt beside him, sheltering him. "You're the one who fought the masked man."

The giant, sitting beside his massive axe, gave a tired nod. "My ward lay sleeping in your wagon."

"Not my wagon, sir," Keiphral said. "My companions and I only just joined it a few hours ago."

FIGHT IN THE FOREST

"All the same, she was threatened by that masked monstrosity, and I stepped in to humble it."

"They're dangerous," Keiphral said.

"Met them before, have you?" the big man asked.

Keiphral nodded. "When I escaped Wildercrown."

The huge man leaned forward, blood running from at least twenty different wounds. "You saw the elf city fall?"

"I did," Keiphral said. "Though it is not a memory I care to remember, even to recall and relate news to an enemy of our foes. But yes, I was there, and so were the Masked Ones. One followed me as I fled out of the Qweth-Wëalda. I escaped, but I think the one I fought was weakened somehow. It did not pursue me."

"Then you and I share common enemies," the big man rumbled. "That should be a good enough start to a new friendship." The man tried to stand, but grunted, fell, and caught himself, shifting his weight awkwardly as he descended to his knees again. Keiphral's eyes, having fooled him into seeing a set of spare weapons and a pack filled to bursting on the giant's back, now saw the truth. Lights, both from torch and firefly, lit upon a pair of cracked iron wings, as broad as a man was tall, encasing the giant like a cloak of plate.

"Angel," Keiphral whispered, thinking of words shouted under burning trees.

The warrior half-chuckled, half-groaned. "No angel, only a sinner unmasked by battle. Doubtless you know my kind. Feel free to forget what I said about new friendships, if you wish. I doubt you would want to be seen conversing with a wretch like me. Though, I would ask you share your story after our fight here is done. If not with me, then with the elf you saw springing away just now. He was not Lohrë, as you thought, but Arwë of Wildercrown. What do you know of Lohrë?"

"Seek Arwë," Keiphral recited quietly. "He and the angel guard a treasure most precious."

The huge man froze where he knelt. "And how did you know *that*?"

"Because Lohrë is not dead," Keiphral whispered. He rose to his feet. "At least he wasn't when he commanded me to leave Wildercrown alongside his lieutenant. I last saw him cutting a path to rescue the Elf-lord."

"Such things would not be known to one not of elvish blood," the huge man said in awe. "You must indeed be an elf friend. Please, hold onto this news, then recall it to my companion when we all walk under Last-Hope's towers. For now, I beg you to finish my task: Find my ward, along with your friend, Dusk."

"What happened to Dusk?" Keiphral growled.

"The lad just left," the man said, pointing away, out of the clearing. "He heard the cries of soldiers at the rear of the caravan and went off to find them while I watched over you. You seem less injured than we at first thought."

"No real injuries, only bruises." Keiphral chuckled, rubbing the tender, swollen parts of his face and shoulders. "But who are you, sir? Who was your ward?"

"My name is Nephtyr Ithar-fel, and my ward is Yeiley. We are both friends to the Qwei-Sillar and to the Hidden

City. We were making our way there when the fomori attacked this train. Go to your friend. I would not be surprised to find Yeiley where the fighting is fiercest. If I can stand, I will follow. Until then, go! And bring me news of her wellbeing."

Keiphral bowed. "My name is Keiphral Morne, and by whatever blood that runs in me, I will stand by your ward."

"Be careful when swearing such oaths!" Tyrith grunted. "You may find yourself bound by them in ways more harrowing than you can imagine. Let your sword and swiftness be your promise. Now go."

Sword in hand, Keiphral nodded and ran toward the clamor of men and monsters.

He had scarcely left the clearing when the sounds of crashing steel and singing arrowheads rose all around him. Horses and oxen ran this way and that, trampling confused fomori as they attacked anyone and anything without plan or reason. The beasts of burden, untethered from cart and driver, fled with wild abandon. Keiphral flung himself out of the path of a bear-like beast with many antlers, the likes of which he had not seen pulling cart or wagon when they had met up with the caravan earlier. It raged past him, breaking half the bones in a stray goblin's body with a single swipe of its massive paw.

An arrow struck the wooden slats of a wagon filled with screaming children, just missing Keiphral's face. He checked to make sure the family was safe within, but a thickset fomori tackled him to the growled, clawing at him and biting at his face. With his sword pinned to his chest by the fomori's girth, Keiphral jabbed a finger into the creature's eye, then clubbed it with a wooden beam handed to him by a smiling Anglorean lad. He tousled the boy's white-blond hair in thanks, then ran off again toward the rear of the caravan.

Keiphral saw men and monsters drop, cut down by knife, axe, and arrow. As he ran, he saw a goblin sidle up to a crying bundle, licking its lips and readying a vicious dagger. Keiphral swept the beast's head from its shoulders, returning the baby to her mother, then he ran for the spot where the fighting was loudest. The deep roars of fomori and high screams of goblins mingled with the shouts of whatever men were left of the rearguard. Keiphral, happening upon the bodies of the fallen protectors, feared the worst. But someone still fought at the back of the caravan, and he charged toward the noise. The road suddenly lay choked with burning wagons, and the gaps on either side were blocked by trees closely packed. Keiphral dove under a flaming wagon, pulling himself forward on elbows and knees, hoping his elvish helm would spare his dark hair from the fire.

When Keiphral came up from under the cart, two goblins fell on him, hacking with shortswords. His mail repelled their blades, but the force of their hairy, beating arms buffeted him this way and that. Keiphral fell but severed the stabbing hand of one creature. He wrapped a strong arm around the neck of the other, wrenching it down to the dirt with him. They landed with a crunch as Keiphral drove his whole shoulder into the goblin's sternum. He rolled out of

FIGHT IN THE FOREST

its grasp as it groped for breath, then cut the legs out from the handless one as it ran about screaming and clutching the bleeding stump of its wrist. Staggering to his feet, Keiphral made short, bloody work of his two foes.

He then stood quiet, listening. All had gone silent, and fear drove him with renewed speed toward the end of the wagon train. Bursting through to the last carts and onto piled bodies of men and cart-pulling beasts, Keiphral encountered a stench and sight that nearly made him retch. The dead lay everywhere, slain by blade and arrow. But the sight and smell of fomori and goblins smoking, burned nearly to the bone, forced bile to rise. He fought back the urge to vomit, then something caught his eye. A gentle glow in the midst of the ugly carnage anchored him, and he stepped forward.

The glow shone in the hand of a girl, the same one he and Dusk had seen wrapped in a cloak in the cart only an hour or so before. Her garb was torn all over, and she bled from various wounds, both shallow and deep. She knelt over a small figure. Her gleaming hand gripped his arm, which to Keiphral, far back as he was, looked to be burned badly. He held back the urge to cry Dusk's name, instead coming over quietly to watch the girl work and defend her from any assault should it come from the forest. No enemy came, and Keiphral knelt down beside his stricken friend.

"Well, Dusk," he choked, "I told you you'd better be ready to use your powers here. Seems you did and made sure every single fomori, goblin, and monster that meant the caravan harm is ashes now."

Whatever work the girl had been doing on Dusk's arm looked now to Keiphral to be at its end. She began dressing it, and Keiphral wondered how many times the task had been done in the days since he had met the young shepherd from Sunreach.

When the girl's task lay neatly wrapped and she had positioned Dusk's arm gently at his side, Keiphral smiled. "Is that his gauze?" he asked her. "Funny that he's the healer, yet we're always the ones patching him up with his own tools."

Without a word, the girl rose. She was tall and slender, and Keiphral could discern her pale beauty even under the cowl of her cloak and despite her many wounds. Her shining eyes searched his, and there was some recognition in them. She then turned abruptly, and like the wind over a dark meadow, she was gone.

"Wait!" Keiphral yelled into empty darkness. "Yeiley, one of your companions is safe but hurt. He saved my life and yours. The other hunts a masked man. Come back with us to the city. We go there to fight and to find answers." There was no response, and the girl never came back.

A groan stirred Keiphral out his tired reverie. Another figure lay squirming beside Dusk. His hands, arms, and legs had been wrapped with the same delicate care as Dusk's. He had stirred awake at Keiphral's call.

"Del?" Keiphral said, pulling the blond-haired swordsman up to a sitting position. "What happened?"

"A devil," Del croaked. "We fought the beasts. I killed the most. But the rearguard fell. There were too many, then only I was left. The girl came. We fought together. We were winning, then they overwhelmed us. I fell. They piled on top of me. Then she—no, *he*—" Del indicated Dusk, who lay straight and in a deep sleep. "That little devil called fire and shadow from his palm. He burned them. He burned them alive, all of them. They're all dead. And he would have burned me, if not for her. He's a devil like them! And devils need putting down." Del shoved Keiphral off, picking up the shards of his sword. When he made as if to plunge the broken blade into Dusk's heart, Keiphral shoved Del in the same way, and the swordsman buckled under his wounds and Keiphral's strength. Del hit the ground in a tangle of heavy limbs. But with fire in his eyes, Del staggered to his feet, weapon poised to strike the boy garbed in elvish armor.

"Don't," Keiphral said, leveling the full, untarnished length of his sword at Del's chest.

"He's one of them," Del spat, pointing his jagged blade at Keiphral's chest with one hand. He kept shut some wound at his collarbone that had opened in the tussle with the pressure of his other.

Seeing the blood pool from under the swordsman's bandages, Keiphral lowered his weapon. "Dusk is no devil. In fact, he looks to have saved you and the girl. Come, Del. Let's find a cart with a horse that still lives, and press on, back toward the Hidden City."

"I won't," Del growled. "Not with you. Not with *him*."

"Del!" came the gruff bark of Sergeant Ethstan. "Stay that blade, boy. We've a lesson to teach you in not pointing swords, whole or broken, at friends."

"These are *not* my friends," Del snarled as the grizzled sergeant approached. Ethstan held a spear in one hand and a sharp hatchet in the other. His armor lay about with scores and cuts, and blood ran freely from a new notch at the top of his nose. He leveled the butt of the spear at Del's chest, pushing the boy a little with it.

"Stand down," he said, danger entering his deep voice.

"Sergeant, I—"

"You are needed elsewhere, Del," Ethstan said. "For now, we make the last run to the city tonight. Another attack will kill us all, so we don't wait for the morning. And we go at a run. Shouldn't take us much more than half a day at that pace. Looks like you've been patched up nicely, which is more than I can say for half the soldiery. The fighting was fierce in front, but we threw off the worst. The rest fled screaming after some light from this way drew them off. Looks like you handled yourself well here too.

"Hey, Del! Don't make your accomplishment turn sour. I've got sweet words for the captain concerning Del, our little layabout, should we make it to Last-Hope alive and should you keep a civil tongue. Now, drop that broken piece of scrap, grab a new blade from the dead—with respect, mind you—and we'll be off in five minutes' time. Am I clear?"

"The boy, Sergeant, he—"

Ethstan flung his axe into the dirt where its blade struck in, the haft standing straight. He grabbed the boy by the collar and hauled him close. "Am I clear?" he growled.

FIGHT IN THE FOREST

Del gazed defiantly at the scarred man for moment. Then his eyes fell away. "Clear, sir."

"Good," Ethstan said, releasing the boy. He slapped the shoulder that was not bleeding openly. "Off to it then, lad. Report to the front when you're fully equipped." With a nod, Del set to searching the dead for new gear.

Ethstan then turned to Keiphral. "That giant back there told us about what happened toward the front," he grumbled. "Said you and the healer-lad handle yourselves well in a fight. I've never heard of a *Veilglorrum*, as the giant called that thing that attacked like an elvish devil. But I have heard tell of masked figures being the terror of man and beast in the norther reaches of late. If you two can handle one on your own, I'd still say I've done well by having you two tag along with my merry bunch. We've lost more 'n half our men in this attack and would have lost more 'n that had you and your boy, Dusk, not been here. Whadda you say, Morne? Care to keep watch over my flock while I shepherd them to Last-Hope?"

Keiphral nodded. "I will," he said. "But where is Elijah?"

"The ol' surgeon's tending the wounded, as always," Ethstan reassured. "My lads 'n I took the brunt of the frontal assault and led it away from the train as best we could. Ol' Elijah was right there in the thick of it, taking wounds of his own as he fought at our sides, all while dragging away the wounded. You and your boy, Dusk, would do right by sticking close to that man. He's a favorite of the prince and my captain, though he be the envy of every lord and lady in Last-Hope. Come away now. The train leaves again, and we of the soldiery are going to have to keep up with the carts on foot. These blasted fomori knocked my poor horse dead, Eternity take him."

"Where can I lay Dusk?" Keiphral asked.

"Bring him along," Ethstan said. "The giant went out like a light after he gave us his news. Then it took five of my men to haul him into a wagon. Dusk can lay in that one with him. Hurry now!"

Keiphral hauled Dusk up into his arms. The boy slept, despite the commotion of soldiers and caravanners running about to make ready for the last leg of the journey to Ephtar-Malas. As Sergeant Ethstan led him to the wagon in which Tyrith lay, Keiphral caught Del's glare. The swordsman, amidst other searchers of the dead, drew out the balanced sword of a fallen friend. After examining the blade for balance and sharpness, Del claimed it for his own. Then slowly, he pointed it toward Keiphral and Dusk, glaring at them as they went.

Keiphral ignored the boy's bravado, and after a few minutes, found the wain Ethstan had meant for Dusk. Listening closely to the sergeant's orders, and nodding his concurrence, Keiphral lay Dusk beside Nephtyr Ithar-fel in the wagon led by the same quiet woman as before. Then Keiphral, wrapping his elvish cloak close about him, set off to make ready for the last run to the Hidden City.

16

HIDDEN CITY FOUND

Dusk stood high on a tower that overlooked a city carved from precious stones. Clouds buffeted one another before a wide expanse of dying daylight, casting the sky in violet and gold. Far below, a battle raged. Stones broke, shields thudded, and walls came crashing down. But he was the light, and he saw the shadow gathering far down on the wall. The growing dark was a danger, but it could not be contained. It burst forth, hungry and horrifying. But from the tower, he called the light, and the light came, beaming in the heavens. Light guided shadow, and together they ruined the seething ranks of assailants as they stormed wall and city. But, though gorged and bloated on the blood of a thousand screaming beasts, still the shadow wanted more. It turned toward the city, leering lustfully at its shining walls and all its people. But the light would not let it have them.

Then a frail voice cut through the chaos. "The storm," it said. It was a man. "It rages on my very doorstep, and I cannot resist it. How many others suffer like me? Will

I ever wake again? Where are my fighting men? Do they win the battle? When will my surgeon return and free me from this living death? I do not want to die, but if I do not escape soon, all the lives in my care will perish, and I should be hacked to pieces, even in my bed. Help me."

But Dusk could not heal or help. He had thrown his skills away, traded them for all-consuming power. Instead of wrapping, sewing, and salving wounds, he instead peeled away the wraps of his false arm. As each dressing fell, the fire inside him burned hotter, brighter, until the last of the wrappings withered into smoke. There was the shadow living upon his fey arm. It was ravenous, maniacal, and ready to devour *more*. Fomori were not enough. It craved the flesh of humans, forcing him to look back to the city as it burned. As he looked, the shadow bit his arm with barbed fangs. Dusk screamed and screamed.

Dusk gasped as he awoke, clammy and shivering. He moved at great speed, but not of his own will. Feeling his neck ache at a twisting strain, he touched the back of his head, feeling a familiar, cold smoothness. "Sleeping again with the h-h-helm on my head," he groaned. "Dream upon d-d-dream of awful things."

"You're alright, Dusk," said the stern voice of Elijah. Through eyes bleary with sleep, Dusk thought the man looked sad, ashamed almost. "Have some water." The old surgeon thrust a capped wooden cup under Dusk's nose.

Shuffling up to rest on his elbows, Dusk took the cup and gulped down several mouthfuls of cold water enriched with herbs. He sighed as he took the cup's rim away from his mouth. Setting it down with a thump, he looked up at the sky whose black and purpling clouds threw a shredded cowl over the wan light of day. "Where are we?" he asked. "What time?"

"Still on the road," Elijah grunted. "The attack ended some hours ago, and dawn came up not long ago. You've done real harm and set fear in the hearts of our travel companions, perhaps revealing too much of who you are and our true purposes. But I think some of these things are on the mend, at least for some of those who saw you slay our fomori foes."

"Harm and purpose?" Dusk asked. "What p-p-purpose do you have for m-m-me, Surgeon?"

"That remains to be seen, given your answers and skills, when I ask for them," Elijah snapped. "All in good time, though. As for the hard planks under your back, you've been put safely into a wagon that makes a final sprint for Ephtar-Malas. The horses are driven to exhaustion, but we are nearly there, and you should see its outer walls before noon. Though, do be mindful of your hurts as you rise again. If you continue calling upon that burning power of yours, we're going to run out of salves and gauze for your recovery. See to it you don't call upon it too often. Though I know you used it rightly both times—against the Veilglorrum, then in service of the Nephtyr's young charge."

"So, that m-m-masked fighter *was* one of the V-v-v—"

"Yes," Elijah said with a tired sigh.

"And Nephtyr," Dusk said, turning to look at hulking form of the angel-man who lay beside him. "He f-f-fought the—"

Nodding, the old man, bearing his own share of bruises and patched cuts, stooped over Dusk. He applied bandages and balm to hurts that stung badly, even in dreams. "I'm not done with you yet. But yes, the Nephtyr, once the worst betrayers and power seekers all. They work now through one of their best to atone. And he keeps watch over a mighty gift. That's all I can say for now. But know that you've done well by the people here. And you've protected something precious, though the world may never know what that thing is."

"What of the Veilglorrath?" Dusk asked, sitting up. "You half-answered the question on the C-c-coast. But you d-d-distracted me with t-t-talk of my m-m-mother before t-t-telling me who they are."

Elijah sighed. "Dark things. I'm sure you remember me wishing not to discuss them, even under daylight. But now it cannot be helped. They are upon us, no longer just a rumor of fear. In the elf tongue, they are named *skyrenders*, who once were elves, Men, even Nephtyr. They shed whatever humanity once belonged to them and bargained their souls for power given by seven wise ones. These wise ones, in the most ancient of days, betrayed all living things and the One who made them. They wrought havoc across the Outer-dark. Do not ask me what became of those betrayers, for I do not know. But a small remnant of their servants, the Veilglorrath, came to Leóhteness-Fal with us, along with one of the fallen wise ones, said to be imprisoned here somewhere. It is said the Veilglorrath wait in the shadows for the return of their wise one. Their sudden reemergence in strength, at the head of these fomori armies, troubles me."

Grogginess and fear fled at the chance to question the old surgeon, so Dusk untied his helm. He set it beside him on the floor of the trundling wagon. Shaking his head, he let the cool, morning wind tousle his hair. He breathed deeply then, preparing his next question. "Who are you *really*, Elijah?" he asked. His amber eyes studied the surgeon as the man finished binding the last of his cuts. "Since I m-m-met you, I've n-n-nearly been cut and killed by m-m-monsters that you and Keiphral s-s-seem to know all about. I'm g-g-guessing I'm in for m-m-more than just healing practice when w-w-we arrive in the Hidden City."

Elijah snorted at that, finishing his work on Dusk. He then moved to the winged warrior. "I am called many things," he said. "Elijah ben Ath-Sweiord, *who-wounds-with-sword*, was my name long ago. Elijah Ge-Cnaewë, *the-knowing*, is my name for those convinced I know something of the world. Elijah Wrathmod or Elijah Formoth-Slaga, both meaning *the slayer*, was my name to a few. *Surgeon* and *healer* suit me best these days. Though Elijah ben Ath is best, for *wounds*, both dealt and healed, concern me greatly."

"Elijah ben Ath," Dusk said. "How came you to b-b-be known by the other n-n-names?"

"Earned, one and all," Elijah said sternly. "And I've entertained your curiosity for the time being. Should you be granted the chance, you'd have my whole life's story in your possession, holding it for ransom amongst your horde of things better left unknown for a boy your age. Now, I think, is as good a time as any to hear of your encounter with the Storm and what brought you to it. I chased after the rumor of you for a long time."

"Very well," Dusk sighed, disappointed. He watched a moment as stone, water, and tree rushed by. The sky overhead was a deeply bruised blue flecked with gold, and leaves turned in the wind. They flew up and away, toward his home in the peaks, miles and miles high, nearly lost to sight. Their slopes faded in a fog of purpling gray as they were diminished by lengthening distance and weakening daylight. "Even morning's f-f-full brightness only shows us the l-l-long shadows of twilight," he mused, forgetting the old surgeon for a moment. Then a thought stung him. "Where is Keiphral?"

"I'm here," the tall lad said, trotting up to the wagon with the clear ringing of his mail. "I'm to watch the middle of the wagon train while Ethstan and his veterans protect the front. Del and our concealed bowmen guard the rear. Figured now was a fine time to check up on you and our winged friend." His eyes flicked to the stricken warrior in the wagon with Dusk. Ten feet tall at least, Nephtyr Itharfel lay beside his broken plate. Elijah had begun encasing him in gauze wrappings.

"A fine time indeed," Elijah agreed. "I'll have the

whole tale of Dusk's wanderings from both of you in turn. Now, before we are interrupted by news or some other invading devilry, out with it, beginning with Dusk." He pointed to the smaller boy, who nodded.

"Fair's fair," Dusk said. His luminous eyes focused on the fading cap of a faraway mountain as he lost himself to memory. "*Greatest in all the world*, they c-c-called me. Although I'd r-r-rather have both my parents alive and w-w-well over titles and p-p-praise. Da left years back. He s-s-said a storm was coming. It would blot out the whole w-w-world, given the ch-ch-chance. He said to be strong, b-b-both to Ma and me. Then I heard a s-s-scream one day m-m-months later. I came back to our c-c-cottage to find her stricken on the f-f-floor. She was s-s-sick, deathly sick. And in my t-t-trying to help her, that's when the p-p-praise began.

"*My* purpose, both then and now, is and was, to heal her," Dusk continued. "From h-h-high up on the darkest meadows of Sunreach, where the w-w-world's light is t-t-too weak to shine, to Glacial Waste now melted, and as far as the s-s-sands of Belrath'ir, I s-s-searched for the cure to her d-d-deadly sickness."

"And that's where your legend began in earnest," Elijah said. "From Hel-Cyriheil, tallest mountain of the North, to Qweth-Coss by the sea, rumor spoke of a bronze-eyed boy who cured the sick better than surgeons!"

"Not just those p-p-places," said Dusk. "But as f-f-far as Quarredhon of the Bolg and the chasms of Weileth, where h-h-hammers strike in the deep without cease. I cured all those I c-c-came across. Most were g-g-grateful. Some hated me for letting their loved ones d-d-die. Others followed me, hoping to learn, only to f-f-fall away disgusted when they saw me simply stare and t-t-talk at plants. But that's how I l-l-learned.

"In listening, I began to h-h-hear. In hearing, I could think. Then they would r-r-respond. I f-f-felt myself grow feral, and flowers y-y-yielded to me nectar, berry, root, and remedy. Thirst and hunger never troubled. I w-w-went without provision. I worked through s-s-sleepless nights and endless d-d-days. I needed a cure. Nothing h-h-helped her. But what medicines I made, I sh-sh-shared with people of my village, the high forests, and p-p-people of the lower places in the w-w-world.

"They ate and d-d-drank of my potions, herbs, and poultices. Men, women, and children g-g-grew strong again. Some ... s-s-some even answered my call back to life when I c-c-cried to them across the shadows. I grew more and m-m-more feral, but Aryka was always there, taming me back to m-m-my humanity. Then v-v-visitors started coming to the c-c-cottage. Most were f-f-from my village at first. But soon they came up from the l-l-low countryside and neighboring k-k-kingdoms. Then they came from countries far and wide, p-p-places I'd never even s-s-set foot. I s-s-suppose I'd made a name for myself.

"But a name wasn't *enough*," Dusk spat. A dark edge suddenly kept his words from faltering. "Daily she died, getting worse and worse, and me failing and failing. Until

HIDDEN CITY FOUND

I found the secret of the Storm and went there, knowing the way almost entirely."

"That's when I found him," Keiphral said, breaking the silent rhythm of his trot beside the wain.

Dusk nodded again. The shadow that had stolen across his face a moment before lifted, and he was himself again. "I walked the Endless Shore, h-h-humming songs and spells. The s-s-sea sang with me, joining its v-v-voice to mine. I suddenly remembered s-s-scenes of battle and glory that once s-s-stained the shores of a darkened world. The song I s-s-sang with the sea spoke of Elderlight. My da once said the name, but he never m-m-mentioned more. The s-s-song told of great ones c-c-coming to Leóhteness-Fal from across time and tide, devising a trap s-s-set for an ancient horror. When it sprang, the great ones f-f-found themselves just as caught and cornered, sparing their w-w-world from the horror, but now sharing this one with it."

"But what's that got to do with the Storm?" Keiphral asked.

"G-g-getting there, Keiph," Dusk said, a wry smile splitting his severe features. "The song s-s-said that, when the great ones threw the horror d-d-down, with its last breath, it cast a lesser f-f-fraction of its power away. It escaped over the blackened w-w-waves before a final blow could be struck. So, to the entire, darkling world, those that were left after that b-b-battle swore an oath. The last living g-g-great ones, immortal and wise, were mariners, b-b-both of earthly sea and Outer-dark.

Victorious but broken-hearted at having left Elderlight, they bound the r-r-remnant of the horror's power to the sea. They did it with their final s-s-strength, then vanished forever."

"Hunters of the Six," Keiphral blurted. Surgeon and healer both looked to him. "'They departed then for the *Star-sea*.'"

"No doubt Keiphral Morne has heard a fragment of this tale from his elvish hosts," Elijah mused.

Keiphral gave a vague nod but said nothing else as he seemed to consider something.

"I sang into the Storm, thinking of my p-p-parents, as its black clouds descended on me," Dusk continued. "I g-g-guess I made an alloy of my parents' memory and the ancient s-s-songs. For some reason, then, I r-r-remembered my plants and flowers t-t-too. Their memory amplified my s-s-song. My v-v-voice rang out over the waves but sh-sh-should have been drowned out in the roaring."

"I heard it!" Keiphral said, roused from his reverie. The metal rings of his mail created a musical rhythm of their own as he plodded along beside Dusk's wagon. "There was you, then another voice; the sea itself maybe. It took up the verse when you seemed unable. It sang back to him, Elijah! The sea sang back! It matched his sadness. The sound was beautiful and fierce. It bid him face the endless water. Out from the elf-woods and through the Dread Coast Storm I struggled. I was half-awake, half in delirium. But then I saw Dusk standing in the rampage, humming, transfixed on the shore!"

Shadow flooded Dusk's eyes again, and he looked troubled. "I didn't expect the l-l-longing for power and vengeance that r-r-reared up in front of me," he said. "I should have, seeing as I s-s-stood at the eye of a Storm. The only m-m-memory I bore then w-w-was the love of my father and mother. I thought of l-l-living the same life as them, and p-p-passing on the right things. But against that l-l-love, the power h-h-hidden by Storm and wave exploded."

"That I saw too!" Keiphral said. "A colossal flood mounted up from the depths. Blackened waters raced up to smite Dusk. There was a terrible scream. But like an ancient rock immovable, I saw Dusk there, and the wave broke over him. But even as it washed backward, the surge swirled and churned and gathered new strength from the ocean. It meant to lash the shore, engulf Dusk in a maelstrom! But he held out an arm to catch all its might in his hand."

"The power was all in a f-f-fury," Dusk said. "The w-w-water touched my mind, hoping to d-d-drown me, but instead, I bound its melody and m-m-memory to me."

"Then all was calm again!" added Keiphral. "The ocean retreated, pure, salty, and powerless. The clouds above parted and went away. And Dusk, dark and powerful, laughed. But the power he held delivered him a blow from nowhere. Out of the water and into his body, the shadow hoped to devour Dusk whole! It tore his flesh, and all I remember is more screaming. That's when I rushed in with my sword to see what service I could be to this man I'd never met but who needed my help. Even as I got there, Dusk thrashed the sand and flung his arm to the sky. Fire and lightning screamed down one last time. It struck him, Elijah!"

"The l-l-last breath of it charred my arm, sealing the p-p-power to it," Dusk said through gritted teeth as he rubbed at his bandages. "In the end, I hadn't f-f-found my mother's c-c-cure; I'd fought, subdued, and stolen it. And before all this is o-o-over, Elijah, I will go back to Sunreach and t-t-try this power on her." He glared at the surgeon as if daring him to contradict him.

"And to think, you knew and did all that with only a few old songs sung by your da as your guides?" Keiphral asked.

Dusk shook his head, turning from Elijah to face his friend. "I told you. It was sh-sh-shown to me."

"How?" Elijah asked, cocking an eyebrow.

"This," Dusk said, grabbing up his da's helm. "My da p-p-passed it down, saying it would help at n-n-need. I p-p-put it on, and it showed me the r-r-remedy I gave to my m-m-mother."

Keiphral eyed the helm, as if trying to recall some half-remembered memory.

"Indeed," Elijah said, studying the helm in Dusk's hands.

Dusk nodded, caressing the burnished steel. "I don't know h-h-how, but it showed me the w-w-way when I was l-l-lost in the labyrinths of Eilath Rut, in T'Rhonossarc. It s-s-sent me a v-v-vision of my da, far away and under the earth."

With his eyebrow cocked up again, Elijah glared at Dusk as if seeking the truth or falsehood of Dusk's story in the lad's face. The old man huffed then. "Very well. Prove to me my trust was well placed."

"Sir?" Dusk said.

"Let's see what you're made of," Elijah said. "You proved to Morne, the travelers, and me that you are powerful. Rumor and evidence both say you can call down smiting fire to burn up your enemies. You've yet to show me your skill with scalpel and herb. I want to see you mend. Then will I trust you with more of *my* story and purpose. Perhaps I'll teach you how you may be able to bend more power, both toward the burning of foe and to the healing of the one dearest you."

Dusk again studied the old surgeon's face, wondering whether some trick was being played on him. Under the tall man's stare, he looked away, considering. As he turned, Dusk thought he discerned a shadow moving in the tree-shade beyond the road. He saw a rippling, heard the snap of cloth, and could have sworn a thick, gray cloak vanished right then into the thickets. But it could just as easily have been the waning light and a stir of the wind in an unfamiliar place. He turned back to Elijah, Keiphral, then away from both. He gave a single nod.

"Good!" Elijah barked, clapping his hands. "We've still a few hours before we reach the city's gate, even at the pace the sergeant has set. Until then, you have full command of my stores of leaf, herb, and root. My tools too. See what you can do to help the sick and injured. I've already passed word that you are my newest surgeon, seeking the city to study and distill new cures for the Wasting Sickness. Convincing, and close enough to the truth. Now, prove me right. To work!"

"I'll go with you to each cart," Keiphral said as Dusk filled his belt pouches and pack with the surgeon's supplies. Elijah jumped down from the wagon then waved to the lads as he made off to find the sergeant. "I need to stop at each one to check on our travelers," he continued. "Come along! It may prove interesting if nothing else."

With a grunt, Dusk hopped down from the wagon, giving Tyrith one last glance. The angel-man looked the pummeled way Dusk had felt under the Storm's thrashing. He hoped for the warrior's swift recovery. But with boots back on the ground and walking, Dusk looked up to Keiphral. He felt bolder next to the bigger boy, and his attention went to those who needed tending. "That one f-f-first?" he asked, pointing down the wagon train as wains wheeled by. Keiphral nodded, and they set off at a run toward the first of Dusk's trundling charges.

The hour following dawn was quick and not as unpleasant as Dusk had expected. His first charges were the children of the wagons. Some were frightened by the battle while others had recovered quickly, laughing and playing games under cover of sheet and tarp. All of them pointed and stared at Dusk's golden eyes, and some jeered at him because of them, even while he worked to heal them. He treated them all the same, with tenderness paired with firm instruction, rough hands, and at times a harsh voice. Not all of them liked him in the end, but the scraps of dark that lay behind the glow of his eyes commanded respect from all. He set fractures, cleaned cuts, and treated the sick, ensuring good work done with haste, for he knew he was needed most in the carts that were loudest. Those ones, farther down the train, bore the soldiers. The men inside had banded together against fomori and other threats to ensure this little vestige of civilization in a world gone to chaos saw the safe end to its long road.

Dusk climbed down from a large wagon driven by a lively Midlothean family of eight who had settled in the desert only to be displaced a few years later by the havoc of the cataclysms there. He waved to them before making his way to the first of the carts that bore the wounded. Groans of pain and screams muffled by close watchers and friends reverberated from the wagon. Dusk checked the fastenings of his helm, making ready to jump up inside the swift-moving wagon. As he ran beside it, matching its pace, he called upon the melodies of regrowth he had learned from all living things. He hummed the tunes such things had taught him. And with the green of spring and golden daylight in mind, he called also the shadow. With his permission, the ravenous power that had taken his arm and slain some hundred fomori in the battle of wains squirmed under his skin. He willed it to the surface. Even concealed by Elijah's dressings, his arm gave off a faint glow. But caring little for who noticed, up he jumped, and under the wagon's cover he went.

Soaked bandages and ugly gashes gleamed a shade of red with which Dusk was all too familiar. His heart hurt to see that these fighting men were barely men at all. Most were little older than he was. Some, dressed in full chain and leathers, had seen *fewer* summers than he had. But, calling for what tools were available, Dusk went to work with a set jaw and a mind only concerned with mending. Those who looked on saw a strange light surround the one whom they had taken for a simple shepherd boy from the darkling peaks southward. By his command, wet lacerations closed. By his hand, skin and muscle torn asunder lay neatly sewn. He did what he could to comfort those whose bones had shattered under goblin hammers. When done with these, Dusk commanded those less injured to hold down their flailing friends while he set grisly breaks that made even the hardest veterans among the soldiery go pale.

Keiphral came by when he could from his patrols. He brought news to Dusk concerning which injuries were to be found in which carts. The lad, even clad in his elvish chain, would run off to fetch clean water and rags or help remove wooden splinters from skin with his honed knife while Dusk stitched up worse wounds. Dusk was glad of the big lad's help, finding true good nature in Keiphral's sense of duty. There was also an eagerness to help in Keiphral that seemed to Dusk to go beyond quiescence. Del, in contrast, though held tightly together by Dusk's sutures and gauze, marched in between the wagons with less honorable intent. Instead of offering help, the swordsman seemed to visit each wain in which Dusk applied his craft, simply to stare and sneer at the younger boy. Dusk ignored him, letting his own sense of duty speak for him. And in this way, the morning passed quickly.

Hours of work left Dusk wrung out, and he had found a little covered cart in which to sneak away. He sprawled across the wooden slats, escaping the moans of the suffering and demands of those concerned. Even as morning's light waxed to its tenuous noontime zenith, he lay thinking, near to sleep.

He had called upon more and more of the shadow to bolster his fading strength during his work. As he did so, a sense of familiarity accompanied its strangeness. That familiarity had grown, and now the shadow was taking a little more control as he faded further into the reaches of his mind. He yielded more trust to the power he had pulled from the Storm, giving it authority over him. His mind, tired though watchful from its perch in faraway places, noticed a personality crawling forth from it. And at the core of that personality was derangement. Dusk's songs of light and life grew quieter, overwhelmed by savage whispers, desires for sudden violence and the silencing of the loud screams nearby. But, remembering his parents, Dusk resisted those dark desires and came fully back to himself.

His mind returned to the fore at just the right time, for the helm chose his moment of strife to stab him with a harsh whisper.

Dusk approaches: Dusk over all the world, forever! the

whisper said. Alarmed, Dusk called upon both the power that lay under his bandages, and his songs of healing, for stability. But he could not reach them. He could only listen, arms pinned to his sides. The voice came again, this time as a chorus. *We have heard tell of your journeys, Heir of Tryllyë. Come to help Malas the Great, have you? That is good, as my promise to stay hid wanes with False-light. My charity is almost spent, gnawed by time and negligence. Ha! Darkling Days approach again, and when they do, and light is gone, oh, we shall eat and eat and eat. This place was not mine in the beginning, but what luck! Punishment turns to greatest reward, and Nephtyr are to thank. Take heed, for Dusk is what you stand against, and Dusk falls, relentless. Oh, how it falls, and it will eat you, and the Light-fearers shall take up the victorious cry. But go now into your city. Enjoy while you can, Heir of Light. Find me, and free me, for you must. Dusk lays its black blanket over Leóhteness-Fal, and you shall play your part. For light shall never fully die, but it shall open doors into Dusk!*

Dusk started awake, looking about. Wind passed through his little wagon, and birdsong twittered in the silvery trees without. Wan daylight shone through the boughs in small blazes of platinum and gold. Air fluttered in, fresh and cool on his face, but all was otherwise still.

"We've stopped," he whispered, sitting up, rubbing his eyes. He peeled back the wagon's cover and started again, finding the long face of Elijah ben Ath as the surgeon was making to poke his head in. He stared at Dusk with stern, gray eyes.

"I've come to collect you," the surgeon said. "I need you at the front of the caravan. But first, some final explaining to do—for my part, not yours. You put my ingredients to good use."

"It is what I am g-g-good at," Dusk said.

"I see that now," Elijah replied, smiling. "I searched high and low for you in the mountains, expecting half the stories to be smoke, the other to be rumor. I never thought I would actually find the man whose quality came close enough to match such lofty praise. Then I found him, and he walks a narrow line, balancing a righteous heart and hardened skill against ravenous power."

"I care nothing for power," Dusk snapped.

"And that is why I need you," Elijah replied.

"I s-s-seek a path home, to m-m-my mother," Dusk said firmly. "Not to fight wars for Ephtar-Malas."

"Eissyr will remain stable for a year and a day," Elijah said. "And that which I gave her is the closest thing there is to a cure for the Wasting Sickness at any rate. You have found power, but not a remedy. And the storm that tears at Ephtar-Malas shall soon blast all the world, should the city fall."

"That's why I n-n-need to go back," Dusk said. "I have both remedy *and* power. Healing song *and* p-p-power to amplify it all the m-m-more. I n-n-need to be with my p-p-people and my mother."

"You wield a power older than the earth itself," Elijah said. "It was meant to stay where it was, imprisoned—part of its power at any rate. And you stole it."

"With intent t-t-to do something g-g-good with it."

"No good can come of it, Dusk, only misery in the end," Elijah said. Then his features softened. "Such was my first thought regarding such things. So, with such convictions, when I saw so mighty a fighter and healer, contesting with the might of ancient evil on the Dread Coast, my plan was to kill you."

Dusk's eyes narrowed at the surgeon, and he sent a message with his mind to the crawling shadow that lay squirming beneath his bandages. *Be ready.*

"Then I simply found two lads," Elijah continued. "Two lads whose friends or families I knew, whose good nature gave me pause, even in the presence of such danger made manifest, and foes chasing. So, I trusted you, a little. But that trust proved treacherous."

Dusk frowned again.

"I came running to the rear of the wain-battle," Elijah said, "and there you stood, hand held aloft, scorching fomori with fire and darkness. I nearly killed you then!"

Dusk's amber eyes flicked to his bandaged arm once more, and it grew hot. *Nearly time.*

"But I decided against that judgment," Elijah said. "Between tending my patients, I watched as you cared for your own. Never have I seen such skill and gentleness, nor such resolve in keeping so great a terror in check."

"Elijah," Dusk said, releasing the shadow's attention. His arm cooled. "The st-st-stories about the b-b-battle on the C-c-coast, the ancient M-m-men chasing the m-m-monster across the s-s-sea—"

"All true," the surgeon said. "I'm sure you've heard all manner of hysteria and deception concocted by the Nephtyri Hegemony to keep all the realms from believing. But yes, the thing you fought by sea's edge was a remnant of one who was once so much greater and more terrible than any ever seen by Nephtyr or Kindred. Any sliver of power from one such as that is mighty indeed. So much so that no one dared challenge it until you, in your desperation."

"I n-n-needed to save her," Dusk whispered.

"I know, Dusk," the man said, holding up a hand. "I don't blame you. A watch was set on those shores, and it has, apparently, gone missing. The Qweth-Wëalda is burning to the ground, and Anglorost is raped by the Swardha-Menn. The deserts are destroyed, and my city lies at the center of all. Fell things are waking, Dusk. And you now play a chief part."

"M-m-me?"

"You," Elijah said. "As I said, you bear both skill and power. And in your healing work, I saw a heart devoid of malice, whose only wish was to do right by his family and others. That, you shall do, unequivocally. And the power you possess, though it be a thing of shadow, may prove a great ward against our enemies."

"What are you s-s-saying?" Dusk asked.

"That my home, its thousands just like you, your mother, your friend Keiphral, and all those children, women, and men, all need you, Dusk. And I have dire need of surgeon and soldier both. Will you not come with me, now that the danger has passed some? Help here, stem the tide of battle from a place of strength, then return home. If it's any consolation, I have ordered the paths up to your mountain fortified, strongly, though quietly. Your people will be safe while you care for mine."

"Elijah ben Ath," Dusk said carefully, "I ask you ag-g-gain: Who are you, that you m-m-may order the muster of soldiers and the b-b-building of fortifications in a realm r-r-ruled by a prince?"

"Come with me, and I will show you!" Elijah said, throwing back the wagon's canvas. Afternoon's golden light seared Dusk's eyes, forcing him to cast his good hand over them. When the glare and pain dissipated, he looked up. Against the gilded sky shone a mountain, split down its center as if rent by a blast of lightning in ancient days. Down from the broken mountain marched towers and winding walls carved from shining stone. Houses and great halls crowded around the mountain as well. Mighty courts lay chiseled into shaded recesses. Each level of the city met the others, connected by networks of bridges that shone like pearls. Water flooded down the mountain in streams of silver. It fell freely here, gathered in cisterns there, or flowed down the tracts of interconnected aqueducts. Turrets, whose caps shone of copper, bronze, amber, and opal, glowed with some inner radiance, even in the diminished light. And before the head wain of the caravan, in ominous contrast to the bright city, yawned a gate of sable stone, guarded by cloaked sentries.

Before such glittering spires, and the high, imposing

HIDDEN CITY FOUND

outer wall that crawled with soldiers in gleaming plate, Dusk swallowed hard. Here lay the last island he had seen in dreams that had been surrounded by a ravening ocean of spears whose tide had not yet come in. Here was where need had driven him, truly, and where he would find his answers. "I will go with you."

17
LAST-HOPE BELEAGUERED

"How tall is it?" Dusk asked of the gleaming wall that crowded all the horizon.

"Nearly a hundred feet at the lowest," Elijah replied. "Thick enough for three men to walk abreast. And that's just speaking of the outer wall. Should the city ever be breached, there are many gates and bridges across which her people may flee, each one more treacherous to take than the last. The Rhonoss Lords long ago built the city in an act of final service. Ephtar-Malas stands as a monument to the victory of the Kindreds and as tower of watch should that which they defeated ever return in force."

"Rhonoss," Dusk said, considering the word. "Del called this l-l-land the Rhonoss Arch when he s-s-stopped us." Dusk saw the sword-boy sneer as he and the last of the rearguard joined the front of the caravan. Dusk was surprised at the lad's ability to overhear anyone's use of his name in such commotion.

"Yes," Elijah sighed, "It's hard to believe, but that sword swinging layabout comes from renowned stock. He used the old name for what we now call T'Rhonossarc, whose foundations were carved by the Rhonoss Lords of old before their vanishing. It was the Qwei-Sillar and Midlotheans, who, keenest of eye, spotted the broken mount during a great battle and retreated there under heavy assault. What they found was an old fortification built into the cracks. So, in that dire battle, those Kindreds looked down and shot their foes with arrow and dart. With such deadly support, Angloreans and Suthesturri, with the Rhonoss and Nephtyr to lead them, fought a battle across these hills and valleys, whose like is never again to be seen in this world.

"The battle was won. But as an unfamiliar peace settled across this alien world, the Midoltheans, with the Rhonoss, founded the city as a light of hope and place of refuge. At the same time, the Angloreans went away west, and the Suthesturri journeyed south, each seeking new lands to call their homes. But highest in honor, and grievously wounded by their sacrifices, were the Qwei-Sillar. Men in this new world gave elves leave to name all things in Leóhteness-Fal before their departure to the forests of the North. So, this city, precious to all the Kindreds, is named *Hidden City* by Men, for it lies in a valley encircled by mountains, rivers, and hills, with no direct road of entry. But its true name is Ephtar-Malas, which is *Last-Hope* in the elf tongue. For had the Qwei-Sillar and Midlothean Men not seen and mounted its ruin when hope forsook them, the war would have been lost. And I pray now that we who have inherited such a seat of glory may defend it as our enemies multiply and hem us in from all sides."

Dusk looked away from Elijah, seeing Keiphral approach with a few other men of the caravan guard. The lad stood awestruck before the resplendence of Ephtar-Malas, whispering, "*Raise the alarm at Last-Hope. Tell the sentries the elves, and they, are invaded.*"

"We will, Keiphral Morne," Elijah said. "Though there is nearly as much within that would threaten my city's safety as without. For though it has always been well-manned and provisioned, strange ideas come down from the upper districts. Brain-addled nonsense tells the people to tear down the sensible foundations of our society—foundations that have kept us prosperous and at peace. As war looms and the captains set rules for the city's defense, the comfortable people seek only comfort over right action. Some of us try to keep those who fancy themselves rulers in the prince's absence in check."

"Absence?" Keiphral asked.

Elijah looked away as if having heard his name called from afar.

Dusk grunted, drawing Keiphral's attention back. "Nothing I've ever d-d-done has come easily or been c-c-comfortable," he said. "Hopefully the r-r-resistance I've faced, the damage to my b-b-body, has forced me to grow s-s-stronger."

"The same for me," Keiphral said. "Though perhaps we've only grown a little stranger in this strange world that I still know so little of."

"No m-m-matter the growth," Dusk said. "It's all been for the b-b-better, I think."

"We hope," Keiphral said, giving Dusk a wry grin.

"We hope," Dusk replied, smiling in response.

"Ah, don't listen to me prattle on about politics and princes just yet," Elijah said with a sigh. "Just know that cooler heads have prevailed for the time being. But I do not know how cool they will stay once the enemy that burned Wildercrown surrounds us on all sides. For now, stay hidden in our crowd of refugees. But be ready to step forward when called. I fear even entry to the city may prove difficult."

The wagons and beasts of the sprawling caravan were already trundling under the city's imposing entrance. Dusk and Keiphral went among the travelers. The boys checked in on those whom Dusk had mended, ensuring bandages and sutures had not shifted or torn. They went to the wagon containing Nephtyr Ithar-fel. The angel slept soundly. Between visits to family and fighter alike, Dusk and Keiphral could not help but turn stunned gazes back to the black granite gate. Its granite blocks were flecked with gold and seamed with silver. The stone portal stood twenty feet taller than the walls. Some fifty sentries manned it, and these were tall and stern, even at a distance.

"The Sable Gate is perhaps most impressive of all the city's constructions," Elijah chuckled as the boys stared. "Made by neither Rhonoss nor elf, it has stood long before any Kindred set foot on Leóhteness-Fal's dark soils. Some say it's always been. Others say the Rhonoss simply carved a gate into its implacable face before walking under it, then disappearing forever. Legend sings of giants in ancient days mining for precious metals. They heaped lumps of black granite, which they found useless, into towering piles, then melted them with fire that burst from their eyes."

"Like Mithweileth-Nal," Keiphral said wistfully.

Elijah nodded, and the conversation continued. But Dusk's attention fled as he peered through the yawning gate and into the city beyond, spying more wonders within. Row upon row of watchful turrets retreated up hills that grew ever upward toward the feet of the broken mountain. The square just beyond the gate bustled with market stands and music. Before he could see more, a hailing call came down from above. Sergeant Ethstan, motioning for Elijah, Del, and his guardsmen, met with an approaching cadre of guards cloaked in red.

Before long, Dusk heard Elijah's voice lash out above the din as his conversation with the guards grew heated. "No time to waste!" he heard the surgeon shout. "We've just arrived, out of battle, and the people are exhausted. We've sick and wounded in nearly every wagon. And I have new remedies for the Wasting Sickness that may soon afflict us all. I've been successful in my travels, and I've found the one I've been seeking for the prince's sake. Where is Aelfnoth? Send word to the captain that Elijah Wrathmod is returned and seeks his audience."

"Forgive us, Surgeon," a tall soldier said. "The city is filled to the brim, and we are only permitted to allow fighting men entry."

Dusk heard a smug, "Hmph," from behind as a heavy arm jostled his shoulder. "Outta my way, *beast*," Del sneered, shoving past him. "You hear that? City wants real men inside, not fire-calling freaks." The swordsman stalked past him and the group, right up to the guards in scarlet. They nodded, letting him and a group of armed caravan guards pass.

"Arrogant git," Dusk spat. "To think I went out of my w-w-way to spare him from my f-f-fire last night."

"Don't worry about him, Dusk," Keiphral said, laying a hand on the younger boy's shoulder. "I spent time with him. He's not half the oaf he seems. What's on his shoulders is heavier than he lets on. My guess is he's going straight up to the wall to look out at what's coming. He loves this city in his own way. I also have a feeling that that one will repay your mercy in kind."

Before Dusk could argue, Ethstan's voice rose above the crowd's as the sergeant growled at the gate guards. "Elijah's the chief surgeon of the city. You know that. And if he's got a remedy and a new surgeon to look after the masses, the soldiery, and quite possibly the prince, then that's more'n enough reason to let them all pass."

"We need fighters," one of the guards said, impassive.

"We have them," Elijah snapped.

"Everyone else," the guard continued, as if not having heard the surgeon's retort, "we're putting on the road north to Qweth-Coss by the sea. Folk there need help with an unusual abundance of fish to catch, ever since the Storm died over the Coast. The Gathilin Bluffs offer some protection away westward. We hear there's hunting, gathering, and fortifying to be done there. Help's also needed farming and storing food in all the country south of here. A guard's been set along the hills that ring the Ephtari Downs. They seek man and lady alike to watch the land all the way to the sea; protect our crops from any who'd burn them."

"I don't bring farmers and fishers," Elijah snapped. "And I certainly don't have time to argue their worth to guards without a captain! I've brought a surgeon and a soldier, fighters both! But if you must have one over the other, then they shall both serve the guard. Both can fight; any among the caravan train will tell you as much. One was trained by the Qwei-Sillar. The other wields scalpel *and* sword and will prove invaluable to your men as both fighter and mender."

"Show me," one of the guards boomed.

Elijah motioned for Dusk and Keiphral. Up they came, one decked in gold and steel, the other wrapped and haggard, looking as though he had been beaten.

"I can tell he's seen his share of battle and loss, more so even than some of us," one of the guards said of Keiphral. "His bruises say as much. And he's already dressed for the roll, armed and garbed like a warrior. Very well! In he comes, and to the wall he'll go after his rest. You'll take him there?"

Elijah nodded. "Along with most of the injured we bring to you, up to the infirmary. I will tend them too and make sure they are fighting fit."

Nodding, the soldier motioned Keiphral through the black-stone gate. "Come forward, lad." Keiphral did so.

"This one," said another guard, kneeling so that his craggy face sat just below Dusk's as he looked at the boy. "This one has seen less battle but more sorrow in his time. Arms and legs seem strong, though one of them is wounded." He looked to the riot of bandaging that wound around Dusk's right arm. "*Badly* wounded."

"All the more reason for him to come with me to the infirmary," Elijah replied. "So that my surgeons may help him before his service on the wall. Once done, he'll be a surgeon himself, mark my words."

"You a shepherd, boy?" the guard said. The man's face was gruff, but Dusk could see a stern, good nature in it.

"I was," Dusk said, picking his words, and the way he said them, with utmost care. "My da was a knight. And my mother a warrior too. He fights now in a faraway country against our foes. And she battles something worse: the Wasting Sickness. So, I became a fighter of diseases, and I've won many battles. And in my search for the final cure, I've become a fighter of ruffians and a slayer of fomori. Shepherd, healer, fighter. All three, sir."

"You make me believe it," the guard said. There was no mockery in his eyes, and they flicked to the haphazard helm on Dusk's head. "That you should bear such a token speaks well of your story and lineage. I have only seen one of its like upon the head of a great warrior. He went away to a new life with his wife and baby boy some fifteen or more years ago."

GARDEN OF ASH

Dusk stared back at the guard, and his eyes caught fire, burning at his wish to hear more about his da, whose helm it was.

"No," snapped another guard. "The boy's too small, too frail. He'll never be an asset to the defense. Not so long as he's injured and without skill at arms. Get you gone, boy! Make use of yourself as fisher, farmer, or shepherd. Leave the fighting to us."

"Aye," Dusk heard Del say from under shade of the black gate. Dusk glared after the fool swordsman.

"Silence, all of you," barked the guard who knelt before Dusk. "Look at him now."

Dusk looked back at the armored man, then to the others who now stood encircling him. Sudden shock drained the color from all their faces.

"Murder," said one.

"Death," gasped another. "Of one kind or another."

"Let him pass," said a third, who looked haunted when he studied Dusk's face. "This boy has killed before, and not just wolves."

"He passes," said the guard who knelt. He stood to his full height before he continued, looking to Elijah. "My post here ends at nightfall, then I sleep until dawn. I walk the lower levels until noon tomorrow, then the wall. I will come to the infirmary then to collect them. Should allow for sleep and a little recovery. You agree, Surgeon?"

"A little," Elijah said grudgingly. "Would that they had a week to recover from the toil they've each seen and done. But half a day of rest will suffice, given our circumstance."

LAST-HOPE BELEAGUERED

"The best I can do," the grim guard conceded. He turned to Dusk and Keiphral. "Very well. I will collect you both tomorrow at noon for the beginning of your training, though I feel I won't need to teach much. My name is Torross Tarian, and you are under my command. I would also caution you regarding people, alleys, and whole prefectures to avoid. But tidings tell me neither they, nor our city, have long to stand. Take these."

He slapped slivers of cold metal into their palms. Dusk and Keiphral studied the Midlothean script and stories inscribed across each of the polished surfaces.

"Clasps for you to wear, defining your post and under whom you serve," said Torross Tarian. "Be wearing them when I arrive tomorrow. Now, in you go."

Both boys smiled in thanks, palming their new tokens. Elijah, giving Torross a knowing look, pushed through, alongside carts laden with goods, travelers, and wounded.

"Dusk! Morne!" Ethstan called. "Glad to see your entry into Last-Hope is granted. Before you go, take these, along with those new badges." He handed the boys small pouches, each of which giving a merry clink as they struck the boys' open palms.

"Your share of the road's wages, given the work you put in to help heal and fight," Ethstan said with a smile. "Two gold Scills a man—more'n a month's wage! And Scribes know what would have happened to this lot if you hadn't come clear outta the woods lookin' out for 'em." He made a motion toward the last few members of the caravan still outside the gate. "Make sure some of it gets back to your mother, eh Dusk? Elijah told me a bit about your plight while we rode together. Take good care of her, you hear? All men should do likewise! Do that unto her and to anyone 'round you, and you'll never go wrong." With that, the sergeant caught up Dusk's uninjured hand and shook firmly. The grizzled sergeant gave him an approving smile and nod, then cuffed Keiphral on the shoulder as well. Then, Ethstan turned to march into the city without another word. Dusk watched him go, crimson cloak billowing, wondering if he would one day grow as tall, as good-natured.

As they passed under the Sable Gate's arch, Dusk caught Del staring at both he and Keriphral. Disbelief painted the boy's face, and he practically shook with fury. They exchanged no words with him, but Del practically strangled the hilt of his sword, the blade grinding in its scabbard. Then he stormed away and was lost to the calling crowds of Ephtar-Malas.

As he and Keiphral entered into the swell of the market, Dusk saw a swarm of men and women garbed in white and gray rush down a great staircase and gather about Elijah. The surgeon greeted them warmly but sternly, and Dusk could see relief and joy in their faces at his return to the city.

He caught bits of their conversation as the robed visitors questioned Elijah about his travels. Remedies he had discovered while gone, the state of the city's medical supplies, and how long he intended to stay where chief among many topics. Dusk heard the surgeon silence them then point to the trundling wains of the caravan as they crossed into the city square. Dusk heard Elijah mention the sick and wounded as the surgeon motioned to the wagons. Then the crowd surrounding him broke suddenly free like a flock of scattering doves and bustled into action. Dusk watched as white-robed men and women jumped up into the carts, checking on the owners and their cargo. Soon, Elijah's company took control and guided wagons and walkers away, up toward what they were calling hospital ward.

Elijah turned to the boys, a glint of pride visible in his stony eyes. "My junior surgeons have managed well while I've been gone," he said. He showed them his first genuine smile. "I go ahead now to make sure the way up is secure for our travelers. I perceive no danger from attackers so close to the city's walls, but be vigilant. As I said before, not all enemies come from without, and not all within the city are friendly, as you shall soon see. The city's guard may have some business for me to attend to before the healing work can begin rightly. If so, and I'm long gone, then explore the city at your leisure. The city is divided into levels by its stone staircases. But be sure to find the hospital ward and the infirmary above the Fourth Stair, which is the fifth level. My surgeons, as you no doubt have picked out by their whites and grays, will let you in and give you each a bed. I will come to you as soon as I can."

The surgeon practically leapt away, and Dusk and Keiphral watched him stride up the stairs the junior surgeons had come down a moment before.

"I t-t-take it that one's the First Stair," Dusk mused. Both boys watched the tall surgeon gain the second level, cross an elegant stone bridge, then climb another Stair and disappear from sight above.

"At any rate, I'd say part of my task is complete," Keiphral said above the combined din of dickering, shouting, laughing, and singing in the thoroughfare. "The alarm is raised, and the guard seem to have their watch over the city well in hand. I suppose we explore now, then wait for real duties to come tomorrow. Should we get familiar with our newest home then, Dusk?"

"*My* task is f-f-far from done," Dusk said. "I would go r-r-right now to the infirmary and s-s-study all manner of their medicines to g-g-get a jump on the new cures I w-w-want to create."

"As for that, I'd say, all in good time," Keiphral replied, pointing a thumb over his shoulder. "Elijah's surgeons seem a bit busybody in the way they do things. They've plenty to fuss over now." He then pointed toward the wagon in which lay the Nephtyri warrior, swooning and bloody with wounds. "Let them tend those who need it most badly first while we explore. Then we'll go up past that Fourth Stair and be at the mercy of the healers for the rest of the evening. There'll be plenty of time to work tomorrow too. Agreed?"

Dusk smiled at the older boy who cut an imposing figure in his elvish garb. He found no reason to resist Keiphral's plan and nodded. "Let's go."

LAST-HOPE BELEAGUERED

Exploring helped ease the boys' anxieties. Dusk had to keep himself from salivating as he and Keiphral passed under pavilions of scarlet, cobalt, and gold, catching the scent of hot bread, butter, and onion. Men laughed and called, peddling tools, candles, and earthenware cups. Fishermen hawked fresh catches and salt by the block while their brightly dressed wives sold intricate lamps and fish oils to fill them. Homesteaders offered honey, wax, chickens, eggs, and grain, while dyers showed the results of their craft in the forms of shirts in shades of deep blues, greens, and reds. A hundred more smells struck them as they continued. The scent of sweet cakes baking was best, but the uninvited tang of manure wafted to them too whenever they passed an animal stall.

"You feel it, Dusk?" Keiphral asked.

"Something strange." Dusk nodded. "Everyone's t-t-trying to put on a s-s-stable face, like all's business as usual, and the cakes are c-c-cooking."

"But the stench is there, at the fringes," Keiphral said. "All the city's going to be like this, I fear, and rightfully so. Come on, let's go up higher and see what else we can find!"

The lads strode under carved archways of white stone and wooden latticework crawling with arrowhead, spiderwort, and heartleaf. They strode up intricately cobbled streets, enjoyed the burble of granite fountains, and stared overlong at mosaics of women fashioned from chips of colored stone and glazed tile. Everywhere they found wondrously painted patterns underfoot, overhead, and splayed across the walls of homes and other buildings.

GARDEN OF ASH

Dusk couldn't help but smile as they crossed a series of bridges in the higher places of the city an hour later. These spanned the sudden drops of gushing waterfalls and moss-covered chasms, pervading the face of the old mountain into which the city had been delved. Standing in the middle of one such bridge, Dusk and Keiphral gazed out over the lower levels and shining spires of Ephtar-Malas. Light shone from across the world, northwestward. Its glory bathed the city in afternoon radiance.

"Bright and pretty, s-s-sparkling stone," Dusk muttered. He looked to Keiphral as the bigger boy turned to him.

"But it could be brighter," Keiphral finished. "That's what the elves said while I traveled with them. And dread rides the wind, just like in Wildercrown."

They stood on the bridge for a while, looking and saying little. Keiphral pointed eastward as daylight shimmered on the surface of the river that cut straight through the city's center. Dusk called it *Dethrai'ar*, telling him that it been the one they had followed and abandoned on the second leg of their journey toward the city, down from Sarith Mel. It now struck a jagged, silvery path through the ground levels of Ephtar-Malas. Little boats and barges crowded it, bearing people, supplies, and wares. Wind off the river and distant sea stirred the hair that peaked out from under Dusk's helm. It flung their cloaks out, and the lads, one tall and one fierce of eye, caught the attention of people passing. Little exclamations made Dusk and Keiphral smile as they stood.

"There he is!" said a woman in hushed tones. "The shorter one with fire for eyes. He sewed up my boy after the battle and was all aglow as he worked! Some even said that odd glow about him grew brighter the more he worked, the harder he pressed himself. That's one who should be helping the prince. That's one who should be right up there on the walls healing our wounded fighters!"

"The tall one looks like an elf, if I've ever seen one!" said an old noblewoman. "If our men were as well-armed and, shall we say, well-proportioned as that one, then we'd have no trouble freeing our country from those goblin wretches! I just hope the prince recovers consciousness and wit enough to use one as mighty as he."

"Something tells me we're about to come closer to this rumored prince than we bargained for, Dusk," Keiphral said as he smiled and bowed at their admirers.

"You think?" Dusk asked distantly.

"Elijah let slip the prince's 'absence' at the Sable Gate, remember? Then, when I asked, he went all aloof. The guardsmen said Elijah's close with him. And now, folk make mention of this prince needing help, being unconscious. Elijah told us to be wary. I think we're best off being wary of *him*, just as we are of goblins, masked men, and fomori. Dusk, are you even listening to me?"

"I'll succeed," Dusk whispered. Sight of the silver river and the now-stormless sea far away brought on thoughts of his parents. Dusk smiled a little then, his words coming easily as he continued. "I'll heal Eissyr and find Treiarn.

The shadow, both within and from outside, are only passing things. For now, faith and courage are enough."

"I hope you're right, even though you've distracted me away from discussing the prince of this city twice now," chuckled Keiphral.

"What?" Dusk asked, considering the city's sprawling gardens and its surrounding golden fields. He felt at ease for the first time in months, almost as if he had returned to a home barely remembered.

"You're hopeless," Keiphral sighed. "Anyway, I'm famished. How's about we find some food and an ale before surrendering to the mercies of the surgeons?"

Dusk approaches: Dusk over all the world, forever! Dusk shook his head, suddenly afraid and feeling as though he were bound up hand and foot at the bottom of a cart again.

"Dusk!" Someone shoved him, hard. He toppled, the fall calling back his sense. His hand snapped to his forehead, meeting the cool steel of his helm. Keiphral held his other, having kept him from falling after pushing him. "You alright?"

"G-g-guess I'm hungry t-t-too," Dusk stammered. Then he laughed. "I'd b-b-bet the newest guards of Last-Hope could w-w-wash down a solid meal with a celebratory ale. We d-d-did just come through a t-t-trial by fire."

"We certainly did," Keiphral said, eyeing him. "And you held the torch. You sure you'll make it, or pass out on the way?"

"Ha!" Dusk laughed, snatching his hand out of the

bigger boy's grasp. "I'll even r-r-race you there. Come on! I think I s-s-saw an inn above the next Stair."

The two boys were silent as they devoured feasts of steaming fish stew and custard tarts. But after they clacked together two large wooden cups of cold beer, and drank as if in contest, they were soon chattering and joking at the wildness of their tales.

"Not surprised by Elijah taking you on as his own one bit," Keiphral said before another mouthful of golden beer. "Seeing as how you mended yourself *and* the caravan's wounded on the way here. And though I didn't see all of it, I did see you trade blows with that masked man. You put a stop to his rampaging quick enough. Barring that, Del himself told me of your arrival at the back of the caravan. He said you burned the fomori to cinder with a will! Had you been at my side during the raiding at Wildercrown ... well, I think it's safe to say I would have been braver."

"Braver?" Dusk asked, nearly choking on his beer. "Keiph, you s-s-stalked right up to the Storm and me, r-r-ready for a fight, n-n-not knowing what to expect. After that, you offered to escort me then j-j-jumped in to fight fomori and p-p-protect the caravanners. You were the one who s-s-stormed in to battle that masked monster. I only s-s-stepped in after I saw your strength."

Keiphral sighed and took a long pull from his cup. "To be honest, I only did what felt right. I don't know who I was before I woke up, Dusk. I only remember pain and fire." He shivered and took another drink. "But, having learned from the Qwei-Sillar what goodness and right action are, I'm trying to mimic them. I hope I wasn't an evil brute before!"

Dusk chuckled at that, then grew serious. "If you were, you're f-f-far from it now, Keiph. You're d-d-doing right by the elves, j-j-just as I'm trying to d-d-do right by my mother."

Keiphral gave a troubled nod. "I just wish I wasn't so scared. Can't help but think that if Lohrë and the Elf-lord are dead because of me, then I know now that there was more I could have done."

"No, Keiphral," Dusk said, growing solemn. "Even had I b-b-been there with you, the end would have b-b-been the same. If an army of elves, t-t-trained by centuries, couldn't stop the fomori, then w-w-what good could I have done at your side? Kill a hundred, maybe two?"

"Maybe more," Keiphral said into his cup.

"I d-d-don't even know what I d-d-did to make the fomori burn," Dusk said. "Del and the g-g-girl, Yeiley they called her? They were in trouble and would have d-d-died had I not helped. That seemed r-r-reason enough for the Storm to jump out of me."

"The girl!" Keiphral said, lunging forward and nearly upending his drink. "Between the two of us, you saw more of her. What was she like?"

"Ho then, lads!" shouted the pudgy innkeep. "Too early in the eve to be roughhousing already! That all begins after dark. Keep quiet, else you're out on your ears!"

Both boys went red, chuckling into their cups.

"She was s-s-strong and quick," Dusk said, contorting his face in remembrance after another sip.

"Pretty?" Keiphral asked.

"Lovely!" Dusk said, his mouth curling into a smile.

"And elegant! She b-b-bore a black sword with golden edges. Sh-sh-she stabbed it through the fomori like they were n-n-nothing but walking water."

"Yeiley," Keiphral mused. "Yes, that was her name. The warrior, Nephtyr Ithar-fel, said so. She may have some part in the task given me by the elves."

"Which is?" Dusk asked.

"Well, before they sent me away, the elves of Wildercrown told me of their Messenger. He was supposed to travel alongside an angel. Together, these two were supposed to bear a precious gift to some secret place."

"You th-th-think the winged warrior—"

"He's the angel the Elf-lord spoke of," Keiphral said. "He must be. And the elf with the bow who went after the masked man. He spoke to you?"

Dusk nodded, forgetting his beer. "He s-s-said his name was Arwë before he left. You called him Lohrë, though."

"I did," Keiphral said, eyes going wide as he gazed past his surroundings but continued speaking. "I thought he *was* Lohrë, who protected me. But their hair and eyes were different. Lohrë was dark, while this Arwë was blond. Dusk, the Elf-lord is father to two sons, one of which is Lohrë. The other is this Messenger they spoke of."

"Who t-t-travels with the angel," Dusk added, pointing a finger at Keiphral.

Keiphral put a hand to his chin. "Then this Arwë, who travels with an angel and bears the same face as Lohrë, must be the Qwei-Sillari Messenger."

"And the girl, Yeiley, m-m-must be the precious treasure!"

"You think?" asked Keiphral. "Could the treasure be a person, not a token?"

"There was s-s-something strange about her," Dusk said, remembering the night before. He found his cup again and took another long gulp. "She had a sort of inner l-l-light to her. It was con-con-concealed by her cloak. But when the cloak p-p-parted, she practically flashed. The light coming f-f-from her blinded the fomori. And now that I think on it, I s-s-saw her burn one of them to a crisp with a touch!"

"I think we have an angel to question," Keiphral said, making to stand. "We should head to the infirmary, see if he's awake before the surgeons begin their fussing over us."

They struck cups and drained the last of their beer. They clattered hard-earned coins onto the table, then left the inn with a wave at the innkeep. After shambling onto the street, they walked out into the cool evening. Both boys looked up to see the golden-blue of the sky chased away by pink and deepening violet. Dusk looked to see Keiphral staring overlong upward.

"Keiphral?" he asked.

"Just thinking about tomorrow," Keiphral replied, staring at the winding wall that guarded the city. He seemed suddenly drained of his drive to question the angel. "You think Del will give us trouble?"

"Bigger k-k-kidds always have," Dusk said flatly. "For me, at least."

"Because of your size?" Keiphral asked awkwardly.

Dusk gave him a blank stare. "That, the f-f-fact that my da left my ma and me, that I t-t-talk to plants and animals, that m-m-my family is poor, *and* that I can't s-s-speak to save my life!"

"I see," Keiphral said, looking away.

His head spinning, Dusk attempted a curt bow. "S-s-sorry Keiph. I've n-n-never been much g-g-good at making f-f-friends. My weird skills and p-p-problems with talking have always kept kids my age at a d-d-distance. And I'm g-g-guessing the life of a s-s-surgeon is going to be r-r-rather detached too. But I'm not a s-s-surgeon yet. And we have a w-w-wall to walk tomorrow. Sh-sh-should we see it before finding our angel?"

"You think we'll get in trouble for sneaking up there?" Keiphral asked, nodding toward the wall.

Dusk grinned. "It's what f-f-friends do."

Keiphral returned a sheepish smile of his own. "Friends," he mused. "Yeah, it *is* what we do." With that, they were off to the nearest gate that would bring them up spiraling stairs and out onto the soaring ramparts of the out-wall, jostling and racing one another as they went.

All was cool, dim, and windy when they reached the top of the stairs, puffing and laughing. But just as they set foot to the wall, high and above many parts of the city, Keiphral froze, and he clutched at Dusk. The younger boy stood straight and firm, frowning at his friend.

"Beer gone to your bowels?" Dusk asked with no sign of his stammer. "Why are you all hunched over?"

"I-I've only ever been up as high as the tallest tree," Keiphral stammered, holding onto the younger boy as a ship clings to port in a storm. "Not used to such heights. Makes my stomach cramp and head swim."

"Really?" Dusk said with a surprised laugh. "It's normally *me* who's weak-kneed. You've never so much as climbed a high hill or mountain? Sarith Mel and its Watchful Hills were nearly as tall! We were there only two days and some hours ago."

"The land was all spread out!" Keiphral hissed, descending to all fours. "And a fall from there would only send you rolling, not screaming to your death."

"Wow," Dusk said, first walking then skipping in circles around the huddled boy dressed in warrior's garb. "He fights man and monster, wields elvish weapons, even runs tirelessly for hours with no water or food. Yet, he cannot stand to his full height when walking the ramparts? What *will* we do with you, Keiphral Morne?" He finished by jumping up on a stone merlon that jutted up from the high walkway, landing gently on the top with one foot. He posed ridiculously with one hand seeming to shade his eyes as he glanced toward the horizon.

"I'm glad to see your confidence increase to such heights," Keiphral retorted.

"That wasn't half bad, Keiph!" Dusk said, hopping down to Keiphral's level. One foot struck the rampart lightly as he stuck out his other leg and twirled in a full circle before coming to a stop, standing over the prone Sojourner.

"What wasn't half bad?" Keiphral snapped, looking up at the younger boy.

"Such great *heights*?" Dusk laughed, gesturing with a flourish and another deft spin.

"More than just a fighter with a pretty face, you know," Keiphral chuckled, rising gingerly. He then looked at Dusk strangely. "No sign of your stuttering up here in the wind, eh?"

Dusk's smile evaporated, and he deflated. "No. Just left the t-t-troubles faraway for a m-m-minute, is all."

"I'm sorry, Dusk," Keiphral said. "You were having a little fun at my expense, so I thought I'd poke back."

Dusk gave the big lad his wry smile. "Don't stop! Like I s-s-said, it's what f-f-friends do. No r-r-reason for me to get down anyway. I'll l-l-learn all there is to know here in Last-Hope. Then I'll r-r-return to Sunreach and call Ma b-b-back from the brink."

"You will," Keiphral said. "And she'll be better than new."

Dusk gave a determined nod, then started shivering.

"What is it?" Keiphral said as his knees wobbled underneath him. Dusk's laughs came in silent gasps until he couldn't contain them.

"You, Keiph!" he said, laughs bursting out, echoing along the wall in the whipping wind. "Still *you*!"

Keiphral, abashed at first, soon found he couldn't contain his own snickering. Then the boys laughed, loud and long.

They laughed until tears fell and they clutched their sides. They laughed until Dusk stopped short and went back to the crenellations. This time, he turned away from the horizon, looking up to the city's highest levels. He froze then, a chill at what he saw running through him.

"What is it, Dusk?" Keiphral said, gaining his feet.

Dusk pointed. High above, on the roof of a tower, stood a pale, glowing figure, gazing northward.

"S-s-same cloak, same glow as the girl from the w-w-wagon train," Dusk whispered without taking his eyes from her.

"Yeiley," Keiphral said.

The figure turned to look down at them as if she had heard her name spoken. Then she vanished, fast as blinking. Before their minds could catch up to her disappearance, the northern wind tousled their hair. Dusk smelled smoke. The boys glanced at one another, then ran to the opposite side of the wall. They looked out in the same direction as the cloaked figure had. Miles away, the clouds riding the northern horizon were awash with a reddish, creeping light.

On the fuming wind, Keiphral heard a familiar sound that set his teeth grinding. "The horns are blowing."

18
A DAY'S DUTIES

"We have to tell Elijah, the guards, the sergeant, everyone!" Keiphral called over his shoulder as he leaped down the steps. Dusk, heavy with drink, was now propelled by terror. He and Keiphral dashed down from the out-wall by the same spiral stair they had used to come up. After agonizing minutes of unending descent, they finally burst back onto the lower streets. Elijah was already there, waiting for them.

"With me," Elijah snapped.

"Elijah!" Keiphral said, practically dancing with excitement. "The marching hordes are only days away. Coming from the North, as I said. The same evil glow, same horns blowing, approached Wildercrown before it fell. We must do something!"

"We saw from higher up," Elijah said, striding up city stairs and crossing ascending bridges, his two dizzy companions in tow.

"We?" Keiphral asked. "Where were you, Elijah?"

"And how d-d-did you know where to f-f-find us?" added Dusk.

"We saw from higher up," Elijah repeated. "I was in the high parts of the city where I had been ordered to return the moment we'd crossed under the Sable Gate. I thought things could wait a day or two, allowing you both some time to rest. But tonight, only one of you will be allowed to."

"Only one?" Dusk and Keiphral said together at the top of a broad Stair.

Elijah led them to a cross-shaped building with spires at each corner. Outside it stood two soldiers, cloaked and armed, but at ease as if simply making a stop on their patrol route. They nodded to Elijah, and the surgeon turned back to the two boys. "As I said, I wanted more time to explain things to you properly. I know this has all been too much too fast. But my hand is forced now, and it may be yet again by other forces 'ere long. My travels took me far abroad and ate up so much time." For the first time since he had met the surgeon, Dusk thought Elijah ben Ath, the leader, planner, and healer, looked unsure of himself.

"No matter," the surgeon said with a sigh. "Had I not gone so far, I may have only met one of you at a time and spent far longer seeking the other. No, this is as right as things may have turned out. And they may yet turn out for the better. But now we must hurry!"

"We don't know you well, Elijah," Keiphral said flatly. "But one certainty about you is you know how to speak yet still say nothing. What is it you're on about?"

At a few low chuckles from the guards who stood within earshot, Elijah smiled. "You know me better than

A DAY'S DUTIES

you think, Keiphral Morne. You are to come with me to the citadel tonight."

"The citadel?" Dusk and Keiphral said at once.

"You're both getting good at that," Elijah observed, walking to the front steps of the cross-shaped building. He waved the guards there into action. They took up positions on either side of the trio. Elijah turned back to Keiphral. "Forgive me, Keiphral Morne. I had hoped at least to let you sleep before dragging you to the top of the city to deliver your message from the Qwei-Sillar. Tonight, however, I must ask you to put aside your exhaustion one more time and go up with me. There, we will discuss the threat of those who, even now, burn the fringes of T'Rhonossarc. With your knowledge of what the fomori, and the goblins they control, have done to the elf-lands, we may form some plan for the defense of the city, well-guarded as it is."

"It's what I've been wanting since we arrived this afternoon," Keiphral said. "Lead the way, Elijah."

Elijah nodded. "We must go quietly," he said. "With only a small escort and no horses so as not to draw undue suspicion. The prince's vassals are private folk."

"The prince and his v-v-vassals?" Dusk demanded as his tall companions turned to leave. "What of me?"

"You, *Surgeon* Dusk," Elijah said, emphasizing the title, "are to follow our plan, as before. Report to the infirmary, subjecting yourself to the mending of my physicians. Then spend the next few days both healing those who need you and learning all you can about this city."

"But I—"

"Know that your mission, once I return to reveal it and collect you for it, shall be of even greater import than the one carried by Keiphral. Rest well, but be ready. For now, goodnight!"

Dusk watched from the infirmary's doorstep as his companions and the guardsmen bustled away, across the grasses, roads, and gardens of the sprawling ward. They climbed the next Stair, even broader and grander than all the ones below it. As they disappeared from sight, Dusk sighed, turning. He made to knock on the infirmary door that towered over him. Before his hand met the sturdy wood of the door, it flew open. A short, robed, bespectacled man with a wisp of white beard on his chin swept him off the porch and into the warm glow emanating from within.

"Young Surgeon Dusk!" the little man said, smiling and hurrying Dusk down a candlelit hallway. "We've been expecting you, of course. Master Elijah spoke highly of you. He told us to look you over and have you get some well-deserved rest before you enter into your split duties. One of your posts shall be here at the infirmary by morning. The other shall be with the guard in the afternoons. So very exciting for us to meet a man who heals with hand and skill, as well as song! It's a rare thing, you know, though not totally unheard of amongst us healers, ho ho! Straight into the city all the way from the high country of the South, I hear of you too. Splendid. I'm doorkeeper this week, so whatever you may need concerning the house and your room, don't hesitate to ask!"

A DAY'S DUTIES

They came into a wide chamber filled from wall to wall with beds, cabinets, cushions, tools, and linen gowns. An occupant lay in nearly every bed. A handful of nervous, white-clad men and women rushed over to greet Dusk and the little physician beside him.

"Here he is!" the bespectacled man said to them, smiling with pride as he presented a dizzy, travel-stained Dusk. "Our newest surgeon is here to join. But first, he needs examining. Look him over. Change any dressings that need changing, then to bed with him! He has a busy week in front of him. Now then, goodnight, Surgeon Dusk!" Before Dusk could respond, the little man was halfway up the hall they had come down, and the gaggle of physicians had already surrounded him and begun their prodding.

The rest of Dusk's night passed quickly as robed physicians fussed over him. He listened to them as they checked him for signs of fever, head trauma, bone fractures, internal bleeding, and Wasting Sickness after his journey and many fights. They took inventory of his collected cuts, applying sour-smelling salves and sutures to all. Dusk marveled at the cool relief such attentions brought to his stinging shoulders and back. He also noticed many heads turn away at his mention of Veilglorrath when they questioned him about the injuries both he and Nephtyr Ithar-fel had sustained. The angel-man had been brought in, patched up, and forced into an over-large bed some hours before.

They paid special attention to Dusk's scoured arm. He noted their faces going dark when they removed the dressings to investigate his Storm-inflicted wounds. The arm always felt weak, shaky, and hot to Dusk. But when the physicians ran him through tests of strength or endurance, they found it stronger and more durable than that of the combined strength of any three hardened warriors.

By the time the surgeons had treated him, given him a change of clothes, and shown him to a private chamber in a high tower of the infirmary, Dusk had no more strength of will even to keep his eyes open. As soon as the door clapped shut behind him, he stowed away his helm and gear. Then he collapsed onto the neatly made bed into a dreamless sleep.

Dusk awoke early the next morning. On a table in the hall outside his room, to his delight, he found a stack of books. The physicians, at Elijah's request perhaps, had brought him a compendium of hundreds of records regarding the Ephtar-Malas' medical practices and theories. Under these was a leatherbound history of the city itself. At the bottom were two books of lore with a brief note tacked on. It stated that the tomes should interest a young boy who had only less than two days ago seen an armored giant and battled a masked creature twisted by shadow.

He stowed the lore books and city's history into his pack alongside his dried food and medical ingredients. He brought the records with him down to breakfast. He sat at a long table, running a trained, gold eye over the many-handed writings of collected theory and practice beside a

A DAY'S DUTIES

plate piled high with eggs, sausages, and dried tomatoes. During his read and feast, Dusk spoke briefly with many of the robed physicians who came and went from the dining hall. He found them all to be good-natured folk, if a bit strange, just like him. They were easy to talk to, given their interest and expertise in all the healing practices he had come to master in recent years.

After breakfast and a bath, Dusk found his way to the physicians' library. The chamber lay on the third floor of the infirmary, consuming an entire wing of the building. Shelf upon shelf of book, scroll, vellum, parchment, and record lined the walls. Dusk gazed at the wheeled ladders and wooden stools that were set all about the vast room for easy access to all heights. He stood enrapt, gazing from floor to ceiling in wonder. A tall physician of forty years or so entered the room and chuckled at his amazement. She then laughed at his surprise when she told him that the prince's archives, up three more Stairs, was a building far grander than the infirmary, and was solely dedicated for the storing and safeguarding of the knowledge of all countries. It apparently stored ten times as many documents as could be found in the infirmary library.

Wanting nothing more than to spend entire days high up on ladders and deep in chronicles, Dusk heard a commotion that drew his attention downstairs grudgingly. A pack of surgeons with rust-red stains spattering their robes hurried new patients down the entry hall and into the ward. The afflicted were refugees out of the West, escaping battle, and every surgeon set to their mending.

Dusk observed the surgeons' treatment of these new arrivals, soon giving dozens of suggestions in those first quiet but tense hours of the day.

Eventually, having taken Dusk's advice regarding salving, slicing, suturing, wrapping, and binding, the physicians argued that he would prove more effective treating patients than offering advice. So the morning passed, and Dusk worked. He performed his healing arts, calling upon song and skill to the mending of every man, woman, and child who lay in the infirmary. When he had finished and the last of the injured lay quiet after Dusk's attentions, Elijah's physicians stared in awe of the strange, stuttering shepherd boy from the mountains who seemed to have worked medical miracles before their eyes.

Just as the robed healers swarmed him, offering congratulations and demanding private tutelage and conversation, another visitor swept in through the infirmary's front door. Dusk recognized him for an elf: tall, graceful, and cloaked in green and gray. The elf's metal-blond hair escaped in streaming strands from the confines of his drawn hood. Dusk watched him make his way to the angel-man who lay in the far corner of the healing ward.

Making quick excuses, Dusk left the cluster of excited physicians and pursued the newcomer to Nephtyr Itharfel's bedside. "H-h-he recovers nicely," Dusk said gently to the tall figure.

"Indeed, he always has," the elf replied. "Though

his battles of late have taken all he has to give, and then some."

"Battles against the Veilglorrath," Dusk whispered.

The elf nodded, haunted eyes searching his stricken companion's face. "The evil ones' number is reduced, though it only be by one. And the price of that one came at great cost to us both. Still, it is gladly paid."

Dusk then recognized what he had taken for the elf's heavy walking stick as the great bow with which he had seen him shoot the masked man. The weapon showed splinters and other damage, its thick string cut. Dusk also noted the wet bundle the tall elf let dangle from his other long-fingered hand. Blood ran from his shoulder, running in crimson rivulets down his muscled arm and onto the bag he bore. On the bundle, red and black mingled together, dripping dark, oozing drops onto the clean infirmary floor.

"Arwë," Dusk said.

The elf turned to Dusk with a grim light in his eyes.

"You're hurt," Dusk said in a low voice. "Let m-m-me help you."

"I've only just arrived from the hunt," Arwë said in a frustrated whisper. "And far too late. The fomori blow their horns. And those we fought in the woods were not even the vanguard of the forces arrayed against us. No. No time for rest. I'm on my way to the top. The prince needs to know that more than fomori march against Malas. I needed to see Tyrith along the way. See to him, Dusk. When he wakes, tell him the prey is slain."

"I will g-g-go with you—"

"No, Surgeon Dusk," said yet another visitor standing in the entrance hall. The voice was cool and grim. The man it belonged to was tall, cloaked in crimson, and broad of shoulder. "You and I have a wall to walk this afternoon."

"Torross Tarian!" Dusk cried, snapping to his best imitation of soldier's attention. "For-g-give me. I was busy with—"

"With your sworn duty, Surgeon," the guard said, chuckling. "Already we've got you torn between vital chores. Such is life during these times of war. You've done great work for our city in a single day. No one begrudges you your skill and success. But come along now for a few hours! There is much for you to see. I saw the elvish outrider arrive, despite his best attempts to enter the city quietly. I have already dispatched an escort as befits the Herald of Wildercrown."

"Keiphral was right," Dusk whispered, eyeing Arwë with awe. But the elf only gave a small nod to Toross.

"He will go when he deems best," Torross continued. "And his guard stands at the ready to take him up. Now, come along, Surgeon, with all arms, armor, cloak, and clasp. It's cold and windy up on the out-wall. Though somehow, I feel you already know that."

Dusk blushed at the big man's knowing smile, then ran off to his chamber to collect his gear.

A half hour later, Dusk stood again upon the soaring ramparts, looking out over mountains and fields beside Torross Tarian.

A DAY'S DUTIES

"You've got steady feet!" Torross said approvingly. "I thought we'd have to teach both you *and* Morne how to walk the wall without looking down and getting sick."

"Walking even the highest w-w-wall is no challenge when you count m-m-mountain goats among your climbing t-t-teachers," Dusk said, taking a lungful of fresh air as it blew out from the west. "The wind's sh-sh-shifted. I don't smell s-s-smoke today."

"It's still there, more caustic than last night," Torross said gravely, searching the northern horizon. "Day's not as bright as it should be, given the fires and reek thrown up over the hills there, just out of sight. Even now, those bastard fomori burn homestead, field, and farm. Our outriders have been coming and going with news for days now. And it's not just those monsters committing the violence. Men have joined them too. The same men who attack Gathilin and the Angloreans. *Swardha-Menn*, as they were called in older times. *Varangi* was an even older name for them, when they joined all the wrong sides in the war that brought us to Leóhteness-Fal."

"You m-m-mentioned needing to teach Keiphral to w-w-walk up here," Dusk said, although his mind flashed with images of fanged fomori marching beside rampaging axe men, with ice in their veins and iron for eyes. "Any w-w-word from him?"

"None, save that his audience with the vassals and captain of the guard was not to be disturbed by any duty," Torross replied. "Must have been important news to sneak him out of guard duty!" The guardsman laughed at that, then looked away eastward. His eyes followed River Dethrai'ar as it carved through hill and mountain toward the Hidden City.

"You also s-s-seem to know much history," Dusk said, continuing his march of the wall.

"Ha! A little, I suppose," Torross said. "I was, after all, taught by your father."

"My fa-fa-fa—"

"Why do you think I plucked you off the street and into my command?" Torross said with a grin. He then grew solemn. "Treiarn is a good man, Dusk. A man of virtue, faith, and bridled strength. But when that strength is roused to anger, then to wrath? Well, let's just say, had all the armies fallen and there been no one left to defy the Nephtyr and all their legions, Treiarn would still have singlehandedly brought their vaunted Hegemony to its end under his boot."

"Armies and empires," Dusk breathed. "I never knew. Da t-t-taught me much about the world and its h-h-history. But whenever it came t-t-to the Nephtyri Hegemony, he would only say the Kindreds b-b-brought it low, ending the l-l-lesson saying, *'Tyrants fall.'*"

Torross clutched his sides, shivering. Then he stood straight and laughed loudly into the wind. "They do indeed!" he said, wiping at his eyes. "Glad to see the old general's still teaching the troops rightly!"

"Have you s-s-seen him recently, Torross?" Dusk asked urgently.

"Come to think of it," said Torross, "I saw Treiarn

A DAY'S DUTIES

pass through the city a while back. Some two years ago, perhaps? I only spoke with him briefly. He seemed urgent to be away. I assumed he wished to be back with you and your mother, given you both were his chief reasons for laying down his arms in the first place. Elijah may know better."

"He only t-t-told me a little," Dusk said. "We've had no t-t-time since our r-r-run to the caravan and then the att-t-tack." His head spun at the mention of any news that concerned his father's whereabouts.

"No time indeed," the tall guard said, rubbing at the dark gray stubble that invaded his jawline. "Well, before Elijah lets the time get away from him and you all the more, know that Treiarn spent the most time with him before he was off again. You know, Dusk, now that I think of it, your father went away westward, not back south. South would have been the way one would expect him to go if he were returning home."

Dusk only frowned, eyes darting back and forth as if to connect the scattered pieces of some convoluted puzzle.

"Don't tell me it's been that long since you've seen him too," Torross said, brow furrowing.

"Two years," Dusk whispered.

"I'm sorry, Dusk," Torross said, going gray as all mirth drained from him. "I thought you knew. I thought you were down out of the mountains with your father's blessing to fight for the city as a token of his goodwill. Does he even know you're here?"

Dusk shook his head.

"What," Torross said, hesitating. "What about your ma, then, Dusk?"

"She's the r-r-reason I'm here," Dusk said through gritted teeth. "Da left without s-s-saying why. He gave me this helm and nothing more. Then sh-sh-she got sick, and I searched for cures and p-p-power. I was on my w-w-way back to Sunreach when Keiphral and Elijah f-f-found me, told me about the t-t-trouble the city was in. I w-w-went with them for a little while but only m-m-meant to go so far before h-h-heading home to heal her."

"Then the assault on the caravan Elijah told us of drove you fully into our arms and away from home," Torross mused.

"Yes," Dusk said.

"You mentioned the helm," Torross said, pointing to the top of Dusk's head. "When Treiarn came here, he arrived garbed in Midlothean fashion with his winged helm. He wore none of the spoils he had won in the Hegemonic Wars. Those few of us who saw him figured he'd passed those gifts on to you. Seems we weren't wrong."

"What do you know of m-m-my helm?" Dusk asked.

"That it came straight off the head of the Hegemony's champion," Torross said. "Your father slew the greatest warrior ever to rise from out of the Nephtyr. Treiarn humbled the angel on the bridge that led to the gates of their high mountain-city. Those gates remain shut, and the Nephtyr remain humble to this day because of your da's victory."

"What h-h-happened after?" Dusk asked.

A DAY'S DUTIES

"Knowing the Nephtyr would never again rise in arms against Ephtar-Malas, nor hurt any other Midlothean, we all went home to our wives. Treiarn, laden with honor, spoils, and promises of power and lands, renounced his duties. He retired away with you and Eissyr, asking never again to be called to action. I would have done the same in his place, my wife having just given birth to our daughter at the time. More so now that I have a son to look after as well!"

They continued speaking of small things between drills and instructions given by Torross. A few hours had passed when Torross caught Dusk looking away, into the darkening sky. The boy gazed up at the highest towers, then to the citadel.

"I'm concerned for Keiphral," Dusk said.

"As am I, truth be told," Torross replied, gazing up with Dusk. "The vassals and prince haven't released him yet, and he's been up there nearly a full day. I could use your friend, and the hope his elvish gear and bearing would bring, on the wall. The prince's condition scares me, and I don't know if we can trust his nobles."

"Prince's condition?" Dusk asked. He turned to Torross, trying to betray neither his curiosity nor his speculations.

Torross gave a frustrated sigh. "Forget I said anything, Dusk. You being my good friend's son has lowered my guard. It's been good reminiscing about him. But, from one guardsman of the city to another, I'll tell you to do your duty with any questions to be passed on to your commander."

"And what do you s-s-say, as my commander?" Dusk asked with a grin.

"To be careful, Dusk." Torross then spoke quietly. "I fear for the prince, for he has not been seen by his people in well over a year. Strange cries travel down from high up when we of the guard are stationed close to his citadel. Even if it's just a sickness the prince deals with, Elijah and our captain are stuck in the middle, with foppish fools on one hand and bloodthirsty foes on the other. Be careful. And, if you please, make little mention of everything we discussed up here today. My counsel to you concerning all these matters is this: If you speak of them again, speak of them only to those whom you can trust. If Treiarn omitted so much from the education of his own flesh and blood, he must have had his reasons. Thank you for your honesty with me. I would expect no less from the son of Treiarn, Knight of Ephtar-Malas and Scourge of the Nephtyr."

"Thank you, Torross," Dusk said, offering his hand to the big man. "It's g-g-good to hear who my da was from someone other than m-m-my ma and those of my v-v-village."

Torross nodded and shook the boy's outstretched hand. "Your father always called me Tor. You should do the same. And when next we meet, the lads and I'll show you and Morne how to fight like men of the city. We'll get shields and spears in your hands. Agreed?"

"Agreed, Tor," Dusk said, smiling.

"Good," Tor Tarian said. "Hurry down, Surgeon, off to whatever other duties you may have tonight. We've not

A DAY'S DUTIES

been attacked yet, but I fear it's only a matter of time. Your watch on the wall is ended for today."

"Sir!" Dusk said, giving a crisp salute. He then bolted for the nearest stairway that would bring him down from the windblown wall and into the relish of a hot meal.

Dusk reached the bottom faster than he had expected, then kept on walking. He had motioned to adjust the fit of his helm, then all thought of warmth and food fled him halfway through his descent. Now he strode aimlessly, lost in thought over the news of his father's past and hearing whispers of where he may be now. As if gliding through a dream, Dusk passed up and down steps and over bridges. Soon, he strayed into unfamiliar wards of the city, failing to think on each one's various functions, offices, courts, and marching patrols of scarlet-cloaked guards. All that seemed to matter was the mystery of his father and what Dusk would do next.

The cobbled road ran a winding, evenly paved path through all levels of the city, feeling firm under his feet as he continued walking half-awake. Not even the shapes of walls and colors of the city wards and all their levels, as different from one another as night was from day, could keep his attention. "You retired," he muttered to himself. "What m-m-made you don your armor again, come b-b-back here? Where were you when I s-s-saw you through the helm, under earth, before those d-d-doors? Where were you w-w-when Ma got sick?"

Gone away to find the light, a voice replied in his ear. *It* is close, and so are you, but he is far away. Bring the light and bring the Key. Hurry. At end of night comes break of day. Seek once-bright Innoth-Hyeil Darrë!

Dusk passed bread bakers, butchers, inns, pawner's stalls, and carven stone houses. The vague memory of a cathedral also pricked his senses with sharp spires and dizzying heights. But these he passed by as well. "Who were you, Da? Do I even know you n-n-now? Would I have known y-y-you then, in your w-w-warring days?"

Cowards all, the Nephtyr were brought low, came the voice again. Dusk put a hand to the side of his helm, listening. *Nephtyr deserve what they were given. They shall be first to fall.*

Dusk passed brilliant mosaics displaying everything from fey folk and lovely ladies to myths and scenes of innovation and magic. Cutting across an alley, Dusk stopped, looking up to see a fresco on a section of high, broken ceiling. Badly damaged and faded, the mural depicted a battle fought under a black sky by tall men with gold swords. "What was it, Da?" he asked of the painting. "That f-f-final sin that broke the dam? What did the Nephtyr d-d-do to send you burning a path right to their d-d-door to kill them?"

He ventured to the lower, less extravagant circles of the city, seeing more wood, less stone in the architecture. The woodworking and patterning that bedecked the more practical and business-like levels of the city caught his eye now and then. But still he walked from street to street, puzzling over Tor's stories, as well as what little

A DAY'S DUTIES

news Elijah had given him since their meeting. Merchants and traders had thrown up their stands on all the lower streets, hoping to attract all manner of passersby before light went down for the evening. Dusk continued, ignoring a variety of trinket-laden stands and shops not far from the Sable Gate.

"What was the Key, Da?" Dusk asked, climbing upward once more. Globes of torch and feylight sprang up throughout the city, casting concentric circles of gold and green upon his ascending path. "Did you t-t-truly steal it? Do you h-h-have it now? I wish you would come h-h-home to us."

Away from home, he took the Key, then stowed, then stalked, then stole it back! His part is done, but yours is here. You found what you need when you came down from your mountain aerie.

"The Storm," Dusk whispered, making to remove his helm. He felt hot and famished, as if he had just run the race again down from Sarith Mel. He needed relief, but the voice that kept up its whispering needed to tell him more before it would let him go. But just then, a name and a face broke his reverie. "Ary," he gasped, and he removed the helm. He shook his head clear of Keys, whispers, and ancient words. Cold, fresh air buffeted his face. He gazed up to see a velvety sky painted with spirals of gold, amber, and purple. His hair blew back, and he huffed, stricken dumb. His bandaged hand hurt, and he found it grasping the railing of a staircase.

"The Stair Elijah and Keiphral climbed up to the

h-h-highest level last night," he whispered, wondering how he had gotten there.

Captivated by the switchback steps and staring at the sky from hundreds of feet above the world in high Ephtar-Malas, Dusk grinned. Knowing his da had walked these steps, he felt more at home here than he had during any part of his journey prior. He breathed deeply and let the wind caress his flushed face. Finally, after worrying over his parents, the darkening world, and war approaching, he let his thoughts stray again to Aryka. The sky darkened, and all he could see in it was her angled face. Then all he could think of were her dark hair and white smile.

"I'm sorry, Ary," he whispered. "I'll return soon, I p-p-promise. And then I'll ask you to—"

"Come on, iss' down here!" The voice cut across Dusk's fantasy, and he turned to see a group of armed and armored guards stomping down the winding Stair.

Not guards, he thought. *Apprentices.*

Doing his best not to be noticed, Dusk replaced the helm on his head, looking away. Then he heard a familiar voice, which pulled a low groan from him.

"Lads! If it ain't the little mountain monster who breathes fire then faints!"

"Hello, Del," Dusk said, turning to face the group of boys.

"What's wrong with his eyes?" a big one said. They were *all* big to Dusk. This one wore a gold clasp at his throat.

"Yeah," sneered another. "Looks like he swallowed a candle and his brain's burning!" The group laughed, the sour tang of ale reaching Dusk's nostrils twenty feet away.

A DAY'S DUTIES

"Ex-c-c-cuse me," Dusk said, shuffling toward the hill that would take him down toward the infirmary's door.

"Wah-wah-what's wrong with him?" mocked one of the smaller boys. This one possessed a bit of a rat-face in Dusk's brief estimation.

"It's just how he t-t-talks," Del said, snickering as he gripped his head and stumbled. He almost barreled into Dusk, who caught the swordsman by the shoulder with a supporting hand. Dusk's cloak fell, revealing his arm's winding bandages as he reached upward.

"I knew Del couldn't hold his ale!" the biggest of the group said, pointing and laughing. "He's green as a leaf, and he said he's the toughest of us all, his dad being cap—"

"I *am* the toughest of you lot," Del slurred, shoving Dusk away. "Just had a bit too much smoke is all, with all the beer."

"Ya, right," said the rat-faced boy. "You're the toughest of us all. Show us by knockin' the glowy-lights outta this kid's head. I don't like the way he looks at me. 'Sides, look at his arm! It's all bandaged up like it's been hurt already. Anyone asks, we'll just tell 'em we saved him from ruffians."

"No," Del snapped. "You want me to prove how weak you sniveling lot are, you'll challenge me yourselfs!"

"All of us put together'll hog tie you and throw you naked at your shiny girl's door if'n you're not careful," the biggest one growled. "And if'n she even exists."

"No, *we* won't," said a tall, dark-haired lad. His hood

was up, and he stood separate from the group of boys. He wore an intricate clasp of hammered bronze at his throat.

"No one asked you, Sen," snorted the biggest one.

"No?" the dark one whispered, stepping forward so that he was face to face with the biggest. "Maybe I'll just shoot those lips right off that fat face of yours?" The group froze, and Dusk noted that this dark boy was the only one of the six who carried a heavy bow instead of shield and spear.

"I'll deal with you later, forest-fairy," the biggest boy spat. He turned back to Del and Dusk. "Go on, then, Del. Hit him. Give him a good one, the way you said you wanted to when you were talking earlier."

Del flushed, the greenish hue disappearing from his cheeks. He grew solemn. "Come on," he said, stalking toward a set of descending stairs. "This was a stupid idea. Let the beast-boy have his perch above the hospital so he can mutter to himself." Dusk relaxed a little. Then four boys blocked Del's way, all except the one named Sen.

"No. Hit him," said the biggest. "Hard." And he shoved Del back toward where Dusk stood. Dusk looked from Del to the hooded boy with the bow, hoping for at least one ally. He wished Keiphral were here. Sen only looked away. Then something clicked in Dusk's mind.

"Shiny girl," he whispered.

"What?" Del snapped, suddenly sober.

"Yeiley," Dusk said. "The g-g-girl from the caravan. Del, what d-d-do you know of her?"

Del's fury seemed to re-ignite, and he advanced on

A DAY'S DUTIES

Dusk, his sandy hair tousled by the wind. "Don't you speak her name, beast!" he roared. "I didn't give you permission to."

Seeing Del's fists clench, Dusk's heart skipped. He whispered the shadow, and the linen gauze on his arm glowed, growing warm. *If he touches me, hurt him.*

"Surgeon Dusk!" came a cry of indignation. "Your watch on the wall ended an hour ago, according to Lieutenant Tarian. As light goes down, your nightly duties begin: You have patients to attend to!" Elijah ben Ath came bustling down the high Stair. Slung about with bottles, bags, and remedies, the senior surgeon stomped right down into the midst of the group.

"Master Elijah," Dusk began. "I—"

Annoyance flared on Elijah's face as the guard boys obstructed Dusk from his view. The surgeon shoved Del into his friends. "Move, oaf!" Elijah barked. "Unless you and your lot were escorting the city's newest surgeon safely back to his post at the infirmary? The infirmary where he is expected by my staff and waiting patients, *sick* patients, who may not survive the night, given his untimely return? I find your better intentions unlikely, though I'm willing to hear them. Explain!"

Del shoved himself out of the arms of his dumbfounded companions, then flung his shoulders back as he stood tall in front of the surgeon. Dusk saw hatred in the swordsman's eyes. "What's it to a crazy, old man like you?" he retorted. "The other surgeons can manage if the one who taught them is half the man this city says he is."

"Del," said Sen. "We leave. Now."

"The only reason the prince keeps you around is 'cause he's *sick*," Del continued, inching closer so that his nose nearly touched Elijah's. "And 'Elijah's the only one who knows the treatment for him,' they say. Convenient is all *I'd* say, given your love for secrets and goings on behind closed doors."

Despite Del's height and barrel chest, Elijah towered over him. The surgeon bent down to Del's level where he fixed the boy with a deadly glare. "Speak of the prince in that way again, *boy*," he whispered acidly, "and maybe I'll just stuff that gob of yours with a vile drug that would do more harm than help."

"You wouldn't dare," Del retorted. For just an instant, Dusk saw him falter.

"Better yet," Elijah continued. "I'll ask the prince for you to be my trusty companion on my next errand across the world for him. Maybe instead of a packhorse, I'll just weigh *you* down and tell everyone you're my bridled donkey. It would suit you well, considering every word that escapes your lips somehow manages to make more of an ass out of you!"

The boys and Dusk broke into a fit of startled laughter, but Del held the older man's gaze for a few defiant seconds. He then folded under the weight of it, looking away. "Come on, lads," he spat.

"Thank you all for assisting the healers of the city," Elijah called to the boys as they departed. "Finest men of Ephtar-Malas, the lot of you! I'll be sure to give your

A DAY'S DUTIES

patrol commander a glowing report." Dusk could almost feel the guard boys shiver at the words as they left. He looked up at the surgeon.

"Come," Elijah grunted. He set off down the hill toward the infirmary. Struggling to keep up with Elijah's long strides, Dusk listened to the clink and jangle of glass bottles and oddments on the surgeon's belt.

"Thank you," Dusk whispered.

"Thanks nothing," the surgeon barked. "I protected those idiot boys from being turned to ash or worse by your hand."

"M-m-mine?"

"Don't insult me," Elijah snapped, halting abruptly before the infirmary door. He reared down on Dusk the same way he had done to Del. "As your doctor who stitched you up after your battles and wrapped your shadow-cursed arm, I'm well aware of what you're capable of. Those boys weren't, and you were about to make them pay for their threats, weren't you?"

Dusk's eyes flicked to the smoldering gauze covering his arm. "Yes," he muttered.

"Yes," Elijah said sharply, backing away in mock study of Dusk. "And here I thought we had an understanding of your using this shadow for healing inside these walls."

"I did," Dusk insisted.

"Yes, you did!" Elijah said. "You saved some twenty lives this morning, according to my physicians. What is the price of twenty lives to you, Surgeon Dusk?"

"Limitless," Dusk muttered. "Priceless."

"Ah," Elijah said. "Then what is the price of four fools who irritate you and seek to do you harm?"

Dusk gave no response.

"The answer is *the same*, Surgeon Dusk," Elijah said, glowering. "You'll find I ask very few trick questions of those with whom I deal. I still honor the agreement we struck in the wains. Assure me my trust is still well placed."

"Trust," Dusk repeated severely. "It goes both ways, Elijah. I just learned today that my father came to this city two years ago. Not only that, but I hear from Torross that he spoke with *you*! Yet another piece of news you seem so easily to omit?"

"Because of trust placed in me," Elijah retorted, "I am sworn to secrecy regarding your father. There are pieces moving in the world whose compulsions are better left unseen, at least for now, I—" As he said the words, Elijah stumbled forward, bumping into Dusk, who flung out both hands to steady the surgeon.

Wondering if he would at some point be forced to bear the weight of every man twice his size and height in Ephtar-Malas, Dusk croaked, "Elijah, have you slept at all since we met?"

"No!" Elijah retorted, shaking his head and standing back up to his full height. "And that's why I have no patience for stupidity and the petty squabbles of children!" He pounded the infirmary door, which opened immediately into the familiar candlelit hallway and bespectacled porter.

"Master Elijah!" the excited little man said. "We were expecting—"

A DAY'S DUTIES

"If you'd care to rise above such things and to act the man you're supposed to be," Elijah said, interrupting the porter and turning back to Dusk one final time. "Then let's get into the house and rest tonight. I will evaluate your treatment of this morning's patients at dawn, and we'll see how well you held back."

"What of Keiphral?" Dusk asked, clearing the threshold behind him.

"Still in the citadel, and being treated well," Elijah said wearily, handing his packs and gear to the doorkeeper.

"And the prince," Dusk ventured. "Del s-s-said—"

"That oaf," Elijah said, "though he would do better with a muzzle than a mouth, has the truth of things. But I will say no more. Now, goodnight! You did well today, excepting our meeting just now. But we shall discuss tomorrow." With that, Elijah shuffled down the entry hall and disappeared.

When he reached his room, the day's duties caught up with Dusk, along with his travels and battles from the night before. As he changed into his night clothes, Dusk asked of his room, "How am I to c-c-continue balancing power and gentleness if forced t-t-to slay then heal one day, then heal then slay the next? How would Da have managed?"

The answer came as Dusk made to remove the helm. As he set his hand to the steel, weariness overcame him, and he fell across his pallet, the world going black to the sound of distant whispering.

19
INTERLUDE: SLEEPLESS DREAM

"Bring your healing powers to bare, for our prince has grown worse and calls out for restoration and help, even in his sleep. So much rides on you, Star Under-earth. Would you not remove the Nokleth's cloak, just for this small healing?"

"Healing the Sickness is no small healing and will take all of my power to do rightly. If I remove the gift of my cloak, I will be found, my light revealed. Will the city be ready when fomori and Masked Ones come to steal me?"

"It will have to be. All hands are forced. The enemy is close. We must try. If the prince survives, then he shall again lead the defense, to the encouragement of Men. If you are not revealed, then the city's fall is guaranteed with time."

"I am ... afraid. Afraid to reveal my light, only to see it fail him, for I fear it will not be enough."

"What then will be enough?"

"The shadow."

"No. The boy is not yet ready. His time spent among

INTERLUDE: SLEEPLESS DREAM

the patients has shone his skill, which is staggering. But he cannot control the deadly thing he wields. Death is all that will come if we bring him up now."

"Bring him."

"I will not."

"Then your prince dies."

"... I will fetch him."

* * *

"I just wish I could have seen him again. He's been gone so long, and our only news of him came from that tall surgeon who helped heal Eissyr just that much more. But the surgeon's gone, same as Dusk, with no other news sent afterward. Now I suppose no news will come up the mountain. Seems all the world is burning, what with the torch-glow and all the booming going on down in the valley below."

"It's a frightful time for us all. But come along, Aryka dear. The Men of the Lower-world have thrown up gates and towers to guard and watch the bottommost reaches of the mountain. They work their way up, building their fortifications ever higher. And new folk will fly here seeking refuge, knowing now the ways west and north are barred. Soon we shall all be mountain-folk!"

"All except Dusk, who fled the mountain to travel among the Lower-worlders."

"He travels to find the final cure, Ary. If he's not home yet, then he's not *found* it yet. Come help!"

"He's not home yet because he went to that dreadful city instead of returning home. I hope the surgeon is right. But how will folk respond if they see him go all feral and beastly? It happened whenever he became overwhelmed in his search for cures. It was like a whole other side of him took over. What happens if that part of him breaks through when he's at his weakest? Sorry, Ma, I'm just worried. What needs doing?"

"Da needs help chopping wood for palisades during the day. Then you'll come in at light-down for supper. Before bed, for a few hours, you and I will carve bows from the ash and yew not reserved for wall-building. Ours is the strongest, springiest timber as can be found on Sunreach. We'll give those fomori-folk what for should they seek to take our soaring fells while our hunters remain watchful, armed, and keen of eye!"

* * *

"Ride on! War ravages T'Rhonossarc and Gathilin, but the Angloreans must be stirred to a fury if they're to win their fights and come to the Midlotheans' aid after."

"And you think you can kindle that fury, Treiarn? How?"

"I stole the Key, and so have stoked the full brunt of the king's hatred. We seek the camps of the Swardha-Menn, thence to show the Angloreans their beloved Key in enemy hands! So ride, you hundred! Ride now to Anglorost, and afterward to Last-Hope!"

INTERLUDE: SLEEPLESS DREAM

* * *

"Lohrë? Where are you, my love? Life has only just begun and cannot end for you so soon, and neither for me. I will find you. But where? And where is the Elf-lord? Shout to me, my love! Anything that will help me find you. We are needed away, for the Fomori Throne must be found again. Awaken, and hear Cyrwedh calling!"

* * *

"Well done, faithful one. Please, help me."

"I will not."

"You must! You're so close now. I saw you solve the twists and turns of T'Rhonossarc's labyrinths without aid and make your way to the Storm. You are small, but you are strongest, most powerful! The armies are yours for the task."

"No."

"All the world will be ruined. The light is gone out of it. Last-light, under Malice, is all that's left. But even what little light is left can help."

"I s-s-said no."

"Release last-light! The Key holds shut the door, and the Coffin entraps last-light."

"No."

"But power will be yours, more power!"

"Enough to s-s-save my mother?"

"That is too small a wish. Think bigger, little one. You shall have everything you could ever want, and more! Power overwhelming, and dominion over all. Just *think*."

"You cannot s-s-save my mother."

"You shall rule, better than the Nephtyr, than the Atrellarrath—nay, the Creator!

"No."

"Why do you deny me?"

"I know b-b-better. My foundation is strong, laid d-d-down by my mother, my father, and by Eternity. And I *am* faithful, but not to you."

"You will be."

"Faithful always, but n-n-not to you."

"Find me."

"I w-w-will, to overthrow you."

"We shall be joined, the lesser and greater halves of power!"

"No."

"You *shall* obey."

"Not you."

"Then I shall find another, for *malice hides a great secret*."

"It may, but there is only l-l-light in the end, and you r-r-rejected it long ago."

"I see. You know who I am; I, who have been whispering to you, guiding you?"

"Eshra."

20

POWERS TO BEAR

"Dusk, hurry!" a voice hissed, yanking Dusk out of his dream of familiar voices. "Wake up." The face of Elijah, stony and cold, stirred him to waking.

Dusk's eyes opened, seeing the outer room and hall doused in flickering gold as candles sprang to life. "Wh-what?" he began.

"Thought you'd awaken to serve only patients of the infirmary?" Elijah asked. "You will. But now, a certain patient needs your help, far above. My world is become yours. Hurry up! Dress and gather tools. Two minutes."

Dusk shook his head, trying to dispel his grogginess. The motion hurt, his head feeling oddly heavy as he rocked it side to side on his shoulders. Then he reached up, felt familiar metal there, and groaned. But his dreams stung his conscience again. Then thoughts of battle and foreboding seized him. "Elijah," he said with sudden fierceness. "The city. We've m-m-missed some-some-s-s-somethi—"

"Don't hurt yourself," the surgeon said. "The city is safe still, for now. News says the enemy waits on the borders of T'Rhonossarc. Fomori harry our supply roads, stealing from any who would dare bring replenishment to the city. However, I think they did not expect to find the Men of Ephtar-Malas, who stand just as tall and powerful with the world's light failing as they stood in ancient days. Up now! Less than a minute."

With a groan, Dusk threw off his blankets. Their absence revealed the gauze as it wound about his chest, his aching arm, and hand. Still lying flat, he looked up and about his little room. Elijah had already gone out. He groaned again, then sat up. He threw his legs over the edge of the bed, his feet slapping stone. Tugging on new trousers, socks, and boots, Dusk shook the sleep from his eyes. As he put his head through a linen shirt, Dusk heard a crash and a curse from Elijah. The surgeon still bustled about in the next room. Dusk grabbed up Aryka's gray-green cloak from the hook he had hung it on. He clasped it absently with Tor Tarian's badge, remembering the fresh scent of Ary's brown hair whenever she would hug him.

"Home soon," he whispered, before going to his cupboard for surgical implements, herbs, and medicines. When he was supplied, he removed the helm, tucking it under one arm. Then, in his haste to gather up the remainder of his things, Dusk jumped when he thought he had seen an ominous stranger pass by his bed, having entered his room noiselessly and without being seen. Instead, he stopped to gaze at the grim, aged face and fire-bright eyes, recognizing them all as his own. The face stared back at him through the looking glass he had passed, and he began thinking of his da. But, shaking his head at the sound of Elijah's hasty footsteps, Dusk moved on.

Bag packed, Dusk rushed into the next room. Soft candlelight revealed a scattered stack of books and a plant whose pot had shattered when it fell from the desk with them. Vellum and cracked paper soaked up water and dirt as he passed. Just as he bent to mitigate the damage, Elijah's voice called, "Downstairs, Dusk! Our guests are waiting."

"Guests?" Dusk mouthed to himself as he crossed the dim room. He made a point to rescue a copy of a book named *The Firas Gospel*, giving it a quick brush with his hand before returning it to its place on the desk. Passing the library then descending the stairs, Dusk sneaked across the ward filled with sleeping patients. But before he reached the entry hall, he spotted a pair of stern eyes staring at him from a dark corner of the room. He made his way over to the warrior who had propped himself up on one elbow.

"Nephtyr Ithar-fel," Dusk said quietly. "How do you f-f-feel?"

"Passing fair, little surgeon," Tyrith whispered. Even with a quiet voice, Dusk could not help but think of distant thunder whenever the Nephtyr spoke. "You and Elijah know your craft. Though, I'm barely able to sleep. I wish I had some news of my friends. But that can't be helped. Where are you off to at such an hour?"

"Urgent errands, I'm t-t-told," Dusk said. "But I'm glad I've f-f-found you awake. Because I *do* bring a m-m-message for you, no more than a d-d-day old. Arwë was here, and he l-l-looked after you for a m-m-moment. He bid me t-t-tell you upon your waking, 'the prey is slain.'"

"Good news, twice over," Tyrith said, flashing the first smile Dusk had seen cross the Nephtyr's scarred face. But his smile fell, and he grew serious. "Any word of Yeiley?"

Dusk shook his head, thinking of the pale figure he had seen amongst the towers the night before. "None that I can c-c-confirm, but something tells me she's s-s-safe. And I'm g-g-glad I could relay at least s-s-some good news to you. For now, I'm off, p-p-probably to help someone else."

"Go, Dusk," Tyrith said, easing back into his cushions. "You've done well by me. None would blame you for disdaining a Nephtyr, but instead you've given earnest care and brought me hope. I will sleep well, and something tells *me* I will see you sooner than expected."

Dusk flashed a quick smile at the warrior's words. He nodded once, then hurried into the entry hall. His relief at having beaten Elijah to the barred front door brought such a sigh that Dusk nearly missed the commotion outside. A thick pall must have crept in over Malas while he had slept. The splatter of falling drops on cobblestone formed a dull cadence. But joined to the rhythm of rain were a chorus of low voices and horses' snorts. Torchlight flickered in through the shuttered windows, and Dusk guessed that a crowd of some dozen or more men waited outside the infirmary.

Elijah thumped a pack in the entryway, giving quick, hushed instructions to the bespectacled doorkeeper, who was still dressed in nightclothes. Something was wrong. Elijah dismissed the little man with a wave. Dusk saw Elijah turn, ashen-faced, then stride up the entry hall. The tall man clapped Dusk on the shoulder as he arrived. Dusk fell in behind him, donning Treiarn's helm and Aryka's hood over it. With a shove from Elijah, the heavy infirmary door swung open. Then they were out in the world, under soaking rain and glaring torchlight.

"Captain Aelfnoth," Elijah said to the group of brightly armored men. Dusk had been wrong. There were not twelve but *twenty* men here, all dressed in scarlet and steel. Nearly half were mounted. The others stood close to their animals, whispering gently. One particularly tall man detached himself from them. He came forward, guiding two horses by the bit.

"Surgeon Bana'Ath," the man boomed. "Straight to the top with us tonight, no stops."

"His condition has worsened?" Elijah said, mounting.

"Not so loud," the captain whispered. "I have only been told to escort you and your best surgeon with haste."

"I'll draw no more attention to our situation with a question than you already have with half a regiment parading through the streets armed for war, Captain. You will at least do me the courtesy of telling me what I'm walking headlong into."

"A parade not by *my* order," Aelfnoth snapped. Then he sighed. "Apologies, Elijah. We were *instructed* to give full escort. Had I had my way, I would have come to your door alone and in the dark. But the Stewards insisted. Mount now, and I will tell you all that's happened."

Elijah nodded, then motioned in Dusk's direction. "He rides with us."

"Your ward?" Aelfnoth asked, brow furrowed.

"My *best surgeon*, captain," Elijah replied. "Give him the same courtesy you'd give me. Now, let's be off. My bones want me out of this rain and back abed before sunrise."

Aelfnoth frowned. "Two guests with us tonight," he said. "Is this wise, Elijah?"

Elijah nodded, looking at a miserable figure standing apart from the soldiers. He hunched beside his horse, almost kneeling. "I'm glad you fetched him," Elijah said cheerily.

"Del?" Dusk whispered. Even in the torch glow, the broad boy's face was drawn and green. One hand held his horse's bridle. The other kept firm hold of his stomach.

"Our self-important swordsman wants a look 'behind closed doors,'" Elijah said with satisfaction. "He said he seeks the prince's inner circles, and, fittingly, his heritage grants him such privileges."

Captain Aelfnoth grunted, then motioned for his men to attend Dusk. The world flew suddenly away from Dusk's feet. Light and rain blurred, and he felt himself hauled into a saddle, where he sat in front of a dark-skinned soldier. From so high up, Dusk watched Aelfnoth pass a horse's reigns to Elijah. Both men mounted, then with a clamor of voices, hoofs, and cobbles, the company was off.

Smooth stone walls and high archways blurred by as they cantered up the endless ramp that paralleled the steps of the fifth Stair. Passing through gates as they made their ascent, the retinue met salutes from men clad in scarlet and bronze. There was no stopping. Each threshold passed overhead with a whoosh and a second's respite from the rain.

Dusk looked up. The sky bellowed, cloud and wind at war. Lightning crawled high above, but thunder growled later, farther away. Drops soaked his hood, but his head remained warm and dry under his helm. *Going to the top of Ephtar-Malas?* he thought.

Yes, hurry to the top to find the door downward, the helm whispered.

Shush, more important things to consider now, Dusk responded. *Could this have something to do with Keiphral, the cloaked girl, or what Del and Elijah had let slip about the prince being sick?*

They rode on for several cold minutes, passing turret, garden, and house. Dusk spied curious faces staring from window hollows fitted with dyed glass and lead for support. He stared back in wonder, pondering just how many months' pay earned guarding wagons could afford just one such glass panel. The upper levels were affluent indeed.

A short time later, the horsemen marshaled one by one into a single column. Their ascent had become a level road once more. But before them now sprawled a smooth stone bridge, so narrow only one mounted man at a time could cross without risk of falling. So far was the chasm between the company and the next gate that the bridge curved away and out of sight as it followed the shape of the cracked mountainside around. The clack of hooves came a little slower as the riders' animals grew cautious. Dusk looked to his left side, noting the walls, high towers, and sentries manning them. Looking to his right, his breath caught. Valley, river, mountains, and misted woods lay all about for miles and miles far below. With no guard rails to keep him from falling and joining the landscape, Dusk clung to his horse's mane.

"How high up h-h-have we ridden?" he breathed. "And how much t-t-time since we left the infirmary?"

"Arwë-Heófness stands a thousand or more feet above the Sable Gate," boomed his riding companion. "And we are perhaps some four hundred above your infirmary. The Arrow-bridge was one of the last gifts to the city, built and gifted by the Qwei-Sillar before they departed northward."

"Arrow-b-b-bridge?" Dusk said. "But it c-c-curves."

The soldier chuckled. "The shape of the bridge has nothing to do with the name, Surgeon. The Elder Kindred, sharp of eye and strong of arm as they were, built us this bridge as a shield from our enemies. The bridge crosses the gap between Dún-Scraeff, the broken mount. It connects the summit of All-Souls to the Prince's Ward. Should a hostile host somehow breach the city to this high point, they would be forced to cross the bridge two abreast, and with no railing. Those with balance enough to cross would die, cut to ribbons from every angle by archers from our towers."

"S-s-seems effective," Dusk remarked.

"And look there!" The soldier pointed a steel finger up toward the taller of the two summits as the bridge's path stretched around it. Dusk had heard the heavy boom of water falling growing steadily for some time. The riders rounded the bridge's turn to see the source of the noise. A roaring waterfall, greatest of the hundred that surged down and into the city, flung its contents into the gap between bridge and mountain. "We control the falls, in a small way," the soldier said. "We dam up melted snow and rainwater from above. Should unwanted visitors survive our arrows, then those above may trigger the water's full release. And our visitors would enjoy the courtesy of a ten-million-gallon drink."

"Genius," Dusk whispered.

"Glad you approve," the rider said, amused.

"So," Dusk said, trying to keep his questions from overflowing. "Prince's Ward?"

"Aye," the man said, a smile in his voice. "Can't blame you for being curious. Very few are ever given the honor of viewing the city's highest ward. And, meaning no insult, I'm not sure why it's been granted to you."

"Elijah?" Dusk suggested.

"His word carries great weight," the rider agreed. "Though it grows lighter by the day, it would seem. We of the soldiery would trust him with our lives. But his recent penchant for causing trouble as often as treating bodies gives some pause."

"D-d-do you think he's r-r-right doing the things he d-d-does?"

GARDEN OF ASH

The rhythm of clacking hooves returned to the center of Dusk's thought as the man mulled over the question. "I do, for my part," the soldier responded. "And the last thing I'll say is this: Keep close to the man. If he sees value in you, go with him to the end. He's more than healing hands and a cutting wit. Things tend to happen 'round ones such as him."

"Things?" Dusk asked.

"Big things," the rider said. "He's seen war and wonder, and the world tends to change because of him. Things of that sort."

"What about a g-g-girl?" Dusk ventured.

The man laughed. "Sorry, lad. Seems I've taken all the time we were allowed. We've arrived." He motioned to the others who were passing under what seemed to be the final gatehouse and into a grand colonnade beyond. They passed through, then riders dismounted swiftly behind him. Dusk's companion climbed down in a smooth motion, then brought the boy down from the saddle with strong hands.

"Thank you for f-f-filling the time and r-r-riding with me, sir," Dusk said.

"The honor was mine, little master," the guardsman said. "And though our conversation was cut short, I have a feeling you'll learn quickly about all that I said, sticking close to Master Surgeon Bana'Ath, mind you."

"Yes, sir!" Dusk said, giving the salute Tor had shown him. "May I know your n-n-name, given the ch-ch-chance to meet you again in the lower st-st-streets?"

The man laughed and gave a crisp salute in return. "Tamru Angharad," the man said. "But friends call me Angry."

"Rider Tamru," Dusk said, taking care not to trip over a single word. "You've no cause to be angry with me yet. My name is Dusk."

"Surgeon Dusk," Tamru Angharad said, surprised by the boy's courtesy. "May tonight's work be swift and successful for both you and Elijah. Now, off you go! My part is done, but you're still in a hurry."

Dusk gave an enthusiastic nod, then took off at a run. Tamru chuckled as the boy departed. "Not just apprenticed to Elijah ben Ath," he whispered, "but surgeon of equal skill and station. Value indeed."

Dusk spotted his mentor. But first came Keiphral, running over from where he had been posted at the gate. The lad clad in elf harness detached himself from the guards there to join the reduced retinue of Elijah, Aelfnoth, Del, and Dusk. Dusk waited for the larger lad. "Made it to the t-t-top first without m-m-me, eh?" he whispered enthusiastically. "Seems I've been p-p-pulled into some secret d-d-duty, same as you."

"Would that I were," whispered Keiphral, clapping Dusk on the shoulder. He shifted his grip on a plate-and-wood heater shield.

"New shield?" Dusk asked, admiring his friend's new armament.

"Assigned when they stationed me at the gate to wait

for Elijah and Aelfnoth," Keiphral said, showing Dusk the bronze and scarlet patterns of the shield's surface. "And *you*, apparently!"

"Any idea what's g-g-going on?"

"Only that they questioned me for hours in the citadel."

"They?" Dusk asked.

"Barons of T'Rhonossarc," Keiphral said. "All sorts of lords and ladies. They had questions about the elf-lands, the Elf-lord, battles, my travels, companions, all of it. After they let me rest, they thanked me for having fought fomori and rescued citizens of the city by setting me atop the Prince's Ward. I'm guard of the citadel! I'm to escort you and the master surgeon straight to the prince's rooms, then await you at the door. Probably should have waited to let ol' Elijah tell you all that. But seeing as how you're going to learn it all anyway, what harm could come of hearing it from me?"

"C-c-couldn't think of a b-b-better doorman," Dusk mocked, jostling Keiphral's shoulder.

"Yeah, well, we can't all be as high as you, escorted like a lord through the city n' all," Keiphral replied, punching Dusk's good arm. "Speaking of lords, the elf we spotted for that instant in the fight for the wagon trains is here!"

"Arwë!" Dusk said. "Keiph, I m-m-met him briefly, yesterday. Tor Tarian n-n-named him Herald of Wildercrown when he came to the infirmary to v-v-visit the angel. You were right! He's g-g-got to be Lohrë's brother."

"Must be," Keiphral agreed. "He came striding up the Stair, crossing Prince's Ward last night, wounded and grim. He looked just like Lohrë. For all his hurts, Arwë went right into the citadel bearing some bloody token. He hasn't come back down, so I'm guessing he's their guest up there."

The sound of retching cut short their conversation. Del, pale and green from his night of debauchery and the ride up, bent over an immaculately trimmed shrub. Dusk and Keiphral looked to one another then stifled their laughter. Del stood and let flash his anger at the sight of Dusk and Keiphral's snickering. The swordsman shoved past them, mounting the steps to the palace.

"What's he doing here?" Keiphral asked.

"Elijah—"

"Surgeon Dusk," came Elijah ben Ath's angry hiss.

"Tell you on the way," Dusk told Keiphral, taking off toward Elijah.

The tall surgeon, already halfway across the well-manicured ward, walked and talked with Aelfnoth. When he caught up with the two men, Dusk nearly had to maintain his jogging pace to match their stride. They hunched as they went, cloaks wrapped tightly about them against the rain. The low thump of their boots on the flooded cobbles was joined by the high staccato clicks of Dusk's smaller, lighter ones. A pattern soon emerged from their procession. Dusk looked back. The escorting guards had left, tongues of torchlight fading as the last of them passed back under the prince's gate, back across Arrow-bridge. Keiphral followed the captain and surgeons at a distance so as to see but not overhear them.

"Since sundown," Aelfnoth said in response to a question from Elijah.

"Have other physicians been notified?"

"No, sir. Only you, and now the boy."

"Probably for the best," Elijah said. "Does anyone attend him?"

"Only his trusted servants," Aelfnoth said. "And the usual handful of fickle noble fools." A raised eyebrow from the surgeon pulled a harrumph out of the towering captain. "They all know what I think of them. They play their games with people's lives while our enemies scheme in the dark. I stand in the gap, reminding our *elite* that goblins, and not common folk, are their enemies. Then *you're* left to stitch me back together after the old men's pockets are lined and the young men are dead. Am I wrong, healer?"

"Oh no," Elijah said with a wry smile. "I think you have the shape of things, Captain. If all the world were run by captains, soldiers, and those who work honestly for their coin, we'd have far fewer losses and far better judgment."

"Alas, for the barring of good men to power and a brighter world!" the captain laughed.

Elijah chuckled with him, and the two men continued speaking quickly and quietly of secret things. The downpour washed away what little he could hear of the conversation, but Dusk found himself gaping at stone stalagmites that struck toward the heavens. Firelight glowed in their windows, which had been bored out of the standing stone. Each tower looked out from the four corners of the prince's level, no doubt offering a view of valley, mountain, river, and all who approached.

When the company had passed through the high ward, Dusk glanced to the side to see another titanic bridge of white stone. It crossed a dizzying gap between the magnificent square and a cathedral, vast and indomitable. Even in the dark of night and storm, Dusk could see that the minster was as widespread as any city. Its buttresses and trellises climbed, layer upon layer, roof over roof, until its vastness clawed at the clouds with silver fingertips—the highest turrets in all of Ephtar-Malas.

Dusk's awe was short-lived, as Aelfnoth and Elijah had crossed the square without so much as a glance. But wonder ignited anew when the captain led the surgeons to the city's highest construction. A bastion, towered and high-walled, lay carved below the greater summit of the broken mountain. Standing nearly as high as the great cathedral, the citadel's walls were unassailable and shone of pearl, even in the gloom. It towered over Dusk, impossibly sculpted, and not by the skill of Men. The companions mounted switchback marble steps, passing sentries with salutes from Aelfnoth.

They climbed for several minutes before approaching doors of hewn quartz. Intricate carvings of surpassing skill decorated panels of the doors' faces. One depicted great jewels in the sky. They shone brightly in one carving, then lay in shattered ruin in the next. Great armies of Men, elves, and winged things were locked in battle with hosts of evil-looking Men, goblins, and cloven-hoofed creatures. And watching over these stood wicked, smiling things holding tablets and styli.

Captain Aelfnoth exchanged a few brief words with his sentries, then ordered Keiphral and Del to join them at the door.

"Be ready, lad," Elijah said to Dusk while the captain gave orders. "I fear we'll both be hard put to it tonight. Don't speak unless calling for tools, medicines, and boiling water. I fear we walk into a den of vipers to rescue a wounded badger. And let's pray he has the resilience of one."

Before Dusk could ask one of many mounting questions, the citadel doors split and swung open. Elijah shook Aelfnoth's hand, bidding him farewell. The towering captain bowed, leaving the surgeons in the care of citadel guards. Dusk watched as Aelfnoth joined Keiphral, Del, and a cadre of soldiers. As the captain spoke, the guardsmen, seeming vexed, nodded reluctantly. Soon, the ringing of Aelfnoth's mail joined the chorus of rainwater as he departed. Four of the citadel guard, armored and robed, escorted the physicians through carpeted and candlelit hallways. The men wore helms whose faceguards were the wings of eagles, their cloaks dark as wine. Dusk imagined Captain Aelfnoth belonging with these silent scions of a more legendary age, rather than a guard commander.

"I like C-c-captain Aelfnoth," he ventured.

Elijah chuckled grimly. "As do I. He's the best knight you'll find, either in this realm, or any other. He's every bit deserving of a place at the prince's side. Though the prince figures him too sharp for the court and wisely appointed him war tactician, guard captain, and the prince's face and voice when Aelfnoth treats with the people. He is honest, courageous, and you could ask for no greater ally in all the city; therefore, he is the target of the city leaders' hatred. They would see him removed or harmed. Though I fear his tongue will land him in more trouble than any foe or plot."

They stopped at another small company of citadel guard who stood at the entrance to another great door. This one also stood tall and imposing, carved of ivory and fastened all about with steel. Elijah breathed deeply, looking every bit the old surgeon hoping to retire. He looked down. "Dusk," he said, disregarding Keiphral, Del, and the dozen guardsmen who stood within earshot. "You've healed the people of your village, and of the kingdoms in the South. You've brought your mother back from the brink of death and contended with dark powers. You nearly cured the Wasting Sickness itself, and you slew a hundred fomori with a will."

Dusk flushed, looking away to hide his embarrassment before the dark eyes of the soldiers.

"If ever there were a time to bring all your powers of healing and more to bare," Elijah said, kneeling to put a hand on Dusk's shoulder and look him in the eyes. "Now's the time. We come to it at last: the reason I brought you here. There are two men in this citadel who need you more than any in all the world. One of them is me. The other is behind this door, on what may be his deathbed should we fail to help him. Understand?"

Dusk's eyes narrowed. "No, Elijah."

"Then all you need know is that we shall both apply our craft here, apply it well, and save a man." He nodded to the waiting soldiers, and they threw open the ivory door. Inside sprawled a luxuriant chamber, guarded by another handful of tall sentries in the corners. Dusk and Elijah entered while Keiphral and Del took up positions on either side of the door, just inside the room.

Servants ran this way and that. Dusk's eyes drank in the flames of braziers and oil lamps whose light flickered off mosaics illustrating ancient histories in piecemeal stories. Stunning patterns and lettering decorated walls, columns, and beveled edges that met the ceiling in riots of gold and lapis. Fine tool work decorated every archway, and each lay festooned with insulating velvet or banners embroidered with the heraldry of knights and great houses. Trinkets and relics lined the shelves of display cases. Reams of wax-stamped parchment, quills, and expensive, deep-toned inks lay strewn across several writing desks.

Deeper inside, several attendants surrounded a four-posted bed. Behind the bed's transparent drapery lay a pale man dressed in scarlet silks and white linens. He was thin, deeply recessed in the cushions, and fought weakly for his life. The servants' heads rose, turning to face the arrival of the citadel guard and Elijah. They bowed in deference to the surgeon. Then they hesitated, frowning at the gauze-wrapped, bright-eyed boy who stood beside the surgeon, all a-clatter with his bottles, bags, and remedies.

"Report!" Elijah snapped, making the servants jump.

A young woman, strands of blonde hair falling from her headscarf and hood, stepped forward. His heart skipping a full beat, Dusk nearly gasped with recognition. Keeping his composure, he stood as tall as he could and tried to look the part of the calculating surgeon as he avoided her opal eyes.

"My lord," she said, her voice a familiar music to Dusk's ear. "This storm seems to have worsened the prince's condition. This Wasting Sickness before caused him confusion and extended periods of unconsciousness, with dreams that would not let him sleep. With the storm's arrival, he does not wake at all, and he bleeds when he coughs. Sometimes we cannot stop it, hence the red wrappings. We have done our best to keep him comfortable, though we can do little else. Please ..." She stepped back, wiping her eyes.

"You have done what you could," Elijah said to her. Then, addressing the surrounding attendants, he said, "Stay near, all of you. And be ready to run for us when we call. Surgeon Dusk here has healed women and men by the hundreds, in more lands than any of you could dream of seeing. You are to pay him every kindness you would me, and run for whatever he needs at his command." A small flourish of nods signaled the servants' compliance. Elijah then motioned for Dusk to drop all supplies onto a nearby table. Dusk did so, gathered his tools, then eyed the blonde-haired girl again. He met her eyes, which sparkled with the same opal sheen he had nearly been lost in when he slew her enemies. She was first to look away.

Dusk took a step toward the girl. "Yei—"

"Pay attention to what you're doing, Surgeon!" Elijah hissed. "If he dies, *we* die, understand?"

"No!" snapped Dusk. "Just wh-wh-what have you g-g-gotten me into, Elijah? Are w-w-we treating the Prince of Ephtar-Malas?"

"I will tell you all after our patient is safe and we're on the long path down to the lower levels," Elijah whispered. "For now, we pull no stops. You will bring every ounce of your power to bear for this man's mending. You will prepare the same remedy as you made for Eissyr. You will sing all the songs of remedy and power, and I will step in where your voice falters."

Hot anger smoldered in Dusk's stare. But seeing the servants gaze in wonder at their quiet argument, he nodded to Elijah, set to untying his packs.

Straightening the helm on his head with a steadying hand, Dusk whispered to it, saying, "I remember the f-f-first remedy. Show me a g-g-greater one if you know, and l-l-let me save this man." And with both light and shadow welling up inside him, Dusk's arm burned under his heavy wraps. He applied his time and tenderness once more, helping Elijah wash and prepare the suffering man on the bed.

Dusk then turned to Elijah. He pointed toward a table laden with their healing elements, then to a cast iron kettle. Elijah grabbed up each, filled the kettle with water, then set it over the fire. Dusk gathered a few other stoppered bottles, phials, and packaged antidotes. He then hummed his power over them before handing them off to Elijah. The tall surgeon poured the ingredients and whistling kettle's contents into a large clay bowl. With each ingredient Dusk cut, shucked, or crushed, the very air surrounding his hands caught alight. Stories of his work that would pervade the city later spoke of the little surgeon whose hands burned red-hot with power, sparks escaping them as when scorching iron is struck by the hammer.

Dusk poured various measurements of liquids from his phials into the bowl, then mixed the remedy gently. When Elijah thought all was ready, Dusk brought his hands together at his chest, as if praying. The boy drew his palms apart, and between them sprouted a golden light. It gleamed through his fingers, flashing gold, silver, and green.

Into the tincture went the globe of light, and it melted the contents of the bowl into glowing liquid gold. The surrounding attendants looked at the medicine, eyes growing wide. Dusk smiled, motioning for them to help the sleeping man to a sitting position. He brought the bowl to the sickbed. Before administering the cure, Dusk looked at Elijah. The surgeon was finishing clearing the man's nasal passages, throat, and chest of phlegm and blood with a set of winding tools. Elijah nodded to Dusk, eyeing the smoking wrappings on the boy's arm.

Breathing deeply, Dusk set his gleaming cure on a nightstand, feeling power seethe under his skin. He caught sight of the blonde girl, who watched him intently. *Who are you?* he wondered at her. But he shook his head. *I can't* care now. This man is worse off than Ma was. I will help him, then her.

"You've come far, Surgeon Dusk," Elijah said, bringing Dusk's focus back to the chamber.

"As far as a prince's bedside," Dusk said without stuttering. "Now to add the latest ingredient." He slit his smoldering bandages from shoulder to wrist with a thought. The power underneath was uncaged. It wanted escape and violence, ten times more than it had wrought against the fomori. But Dusk stayed its murderous intent with a will, forced it to mend, not to mangle. Shadows stretched at odd angles, formed shapes that seemed to grope for the boy as he hummed louder. Countering the serenity of his humming, Dusk began singing the harmony of the sea's song as it thrashed under the Storm. When he stopped, both songs echoed in the murky chamber. Then he struck up new songs in harmony and discord with them. Surrounded by such music, Dusk began his ministrations.

With a master's skill, Dusk worked tirelessly inside the opulent house, repairing the damage the Wasting Sickness had wrought on this man whom Elijah had claimed needed curing most of all. The work took hours, as Dusk and Elijah only gave the man one mouthful of Dusk's gleaming draft at a time. They would administer one gulp then allow the weakened man periods of relaxation afterward so as not to upset his throat and lungs with fits of tearing coughs. Attendants traded posts, shifting in and out of the grand chamber. They stood close at hand offering gifts of time, support, and singing. Attendants also delivered new slices of roots requested by Dusk. Some also brought packs of seeds, stacks of weeds, and gave the surgeons cups of cool water to drink.

When the bedridden man seemed to emerge from his dreadful coma, he coughed, beginning a fit that lasted agonizing minutes. The surgeons did all they could to stop the man's throat from ripping under the strain, bringing up blood. They were not successful, but continued their ministrations while servants applied white rags that returned to their hands stained with crimson.

After some time, Dusk finally delivered the last drop of the cure, humming a new song of power. But the sound faltered, his strength giving out under the pressure of the shadow in its incessant desire to kill instead of repair. Dusk's strength gave way under the restrained shadow, which burst from his arm. It leaped into all corners, drowning the chamber in darkness. Knowing the ailing man was a hair's breadth from either recovery or death, Dusk looked with pleading eyes to Elijah for words that would fill the broken song. Elijah stepped in, his rich baritone accompanying Dusk's rhythmic hums. Elijah's song pressed the shadow back toward slumber. Some measure of peace spread through the stony room. Then the two surgeons lay a blanket of healing power over the man on the bed. Like two strong hands that pulled him out of the thrashing sea as he floundered, Dusk and Elijah brought the man back from the brink of death. And like a ship of rescue unlooked for in a storm, the same strong hands hauled him onto the solid deck of life.

But just as the healers' songs reached their crescendo, there was another faltering. One song sang beautifully low, calling for peace and restoration. The other became harsh and discordant, then failed in its harmony altogether. Dusk abandoned the melody. Then, a single, unwelcome note rang in the chamber. With it, Dusk whispered a word. "Eshra."

The man on the bed screamed. Thunder cracked. Bloody coughs soon drowned the screams, then shadows reclaimed the chamber. Fear struck the surgeons, and they looked to one another in desperation as the man heaved, wheezed, and changed. Dusk thought quickly. He had kept the Storm's fierce power at bay this entire night, and no shadow had entered the remedy. But here it was, raging in the chamber, casting everyone down and thirsting for blood.

Elijah was shouting words with a will as strong as iron. But even he quailed before the writhing shadow. The weight of the air in the chamber increased, crushing all within, even as they lay helpless. The shadow reached up, out from Dusk. It loomed over the bedridden man. But with fire in his eyes, Dusk stood, defying Sickness and shadow. Then the air went silent like an indrawn breath, turning to ice in all their lungs.

Release me, a voice commanded in Dusk's ear. *Release me, and I will save him.*

Elijah, with sweat coursing brow and face, drew up to

his full height, regaining power and wit. He roared at Dusk. But no sound escaped the surgeon's lips as Dusk listened to the deadly voice from inside his helm.

"To s-s-save him," Dusk whispered, resisting the Storm no longer. "To save us all." His eyes suddenly clouded over, their melted gold fading to black. Dusk's whole arm blazed with agony as power encircled both him and the man who drowned in shadow. Power went out from Dusk, but it worked no salvation. Elijah then leaped at Dusk, and his hand cracked across the boy's face.

"Fool goatherd!" Elijah thundered, but too late. Up from the bed rose not the sickly man, but a thing of twitching shadow. It fixed baleful eyes on Elijah. Then, with a swiping arm, it struck him down. White fangs split the shadow-man's head, and it stooped over Elijah's body.

21
MALICE

Fury overwhelmed all sense, and Dusk howled at the creature before it could bite the surgeon. It stopped, glaring at him. And he knew it now saw a beast instead of a boy, for Dusk knew he was hunched and terrible, his raw, feral power having taken control. Dusk's mind was a spinning hurricane, but it latched onto the tail of the shadow, *his* shadow, as it fled from him and sought to invade the near-dead prince.

You defy me, Dusk-healer! screamed the voice inside the helm. Dusk had become the creature he had tried so hard to hide, especially from Aryka. But the helm, words and all, still sat atop his head. *My power belongs with one who will listen.*

Eshra, Dusk responded, *the Storm and I are one. You were too weak to cling to power.* The prince, now a writhing shadow, towered over him. *I sacrificed my arm for power to destroy the Wasting Sickness. The power is my arm now. If you take my arm, I'll take your head.*

Power is for ruling, not for healing, fool-human! The

shadow thrashed at Dusk's muzzle. The Dusk-beast smashed the shadow's head into a stone column. Dusk could not control the Storm as it grew in his fading mind, and he flailed madly at the shadow. But the prince-shadow was strong and raked him with its claws. It tore his shoulder, spattering black across the floor and bed. The shadow caught Dusk by the throat, lifting him off his clawed feet.

Wind shrieked in Dusk's ears, and he crumpled the thing's chest with a vicious kick. Both monsters crashed to the floor. The Storm in his mind then blew back a little as Dusk felt his jaw break. The man-shadow's arms swept across the floor and pounded Dusk's head repeatedly. Then lightning struck, blinding Dusk, eye and mind. He screamed, hauling the shadow up by its hide with ten times his strength. Then Dusk slammed its head into the floor, cracking stone once, twice, then three times. But before Dusk could force the shadow down a fourth time, it tore itself from his grip. It reared on him, then bit him, neck and shoulder. Pain and outrage exploded as Dusk felt bone and sinew snap. He fell, his feral body curling around the grisly wound. The Storm scattered from his mind.

The man-shadow dug its clawed hand into Dusk's ankle, yanking him toward it, crushing bone. A treacherous wind from Dusk's mind blew away the black clouds, then the Storm was gone entirely. It drained out of him to join with the power of the prince-shadow.

Just as it entered into me on the Dread Coast, Dusk thought as all faded to black. The best had gone, and he was only a shepherd boy, hanging broken in the shadow's grasp. But as the ruined prince made to swallow Dusk whole, all turned to silver light. A peace as pure as glass calmed the chaos and agony of Dusk's mind and body. Then a word heavier than the cornerstone of the earth struck the prince-shadow. Dusk screamed without a sound, then all light went out. And in his dreams, strange words echoed in the dark, and clouds of vermilion and violet exploded with shafts of crashing lightning.

* * *

Keiphral Morne shot through the room like an arrow. *Seek the prince.*

"Malice hides a great secret!" Keiphral cried as he tore his elf-swords from their sheaths. He swung a wide cut past the prone bodies of Dusk and Elijah and the gleaming figure who stood over them. He struck the dark monster as it stood stunned by the figure's radiance. It reeled as he struck again.

Too late! he thought, stabbing with one blade, slicing with the other. *Should have reacted faster. But how could I have known? The prince, a monster? Wait, what's that?* He flung himself down, under the arcing slash of a blade. Del's stroke carved a chunk of thick shadow from the prince's side. The shadow crashed into the surgeons' table, showering the room with fragrant antidotes and shards of glass.

But the creature of swirling shadow recovered and reared on the two guard boys. Keiphral and Del fought together. One feinted, the other attacked. Then the first yanked the second back, out of reach of their swiping, seething foe. But one thick, shadowy arm struck Del off balance. The other lashed its rending claws across Keiphral's chest, tearing his coat and knocking him against a stone pillar. Dazed, but aware enough to know that his elvish mail had blunted the blow, Keiphral rushed back in.

Too late again, he thought.

Del, aiming a swipe of his blade that would have cut the man-shadow's head cleanly from its shoulders found his sword caught in the beast's sharp fangs. It bit down hard, and Del's sword broke. The prince swept him aside with a massive, shadowed arm. Keiphral heard the boy's head bounce off the stone floor as he dashed in, stabbing the shadow through the heart. But Keiphral's blade passed through with no resistance. The dark thing cuffed him across the chin, sending him sprawling to meet Del on the floor.

Keiphral rolled away just before the creature tore the floor with its claws. He clambered to his feet, ducking a dark, lunging arm. Dropping a sword, Keiphral chopped down with the other and cut off the arm above the elbow. The man-shadow loosed a shriek of rage that seared Keiphral's eardrums. With both hands, the boy clutched the sides of his head. Pain and darkness exploded as the shadow's unsullied arm crashed against Keiphral's head. The blow sent his elvish helm flying. It clattered away, little more than a mangled lump of steel. Keiphral felt blood run down the sides of his face and did not hear his sword drop uselessly to the floor. Above him stood the beast, rearing back to take his head with its claws. Then he caught a glimpse of something shining in its palm.

Trinket on a chain, he thought. *No matter. It is a riddle for another to solve. Goodbye!*

But just as Keiphral prepared to leave Leóhteness-Fal, the shadow's arm swept downward and crashed into an orb of golden light. The beast's savage strength rebounded off the impact, and a thunderclap struck the room. Everything in sight burned away in a wash of white fire. Keiphral heard the whining of some hurt and pathetic thing. Then he felt firm hands gripping the sides of his head. Out of the light, a face appeared in front of his. It was all he wanted to look at, and he felt the throbbing pain in his ears ebb gently away. Her eyes shone like burning crystals, and her face, pale and lean, was—

"Star of Outer-dark," he whispered.

"Star Under-earth for now," she replied.

Keiphral's heart leaped at the simple joy of his undamaged hearing and the gentleness of her voice. He looked up and lost himself in bewilderment of her. All that mattered was the touch of her hand that now cradled the back of his head while the other rested on his cheek. He did not want to move. But a name consumed his conscience.

"Yeiley," he said.

"Kel," she replied.

"It escaped."

Glory fled the room, replaced by the glow of a dying hearth fire. It was the only light that had not been snuffed out in the fighting. Yeiley had drawn up the hood of her cloak, and her eyes retreated into shadow. Wonder flickered as her light vanished, replaced by his desire for knowing. "My name," he said. "I don't know how it is mine, but I know it is. How did you know?"

She pointed to the boy who lay with his face down on the stone floor. Blood poured from his shoulder, and one of his legs stuck out, bending at a strange angle.

"Dusk!" Keiphral cried, leaping to his feet. The movement set his head spinning, his stomach lurching. He collapsed on the floor beside his friend, grabbing the lad's good hand and sobbing. "Oh Dusk! What did you do, you fool! We thought you would heal the prince, not make him into a monster! Who are you? And how deep does your power go? Is there anything you can't do? Will you even survive this thing you've done?" Then he saw the fire's coals reflecting off Dusk's forehead and realized his friend's helm released a small radiance of its own. He felt compelled to take it for himself, knew he must. His hand touched the burnished steel, and once more he heard the voice from the beach inside his head.

"*Kel,*" it said. "*Seek shadow. Free the light. Malice hides the Garden.*"

"The Garden," Keiphral breathed, then lowered the helm onto his head. The instant it touched his brow, Yelley's opal eyes lit with sudden perception. She recited to him,

"*Light's Heir shall seek for Garden-hid.*
Deep under earth, to find her worth.

> *Stars' Sailor flies from marching flame,*
> *Dusk-healer plays the Shadow's game.*
> *Scribe's deadly slaves both men shall fight*
> *to wake the world from endless night.*
> *Wither they go, Heir shall follow*
> *and Garden's Key they will find, lo!*
> *Night's pow'r is spent, soon breaks the day.*
> *Seek once-bright Innoth-Hyeil Darrë."*

"Cailus," Keiphral whispered, the memory sharp and bright. "Those were his words. And he was first to name me Sailor."

"My people spoke the words and knew you would come," Yeiley said, putting a hand on Keiphral's shoulder. The touch was light but firm, as if she greeted an old friend she had not at first recognized after years spent apart. She drifted away from him then, crouched to the bloody floor. She wrapped Dusk in her arms and in the folds of her cloak. Radiant tears fell from her eyes as she cradled his head. Then she whispered into the wounded boy's ear, "Dusk-healer. Leave has not been granted for you to depart. Return to us now, though sleep a while. Your strength is needed, and you must follow after us."

Yeiley drew back the hood of her cloak, and light filled the chamber once more.

This time not nearly as bright, Keiphral thought, staring as Yeiley held Dusk's body and sang to him until color flowed back into his pallid face. Beyond the skills of any surgeon, the shining girl knit together bone, muscle, and skin with light. Keiphral gasped as he saw, from the protective circle of her arms, Dusk take a gulp of air. The small boy then breathed easy, as if softly sleeping.

Keiphral threw his arms around them both. "Thank you," he choked.

Yeiley, holding a lad in each arm, laughed a little, and the sound rang in the chamber, dispelling shadow.

But Keiphral shook his helmed head, growing urgent. "Hurry!" he said and pulled away from her. "The prince-shadow meant to kill me with that final lashing. But you stopped him, your light flaring. It flashed off something he held. I didn't know what it could have been. But after hearing the full message from your people, I know that the prince holds the 'Garden's Key.'"

Yeiley nodded, then asked, "Guarded by the Princes of Ephtar-Malas?"

"Perhaps the safest place in the all the world for it," Keiphral said. "Think of the words of your people: We, the Heir, the Sailor, and the Healer, have all made our ways to Last-Hope. With guidance from the Qwei-Sillar, we sought protection. We hoped to form a plan, figure out what and where this Garden was. But it is the city itself, don't you see? Ephtar-Malas, not *malice*, hides the secret. The Key is revealed, and so must be the Garden."

Yeiley set Dusk's head gently on the floor, considering Keiphral's words. "The Atrellarrath put their trust in Elves, Nokleth, and Nephtyr," she said. "It is little surprise to learn that Men, too, are wrapped up in the story of our redemption. Whether their part is for good or ill remains to be seen. We were told we would come to know utter faith, for we could not save ourselves no matter how powerful we became."

"Rely on me, then," Keiphral said, springing into action. He gathered what little supplies as could be found in the prince's bedchamber. "If we don't know what role the prince-shadow plays, then experience says it must be for evil. We can't wait. If we don't find out where it went, what it's up to, then we'll all be hearing the enemy screaming Eshra's name before the Sable Gate soon enough. Then there won't be any plan at all."

"Will you go with me to the Garden, then?" Ithyeil asked as Keiphral slung a water bottle on a string about his shoulder. He gathered up little pouches of food and sheathed at his side the swords he had let fall during the fight.

"I'm going after *him*," Keiphral said, determination deepening his voice. "If the prince is become a servant of this *Eshra* and is driven by her power, then his goal must be the Garden too. If not, and he is under some spell triggered by Dusk's magic, then we must free the Prince of Ephtar-Malas all the same. Either way, Heir of the Atrellarrath, the answer is yes. I will go with you. You seek a Garden. I seek a prince. And yours is the only power that could contend with the shadow. And I fear both our goals are wrapped in it."

"What of Arwë and Tyrith?" she asked. "We will need to send word to them; your other friends as well."

"Elijah and Dusk will recover quickly," Keiphral said,

searching cabinet and drawer for gauze, medicines, and string. "They will follow us shortly. As for the elf and angel ..." He saw a pair of wild eyes gazing out from the carnage the battle had made of the tables, wardrobes, and floor surrounding the prince's bed. There, he dug Del out of the rubble, who gazed at him with wide-eyed wonder. "Del," he said, shaking the swordsman. Keiphral dragged him to a sitting position against the prince's sickbed. "Our companions, along with the citadel guard, will want news of us. You saw all that happened?"

"Didn't miss a detail," Del said wistfully, as if dreaming.

"Good," Keiphral said, clapping the boy on the shoulder, making him jump. He then turned to the girl who had drawn her cloak about her and readied her rapier of black and gold. "Your friends called you Yeiley, though somehow I doubt that's your real name. What is it?"

"Ithyeil Stëorra," she said. The name sounded like music to his ears.

"Ithyeil Stëorra," Keiphral repeated, shaking the dreams from his head. "We have a Garden to find and a prince to catch. And if Innoth-Hyeil Darrë truly lies at the heart of Ephtar-Malas, then we also have a people to redeem. You saw which way he went?"

She nodded, pointing to what looked to be a door of stone, thrown open. It stood sequestered into a darkened corner of the chamber.

"Secret doorways into the dark," Keiphral mused. Then he gave a frustrated sigh. "I have no tinder." But then he gave Ithyeil a wry smile. "I only possess daylight itself!"

She gave him a flat stare. "Only to be used at need," she said. "And even then, I fear I've both revealed and used too much."

"Need drives us," Keiphral said. "Dark paths below the city should prove little challenge, even if you remained cloaked. Now, away!" And off they ran, out of the prince's chambers by the secret way and into ancient darkness below the city.

* * *

Arwë burst into the chamber, bandaged wounds screaming at his exertions. A dozen citadel guards flanked him, and he scanned all the room in less than a second. He considered every detail. A company of guards lay unconscious, strewn about the chamber. Elijah ben Ath's scuffle with whatever foe had breached the chamber had ended with the old surgeon sprawled in a tangle of limbs. Eleven unconscious house servants and two serving girls lay spread across floor, bed, and desk, as if some force had blown them all off their feet. Most curious of all was the young surgeon, Dusk. He lay as if sleeping in restful bliss, completely unharmed. Near him sat the crumpled form of a soldier who had propped his back against the only bed in the chamber. His eyes lay open, wild and horrified, even as he sat at ease.

Arwë made a motion to the soldiers. They fanned out,

securing the room before checking the injured. He crossed the chamber, noting spilled blood and broken stone. With smooth motions so as not to agitate the boy with the haunted stare, Arwë knelt before him.

"Swordsman," he said gently. Even his single, quiet word forced the boy to jump.

The lad stared into Arwë's placid eyes as if looking for an answer to the terror he had just seen.

"Explain," Arwë said.

"L-l-lord!" Del managed. "H-h-he went wild, sir!"

"Who?"

"The surgeons, I think?" Del stammered. "No! It was only one of the surgeons, since the big one's out cold." He glanced toward the sprawled form of Elijah. "Or maybe it was the prince, rising out of his bed like that. He was like a wild thing out of the savage elf forest—er, begging your pardon, sir!"

"Wild thing?" Arwë asked, ignoring the quip.

"Yes, sir!" Del said. "Tall and terrible—shadowy! I've never seen a man in such a state."

"A man in a mask?" Arwë said. "Like the ones we fought on the road, below the Watchful Hills?"

"No, sir, the prince!" Del said. His eyes shot from side to side as if trying to grasp at the scattered details. "The surgeons, sir, they seemed near to healing the prince after his near two years infirm! Then the little rat—er, I mean Dusk, I think his name is—whispered a strange word, louder than all the strange singing they were doing over the prince."

"Swordsman," Arwë said, meeting the boy's gaze, not letting him look away. "Remember well what you are about to recall. What was the word the healer spoke?"

"A name, sir. Eshra."

Arwë's brow furrowed as his eyes traced the memory of his first having met the strange healer. He thought back to the fight in the forest, then up to the morning he had arrived in the city. He had seen Dusk kneeling over Tyrith at the infirmary. He had given Dusk his message to Tyrith. Had he delivered it? Was Tyrith alive still?

"So earnest," Arwë whispered, gazing in awe at the sleeping boy who wore skill and power so easily. "Could a servant of the enemy have slipped so easily into our closest circles?"

"I don't know about that, sir," Del said. "Dusk was one of the first in the room the prince attacked, after Surgeon Elijah."

Arwë's hands clapped the boy on the shoulders. His nails dug in. "Tell me everything."

Abandoning all pretense of formal speech, the boy's words poured out of him. "The-the little rat—er, I mean Healer Dusk—went inta' th'chamber with the old surgeon, sir, to heal the prince, I think, and-and-and I heard the serving girl give the report. Then hours went by, and we-we watched the door and talked to the citadel guards n' asked 'em how it came to be that they had got their way inta' the highest ranks and—"

"The *attack*, soldier," Arwë sighed, snapping his fingers.

"Right!" Del said with a nervous chuckle. "All that

night was brimming full with strange songs 'n lights 'n things I never seen, and a tension was in the air, sir, like never I felt. I guess thass' why ol' stick inna' mud Aelfnoth stationed us here: so as we could see a bit o' magic or power from the outside world, since he said he wants us with him, y'know, seeing what he sees 'n all. Anyhow, the strangest and worst of all the songs was the loudest, 'n it seemed sung only by Healer Dusk, against the tall one, sir. And all of a sudden, the prince! Sir, he was up, all dark and terrible, as I said, thrashing about and striking at anyone near enough! Thass'when ol' dung-face *Kay-full* 'n me jumped in and were forced to club the poor prince afore' he hurt anyone else. But he got the better of me, swept me aside like wheat in the wind. Then Kay-full stood alone as things went dark for a bit. I thought the prince's shadow got the better of Kay-full, but then there was a flash of light, then a girl, then—"

"A girl!" Arwë cried, wrenching the lad to his feet. "Was she cloaked, with blonde hair? Eyes the color of pearls?"

"Y-y-yes, come to think of it, sir!" Del said, his head lulling on his neck with the sudden motion. "She jumped in, and there was light and an awful crash, then there was screamin,' and thass'all I remember."

"Keiphral Morne," Arwë said, continuing his scan of the room. "A girl with shining eyes, and the prince. Blood coats the floor, and the carnage of their battle is everywhere. But all three escaped, that way." He pointed, tracing two pairs of footprints to a hinged slab of stone.

"Oh, right!" the boy said, stepping away, out of the elf's grasp. "When Kay-full and the girl stood together talking, sir, there was something about healers, scribes, and gardens. They mentioned the city, that it was built over something great. And that's where they were headed: deep down, below the city, down through the broken mountain, after the man-shadow prince! What I do remember from their rambling was, 'Heir shall seek for Garden-hid! Deep under earth, to find her worth.'"

Arwë's eyes widened. "Keiphral and Dusk ... *Scribe's deadly slaves both men shall fight, to wake the world from endless night.*"

Del nodded. "What's it mean, sir?"

"Stay here and care for any who awaken as best you can," Arwë snapped. "Await Captain Aelfnoth. He will surely be here with a regiment of Malas' finest soldiers, all too late." With that, Arwë turned, striding out of the room, leaving Elijah, Dusk, and Del in the competent care of the citadel guard.

"Lord!" called Del from the chamber's door. "Where go you now?"

"To wake an angel," Arwë called over his shoulder. He made his way out of the citadel, which now swarmed with soldier and servant. He crossed prince's ward and Arrow-bridge, then down half a thousand steps, seeking the infirmary.

22

PROMISES

Dusk came screaming out of dark, crying out clearly. "The girl! Where is she? She can help. She is the light. I didn't see it before, but she is! Elijah, we must find her. She saved me. I was bleeding. She can save my mother!"

"Peace, Surgeon," rolled the cool voice of Elijah. It was the one Dusk knew the older surgeon only used with severely ill or wounded patients.

"Not dead, nor even wounded," Dusk marveled, rubbing at his shoulder and ankle.

"No, neither," Elijah said, amused. "But you lost a great deal of blood, and a great deal of time has passed."

"How long?"

"Three days since the morning of the healing," Elijah said.

Dusk opened bleary eyes to latticed stonework above. Incense burned close by, and the over-bright light of day mingled with the glow of tallow candles. He turned his head side to side, recognizing the walls of his modest room at the infirmary.

"I feel g-g-good," Dusk said, feeling the clarity of his words slipping. "But everything's c-c-colder, darker, like something's missing from the world."

"The hands of the Atrellarrath have been laid on you, Dusk," Elijah said, sitting in a cushioned chair beside his bed. "Though he be healed in body, no man comes through such a thing unscathed."

"I just w-w-wish she were here," Dusk continued. "In all my dreaming since having my n-n-neck nearly broken by that sh-sh-shadow, all I c-c-could think of was the g-g-girl, her face, her v-v-voice." He stopped suddenly, blushing deeply, expecting the surgeon to laugh.

But Elijah only gave him a solemn nod.

"Elijah," Dusk said. "She stopped the prince, then h-h-healed me after I f-f-failed."

"And went on, chasing the mad-shadow prince, as they're calling him, into the depths of the city, below the broken mountains," Elijah said. Then he looked troubled. "As to failures, I wouldn't go so far as to say your attempt at mending *failed*, Surgeon Dusk. Your strength simply gave out at the end. And your power, seeking destruction, grasped at whatever it could to keep you from forcing it to heal against its will."

"But I did force it," Dusk said.

"You did!" Elijah said with a smile. "Forced it to good purpose. And all it could do was lash out, and in this case, swear the name of the one who made it."

"Eshra," Dusk whispered. He then looked to the surgeon. "What am I, Elijah?"

"A lad of remarkable skill," Elijah said. "With a penchant for getting into trouble, even when under the sleepless scrutiny of surgeons, servants, and a company of soldiers!"

"But what w-w-was all that, and who are you, truly, Elijah ben Ath?" Dusk demanded, cutting through Elijah's attempt at levity. "You f-f-forced me to heal the P-p-prince of Ephtar-Malas before I could g-g-get the full measure of his s-s-sickness. Did you know that g-g-girl, the Atrellarrath? What else are you k-k-keeping from me?"

"One question at a time, Surgeon," Elijah said, standing, and beginning to pace the chamber. "As to what all that was: either the kindling or burning of Last-Hope. The prince has been sick for some time. His nobles were all but ready to sell us and the city to the highest bidder while the men march up to die on the walls. War is coming, whether we want it or not. The prince's vassals would exploit it for the chance to line their pockets before attempting to escape the city as it's destroyed by fomori. The fool *elite* don't realize there is no place left in the world that is safe. With the prince's recovery, I had hoped his voice would return reason and some sense of unity to the city. With him gone, and rumor of him turning to some fearsome shadow-creature spreading by word of the servants, I fear the vassals will go on bickering amongst themselves. As they do, our real enemies will continue destroying our supply roads and pitting us against one another until they eventually take our city. They are united against us.

"I *am* sorry for bringing you into the fray so quickly,

Dusk. I thought you would have had more time to practice crafting your cures while you put in professional time at the infirmary. You had no time at all to recover strength from our departure from the Dread Coast. But the prince's health turned for the worse. He would have died that night had we not intervened. It was a risk I needed to take. And while it bit us at the beginning, some hope may be found in it still."

"How s-s-so?"

"To answer your earlier question," Elijah said, "I have known about Ithyeil Stëorra, whom you know as Yeiley, for some time. I should say, I knew of her birth, though I only met her after she had escaped the fighting at the caravans and made her way to the top of the city to find me. I did not know when she would arrive in Ephtar-Malas, but I have long listened to the turnings of this world. Verily, I sensed the cries of her people from far below the Nephtyri city of Galataeum. I knew she would come here. So, I have moved many people to help along the plan laid down in the Atrellarrathi prophecies. Now that she has come forth and the plan ripens, she's become my charge, as surely as she is Arwë's.

"As to why I am hopeful, I am happy to tell you that Keiphral Morne is alive and well. He and Ithyeil fought together and threw off the prince's attack. They pursued him into the caverns below the city. As we speak, I think they both quest in the dark reaches under the mountain, seeking the mad prince and the Garden built by Ithyeil's people."

PROMISES

"I'm g-g-glad you awoke me to help, Elijah," Dusk admitted. "And that we worked hard to s-s-save the life of the m-m-man who may have been able to s-s-save the city."

"As am I," Elijah said, stopping his pacing and turning to face him. "Though I pray we are not too late and that Keiphral and Ithyeil find him. Whether the prince is turned fully to a thing of shadow, or died in that bed and a thing of shadow simply stepped in to take his place in this world as he left it, I do not know. I do know he was near to death and walks now, in one form or another, because of you. As for me, you've no reason to doubt I truly am chief surgeon of this city. But I serve in other capacities and have not always been a surgeon. My home is Elderlight, not Leóhteness-Fal. That will suffice for now."

Dusk's eyes widened to full golden discs. "Elderlight," he breathed. "The legend p-p-passed down by my father."

"Legend indeed," Elijah scoffed. "Well, in holding so high an honor as to attend the lords of Ephtar-Malas, this *legend* is granted certain access, as you have seen. I am afforded certain permits for travel and requisition. Because of this, I am also allowed to act as voice of reason to the populace. That means I tell the truth to all people, even if that means scaring them or speaking against the will of the nobles. When none seem to listen, I enlist the help of others, namely a weary Midlothean knight who sought peace from war, a certain Elf-lord and his resourceful sons, as well as others. I am both loved and hated for my voice and for my deeds."

"Del seems to have a l-l-low opinion of you," Dusk remarked.

Elijah darkened at Dusk's mention of the haughty swordsman. "That oaf's part is yet to be played. And though I cannot yet see it, I think, and hope, it will be great indeed."

"You make a g-g-great many moves in this g-g-game," Dusk said, eyes narrowing. "Were the g-g-girl and my f-f-father counted amongst your g-g-game pieces as well?"

"In a way," Elijah sighed. He paused as if considering his next words carefully. "When I heard stories roll down from Sunreach, I hardly expected to find Treiarn's son at their source. Then, considering the knight's story and his insistence on returning home to you and Eissyr after a life of war and glory, I considered a deeper meaning. So, I sought you, both in attempt to help your mother and to confirm you as Heir of the Atrellarrath. When I found you and Keiphral Morne on the Dread Coast, I thought I had found the Heir, that all my worries and dealings with elves and knights and angels had been overblown."

"And n-n-now?"

"Now I know you are certainly not the Heir." Elijah laughed. "But you are an Heir, Dusk. Your skills at healing contradict your possession of a terrible power. And, given what was said of your transformation in the prince's chambers, you still give me pause. I'm not sure what to do with you."

"Just don't k-k-kill me," Dusk said, half-joking.

"Oh no," Elijah said, clever eyes flashing. "I think I've a

PROMISES

good enough part for *you* to play. For now, know that Ithyeil Stëorra seeks a very real place of Last-Hope for her people. This city, though unbeknownst to the Qwei-Sillar when they named it, is the source of that hope. We have not seen the last of Ithyeil, and she will have perhaps the greatest part to play in this tale we now find ourselves wrapped up in."

"Somehow, I knew it f-f-from the start," Dusk mused. "She didn't s-s-seem to approve of my p-p-powers when we met during the b-b-battle."

"Yes, but for her disapproval, it seems light and dark couldn't help but both be drawn to serve when each was needed the most."

"Light and *dark*?" Dusk asked, hanging on the last word. He stared at his itching arm, which had been freshly re-wrapped. He then turned back to Elijah.

"I don't know yet, Dusk. I have only theories and no answers for now. But if you give me some time, I will find them, for both our sakes."

Dusk nodded.

"Now then," Elijah said, striding toward Dusk's wardrobe, "if you're as refreshed as you say, how about you come join us in the library?"

"Us?" Dusk asked.

"Oh yes," Elijah said, opening the wardrobe's double doors and questing inside. "We must make you ready. Your wounds closed nicely, and a little Atrellarrathi magic on Ithyeil's part made it as if you were scarcely wounded at all."

"I wish she could have t-t-taken the memory of my wounds too," Dusk said, shivering.

"So would any veteran who's seen service in war," Elijah said, stopping his rummaging to look back at Dusk. "For now, duty should provide enough distraction to help mend the mind a little. So too should being surrounded by friends. Now then, out of bed! There is much you must know, and more that I must tell. We arranged for new clothing to be tailored in your size. Your choices arrived earlier this morning, free of charge. It's a small token, given your great deeds to the prince's house."

"You have s-s-such authority?" Dusk asked.

"Indeed," Elijah said, smiling. "Hurry now! Bathe, then dress. We will need a good deal of time, but we can discuss it over your breakfast in the library."

Dusk found getting out of bed to be no great pain. Elijah lay Dusk's new garb and gear on the bed, then promptly exited the room. Dusk stretched, finding only a gentle soreness in the shoulder the prince's shadow had bitten. He bathed in a deep tub in an adjacent room, having been brought steaming buckets of clean water by the fussy surgeons. When done, Dusk chose his favorites among the spread of clothing that had been tailored for him. He decided on a pair of sturdy, brown, leather boots that reached his knees. He also chose black serge trousers and a green and gray tunic to match the cloak Aryka and her mother had woven for him. He examined the cloak closely. It had been ripped and shredded during his battles, but someone had taken the time to mend it. His eyes watered as he whispered a prayer of thanks.

PROMISES

Dusk left his room, meeting Elijah at the top of the stairs. Both surgeons made their way to the infirmary's library. At the room's entrance, sheaves of vellum, ancient scrolls, and old maps lay strewn across a dozen tables. Around the tables paced several figures, mostly recognizable by Dusk. Captain Aelfnoth, one hand on the hilt of his sheathed sword, greeted them with a salute as they entered. Dusk marveled at the knight, who stood nearly to the staggering height of Elijah. Just as they exchanged greetings, a soldier bustled in with tidings from lower in the city, drawing the captain away.

Amongst the spread of books and loose pages, Dusk spotted Arwë at a table. The elf, covered all over with gauze and bandages, pored over manuscripts written in flowing elvish runes. He spoke in urgent whispers, reading from one of many missives.

"Note forty-three," Arwë said. "*Upon our deciphering of Messenger Arwë's compendium on his mission to the realm of the Nokleth, we have come to new conclusions regarding their excavations of the Quarries beneath the Glacial Waste. Ancient sources, pulled from the deepest corners of Wildercrown's libraries, speculate that the giants of yore, Weileth-Zhul, as our forbearers named them, were builders of many great things that decorate Leóhteness-Fal to this day. One such source, though not elvish, but deciphered from ancient Mannish (potentially the tongue of the Rhonoss?), mentions the name Adùnaton. The name is referred to in other records as 'The Crown.'*"

A recovered but visibly injured Nephtyr Ithar-fel sat

near the table with his companion. His seat was a lush couch built for three to sit across, but it acted to the huge man more as a small armchair. "*Adùnaton,*" the angel rumbled. "Mentioned in other letters you carry, yes?"

"Yes!" Arwë laughed, slapping the table. "It proves the knight's story is true, corroborated by sources hundreds of years old!"

Dusk looked beyond the elf and angel and saw Del sitting in a corner. The gruff lad leaned forward in a chair, honing a set of battle knives by a fire that burned merrily in the hearth. He scoffed when his eyes met Dusk's, and he doubled his focus on the care of his knives.

Then, beside the table to which Tyrith had pulled his couch, stood a man Dusk had never seen before. He was small, perhaps four feet in height. His beard shone with gems, and his skin was iron-gray. He listened while Arwë and Tyrith bantered while he drank beer from a flagon as large as Dusk's head. When his cup struck the table after a long drink, the man eyed his own pile of messages and reports. Most important to him seemed to be a great map of Ephtar-Malas. More specifically, it was a map of the mountains under the city, scrawled all over with what Dusk assumed to be secret roads and passages cutting this way and that through the mountains' core.

When he had finished consulting with Aelfnoth, a messenger, and one of his physicians, Elijah turned to the library's inhabitants. "My friends," he said. "I am sorry to call you here under such circumstances. But you are most trusted of my companions, and I thank you for being here in this strange hour. I've asked you all to come because of what has happened within our walls. Though that which may happen from without will be of grave concern in due time. Let us begin with things outside our walls, for though more deadly, I think they will prove simpler."

Elijah looked to Aelfnoth, and the armored captain motioned for Del to stand beside him. When both men marched up to a separate table, Dusk noticed the miniature units of soldiers that stood atop a mat spread across its surface. Aelfnoth moved the soldiers about with careful consideration, and Dusk saw that the mat upon which the captain placed the ranks was an overlarge relief of the realm of T'Rhonossarc. Dusk looked up to the captain as Del stepped around the edges of the table, adjusting supply lines. It was then that Dusk noticed the sweat and grime that had calcified around both Aelfnoth and Del's temples and cheekbones. Captain and squire looked to have just come up from whatever errand they had recently run for the city. Mud caked their boots, and their cloaks hung about their shoulders in tatters. Fresh dents and scratches also formed crosshatch patterns up and down the legs and arms of their armor. Both men wore tired looks now that they had stepped into proper firelight.

"Despite their ferocity, the out-battles go well," Aelfnoth's deep voice boomed. "The men fight fiercely for their homesteads, and I've sent large garrisons to the hills of Sarith Mel, Midloth Wil, Eilath Rhut, Midloth Audreth, and Pathsellen." He indicated several of the Watchful Hills that guarded the northern reaches of T'Rhonossarc. "The men have rebuilt many of the old watchtower ruins. I also ordered them to construct walls linking the new towers. This goes well, as the fomori, though great in number, shy away from places of strength. They seem only to attack small farms or anything they think they can ruin then run from. We have put a stop to this as well, as I have ordered constant cavalry patrols in the north fields. They have orders to charge down any invading force, no matter how small.

"Tyrith the Fell, as the men call him," Aelfnoth continued, amusement coloring his voice as he looked to the Nephtyr, "has also helped considerably in keeping goblins and fomori away from the edges of the princedom. With his recovery from the battle at the caravan, and fear of him spreading among the fomori, we are able to dispatch him to the outskirts. We know that when Tyrith arrives, the enemy will flee in terror."

Dusk looked over to the towering Nephtyri warrior, only now realizing that the wounds he bore were newly accumulated. Tyrith simply gave a humble nod. "So long as I keep my wings covered, the men think me a natural, if tall, Midlothean," he rumbled. "Only when I let the fomori surround me like a sea do I reveal what I truly am."

"Ah, the avalanche is being modest," Arwë chided, clapping a long-fingered hand on his companion's shoulder. "Tyrith nearly single-handedly struck down a hundred goblins when he was recovered enough to join us. And that was only yesterday!"

"Hmm, the elfling fails to mention the song played by

his bow," the giant man said. Blue light flooded from his eyes and mouth as he smiled. "Arwë and a contingent of the city's marksmen shot our foes from horseback when they joined the scouts yesterday. They cut down half the enemy line assailing the northern farmlands, then trampled the survivors into dust."

"Ha! He boasts," laughed Arwë. "An eventful week it has been since you fell asleep, young Dusk."

"Yes, it would seem even loudmouthed Delphan proved his worth by splitting more goblin skulls than the common soldier," Aelfnoth noted with a knowing smile.

"What!" Del snapped. "I ain't an amateur!"

"No," snapped the captain. "You're better trained and more highly skilled than half the soldiers at my command. It's too bad you're a bored, thick-headed layabout who tends to torture those who are less adept in their skill. But you'll learn on whom to take out that anger, even if I have to dangle you by your thumbs in front of a hundred bloodthirsty fomori to get the lesson across."

At Del's shock, Elijah chuckled. "Continue the report, Captain. Surgeon Dusk needs to know why he's here."

"Aye, lord," Aelfnoth said, returning to the map. "We are well supplied, with provisions enough to last months. We include refugees from the South, along with our own women and children in our accounting of the populace. The Enemy has fallen back for now, preferring sorties in isolated parts of the countryside to open war. Our farmers, hunters, and traders send caravans to gather what crops they can from the outer fields that haven't yet been burned. Caravans go also to the farmland south, on the Ephtari Downs."

Aelfnoth raised an eyebrow to Del. The swordsman stepped forward, clearing his throat.

"We've sent scouts to Westreach, the Quarries, and beyond the Glacial Waste to the Ruined Desert," Del said, suddenly shaking. "Their m-mission is to gather what troops and ... and mercenaries they can find to the Hidden City."

So, the bully stutters as well when under pressure, thought Dusk. *I'll just secret that bit of information away for another time.*

"Our p-promises," Del continued, "should these mercenaries help us, are wealth and assurance that both the fomori and goblins will be wiped out forever should we win here. D-do not mistake the captain's good news for v-victory, however. This battle is not yet won. In fact, battle has not truly begun. We ... we have only dealt with small companies of goblins and fomori. Our scouts report that tens of thousands of fomori march down out of the Qw-qweth-Wëalda by the week. Sh-should they choose to fight a full war, we will not win, garrisoned, defended, and provisioned as we are. This is where we rely on ... Surgeon Dusk." Del's agitation turned to disgust as his eyes met Dusk's.

Taken aback, Dusk looked to the toy soldiers on the table, then to the elf, the angel, and the boy who had bullied and berated him. He gaped at the captain of the knights of Ephtar-Malas, then at Elijah ben Ath. "But I f-f-failed," he whispered. "I couldn't s-s-stop the prince from d-d-dying or otherwise succumbing to the sh-sh-shadow. We've lost Ith—"

He looked askance at Elijah, who nodded his permission for Dusk to speak openly. "We've lost Ithyeil, who would be of as m-m-much help and might as Tyrith or Lord Arwë, g-g-given her powers. And the prince r-r-runs wild beneath the c-c-city!"

"You harnessed a power that cast a pall over the North for centuries," said Elijah ben Ath.

"You used that power to save Tyrith and me from certain death at the hands of a Veilglorrum," Arwë added. "As you saw in the infirmary, that one now lies headless in the forests east of here, thanks to your intervention."

"You fought bravely when the prince turned on you," said Aelfnoth.

"And you, Dusk," Elijah continued, "revealed your power in the battle for the caravans at the same moment that Ithyeil was forced to uncloak herself. And your revelation may be what still keeps the fomori from understanding what the Heir of the Atrellarrath is capable of. Their only knowledge of such a people's existence resides in legend. Qwei-Sillar, Men, and Nephtyr the fomori know well, having fought all three Kindreds in the Fomori Wars two centuries ago. These they fear but can overwhelm with their surging numbers. But the fomori certainly did not expect one of their armies, more than one hundred strong, to be burned to ash by a boy with lights in his eyes!"

"W-w-what are you—?"

"We're saying we have another favor to beg of you, master-healer," Elijah said. "Though we know we have no right."

Overwhelmed, Dusk simply said, "Ask."

"Ephtar-Malas remains leaderless," Aelfnoth said. "The prince's illness has kept him out of the public eye for over a year. For once, this works to our advantage. Thus far, the vassals have entrusted the city's safekeeping to me, but not out of love for me."

"You see, Dusk," said Elijah, "Captain Aelfnoth has managed to keep order in the city, thanks in no small part to his courage and competence. The soldiery is loyal to him, so the city remains hidden, protected, and orderly."

"But," Aelfnoth sighed, "we live on borrowed time. The Enemy is relentless in its search for us. Their incursions onto our roads, farmlands, and now the Watchful Hills only make our city's revelation to them a matter of time. Therefore, Surgeon Dusk, your task is this: Find the prince. Whether alive or dead, man or shadow, the city must have him back if we are to stand any chance against this present darkness. I ask you this as a man who sees competence in others and has seen a great deal of it in you, even for your short time on the walls and in the infirmary."

"And as consequence for waking the shadow inside the prince and attempting to quell it," Elijah added, "the Heir of the Atrellarrath has revealed herself. The Enemy knows she has come forth and will stop at nothing to capture her and her power. But where there is light, so too must shadows be cast. So, you have come forth, Dusk. And you have, no doubt, confused the Enemy to no end."

"Me?" Dusk asked.

Arwë stood. "At every critical strike, you have been there, Healer. You stole a power the Enemy would have used to terrible ends. The Veilglorrum saw you in the woods before I let it report to its kin and before I killed it. And such a display of dark and light within the prince's chamber has not gone unnoticed."

"Dusk," Nephtyr Ithar-fel rumbled. "The Enemy believes *you* are the Heir of the Atrellarrath."

"But I'm n-n-not!" Dusk said, looking around at them all. "I came here b-b-because Keiphral and I were under attack, then stayed because of Elijah's p-p-promises. Helping the people was a g-g-good thing and it helped me r-r-refine some of my skills. But, my lords, I m-m-must fulfill my task. And that is to heal and protect my mother!"

"You will, Dusk," Elijah said with a placating gesture. "But not before we make safe the city. No one leaves, even if we wished them to. As Aelfnoth has reported, we are surrounded on all sides. I told you the truth when I met you, and still do now: There was no safe way back to your mountain then, and there is no safe way there now."

"Then I will blast a way through with this power of mine you all seem so fearful of and enthralled by," Dusk snapped without faltering.

"Not necessary, young master." The little man with blue-gray skin had spoken for the first time. He stepped forward. The top of his head only reached as high as Dusk's shoulder. His voice was rich and deep, as if the earth itself now spoke of the many things it had seen in the long years that wheeled by overhead. "There is another way out of the city. It passes under and out, into the mountains beneath the Glacial Waste. From there, you would skirt the Waste east and south, until you come again to the feet of your mountains. The journey would take weeks in good weather. And that road may not be free from peril."

Dusk stared wide-eyed at this small man with a voice nearly as deep as Tyrith's. Then he asked, "Nokleth?"

The little man barked a laugh and, seeing Dusk's hand and arm wrapped tightly, grasped the boy's off-hand. The man's skin was cold against Dusk's, almost metallic. His eyes, to Dusk's surprise, were lit from within just like his, except they gleamed the color of sparkling emeralds. "Indeed, young healer!" the man said merrily. "Tarthuin Da'rannithest is my name! Though my friends call me Graysword."

"R-r-rumors of the Stone-folk came up my m-m-mountain!" Dusk said, his anger turning to delight. "I never thought I w-w-would get to see one. But why, Graysword?"

"Ha!" Tarthuin laughed. "A story for another time. Perhaps along our journey?" He looked to Elijah.

The surgeon nodded. "As I said before, Keiphral Morne and Ithyeil Stëorra pursed the prince's shadow down into the Dún-Scraeff. If prince and Heir truly seek the Garden of Light, mentioned by Arwë's writings and the whisperings inside the ears of the Qwei-Sillar, then it must lie under the city. And Tarthuin, a friend, summoned by both

PROMISES

Arwë and me, has traveled those roads. He will guide us in our journey."

"Guide *us*?" Dusk asked.

"You didn't think you'd be traversing the lightless depths of the Dún-Scraeff all alone now, did you, Healer?" Arwë laughed.

"I d-d-didn't think I'd be traversing the lightless d-d-depths of the Dún-Scraeff at all," Dusk retorted.

At Arwë's silence, Dusk turned to Tarthuin. The little man, though solidly built and stern of feature, gave Dusk a sympathetic smile. "Whatever path we take, young master, I will lead you out again, back to your country, should you wish it. You have my word. For I go that far in the return to my Quarries after we find this girl, Ithyeil."

"We seek the Heir, Dusk, for she is my charge, as well as Keiphral's now," Arwë said. "Once we find her, bringing her safely to the road appointed her, my hope is to return to Wildercrown. I will find my father, if he yet lives—my brother too. If the stories Keiphral told Tyrith of Lohrë walking the earth once more are true, and if he wasn't buried in the ash of Wildercrown, then finding him and the Elflord are *my* tasks. Until we part ways, me to my city, and you to your lightless mountains, then I am your companion."

Dusk looked to Tyrith, who was downcast. The angel grumbled. "I stay behind for now to help with the city's defense and to draw our foes' attention. The fomori thinking the Nephtyr slain to the last fifteen years ago certainly makes for amusing faces when I land among them, axe swinging."

"Would that I could go and continue fighting back-to-back with an elf of Wildercrown," Aelfnoth said, dark eyes flashing angry inside his winged helm. "But, as is my duty, I remain here, protecting Malas, both from Enemy and itself. At least I'll have an angel for company. But in my stead goes the oaf." He shoved Del forward, who squawked at the captain.

"Del?" Dusk groaned.

"Del," Elijah confirmed. "He is nearly the match of Keiphral for strength, just as the potential of your shadows matches Ithyeil's for light."

"He is also the only witness to have seen the fight within the chamber almost in its entirety," Aelfnoth said. "He knows what it is you're up against. And we know he won't back down from a fight."

Del sneered at that then met Dusk's eyes. Both boys glared at one another, snorted, then turned their backs.

Elijah chuckled, then continued. "With one of the stout Nokleth, an elf who slew one of the Veilglorrath, and me at your side, we will keep the Enemy guessing. And when our task is done, we will see you off, along the dark road Tarthuin spoke of, then up to your mountain and mother. And though you will travel alone from that point, you shall have with you the goodwill of Ephtar-Malas and all its people, forever. Will you go with me one last time, Dusk?"

Dusk looked around the library at the earnest faces who stared back. He breathed deeply. "I did not ask f-f-for any of this, be it p-p-power, reputation, or grand quests. But for all my f-f-failures, none of you have blamed me.

PROMISES

You've only b-b-been there when I've g-g-gotten into trouble. If this is the only r-r-road home not blocked by enemies of the city, then I w-w-will go with you to help Keiphral and Ithyeil."

Elijah nodded then addressed the assembly. "There is still much to discuss and many questions that need answering. All of you have my thanks for your efforts in keeping this city safe. Your sacrifices in keeping the Heir unhurt and your walking of the strange paths you and I have been set on are to be commended. But now make ready for the next task. We've already let too much time escape us. Gather what provisions you can, and make for the prince's quarters. I will meet you there in two hours. You will pass unhindered by any guard as you pass up to the citadel. Farewell for now!"

23

THRESHOLD

Two hours passed, and Dusk and Elijah stood in the prince's chamber once again. Servants had tidied the debris, but the secret stone door lay open for all in the chamber to see. Darkness seemed to seep into the room from its yawning maw.

The surgeons, with help from the bustling physicians of the infirmary, had loaded their food and necessities into leather travel packs. Leaving instructions to be carried out in his stead, Elijah had led Dusk back to the prince's chambers as quietly as he could under the tumult of midday brightness.

The guards and servants of the citadel had greeted them politely, albeit solemnly, and the silence of the chamber forced evil memories back into Dusk's mind. While they awaited their companions, Dusk busied himself by checking over their stores of food, clothing, and water. When done with his fussing, his mind lay a little clearer. But always his attention came back to the open door. He stared through it, and a creeping freeze spread

THRESHOLD

from his fingertips and up his forearm. A shiver rattled through him. His eyes, captivated by the terrible doorway, suddenly found themselves gazing intently at his bandaged palm. The wrappings squirmed before his amber stare as if snakes seethed underneath. And every other time he blinked, Dusk would catch a puff of shadow rising from the flesh underneath.

"Surgeon." Elijah's voice cut across Dusk's reverie. "Our companions approach."

"This power, Elijah," Dusk said, as if from far off. "It's going to take the whole of me. And it isn't good."

"You bent it to the healing of many," Elijah said. "And you will do so again."

"But for how long?" Dusk asked, the cadence of his words strangely perfect. "I thought I was doing right by my mother in stealing it. Then I slew fomori by the hundreds and turned into a beast of shadow who nearly slew a prince. What have I t-t-taken out of the world and into myself?"

"Something great," Elijah said, approaching the boy the way he would a startled hare. "Something that has been used to deadly effect, but to good ends also, now. And no matter how powerful you become, how far you walk, how many men you slay or mend, the choice will always be yours. And for every single one you make, there will be consequence, good or ill. If you want my advice, I suggest making the good ones!" He lay a hand on the boy's shoulder. The motion dispatched the icy crawl and shadows beneath. Dusk looked up at the old doctor, who flashed him an encouraging smile.

"But how will I know the g-g-good from the bad?" Dusk asked.

"When the right moments come, you'll know the difference," Elijah said, releasing Dusk's shoulder. "And if it's any help, know that you have done well by the people of this city, by your family, and by me. For now, we've a job to do, and that's to help Keiphral and Ithyeil. Understand?"

Dusk nodded, the old man's stoic presence grounding him. And, as footsteps sounded in the outer hall, Dusk shivered again, this time at a cold truth that had been gnawing at him. "Even with my f-f-full power," he said, breaking the silence again, "I would not have b-b-been able to heal my mother."

He looked to Elijah, who stared forward grimly.

"Had I g-g-gone alone back to my mountain and m-m-my mother," Dusk continued, "I would have killed her, just as I d-d-did the fomori in the forest. You and Yeiley were the missing pieces I needed. Death w-w-would have been the result, otherwise, without the two of you at my side."

Elijah sighed then nodded. "It would seem so. But you did well with knowledge both given and earned. I also knew my remedies would keep your mother alive. So, there was some time. And seeing you work, I saw that the power you took from the Storm, and the life-giving tasks you put it to, would not turn out altogether evil. Perhaps, as you explored the darker, mightier facets of your power, I could both put you to good use as a surgeon while also trying to help you hone the more benevolent side. And

THRESHOLD

maybe one day, we both could find a better cure for the Wasting Sickness. Against all hope, I also wanted the Heir to appear. I had hoped we might also convince her that her help was needed on Sunreach and that Eissyr should be the first of her patients."

"A great d-d-deal of hoping, Elijah," Dusk said, unsure whether to look kindly on the old man for forming him into a better healer, or angrily on him for guiding him to Ephtar-Malas with half the truth.

"It seems to be what I'm good at these days," Elijah replied with a sigh.

Arwë strode into the chamber. The elf stood tall despite his hurts, garbed in green and brown leathers. He bore his bow in one hand, armed all over with knives and many vicious arrows. In the crook of his other arm, he held a collection of notes, looking just as ready to sit and read as nock an arrow. On the elf's heels marched Nephtyr Itharfel, whose bright eyes and broken wings lay hidden under hood and cloak dyed the city's dark scarlet. A newly forged battleaxe the size of a man rested between his shoulders. The plate he wore looked to have been battered and patched more than once.

A clash of mail accompanied Captain Aelfnoth and his Knights of Ephtar-Malas. The captain arrived clad in full plate, like Tyrith. He stood tall, armed to his teeth with hammer, mace, shield, and at least three long knives. "We prepare a sortie for the goblins harrying our wagon trains to the west," he said upon the gawking of his companions. "But we wish to see you off and wish you well."

Standing just taller than the captain's heavily girt waist, Tarthuin Graysword flashed platinum teeth at the grim assembly, smiling wide. "The Undercity!" the stone-skinned man cried at them. "Long have my kin dreamed of the Atrellarrath's creations under-earth. If all my wanderings away from my mines lead me to naught, I will have at least seen the majesty made by the Light-folk of old. What fun!" Dusk noticed Tarthuin's hauberk as the Nokleth laughed. It looked to be crafted from rock and concrete, and its plates flexed with every movement of the little man's body.

"What *danger*," Arwë corrected. "Though, knowing what little I do of your folk, these types of expeditions into dark, perilous places excite rather than frighten them."

"Right you are, tree-runner!" laughed Tarthuin, who reached up to slap the elf on the back, nearly spilling the deadly contents of his quiver.

Amusement softened Arwë's features as he settled his arrows. He studied the Nokleth for a moment, then said, "You seem well-prepared for the task, Stonemaster."

Tarthuin smiled wider, hefting a sword that looked to have been carved from solid stone onto his shoulder. "The Herald of Wildercrown is too kind." He laughed. "Though I'll soon beg more of the famed courtesy of the Qwei-Sillar during our jog and ask that you tell me all there is to know of your beloved city, namely of Mithweileth-Nal! The Giant's Ring is a dream of my people, second only to the underground gardens of the Atrellarrath."

"Alas!" said Arwë, bowing his head. "That I should be forced to recount the sorrow of a place so beautiful laid waste, friend Graysword. I fear the city is thrown down, and goblins, fomori, and fell Men even now desecrate my home and the Gleaming Wall. My father, the Elf-lord, may also lie dead in its ashes. I long to return, to fight for what's ours. But duties here concern me just as greatly. As I said in the infirmary: One day I will return to free the Qweth-Wëalda."

"Fear not, Master Elf," Tarthuin said, offering a gray hand to Arwë. The elf looked down at Tarthuin, clearly surprised to see the Nokleth's verdant eyes suddenly solemn and fierce. "Once we've helped the Atrellarrathi lass, escorted Dusk out to his home and hills, and brought even a small measure of light back to Leóhteness-Fal, then I will go with you to Wildercrown. Perhaps I'll stop home first then arrive to help you and yours with a legion of angry, stone-throwing Nokleth. That'd be a sight! The Stonecrafters' first fight alongside the Elder Kindred. We will help take back your home for the courtesy you've shown us. This I promise, not just to you, but to the dream of seeing the Giant's Ring in glory."

Arwë stared in wonder at the little man made of stone. Then a smile pulled at the elf's mouth, and he shook Tarthuin's hand. "Accompanied by Nephtyr and Nokleth, I cannot lose," he said quietly.

"Never neglect Men, Messenger," boomed Aelfnoth, who stood close by. "It is long since I have seen the argent trees. And I should like to do so again when all this is over, even if I am to scour the Qweth-Wëalda of every druel-dripping fomori myself. With the prince's leave, I would journey with you to the elf-lands as well."

GARDEN OF ASH

Seeing his chance, Dusk chimed in. "I would see Wildercrown as w-w-well. Keiphral and Ithyeil need our s-s-support, then I g-g-go to my mother. But if we've ch-ch-chased away the dark by helping Ithyeil, then I w-w-will come once my mother is healed."

"My friends," Arwë said, hiding his emotion, "I cannot thank you enough."

"But my purpose is also split, l-l-like Tarthuin's," Dusk added. "I w-w-would hear all there is t-t-to know of my father's j-j-journeys from you, M-m-master Elf. What better way to p-p-pick up his t-t-trail than to journey with the one who s-s-spoke to him last?"

Arwë nodded. "You may even hear a little from his writings when we come to rest. There is still much to learn from Treiarn!"

"Where is Delphan?" Elijah growled, looking around the room.

"Here, old man," Del snapped, striding in. The cantankerous lad was armored head, hand, and foot in bronze mail. His armaments rested atop a scarlet tunic. Sturdy chain clashed under both. Dusk saw that Del had obtained a new sword as well. Then he saw Aelfnoth approach the swordsman. The tall captain addressed Del with stern, quiet words and a pointing finger. Del stood defiantly, puffing out his chest. But then he gave the captain a grudging nod. Aelfnoth returned it, then stepped back.

"Now that we're all *here*," Elijah said, glaring at the swordsman, "we make final preparations. Arwë, what more is there to know before we leave?"

THRESHOLD

"*Malice hides a great secret,*" Arwë recited, opening his collection of manuscripts. "Del told me Keiphral Morne said the words before he struck the prince. The prince, Del said, even as half-man, half-shadow, bore a key. Del also says Ithyeil named Keiphral *Thalassean* after the prince had escaped. Keiphral told her that, 'they have a Garden to find,' after she mentioned, 'Innoth-Hyeil Darrë.'"

"What do you make of the lad's story, Messenger?" Elijah asked.

"The voices of the Atrellarrath, burned into the minds of my people, spoke of a Key and a Garden," said Arwë. "If we find Ithyeil, we are sure to find these things as well. And if the Garden they spoke of is indeed Innoth-Hyeil Darrë, then all these may prove the secret, and we will be hard-pressed. For the Atrellarrath have said the Garden, bereft of light, will prove a treacherous place indeed."

"What of the Thalassean?" asked Del, surprising the others with his curiosity.

"Messages from Wildercrown, and from the Atrellarrath, used the same names," Arwë replied. "Though Elijah may know more of the Thalasseans."

"Legends passed down from an ancient age," Elijah said. "The Thalasseans were seafarers said to have been so highly skilled at their craft that they fashioned ships able to traverse the Outer-dark, or *Dark-sea* as some call it. They came to Leóhteness-Fal by means other than those of our ancestors and the Nephtyr. But they fought in the early wars the same as any of the Kindreds."

"As to the Garden," said Tarthuin Da'rannithest. "It is a legend of the Atrellarrath, said to have been hidden, both from them and the Nokleth, who are native to this world. This Garden is rumored to house some secret vestige of light, vital to both our peoples. Though the story is so heavily rooted in myth, it is hard to know which pieces of it are to be believed. Its Key was only to be revealed to the Atrellarrath by what prophecy calls *latecomers*."

"All this is to ask, Dusk," Elijah said, "that, while you wore the helm given by your father, did you ever see things that were not there, hear voices you would never have otherwise heard?"

Shock struck Dusk just then, and he clapped a hand to his forehead. "The helm!" he cried. "How could I have f-f-forgotten? Did I w-w-wake up w-w-without it? Where has it g-g-gone?"

"Kay-full took it," Del said. "I saw him."

"Why?" Dusk asked.

"How should I know?" Del retorted.

Dusk glared at the bigger boy, then looked around at his companions. Feeling no need to lie, he nodded. "The helm first sh-sh-showed me the exact compound of m-m-medicines to give to my mother to st-st-stabilize her during her worst s-s-seizure. Then it showed me the p-p-path to the Dread Coast where I d-d-defeated the dark power within the Storm. I saw Ithyeil and her p-p-people trapped under Galataeum. And I h-h-have dreams whenever I f-f-forget to take it off at n-n-night."

"What sorts of dreams?" Arwë asked.

THRESHOLD

Dusk hesitated. "Of war," he said. "Of the p-p-past. Of our p-p-people's coming to this world."

Silence descended upon the room for some time as each man considered the implications of Dusk's visions. Tyrith spoke up. "If this trinket is imbued with some clairvoyant power as Dusk describes, then one thing is certain. While Dusk's helm rests atop Keiphral Morne's head, it must lead him and Yeiley to her goal: Innoth-Hyeil Darrë. You see, my young friend? Even in the dregs of what you have called failure, you have succeeded!"

"B-b-but Tarthuin said the Key to Innoth-Hyeil Darrë was only to b-b-be revealed by latecomers."

"It has been revealed, Dusk," Arwë said. "The shard the prince held, described by Keiphral to Del, must no doubt be the Key the Heir sought. Remember also, that you, Dusk, came down to the Lower-world to take power only months ago. Keiphral awoke scant months ago as well, according to news brought to me by his companion, Cailus. And Ithyeil, according to Arwë and Tyrith, only exited her waiting place under Galataeum and into their company a month or so ago. You three, who fought the prince's shadow, are latecomers to this strange tale."

"I see," Dusk said. "But what of the prince's secret door that l-l-leads under the city? You said the p-p-passage takes twisting paths that do not c-c-come to light. How will we f-f-find this Garden?"

"That's why I'm here, lad," said Tarthuin, bowing low. "We Nokleth have an understanding, one might call it, with our lovely, light-starved earth. Put me on a path underground, and I'll see you to its end, regardless of its branching!"

"Indeed," Arwë laughed. "I've only known the Nokleth a little while, but you can trust Graysword when he says he will lead us into and out of any place under the earth. And I have little fear that the Garden will be shut to us when we arrive."

"And what will w-w-we do when we f-f-find Keiphral and Ithyeil?" Dusk asked.

"Offer whatever help they need," Elijah said. "Whether in a fight, or in bearing some burden. So we must be prepared for anything."

Aelfnoth spoke then, saying, "My prayer is that the prince remains unharmed should his shadow attack you or your charges. I would ask that you question the Heir and Keiphral Morne whither the prince went and if they slew him. In life, the prince always spoke of fulfilling his solemn duty. That was to protect the people of his country and 'to stand guard over that which we have built over top of forever, until light returns.' Those were the words he used, and my heart tells me he held that Key for good reason, not ill.

"The Heir gave Keiphral Morne the name *Thalassean*," Aelfnoth continued. "If old legends and the alliances forged between our ancestors are to be trusted, then we must also trust that the right people seek the Garden. The prince also often spoke of keeping oaths to our ancestors. I think he did before the shadow took him. But now, I must keep mine to the people of this city and shield them from the host arrayed against us."

THRESHOLD

"Very well," Elijah said. "Whatever other tidings we may already have at our disposal, our elvish Messenger shall have to read to us along the way. For now, let us see the secret door!"

The small company came to the stone door in the chamber's corner. Dusk shivered at the darkness that poured from it. He gripped the icy squirming of his bandaged arm with his good hand. Then his companions stood all around him. Each peered through the threshold, down onto a rough path that descended steeply and away from the reaching light of the chamber.

Aelfnoth came among them to see. The knight looked down into the cavernous expanse below. "Go with the blessings of the Men of T'Rhonossarc," he said. He looked to each of them then. "Descend into the unending dark beneath Ephtar-Malas. Help the Heir of the Atrellarrath fulfill her goal, to the benefit of us all. And, if that which you find be a weapon, return it to the surface so that it may be used against our enemies in this time of greatest need! And be ready for a fight. I promise one will be waiting. Farewell!" With that, Aelfnoth nodded to them, clapped Del on the shoulder, then joined his knights. The plate-clad retinue marched out of the chamber, down into the city, and to war beyond.

Elijah nodded to Arwë, who ignited a torch off one of the chamber's braziers. The elf took his place at the back of the small company, holding his fire high. Elijah breathed deeply, nodded to himself, then plunged down the rocky path with his friends behind. Their journey into the ghastly depths of Ephtar-Malas had begun.

24

DESCENT

In our humbling of the Nephtyr, I took with me a collection of their champion's writings, thinking their worth would only go as far as giving me a story or two to tell my children when I'm old and gray. Though now that I read them for the first time during my stay with the Atrellarrath, I've found something strange. While most entries detail the history of this world as written by the Nephtyr, one is far older and seems to be written on a skin sheet the likes of which I've never seen in all my travels. Its writing is ancient mannish, perhaps coinciding with the Rhonoss Lords who vanished shortly after the Kindreds' arrival on Leóhteness-Fal. If ever I have the time, I will need to check this piece of writing against the historical manuscripts collected by Qwei-Sillari scholars to prove its truth or falsehood. In lieu of such methods for authentication, I shall, here, simply state the facts.

The writer refers to a strange ritual, or 'sin,' committed by the Nephtyr, long ago. I cannot speculate here, as I have no proof; therefore, I will simply append the scrap of old,

DESCENT

seemingly Rhonoss, writing here, along with my translation, for later study. It details, seemingly firsthand, events that occurred a mere handful of years after the arrival of the Kindreds to Leóhteness-Fal. If true ...
—*Notes Regarding the Kindreds,
Written by Knight Treiarn the Midlothean,
Under Galataeum*

Arwë sat shirtless on a broken pillar of crystal, reading by light of his torch while Dusk set about rewrapping his aggravated injuries. The company had breached the prince's door and begun their march just after noon. By Arwë's guess, they had walked for some six hours. The path had been dark, haunting, and lovely. Crystals rose out of ancient pools, and rivers flowed into waterfalls, cascading into deep, dreadful places. They turned many corners to find ancient fortifications, the stone having sunken far down. But castle walls and other shafts of stone stood buried but undamaged, in some sinking of the earth long ago. Towering stalagmites, formed by thousands of years of water droplets falling undisturbed from the black ceiling, rose all around the company as they had followed the stony back of Tarthuin Da'rannithest.

Their path had been lit by Arwë's torch as much as by little flowers that shone white and violet in softly burbling stream beds. They had walked beside mushrooms as big as houses and crossed bridges carved in old days by expert craftsmen. Tarthuin's guidance had taken them through one of seemingly dozens of caves, looking to have been bored into the bowls of the mountain by the slow grind of giant, crawling things. And just as the path through the tunnel became too narrow for them to walk two abreast, out they came into a glorious expanse that stretched away, dark and deep. They had watched a great flowing river charge down from somewhere above. It roared away and down, either direction drawing the companions' eyes hundreds of feet, to be lost in distant gloom. It was at this cave mouth that Arwë had felt blood run warm again under his leathers. To his chagrin, he had called for a stop, and Dusk sat him down. The boy had uncovered his wounds and found them freshly opened.

The company had agreed to find a high place where the paths could be watched and they could rest. So, they had made their way up onto a high, flat plateau. It was big enough to house a few of them while one stood watch and the others scouted. So, as Dusk applied his craft, Arwë set to studying Knight Treiarn's works. With sharp eyes on the knight's notes, and ears aimed toward the road up which Elijah and Tarthuin had gone to look ahead, Arwë found a scrap of stretchy skin amongst his missives. It had been the one mentioned by Treiarn, and Arwë had pulled it from its place at the bottom of the parchment sheet. Arwë read through the knight's translation of the ancient text into mannish.

Nephtyr swore to Rhonoss and last of Ephtarrath to use their power to keep shut the Witch-Scribe forever. That is why we all chose this Leóhteness-Fal: to bury one of the Six, diminish their strength while the greater battle rages across Elderlight. The Witch-Scribe was to be kept in a thing the Ephtarrath had forged and named 'Dark Seed.'

"Dark Seed?" Arwë whispered.

"What is that?" Dusk asked. Arwë looked up to see the boy's eerie amber eyes studying the strange script as he wrapped Arwë's shoulder.

"Where is Delphan?" Arwë replied.

"Sleeping already," Dusk said dismissively. "What are you r-r-reading?"

"Part of a missive that has long gone uncared for," Arwë said. "Since we wait for Elijah and our Noklethi companion to scout the way, I figured now would be as good a time as any to review your father's notes on the Atrellarrath and the world's history."

"My f-f-father gave notes to you d-d-detailing his travels?"

Arwë nodded, then sighed. "Treiarn assembled whole manuscripts regarding the Atrellarrath only. He transcribed all that they told him of themselves into one assemblage of documents. Your father speaks little of himself. But I've just now come to a different part entirely, and it may interest you and the rest of us."

"Yes?" Dusk asked. The lad's eyes glowed like hot coals when his curiosity was roused.

"Though it triggers a memory too," Arwë said. "And it is not one I care to recall."

"Of my f-f-father?"

"From when he gave me this collection," Arwë said,

gesturing to the vellum codices wrapped in leather. But he trailed off, simply whispering, "The Dark Seed."

"Arwë?" Dusk asked.

Arwë barely heard the lad speak his name. His eyes studied the page's script, but they weren't reading. He recalled terrible brightness, and words roared in a deep place instead. "Just like the caves in which we find ourselves now," he breathed. Then the memory struck. "Tyrith!" he cried.

"Arwë?" Dusk demanded. Concern furrowed the lad's brow.

"Under Galataeum, down the mineshaft and on the bridge," Arwë said, the words spilling from him as he stood. "Tyrith was first to touch the power stored up within Yeiley. Then wild things flashed in his eyes. He seemed to see the world as it would be, would that *he* were chief of her power and all things were to bow before him."

"I d-d-don't understand," Dusk said.

"Listen!" Arwë hissed. "Tyrith's words when Ithyeil's light touched him were, '*I shall find the Dark Seed, crush her in her Coffin ... all Six shall kneel before me. Galataeum shall be torn open, and in its place, a greater kingdom will be set, in my name ...*'"

"That doesn't s-s-sound much like Tyrith," Dusk said.

"No," Arwë agreed. "And I think they were not all *his* wishes. I think Ithyeil's power struck him with a moment of foresight—a prophecy." His ears pricked up at the approach of quiet feet. Both he and Dusk looked up the road. Two shadows, one tall, one not, approached at speed.

"You said it was your desire, Tyrith," Arwë whispered, stepping away. "What if they were not *your* desires, but someone else's? What if you saw a glimpse of the Enemy's intention for the Heir of the Atrellarrath? Their goals are linked, the Heir and the Enemy. One seeks to free the light imprisoned within Leóhteness-Fal. The other seeks freedom *from* its prison, buried and locked within Leóhteness-Fal by—"

"By light of the Atrellarrath," Dusk breathed. The lad had been keeping pace with Arwë, trying to wrap his injuries, even as he cast about. "What does the n-n-next part of my f-f-father's note say?"

Arwë bowed his head, scanning the vellum scrap quickly, saying, "A Rhonoss chronicler seems to have written it," he said. "He wrote just after the Kindreds' arrival upon this earth, after their scattering, if he is to be believed. The chronicler speaks of oaths taken by those who first arrived, which matches the story given by Treiarn."

"What does it s-s-say?" demanded Dusk.

"I'll read it all," Arwë said, holding up both the skin page and the knight's translation. "'*Nephtyr fought the Scribe at terrible cost. But they overcame, sealed her in the Seed. But when they won the fight, and while Kindreds battled Scribe's goblins and Men, Nephtyr swore a new oath. I am witness to this, for I traveled among Nephtyr, guised as one. I am Rhonoss, but I was tallest, broadest, and best suited to spy in their midst. In this guise, I saw Nephtyr commit a great sin. Nephtyr had met a people named Tryllyë, befriending* them before Kindreds arrived on their heels to Leóhteness-Fal. Tryllyë revealed to Nephtyr their most treasured secret: a Garden of insurmountable beauty. I cannot repeat the name. It was spoken in a fey tongue. But here, my best guess, by sound, is that last syllables were DAH-RAY. This Garden contains great power and meaning, both to Tryllyë and to others who came before us. But the last of Rhonoss built a great city over it: the Last-Hope of our people, for all to come and find protection.'

"It seems a great deal of time passed between the before entry and the next. For the second part reads, 'I am right, was right all along. In Nephtyri fashion, the Winged Ones, traitors and tyrants both, sacrificed Tryllyë. So Tryllyë, not Nephtyr, would keep shut the Seed, which looks more a Coffin. Nephtyr, unchained to their sworn duty, shall seek to be kings over ashes of this world. And buried beneath the city in ashes of the Garden, lie Coffin-Seed and Scribe.'"

"They had brought with them a great evil, tricked it into a trap," Dusk recited, the memory of his vision from weeks before sparked by the chronicler's account. "They sought to bury it deep and in darkness forever, but needed power to keep it shut."

Arwë's eyes met Dusk's as the boy sat him down again to finish his ministrations. "The Nephtyr betrayed the Atrellarrath and enslaved them. The Nephtyr used the light of the Atrellarrath, which is purest power on this world, to bury this most-evil thing."

"At the heart of Innoth-Hyeil Darrë," Dusk breathed.

"Under Ephtar-Malas," Arwë growled.

DESCENT

"Ephtar-Malas," Dusk whispered, "conceals the Coffin."

"What?" Arwë demanded, grabbing the lad's collar.

"S-s-somthing my mother said in her d-d-delirium," Dusk said. "Sh-sh-she mentioned armies marching under-earth and a prince lying dead."

"Elijah Wrathmod!" Arwë said, snapping back to his feet.

"Arwë?" asked Elijah, returning to the circle of firelight alongside Tarthuin. The old surgeon read the disturbed look in Arwë's eyes.

"Ithyeil Stëorra means to fulfill her duty by releasing the light of the Atrellarrath out of Leóhteness-Fal and into the Outer-dark," Arwë said, showing the surgeon the scrap of story. He cast about for his shirt and armor. "In the battle for the caravan, Keiphral Morne swore an oath to Tyrith, saying he would serve her, to whatever end. And such oaths are never easily broken."

"I had guessed as much," Elijah said as he read. "Though I wish we could have waited, alas! I may have done the same as him, hoping to hunt down the prince's shadow before it could do more harm. But if Ithyeil pushed him to do so, I cannot say I blame him, for fear of breaking oaths."

"Elijah," Arwë pleaded. "The light of the Atrellarrath that is buried within Leóhteness-Fal keeps shut the Coffin, which *is* the Dark Seed. The Seed is the prison that confines one of the Dark Six who ruined Elderlight. It is the Witch-Scribe, Eshra! If Ithyeil releases the light that holds shut the Coffin—"

"Up, all of you!" Elijah shouted, garnering an annoyed snore from Del. The surgeon turned back toward the path up which he and Tarthuin had just come. "Up and forward to the end as if all your lives depend upon your haste—for now, they do!"

* * *

Keiphral Morne and Ithyeil Stëorra stood before a clockwork door. All was dark save seven cold lights that flickered far off in the surrounding black. Days of travel in the gloom under the broken mountain had gripped Keiphral's heart. And even though Ithyeil's light guided and protected them, her power had waned over the days, and now she was little brighter than a candle in the gale. Keiphral felt heavy and more afraid than he had been in the tunnels of his Tomb. Even now, his awakening felt so long ago. His mind felt twisted and dull, and he wondered if Lohrë would recognize him should he ever see the elf again.

"Lohrë," Keiphral whispered. The word spilled from his mouth in a cloud of icy mist. He drew a breath, but the air froze his throat. He coughed a rhythm of small explosions in that deep, cold place. A lyrical voice, bright and warm, sang him to expectant silence. Its beauty filled his mind, carrying a memory of starlight. But he could not remember until he understood what it said.

"Keiphral," whispered Ithyeil. Shining shards of memory collided, each cutting into the other before anything

DESCENT

coherent could form. A low moan escaped Keiphral's lips. The rocks under his feet froze and bit. Waves lapped nearby onto a shore of stone somewhere far below. The wind that pushed them was suffused with the familiar, ancient scent of a black lake under the earth.

"Close your eyes, if you haven't," she whispered. Deep in the ensconcing black of Keiphral's eyelids, a tongue of red fire caught then flared to a fury. *Light.* It flickered into his vision as his eyes ached with their opening. Light chased away the dark with beams of white-gold as his widening eyes devoured the sight. They had been starved of it, and he needed more. He refused to close his eyes. But they burned and hurt, drawn to starlight even though the world itself was too old to remember it. Then, as if he had been given a long drink in a desert of dark, Keiphral saw soothing coolness, this time in the form of a woman. He held back his tears, remembered his name, and hers, to his relief.

"Star Under-earth," he said, sick at the desperation in his voice.

"I am here, Keiphral," Ithyeil replied. "Fear not. I've drawn back my hood." He beheld flowing hair that burned with white fire, opal eyes set in an alabaster face.

"You've no strength left," he said, captivated.

"Enough to get us there and back," she breathed. "But no more. We must hurry."

With a will, Keiphral looked away and found with her radiance that they stood at the brink of an obsidian road. The black rock underfoot glittered a thousand colors before the glory of Ithyeil's power. They had followed the mad shadow-prince to a precipice and the end of their road. An infinity of light-flecked waves sparkled off a lake in the dizzying deep below. Keiphral forced his eyes shut for a moment, putting a hand to the helm.

Kel, it whispered to him as a stiff, cold wind pulled at his cloak.

I am here, Keiphral replied, eyes opening again. In front of him and below, down the final stair, stood the clockwork door. Fifty feet high, it rested in a column of silver-seamed rock. Sigils and mechanisms jutted out at every angle, glowing sapphire and white from top to bottom. The door's glass-and-iron surface marked the utter end of their labyrinthine journey through the dungeons beneath Ephtar-Malas and its broken mountain. The same compulsion that had driven Keiphral to claim Dusk's helm for his own bid him come down from the precipice. He descended the steps until his boots struck the last bit of black road before the door. He took halting steps forward, and the door loomed even higher before him.

Keiphral held no key but beheld the door ajar, cracked just enough to allow a man through. He touched the door's cool mechanisms, but fear gripped his heart with icy fingers, and he recoiled. "We shouldn't be here," he snapped, turning to a burning Ithyeil, who had come up behind him.

"I will protect you," she said, "no matter what we find in the Garden of Light."

"It's not light that I fear."

"Keiphral Morne," she said, her patient tone growing

haggard. "We've traveled far in the dark. We're tired. Our people, yours and mine, hang by a thread over the fire. The Qwei-Sillar are fallen. Ephtar-Malas is soon to follow should we fail here. Let us get this done, for redemption, the saving of a life, and the world kindling."

"*At end of night comes break of day,*" he whispered.

"*Seek once-bright Innoth-Hyeil Darrë,*" she replied.

"We've come to the end of night, at the end of this glossy road," Keiphral murmured, not quite sure at what he was saying. "Such blackness."

"And now for daybreak!" Ithyeil said, her smile suddenly gleaming as she grabbed his hand. "Together," she said.

"Together," he repeated and put a hand to the door once more.

The moment Keiphral's fingers brushed the polished surface, the helm cried out to him. He convulsed, gritting his teeth against the shriek. But still he stood, bolstered by the door. He opened his eyes, but they were not his own. His arms were wreathed in shadow. His hand still held the door, the other, the gleaming Key.

"Through the prince's eyes," Keiphral hissed. With tentacles dripping black, he found the lock and fit the Key to it. Its turning threw back a hundred clockwork latches. Clicks, ticks, clacks, and metallic snaps punctuated the dark expanse. Astral gears above turned. Teeth of light spun, met, and separated, like the inner workings of some machine assembled in dreams. Then the great door swung on silent hinges, opening just a crack. Smoke and pale light poured from the threshold. Keiphral blinked. The memory passed. His hands were flesh, gauntleted, and *his* once more.

"The prince was here and lies within," he whispered. "Your light stopped him before. Be ready."

Ithyeil stepped forward, burning brightly.

Keiphral and Ithyeil gazed through the door and into another world. What they thought would have been a dark cavern yawning deeper into the blackness of the mountain instead was a window, opening to a land that stretched far under a clouded sky. They stepped out of dark and onto soft earth. Gray flakes tumbled down, landing on the gray earth. Their feet cut gray imprints as they walked toward a gray horizon. A single, gray tree, bent and mangled with age, drew them down a cobbled path, covered with gray dust.

Ithyeil halted, gasping as her hand went to her mouth. "Belfaerilorn," she whispered. Her eyes brimmed, shining in the light emanating from her.

"What is it?" Keiphral breathed.

"The tree my sires spoke of. It is the source of the Garden's life. We've found Innoth-Hyeil Darrë, where the Tree, grown from the last of the Creator's light that remained on Leóhteness-Fal, lies at the center. It is dead. All is ash."

Keiphral looked up at the gray snow that fell all around them. All the strange world was quiet, and no wind blew. "Ashes," he whispered, snatching a flake between his fingers.

DESCENT

"All is lost," Ithyeil sobbed.

"No," Keiphral said. "All is stopped, frozen. But you, Ithyeil, your coming here brings it to life again. Look!" He pointed upward. Deep azure bloomed in the gray expanse, like a single drop of ink invading a blank page. He smiled, pointing again, this time to the tree's roots. "We've found what we've come here for. Look again! I see a box with light pouring out from its hinges and cracks. You must not see it past your own brilliance. Hurry! Some treasure must await us. But beware the prince's shadow."

"I fear we've found no treasure here," she breathed, crystal tears falling.

"Now I'm the one protecting you, telling *you* not to lose heart," he said, taking her hand. He pulled her with him, toward the leering corpse of the tree, Belfaerilorn. But Keiphral looked at Ithyeil after they had trudged through a gray creek and passed under the tree's gray branches. Her light diminished with each step they took toward Belfaerilorn's trunk. At its withered roots, covered in ash, lay the box. Keiphral released Ithyeil's hand and knelt down to the box. It looked to have been carved from a single slab of black quartz. The tree's dead roots gripped it tightly, like so many ancient chains, gone to rust. He examined the light emanating from inside.

"Kel," said a woman's voice.

Startled, Keiphral staggered back, putting a hand to the helm he had taken from Dusk. But the voice did not belong to the helm. It was real. And it was more compelling, more interesting, and more powerful.

"I am here," he said.

"You and the Starling have done well to find me," the woman said. Keiphral looked at the box to see the light within flashing with each spoken word. "My power, hidden by the Dread Storm, has been taken. But it comes here, even as we speak. My servant awoke by its touch. And even though I was resisted for a time, I need only call, and it shall come. Then all the pieces shall fall into place, as I'd planned so long, long ago. Well done!"

"Keiphral," Ithyeil warned.

He turned to her, then caught her as she toppled.

"Yeiley?" he asked, dropping down with her.

"Truest of boons is your arrival," said the woman's voice. "Unlock now the box, and release the Light of the Atrellarrath for all the earth!"

Keiphral looked to Ithyeil and cradled her in his arms as all strength ebbed from her. "She—" Ithyeil said. "She tells the truth. Light *is* contained within. You were right, Keiphral Morne. But now that we are here, I think your words of caution from before ring true. We should leave, wait for the others, for they are surely following our trail."

"No, Ithyeil!" Keiphral cried. "We've come too far. And who knows what evil that skulking prince may be up to in this place of magic? Maybe we were fools for coming here so soon, me with my wounds, and you having wasted yourself to give life back to Dusk when he was nearly dead. But you said it yourself: We must redeem the world, our friends, and your people. Just as the dead sky here promises potential for life, so will Leóhteness-Fal brighten once

DESCENT

we release the trapped light of your people. This is our chance to restore the Atrellarrath and blot the stain of the fomori and masked men from this world for good. Now is the time."

"Yes!" cried the voice from the box. "Release light for all the world. Unlock me from this prison, and bathe in power!"

Keiphral came to his feet, clutching Ithyeil to his chest. With the Heir in his arms, Keiphral came to the foot of the withered tree and stood before the box. "Together," he said to her again. But as they reached trembling hands toward the gleaming box, Ithyeil screamed. A shadow darted from behind the tree, and pain crashed between Keiphral's eyes.

Blood poured from Keiphral's nose, and he and Ithyeil toppled into a pile of ash. Ignoring Keiphral, the prince's shadow loomed over Ithyeil, desire gleaming in its eyes. Drawing a blade as the shadow reached for her, Keiphral stabbed it in the back, this time parting flesh. His arm drove the blade out through its stomach. It screamed and squirmed, wrenching the sword from Keiphral's grasp. Keiphral took his other elvish blade and deflected the prince's lashing arm with a flurry of parries. To Keiphral, the monster seemed emaciated. Its swings were slower and weaker than they had been in the stone chamber. Keiphral spent little of his strength defending himself to keep its attention while Ithyeil pulled herself through the ash toward the bright box.

Keiphral beat away a clumsy swing of the shadow's

arm, shoved it off balance, then struck it between the eyes with hilt and fist. It crumpled to the ground, dripping shadows, clutching at its face.

"One broken nose for another," Keiphral spat, blood running in channels down his mouth and chin. He glanced away, seeing Ithyeil lay hands on the box under the tree. "Light has won. No more shadow," Keiphral whispered. But a sickly grating sound forced him to turn back. The prince drew the sword from its chest, then swung it hard. Keiphral swung with all his might. Their blades locked with a crash. Keiphral snarled, pressing all his strength into the prince's guard. But the shadow's strength seemed bolstered, and it overwhelmed him.

The relentless strength of the Veilglorrath was as nothing to this, Keiphral thought desperately. Then he saw Ithyeil lying sprawled across the box. Her power had run dry with her exertions. But she raised her hand one final time. A blast of radiance smote the shadow.

Now! Keiphral overpowered the shadow with one final lunge of his dying strength, then struck it down. It fell, rent in half, and Keiphral dropped to one knee, gasping for life as black flooded his vision. Wanting nothing more than to lay in soft ashes, Keiphral closed his heavy eyes. But another ugly sound sent them snapping open once more. The prince's shadow was crawling. It inched toward Ithyeil, who lay only a few feet away.

Keiphral roared his body into action, beginning a slow chase to catch the groping shadow. "No," he grunted, grasping for his sword hilt, finding none. "Leave her.

Fight me." His hand nearly caught the beast's wrist, but it hauled its broken body forward. "No!" Keiphral howled, stretching his arm to catch the shadow by the ankle. It paid him no heed, reaching its goal and laying a claw on Ithyeil's white hand where she touched the box.

A savage wind blew the box's lid clean off. Severed root and shattered stone showered the dead tree. Its branches shivered, and a crash like thunder boomed up into the gray sky. The tree bent double to the raging wind, and all the world seethed with ash.

"Well done, Thalassean!" cried the woman's voice, ferocious and wicked over the blasting wind. "Light and shadow both were needed to set me free. You've found and brought them and so have released your queen. The Witch-Scribe shall write a new ending to his world, and the Atrellarrath are first to be erased!"

Keiphral stared, stunned as a shadow blacker than the Outer-Dark beyond the world rose from the box. It grew and grew until it devoured the sky. It swept down, snuffing out Ithyeil's light. The Heir's scream tore him from inaction, and he found his sword, raising. It exploded in his hand. Then a weight heavier than any he had ever felt crushed him to his knees, then onto his back. Ash and earth choked him as he fought for life.

Then something forced open Keiphral's eyes. He saw a face in front of his. It was a woman. He gasped, not at the crushing weight and invading shadow, but at the eager smile that split her lovely face. An angry light pricked her eyes. She held pale hands before her, as if pushing herself up against a pane of glass. A crack formed in the space between them. The crack splintered, then the space between them shattered completely. Her smile went manic, then a cry of despair pierced his waking dream. The voice was his own.

"Eshra," he choked, tasting blood. "No." All was spiraling dark, and pain was everywhere. He made to draw a breath, but the mountain on his chest and ash in his throat forced him to convulse. He recalled no beauty or light as he lay once more under-earth, in his tomb.

GLOSSARY AND PRONUNCIATION

A NOTE ON PRONUNCIATION

Whenever the "ei" combination of letters is used, it is ALWAYS pronounced as the long "Ā," as in the number "eight" or the word "way." Because of this, our main characters' names are pronounced "TRAY—jin" and "KAY—frull," not "TREE—jin" and "KEE—frull."

Whenever the "ae" combination of letters is used, it is ALWAYS pronounced as the short "a," as in the words "ash" or "apple." Because of this, Aelfnoth's name is pronounced "AL-f—noth," not "AIL-f—noth." The only exception to this rule is found in the name "Galataeum," in which the third syllable rhymes with the word "day."

GLOSSARY OF TERMS

Aelfnoth—Short "a" sound, as in "ash." "Alf—noth." The first syllable rhymes with the name "Ralph." The last syllable rhymes with the word "cloth." Captain of the guard and field marshal of Ephtar-Malas.

Anglorost—Rough, misty, mountainous country to the west, ruled by the Angloreans.

Arwë—"Are—way." The Messenger of Wildercrown. Brother to Prince Lohrë and second son of the Elf-lord, Arwë was born sick and without the use of his legs. Upon leaving Wildercrown on the eve of a great battle that would take his life, Prince Lohrë, Arwë's brother, gave to Arwë a secret power that healed him completely of all ailments. Arwë has since used his new body and skills to become a great hunter, spy, runner, and communicator for the Qwei-Sillar.

Aryka—"Are—icka." Dusk's childhood friend and fellow caretaker of both Eissyr and Dusk when he returns in fey moods from his wanderings abroad in search of his mother's cure. Aryka is the only person who is able to calm Dusk once the inner beasts of his power are released.

Atrellarrath—"Ah—trell—ah—wrath." Remnant of a once great people who were considered to be the First-Born on Leóhteness-Fal and closest in likeness and power to the Creator. They constructed wondrous works of architecture and went so far as to create vessels that would store up light in order to bring light and warmth to all corners of Leóhteness-Fal. But they failed in their sacred duty to bring light to corners of the *universe*, and so suffer from a

GLOSSARY AND PRONUNCIATION

terrible curse: a seemingly endless cycle of renewed power, only to be conquered and enslaved once more.

Belrath'ir Desert—"Bell—Wrath—Ear." A vast desert country to the south of T'Rhonossarc. The Suthestur-Menn, a branch of the Mannish Kindred, claimed it for themselves after the end of the war that brought the Kindreds to Leóhteness-Fal. It is desolate and treacherous, but also home to majestic treasures and mysteries that attract the stoutest adventurers. A cataclysm was recently visited upon the desert sands, and war consumes nearly every corner of the desert. The people there flee across Leóhteness-Fal, seeking solace.

Cailus—"Kai—Luss." Armor-bearer to Lohrë of Wildercrown. He was said to have possessed the keenest sight of any living being on Leóhteness-Fal but was unable to see the stroke that took him in the back, killing him during the final battle of the Fomori War.

Cyrwedh—"Keer—Weth." Master archer, tracker, and Queen-in-Waiting to Wildercrown before the Fomori War. She was wed to Lohrë and is said to have fought sword to sword with the last lords of the fomori over his corpse when he died in battle.

Dún-Scraeff—"Dune—Skraff." The cloven mountain in which sits Ephtar-Malas.

Elf-lord—Ruler of Wildercrown for more than four hundred years. His cunning has kept together the minds and hearts of the disparate Qwei-Sillar who abandoned their high calling after a bloody sacrifice they made long ago for the greater good.

Eissyr—"Eh—seer." The first syllable rhymes with the word, "day," NOT the word, "key." Wife to Treiarn and mother to Dusk, Eissyr is considered by the people of both Ephtar-Malas and Eth Gathilin to be a shield maiden of old. She has fallen deathly sick in recent years, and there seems to be no cure.

Ephtar-Malas—"Eff—tarr—malice" (pronounced nearly the same as the word "malice"). Also known as "Last-Hope" and the "Hidden City," Ephtar-Malas is the cornerstone of civilization for all people not originally born to Leóhteness-Fal.

Ephtarrath—"Eff—tarr—wrath." The collective name given to all elves before tribal divisions. It is considered an appropriate name for any elf who lived upon the lost world of Elderlight. The Qwei-Sillar are descendants of a tribal branch of the Ephtarrath. The name invokes sorrow in the Qwei-Sillar, for they fear they have not lived up to the name given to their brave ancestors.

Eth Gathilin—"Eth—gath—ill—inn." The first syllable rhymes with the word "death." Capital city of the Anglorean Kingdom.

GLOSSARY AND PRONUNCIATION

Fomori—Men, women, and elves once counted among the Kindreds who came to Leóhteness-Fal. They turned their backs on their people, traditions, and their Creator, trusting only in power. They struck away north to form a kingdom of their own. In their thirst for power, these people subdued all the northern reaches of the world, away from light and hope. They were mercilessly corrupted by their own consuming hatred and lust, and by the dark powers and lures of Leóhteness-Fal. Hundreds of years passed, and when they were no longer recognizable as descendants of the Kindreds, the anger of the fomori burned to rule or destroy all the world that still resembled their ancient past. All they needed was a sign in which to conquer.

Galataeum—"Galla—tay—um." Capital city of the Nephtyr. It is utterly impregnable, according to Men, elves, and others who have seen it firsthand. It sits in the crater of a dormant volcano, which the Kindreds named Goldenmount. Its doors closed at the end of the Tyrants' War, some fifteen years ago, and have not opened since. The Nephtyr shut themselves in, and since then, none have been seen wandering the Outer-world.

Innoth-Hyeil Darrë—"Inn—oth—H-Yale—Darr-ay." The second syllable rhymes with the word "cloth." The last syllable rhymes with the word "day." Greatest creation of the Atrellarrath, the People of Highest Light built the Garden at the height of both their power and pride. The

Garden is said to have been first constructed far underground so as to hide the flashing of its light from the Creator. After centuries of complacence, The Atrellarrath simply let the Garden overflow with their power, beauty, and light, allowing all of these things to burst out of the earth and rupture the surface of Leóhteness-Fal.

Ithyeil Stëorra—"Ith—Yale—Stay—aura." The first syllable rhymes with the word "myth." A girl released into the world by a people known only as the Atrellarrath. She hides under a concealing cloak made by the Nokleth, but when she is uncovered, no one is left unchanged by the outpouring of limitless power she wields. To cross her would be folly. But to control her would mean utter domination.

Keiphral Morne—"KAY—frull." The first syllable rhymes the word "day," NOT with the word "key." The Sojourner who crashed to Leóhteness-Fal on a ball of fire. His arrival on the darkened world sparked the Fomori War, when the fomori took the flaming tail of his arrival for a sign that they were to conquer all the world with a power that had been promised to them since the coming of the Kindreds.

Kindreds—Peoples who were not born to Leóhteness-Fal. The Kindreds are comprised of the Nephtyr, Men, and elves.

Leóhteness-Fal—"Lay—oat—enniss—fall." The planet upon which tales of the Kindreds such as this take place. It has no moon, no sun, and there are no stars in its sky.

GLOSSARY AND PRONUNCIATION

If not for two powerful sources of light and warmth set in its northern and southern reaches, the Glacial Waste would conquer all the world's surface.

Lohrë—"Low—ray." Heir to the Oaken Throne of the Qwei-Sillar. He is said to have been slain in the final battle of the Fomori War, two hundred years ago.

Midlothean(s)—"Midd—loth—ian." The second syllable rhymes with the word "cloth." The last syllable rhymes with the name "Ian."

Mithweileth-Nal—"Myth—wail—eth—nahl." The shining protective wall surrounding the elf city of Wildercrown. It provides light and sustenance to the surrounding forest and land and is said to have been erected by a giant.

Nephtyr Ithar-fel—"Neff-tier—ith-are—fell." The third syllable rhymes with the word "myth." Supposedly the last of the angelic Nephtyr, Nephtyr Ithar-fel, or "Tyrith" for short, has dedicated himself in service of the Kindreds which his people sought with such vehemence to slay and enslave. It is not known whether the Nephtyr are alive or dead behind their impregnable walls, but Tyrith is the only one of their kind to have ventured forth from their Hegemonic territory in fifteen years.

Nokleth—"Nawk—leth." The first syllable rhymes with the word "hawk." A strange, stone-skinned people who are good-natured and possessed of a will to dig to the roots of the world. They have only recently been discovered, as they have lived underground for countless ages.

Qwei-Sillar—"Kway—Sill—Arr." Elves who abandoned their traditions of persistent watchfulness over an ancient cadre of enemies known as the Dark Six. They did not abandon this duty lightly, since their freedom from the Dark Six, and from the tyranny of all Kindreds, was bought with their own blood.

Qweth-Wëalda—"Kweth—Way—all—duh." The northern forests of Leóhteness-Fal that cover more than a million square miles in living darkness. The forest is home to elves, beasts, and fae, and no soul is rumored to have ever crossed its full expanse and lived.

Sunreach—Tallest mountains in farthest southern reaches of T'Rhonossarc.

Suthesturr-Menn—"Suth—ess—stir—men." The first syllable is pronounced as in the word "Southern." A branch of the Kindred of Men, the Suthesturr-Menn rule the southern deserts of Leóhteness-Fal.

Suthesturri—"Suth—ess—stir(y)." The last syllable rhymes with the word "hurry." See "Suthesturr-Menn."

GLOSSARY AND PRONUNCIATION

Tarthuin Da'rannithest—"Tarth—oo—inn / Darr—ann—ith—esst." A Noklethi warrior who is far more sociable and outgoing than others of his reclusive kin.

Treijan Dusk—"TRAY—jin." The first syllable rhymes the word "tray," NOT with the word "tree." Healer of Sunreach and son to Treiarn and Eissyr. He grew up a happy if aloof shepherd on the heights of the southern mountains, until his eyes turned the color of molten metal at the same time that bad news began to reach his people from the lower-world. When Eissyr fell sick, he bent all time, skill, and concentration toward healing her.

Treiarn—"TRAY—arrn." The first syllable rhymes with the word "tray," NOT with the word "tree." A strange figure according to all who've ever met him, Treiarn is said to have been a knight of colossal renown who retired to the mountains after nearly single-handedly winning the Tyrant's War.

T'Rhonossarc—"Trone — oss — ark." The first syllable rhymes with the word "throne." First land upon which the Kindreds landed in their arrival on Leóhteness-Fal. It is comprised of mostly stony hill country that is home to some of the most fertile land for farming and grazing in all the world. Because of its centralized location in Leóhteness-Fal, the Rhonoss Arch, as it was named in ancient days, is witness to the founding, flourishing, and erasure of whole empires.

GARDEN OF ASH

Tryllyë—"Trill—yay." See "Atrellarrath."

Tyrant's War—Begun by the Nephtyr after the end of the Fomori War. The Nephtyr used the power vacuum created by the slaying of the fomori to invade all lands north of the Qweth-Wëalda.

Veilglorrath—Elves and Men who have been given themselves fully to the abyssal darkness of Leóhteness-Fal. They believe only in power and domination, and they serve primordial beings whom they believe to be gods. They wear masks whose faces match the god they serve. Their dark devotion gifts them nearly supernatural speed and strength.

Weileth-Zhul—"Way—leth—Zhool." Giants of myth, the Weileth are said to have once stood a thousand feet tall and more. They are rumored to have created cast wonders alongside the Atrellarrath, but no record can verify so ancient a claim. The afterglow of their ruined works still shine in the Mithweileth-Nal, and in the under cities of Galataeum and Ephtar-Malas.